D0852751

GUILTY KNOWLEDGE

E. Howard Hunt

GUILTY
KNOWLEDGE

A TOM DOHERTY ASSOCIATES BOOK

NEW YORK

GUILTY KNOWLEDGE

Copyright © 1999 by E. Howard Hunt

This book is printed on acid-free paper.

Book Design by Richard Oriolo

A Forge Book
Published by Tom Doherty Associates, Inc.
175 Fifth Avenue
New York, NY 10010

Forge® is a registered trademark of Tom Doherty Associates, Inc.

Library of Congress Cataloging-in-Publication Data

Hunt, E. Howard (Everette Howard)
    Guilty knowledge / E. Howard Hunt.—1st ed.
        p.   cm.
    "A Tom Doherty Associates book."
    ISBN 0-312-86760-3 (alk. paper)
    I. Title.
PS3515.U5425G85   1999
813'.54—dc21   99-24567
                                                       CIP

First Edition: June 1999

Printed in the United States of America

0   9   8   7   6   5   4   3   2   1

This book is dedicated to the memory of

Frank Rollins, Jr.

(1918–1998)

He shared with all his gift of laughter

and so enriched the years we lived.

GUILTY KNOWLEDGE

ONE

———

MY SECRETARY HAD listed the day's last appointment as:

Mrs. A. Stokes
Reference: Gurney & Steiner
Subject: Personal/Private

I buzzed Mrs. Altman on the intercom and asked if she could expand on the notation.

"Sorry, Mr. Bentley, that's all the information I was given."

"Gurney and Steiner referred her?"

"Uh—not exactly. She telephoned yesterday and said Gurney and Steiner handled her routine legal affairs. I suppose she mentioned Harris Gurney to establish bona fides. She's here, by the way. May I show her in?"

"Give me a minute, I'll buzz you."

Turning my chair, I looked out the window at Lafayette Park, green in the early spring mist that had been hovering over Washington all day. Beyond the park, the White House was dimly visible, and cars moving along Pennsylvania Avenue had their head-lights on.

Mrs. A. Stokes, I mused, to see me on a personal/private mat-ter. Hod Gurney, the firm's senior founding partner, was of counsel, no longer active day to day, and probably not even in Washington. We were old enough friends that I knew he cruised his ketch to the Caribbean at first snowfall, returning after Easter. And Easter was weeks away.

But the lady had used Hod's name for access, and because his firm took only clients from the major millionaire class, I felt an oblig-ation to see her. I could have phoned Saul Steiner for a rundown on my visitor, but I didn't want to keep her waiting. I could talk to Saul later if I felt it advisable. Meanwhile, she could speak for herself.

So I buzzed Mrs. Altman and said I would see Mrs. Stokes.

When the office door opened I rose and pointed to a nearby chair. With a slight nod the lady walked to it and seated herself. "I'm Amelia Stokes, Mr. Bentley, and I appreciate you seeing me on short notice."

"If you're a client of Hod Gurney's you come well recom-mended."

"Thank you." A gloved fingertip adjusted the dark glasses she was wearing. Most of her hair was concealed under a sort of tam-o'-shanter but what I could see was ash blond. She was wearing a light gray tailored pants suit and a beige silk blouse with a ruffled match-ing cravat. Her complexion was pale, possibly ivory-hued, and her teeth were white and even. She seemed to be waiting for me to say something, so I eyed my appointment pad and said, "Private and personal, Mrs. Stokes?"

"All of that." She smiled faintly. "To avoid any misunderstand-ing I should admit that Gurney and Steiner didn't refer me to you."

"I considered the possibility."

Uncrossing her legs, she leaned slightly forward. "I'm sure you remember General Walter Ballou."

"Now deceased," I nodded. "I attended his funeral at Arlington . . . that was some years ago."

Her turn to nod. "The general was my uncle, and his daughter Francine—"

"—would be your cousin." I paused. "Making Matthew Revelstoke your grandfather."

"Exactly. You have a mind for detail."

"I remember my brief brush with one of the Eastern Shore's great fortunes."

"Oh, it wasn't all that brief, Mr. Bentley, and it was much more than a brush. Francie described the very considerable service you rendered her father—and her—though without much detail."

"I thought that was a closely held family secret."

"It was—and is. I mentioned it by way of explaining why I've come to you."

I shook my head. "That was quite a while ago, Mrs. Stokes. Hod Gurney recommended me to the general as someone who might be able to get him out of a tax bind. I was a CPA then, not a lawyer, and the general's problem had nothing to do with taxes."

"It was blackmail."

"That what Francie told you?"

"Yes." She paused. "I guess you know she died in a plane crash three years ago—flying her plane across North Africa, or trying to."

"So I read." And not without sadness. Francie Ballou had made a strong and lasting impression on me, and I'd been responsible for the death of her blackmailer. A beautiful, rudderless young woman with far too much money. "She left a daughter," I remarked.

"Isabel. Being raised by her brother, Win, in New Zealand."

Outside, fog was obscuring the White House—the normal state, I reflected, even on a sunny day. "So what does bring you here?"

Her mouth tightened. "A distressing situation. In racking my brain for someone who could help me, your name surfaced."

I set elbows on the desk. "Since we're into frankness, I don't represent parties in domestic disputes or do general trial work. My practice is limited to financial matters and I normally represent clients in the federal tax court. Finally, I don't welcome clients who approach me under false pretenses."

She stiffened. I got up. In a controlled voice she said, "Even if there's a compelling reason, Mr. Bentley?"

I said, "What was yours, Senator Bowman? I've seen you a hundred times on television—dark glasses aren't much of a disguise."

Sighing, Senator Alison Bowman removed and folded them. "Since you recognize me—and I made sure you would—consider my position. Because I wanted to consult you on a very personal matter I couldn't have my staff arrange an appointment. Nor did I particularly want to be seen entering this building."

"Why not? It's full of lawyers."

She shrugged. "Suppose I were trailed to your door—political enemies could start a rumor that I'm in financial difficulties. In any case, Mr. Bentley, I'm sorry we got off to a bad start. It's my fault, but I felt minor deception justified. Can we . . . start over?"

"I'm agreeable, Senator," I replied, and sat down. "As a professional courtesy, and because I've admired you as a lawmaker I'll hear what you have to say. But before that, does your husband know you're consulting me?"

"No."

"Is he aware of your problem?"

"Harlan Bowman and I communicate very little, Mr. Bentley, haven't for a long time. No, he is definitely *not* aware of my difficulty. In fact, I hope to conceal it from him forever."

"All right, I'm beginning to understand your desire for confidentiality. Give me a dollar."

She blinked. "A—dollar?"

"To establish lawyer–client relationship."

She opened her clutch purse and said, "Sorry—nothing smaller than a ten." She laid it on the desk. I took nine dollars from my billfold and gave them to her. Then I wrote out an informal receipt acknowledging a one-dollar retainer from Senator Alison Revelstoke Bowman, and signed it Steven J. Bentley, Attorney-at-Law.

After scanning it, she put it in her purse. "You do things by the book."

"From hard experience. Now, suppose you tell me—under seal of confidentiality—what your problem is, and how you think I might help you."

She didn't reply at once, but rose, slowly rounded the desk and gazed out at the near-dark sky. "All those people," she said musingly, "all our beautiful buildings—this Washington of ours is a cesspool of slimy snakes."

"Not entirely, Senator. There's you—and me."

"Yes, present company excepted." She sighed. "I'm nearing the end of my first term as senator, and I've heard rumors that I won't have a second term. Some pundits even say I won't be renominated."

"Oh? What I've heard is that you're a definite presidential possibility, your party's nominee."

"That's Washington gossip but it's good for my self-image." Her face tightened. "Being a candidate is far from my thoughts. Right now I have more immediate worries—my enemies."

"Every politician has enemies."

"Yes, but some are active within my own party—portraying me as a rich bitch who bought her seat with her family's money."

"It was never concealed that as a Revelstoke you had access to almost unlimited funding. But what senator doesn't dispose of a private fortune?"

Turning, she said, "There's that, of course, but the charge is painful, nevertheless. And that it springs from within my own party—my supposed supporters—is hard to rationalize." Gracefully, she returned to her chair and faced me. "Logically, I should start with my marriage. I was thirty when I met Harlan Bowman. After Bryn Mawr I took a graduate degree at Penn in child psychology, found a job in the state Office of Juvenile Protection, and won election to the state legislature. Harlan was already there, ten years older than I, and the owner of several car dealerships. I met him when I was assigned to the Human Resources Committee, and we began dating. He was divorced—somewhere in his background

was a discarded childhood sweetheart—and we were mutually attracted. He courted me persistently and after a year I agreed to
marry him." She looked away. "Big Mistake Number One. Anyway,
I was on a career track, no children for me, and that was agreeable
to Harlan. The party nominated me for Congress, and I served two
terms before deciding to run for the Senate. All okay with my husband. We had our condo in Philadelphia, and I kept my apartment
in the District, but gradually we grew out of touch. A weekend a
month isn't really enough to keep romance alive, and when our accountant asked me about some rather veiled expenses I realized my
husband was maintaining another establishment—and a woman."
She swallowed. "It was a terrific blow to my pride but I didn't confront him, as in retrospect I think I should have. Instead, I buried
myself in my work, became a sort of spokesperson for economically
powerless, mistreated women, and gained a degree of distinction in
that role."

"I know—and I respected you for it."

"Thank you. Uh—mind if I smoke?"

"Not at all. I'm not one of the Brown Shirt antinicotine storm
troopers." I leaned across the desk to light her cigarette. "Enjoy."

"Oh, I do." She inhaled and exhaled relievedly. "Do you
smoke?"

"Occasionally. Used to be a pipe, but now it's mostly cigars. I
don't suppose you've considered divorce?"

"It would be political death, and I'm not ready for that. When
I leave the Senate I want it to be of my own volition. There's a tena-
cious streak in my genes."

"And a compulsion to succeed."

"Yes. I've failed only in my personal life, but so far that isn't
public knowledge." She paused as though to collect her thoughts,
and said, "Not wanting to spend another Christmas and New
Year's alone in my apartment, I took a ten-day cruise to the Caribbean. It was my first real vacation in a long time." She inhaled deeply
and exhaled smoke away from me. "I wanted to get away from stress
in a calm atmosphere where I could do what I've needed to do for
a long time: sort out the basics in my life, evaluate my marriage
and the direction of my political career. I thought I might be able to

determine whether what I have is as far as I want to go, or whether I should try for more."

"Were you able to?"

She shook her head. "Unfortunately, no." She breathed deeply. "Coming here under a false name in a quasi-disguise is what I should have done on the cruise, at least made an effort to protect my identity." Her lips formed a slight smile. "Funny how we realize after a wrenching event what we should have done to prevent it."

"Not funny, human nature."

"I suppose the idea never occurred to me because I'd never traveled incognito, always having been with my husband on trips."

I nodded, said nothing.

"Anyway, I was seated at the captain's table, a distinction I didn't request, and among others was introduced to a younger man who gave his name as Thomas Brooks and said he was a Chicago stockbroker. Tommy was handsome and personable, just divorced, he told me, and it seemed that we were two lonely people thrown together by the vagaries of the cruise." She stubbed out her cigarette and sat back. "Skipping the preliminaries, Mr. Bentley, on the third night we began sleeping together. Sometimes in my suite, alternately in his stateroom. We agreed that ours was a brief affair ending when the ship returned to port. No holdovers, no contact, no reprise of an enjoyable diversion from reality. I thought that was the end of it—until I received a phone call from him saying he wanted to send me a souvenir of the cruise, and asked the address of my apartment. His request seemed harmless, so I told him where I lived, and three days later found a videocassette in my mailbox."

I said, "I think I know where this is heading," and pushed a writing tablet across the desk. "Better give me your address, and your private phone number. If you have a personal phone in your office, I'd like that number, too."

Silently, she wrote on the pad in a style I recognized as endemic to eastern girls' schools, and returned it to me. Her expression was strained as she said, "I assumed the tape would show our shore excursions and some shipboard shots. But when I played the tape I was sickened by what it showed."

"Intimate footage of the two of you."

"Yes." She looked away. "Tommy had a concealed camera in his stateroom, the bastard."

"How much does he want?"

"Fifty thousand dollars."

"Delivered how?"

"A typed note said he'd contact me later."

"Giving you time to consider the consequence of not paying."

She nodded slowly. "Now you know why I've come to you. Mr. Bentley, what shall I do?"

T W O

———

"THE FIRST THING you do is stop calling me Mister. Since we share your most occult secret we can shed formality."

She drew in a deep breath, held it before exhaling. "Steve?"

"That's it."

"Then please call me Alison." She managed a weak smile. "Ali among my family."

"Alison," I repeated. "Ali. I like both. Okay, I'm sure you could pull together fifty thousand dollars."

"Easily." Her nose wrinkled. "You think I should pay?"

"Not exactly. I think you should appear to be willing to pay. Look, you're a highly intelligent woman—surely you know that a blackmailer's first bite isn't his last. Right now your Tommy is testing you. Your response will tell him how far he can go."

Alison nodded slowly. "I understand—but, please, he's not 'my Tommy.' I guess he's any woman's Tommy."

"Any woman who seems vulnerable to his practiced eye."

"You're suggesting he's done this before?"

I shrugged. "Seems like he ran a pretty smooth operation. Seduction, lights, camera, the demand note—nothing on impulse. Question is, was he an independent operator, or was he hired to compromise you?"

"Hired? By whom?"

"You said you have political enemies, people in both parties who covet your Senate seat. Four years ago you won by how much?"

"Fifty-four percent."

"Low enough to suggest that personal scandal could eliminate you next time, or even force you to resign and vacate your seat." I paused. "Get along with your governor?"

"Of necessity."

"And if you resigned he could appoint a crony to your seat, even appoint himself."

She nodded. "That's true. Oh, Steve, thank God I came to you. Since Tommy's call—ugh, I loathe the name—I've barely been able to sleep, hardly think, but you're putting the situation in perspective, organizing my thinking." She sighed relievedly.

"You have more organizing to do," I told her. "Are you good at lists?"

"Helpless without them."

"Good. I want a list of all your staff employees and relevant bio information—married, divorced, drunks, dopeheads, gamblers, womanizers. Gather the information quietly, by which I mean don't start asking questions. Pull everything together—you can get salary figures from the Senate payroll office—and note how long you've known each employee and the length of his or her employment with you. The sooner I have the information, the better."

"I'll work in my office tonight."

"No, don't work there, assemble the raw information and put it together in your apartment."

She sat back and gazed at me. "You think this was an inside job?"

"You were set up by someone who knew about your holiday cruise. Who made travel arrangements?"

"The Senate travel office."

"Who on your staff actually dealt with the travel office?"

"Let's see—I asked my secretary but my media specialist said it would be his pleasure to handle things."

"His name?"

"Arnold Munger. But my plans were known by the entire staff. I gave them a pre-Christmas party, and they gave me an office sendoff the day before I left."

I wrote down the name Munger. "Very likely you have a complete list of passengers from the cruise?"

"Yes, I kept it as a souvenir. You'll want that, too?"

"Yes. Checkmark any names Tommy socialized with. Ah, do you happen to have Tommy's business card?"

She shook her head.

"That suggests he's not who he told you he is. Brokers usually scatter business cards like confetti." I paused to focus my mind. "Any chance you have a photo of Tommy? Say, from the shipboard photographer?"

She shook her head.

"How about the videotape? Is he recognizable enough to pull a still picture?"

She blushed. "The tape shows only his back—his naked back—but *my* face is there and very recognizable."

"So he positioned the video camera to show an unidentifiable white male covering you, while you looked at the camera."

"Oh God." Her hands tightened into balls with white knuckles. "I'm so ashamed. You can't possibly understand how ashamed I am."

"Look, Ali," I said sharply, "you weren't ashamed before you saw the tape, you shouldn't be now. Don't drown in self-pity, it'll paralyze you and I have much for you to do. Now, where is the tape?"

"In—in my apartment."

"Tomorrow morning when banks open put it in your safe deposit box. Your husband doesn't have a key?"

"No."

"Or power of attorney?"

She shook her head.

"Good. By the way, where was Harlan while you were cruising the Caribbean?"

"Before I left he told me he planned on Christmas with his parents in Omaha. The rest of the time I suppose he was in Philadelphia—doubtless with his lady love."

"I'll want to know about her—name, address of the love nest, anything you learned."

"All right, but I know very little. Steve, you think Harlan might have—?"

"It's not unknown for husbands to compromise wives for various reasons, including financial gain. But that may well have nothing to do with your problem. Still, you might consider his possible motive."

"I will."

"Do you have a tape recorder in your apartment?"

"One I use to dictate staff memos and speeches."

"Phone mike? Little black suction cup?"

"I—let me see—I think one came with the recorder, but I've never used it."

"I'll get one tomorrow, just in case. Now—and this is important—don't answer your apartment telephone until you can record incoming calls. Let your answering machine earn its keep. Tommy won't speak to a machine. He won't want a record of his voice, and more significantly he'll want to talk to you, his victim, determine how intimidated and ready to surrender you are."

"An hour ago I was almost ready to give in. Now, with all you've said in my mind, I know I won't have to."

"Good, that's a long way toward winning. Now, the most secure place to give me the material you'll be working on tonight is at your apartment." I gave her one of my cards and added my home telephone. "Call me tomorrow when everything's ready and I'll come by."

She smiled wanly. "Looks like a late-nighter for me."

"In a worthy cause." I left my desk and went to the corner cellarette. From it I took two small snifters and added Hine cognac to each. Alison took one and our glasses touched. Before sipping, she said, "I think a toast is in order, don't you?"

"Definitely. Look, Ali, cancel your guilt trip, let me handle the grief."

"Willingly." She raised her glass and murmured, "Death to my enemies."

"Death to your enemies," I echoed, and drank deeply.

Having no idea how prophetic our toast would be.

THREE

———

IN THE MORNING I phoned Patrick Moran, the investigator I customarily used. Pat had served in naval intelligence before becoming a metro detective, a job he left in disgust at departmental politics. He was a big, good-looking Irishman, a practicing Catholic, and an alumnus of AA. Pat liked most people and had a flair for ingratiating himself with subjects he wanted to question. He was licensed in Maryland, Virginia, and the District of Columbia. I had found him low-key, close-mouthed, and remarkably effective. His voice greeted me with four bars of *Kathleen Mavourneen* before wishing me 'Top-o'-the-morning,' Steve.

"And the same to you, me bhoyo. How soon can you come in?"

"Office? Oh, give me an hour, lad, and I'll be at yer service."

That gave me ample time to receive Mrs. Maude Forsythe, a widow in her early eighties whose two children were already squabbling over their inheritance. "And I'm not even in my grave, Steven," she said resentfully. "Ashley, that's the daughter who ran off and married that Canadian I disapproved of, thinks she deserves two thirds of my estate because she has children. Bryan, divorced and childless, says he could remarry and have children, so he wants the estate equally divided."

"What do you want?"

"I've been contemplating one third for Ashley because she went against my wishes, but her children will have to be educated, so I guess half of everything is fair." She eyed me over her half-moon lenses. "What do you think, Steven?"

"Fifty-fifty won't give them reason to challenge your will. The fact that one heir has children and the other does not isn't actionable in any court I'm familiar with."

"And my will is solid, is it not?"

"Mrs. Forsythe, a will is like a divorce, solid until challenged. If you want, I'll talk to your heirs, explain the facts of life and get them off your back."

"Oh, Steven, I would so much appreciate it."

"It's best if both come at the same time; then they can't speculate about uneven treatment."

"I'll arrange it, and make an appointment." She paused. "Now, before I leave, might I have a sip of that excellent sherry to ease me on my way?"

"With pleasure." I uncorked a bottle of Solera Antigua and filled a thimble glass. She studied the golden liquid appreciatively, before first sipping, then draining the glass. Handing it back to me, she said, "Steven, I'm glad you're not a drinking man like my late husband. If you were there'd be no sherry for me."

"Right you are," I agreed, and walked her to the door.

Two phone calls had come in while we were talking, so I returned them and made notes for Mrs. Altman. By then Pat Moran was there.

"What is it today, me laddy?" he asked in a pleasant tone.

"A small job in Baltimore. I want a photograph of a passenger

that might have been taken on the PanCaribe cruise that left Baltimore for points south just before Christmas."

"That's pretty far back, lad. Those photo concessions don't
usually keep prints more than thirty days."

"But they keep the negatives."

"True," he nodded. "Name?"

"Thomas Brooks is the name he went by, allegedly a Chicago
stockbroker. Late thirties, handsome, a charmer. Sat at the captain's
table during the cruise. Confidence man, and worse."

"How much worse?"

"A scumbag who preys on lonely women—ought to be cas-
trated. I want this done fast, Pat."

He got up. "I'll handle the cruise line photographer and get
my office tracing the Chicago end. What if he's a legitimate broker?"

"I'll want bio including Dun and Bradstreet."

"Will do. Oh—can I lay around incentives at the photo lab?"

"Whatever's necessary." I called Mrs. Altman on the intercom
and asked her to draw a check for five hundred to Patrick Moran's
agency. "Pat's not to be trusted with personal dough."

He grinned. "How well you know me. Bill you later."

"But not before I see results."

After he left, Mrs. Altman asked what account the advance
should be charged to. "Amelia Stokes," I told her, and left the building.

On Pennsylvania Avenue I went into an electronics shop and
bought a phone microphone and a pair of long-running audiotapes.
Walking back, to ward off morning chill, I stopped at a sidewalk
bistro and had steaming coffee laced with rum. The Barbados brand
reminded me, if I needed reminding, of Alison Bowman's Caribbean cruise.

For a politician, I mused, she was a remarkably attractive
woman, and highly intelligent as well. I'd had Congressional clients, but she was my first senator, and so I felt I was moving up a
notch in the inner Beltway world. Not that anyone cared.

As I sipped my coffee I thought back to her late cousin, Francie Ballou, who had so deeply fascinated me in younger days. Both

belonged to American financial royalty, but one had squandered her life, while the other had made much of hers.

And there lay the difference.

Moodily I left the bistro and walked back toward my office, stopping at the wine merchant's where I ordered a case of Solera Antigua delivered to Mrs. Forsythe's mansion on Foxhall Road. I could afford the courtesy; my retainer alone cost her twenty-five thousand a year.

In my office I worked on pending matters, arranged to hire a temporary lawyer to work on an involved case, and had lunch at my desk. A little after three Mrs. Altman said Mrs. Stokes was on the line.

"How are things going?" I asked.

"Quite well. Incidentally, I'm at a pay phone inside the building."

"Good precaution."

"I stayed up until after three compiling everything you requested, but I couldn't find that suction cup thing."

"I have one."

"If you're free, why not come by at, oh, five o'clock? We can go over everything in privacy, and I'll reciprocate yesterday's drink."

"Look forward to it."

Her apartment building was off Connecticut Avenue by Belmont Road, just short of Taft Bridge. A venerable edifice in a quiet, long-settled neighborhood, its gray stone facade was mostly covered with budding ivy. No uniformed doorman, so I moved into the entry and pressed the speaker button for number 301. Presently she spoke, I answered, and the door lock buzzed open.

Riding the old walnut-paneled elevator, I reflected that the building had been erected between wars at a time when construction was durable, no expense spared. The inhabitants were likely to be retired admirals or their widows, former financiers, and elderly politicians. It was the sort of place my parents would have enjoyed if they'd had the money.

The hall corridor was thickly carpeted in a blue-gray shade, and no sound penetrated the varnished oak doors along the way. I rang her door button and in a few moments the door opened inward.

"Welcome chez Bowman," she greeted me, holding the heavy door aside until I was in the marble-floored foyer.

She was wearing a loose-fitting, low-cut blouse of silvery material and flowing pants of the same shimmering fabric. The hip-length blouse was gathered around her waist by a loose belt of large silver links connected by black braided cord. Heelless slippers were colored silver speckled with black. A gauzy silver scarf was tied around her neck, its long ends off-shoulder. Makeup brought life to her cheeks, and neutral lipstick accented her full lips. I felt like whistling in admiration. Instead, I looked around.

There was a step-down to the sumptuous living room's beige-tiled flooring. Colorful Navajo and Mexican rugs covered sections of the tile and gave a pleasantly warm appearance. Furniture was traditional British design, except for a crescent-shaped sectional covered with mocha leather. Within its contour stood a broad coffee table on which my hostess had set snacks and raw veggies. The walls held paintings and lithographs by French impressionists, and a spectacular work by Dali. "Yours?" I asked.

She laughed. "Hardly. On loan from the Corcoran—one of my senatorial perks. Are we drinking?"

"I hope so."

"Then please do the honors." She gestured at a wet bar in the room's far corner. "This time of day I usually favor a mart. You?"

"Stimulates the taste buds." I went behind the bar, found the ingredients, and as I was mixing them noticed a life-size portrait on the wall. The subject was wearing a suit suggesting the Civil War era, a broad handlebar mustache, and a dour expression. Memory jogged, and the senator confirmed. "Josiah Revelstoke. The original gun- and rum-runner. Starting life as a New Bedford whaler, he was neutral during the War between the States." She took her glass, added a pearl onion to the martini, sipped and continued. "Sailed contraband cargos between Savannah and Philadelphia to the advantage of both sides—and of course himself. So by war's end he was quite wealthy."

I tasted my drink. "Never in the slave trade?"

"I never heard he was, but who knows? During the war he was paid in gold by both sides. Gave him heavy leverage to buy up confiscated plantations and Confederate factories." She smiled. "Wherever a choice property was available old Josiah was there, gold in hand, with an offer the destitute couldn't refuse."

"Your mart okay?"

"How much vermouth did you use?"

"About four drops."

"Not that much in mine. Cuts the fuzz right off my tongue."

"So your ancestor's profiteering gave you a social conscience."

"Possibly. But I evaluate things as they are today, not as they were then."

"And you're the first Revelstoke to enter politics."

She nodded. "One possible exception. President Andrew Johnson offered Josiah the governorships of Carolina, Georgia, Florida, and Alabama. That was definitely political."

"What an opportunity to loot!"

"It certainly was. But Josiah said no thanks, preferring to warm the bench and watch his fortune grow. So I have no carpet-baggers among my ancestors."

"Just a legendary blockade-runner."

She drained her glass and set it on the bartop. "Part of the legend has Josiah as the model for Rhett Butler."

After replenishing our drinks I eyed the oil portrait. "Doesn't look like Rhett."

"Who could?"

"Right. Don't make 'em like that anymore." With our drinks we moved toward the coffee table. I took the phone mike from my pocket and asked, "When Tommy telephoned, you took the call where?"

"Bedside phone."

"How did he get the number?"

"Foolishly I gave it to him during the cruise."

"Show me the bedroom phone, and bring your tape recorder."

I waited at bedside until she produced an expensive recorder. Then she sat on the bed while I attached mike to recorder and plugged it into a wall outlet. I replaced her audio cassette with one I'd brought, saying, "This takes twelve hours of recording, so activate the recorder when you go to bed and stop it in the morning. Rewind the tape or put in this fresh one. In fact, let's start now." I pressed the Record button. "Now we can forget about it."

She rose and we left the bedroom. As we moved toward the coffee table she asked, "When Tommy calls, how do I respond?"

"Tell him you're prepared to meet his demand, but only if you're buying the original video and all copies he may have made. He'll agree, of course, so you then ask how he wants payment made. Cashier's check, cash?"

"And then?"

"After he's chosen cash, say you need a few days to get it without occasioning comment. Tell him you have to sell some securities. He shouldn't worry because he has your political life in his hands."

"And my heart will be in my throat."

"He'll expect that, he's victimized women before."

"Please—it sickens me to think of his treachery."

"Part two is getting the tape or tapes from him. Doubtless he'll promise to send them FedEx after he has the money. That's no good, of course. Insist on simultaneous exchange in a private place. If you can get him here in your apartment I'll be on hand to take charge." I smeared a cracker with cheese and munched it. "Any questions?"

"No, but it's a pretty scary scenario."

"Of course it is, but stay cool. Very, very cool."

She sighed. "I'll certainly try. But you'll be here when he comes?"

"Definitely. Now, I'm checking into his supposed Chicago background. I doubt he's really from there, much less a stockbroker, but I want to eliminate the possibility. Meanwhile, my investigator is looking for a shipboard photo of Thomas Brooks from the photo concessionaire, but chances of that aren't good. However, cruise line passenger records will show how Tommy booked the cruise—

in person or through a travel agency—and how he paid for it. If I can get to him before he comes here, the problem is solved."

Her face tightened. "With violence?"

"I prefer avoiding it in favor of reason."

She lifted her glass to finish her drink. "Let me show you what I've collected."

We entered an office next to her bedroom and she pointed to a thick fiber envelope on the desk. "Everything's there, Steve."

"Fine, I'll take it with me." I glanced around, noticing a computer and a Caller ID device. I removed it from the office phone, and plugged it into her bedroom extension. "Should have thought of this earlier, but I'm rusty on electronic surveillance—haven't needed it for years. He'll probably call you from a pay phone, but the Caller ID will indicate what city he's calling from, and that could be useful."

"I understand." She glanced at the table clock and said, "It's getting on toward six, Steve. If you have no dinner plans, perhaps you'll share a casserole with me."

"With pleasure."

"I thought it might not be advisable for us to be seen dining in public, so I prepared a small dinner." She laughed apologetically. "Though I'm no Julia Child in the kitchen."

"Who is? I could have brought wine if I'd—"

"Next time." She disappeared into the kitchen. I heard appliance doors open and close and presently she reappeared, a wine bottle in hand. "Chardonnay okay?"

"Always."

She gave me the bottle and I went to the wet bar, found a silver ice bucket, set the Chardonnay in it, and surrounded it with crushed ice. From the dining room she called, "We have time, let's do the martini thing again."

So while she set the table, I mixed another shaker of marts and refilled our glasses. After tasting she said, "Oh, yes, even better, Steve. You do have a way with gin."

"Legacy of a dissolute life."

She laughed. "I doubt that. But were you as buttoned-down when you knew Francie?"

"Not hardly. But when I took up the law I developed a more serious approach to life and career."

She turned the glass stem and gazed at the clear cocktail. "Would I have liked you then? Francie did—she liked you a great deal, and was so grateful for all you did for her and the general. Now I'm grateful she told me about you."

"Your cousin was young and impressionable. I'm afraid she exaggerated my involvement."

"I'm sure she didn't, having seen you in action. You're resourceful, Steve, a quality I admire. And you have a fixed view of what's right and what's wrong. You don't equivocate."

"That's not a lawyerly trait."

"Not generally." She sipped her drink. "Earlier today I spoke with Harris Gurney, told him I'd asked you to resolve a sensitive personal problem."

"What did he say?"

"Told me I couldn't be in better hands. He's in Marsh Habor, by the way, and invited us to join him for some cruising. If—is it something you'd consider?"

"Very seriously. For several years I kept a boat at the Corinthian, used to see Hod polishing brightwork on his ketch."

"You don't have the boat now?"

"I was using it only every month or six weeks, business pressure being what it was when my practice was developing. Reluctantly I sold it."

"Were you in the navy?"

"Army. Served in Vietnam. Took some shrapnel in my leg six weeks after arriving. Returned to ZI for treatment and recuperation. The war ended—at least the fighting did—and I was discharged."

Her expression showed concern. "And your leg?"

"Good as new. Fully mobile, just some white puckers where the junk was extracted."

She looked away. "You're so much a part of the real world, and my life has been so sheltered from unpleasantness." She paused. "Until that damn cruise."

I shook my head. "A year from now this will exist only in the far reaches of your mind. We'll drive a stake through its heart and go on from there."

Impulsively she pressed my hand. "Oh, Steve, when you talk so confidently I feel as though it's already behind me."

"For practical purposes it is."

In the kitchen a buzzer sounded. She started, unclasped my hand, and stood up. "Dinner bell. I've salad greens crisping. While I bring on the food you might pour the wine."

After wrapping the ice bucket in a colorful bar towel I carried it to the table, uncorked the bottle, and half-filled the glasses as I'd observed sommeliers doing over the years. Alison brought on the salad bowl, served two salads, and returned from the kitchen with a steaming casserole in an insulating wicker basket. After seating her I took my place on her right. "Looks terrific."

"I hope you're not allergic to shellfish."

"If I were this would be the wrong city for me."

"I should have asked, but I'm glad there's not a problem. Lobster, shrimp, chives and scallions in a cream sauce." She began her salad and I started on mine.

We were partway through the main course when the telephone rang. Alison froze, stared at me apprehensively until I said, "Bedroom phone, go answer."

"But, Steve—"

"Just remember your lines, okay?"

"Okay."

I trailed her to check recorder function and waited to learn if Thomas Brooks was calling.

"Hello," she said hesitantly, then, "Oh, it's you. Where are you, Harlan?"

Her husband. I went back to the table and treated myself to more wine. When she returned she said, "A rare call from Harlan. Wanted to know if I have weekend plans." She picked up her glass and drank. "I said I did. Oh, the digital ID showed he was calling from his girlfriend's place." She swallowed. "I rewound the tape and started the recorder again. Is the casserole okay?"

"Didn't I say it's delicious? You prepared it?"

"Sorry you asked that. Actually it's from Ridgewell's. I don't have time or talent to do much cooking so I phone orders from their list, and they deliver. I keep the meals frozen until needed."

"Hats off to Ridgewell's." Washington's oldest and most expensive purveyor of epicure cuisine.

"But the salad is mine."

"Also perfection." I added wine to her glass. "If your husband pops in he'll ask about the bedside phone and recorder."

"I don't think there's a risk of that. Harlan hasn't entered my bedroom for at least two years. It's part of our understanding." She paused. "I don't mean to imply an open marriage, we just don't invade each other's space without advance notice—permission."

"Very civilized."

"That's one description." She held out her empty glass and I added wine. "Steve, I don't mean to pry, but I assume you're not married—because if you were you wouldn't be here."

"True."

"Were you ever?"

"Married? Lasted a little over two years, ended four years ago. Sammy was an artist, very mod, with a sort of pixie quality that attracted me but didn't wear well." I drained the bottle into my glass. "She had a studio in a Georgetown loft, spent a lot of time there. When she'd come home her hair was redolent of pot, and sometimes I'd see white frosting around her nostrils. Our circles and interests were mutually exclusive, self-contained." I took a deep breath. "One night an artist friend called from her studio. Said she'd passed out, what to do? I told him to call 911 and stay with her until I arrived. Naturally, he took off, and I got there just after the ambulance did." I paused. "The paramedics tried to keep her alive but she died in the emergency room at Georgetown Hospital—massive heart attack. Actually, cocaine overdose."

"I'm so sorry, Steve."

"Basically, Sammy was a good kid but we were far from right for each other. She had no interest in law and I had limited appreciation of art—still don't know much about it. But incompatibility doesn't surface until after the marriage when masks are off."

"That's my experience. And when the glow dies the drudgery

moves in, becomes overwhelming." Her features were taut as she spoke. I said, "But you see yourself locked into this marriage?"

"I believe divorce would kill my chance for reelection."

"And you want to continue in the Senate."

"What else am I to do with my life? I worked hard to get where I am, and I like being useful on the national scene."

"Have you thought of a quiet divorce in some distant venue? St. Thomas, say, or Mexico?"

She shrugged. "Divorce is divorce, a handicap to any politician. Besides, Harlan wouldn't leave quietly, macho pride being involved. He'd want a good deal of money, though I could afford to pay him off. It's just that, well, I haven't given a lot of thought to the marriage. He's not underfoot, and he's available for mandatory social functions, like White House receptions and banquets. So I guess he has his uses. Anyway I've grown accustomed to the situation."

"As your attorney, Ali, I have to ask a personal question: Aside from Thomas Brooks is there anything in your background that you wouldn't want made public?"

"Such as old lovers? Before Harlan I had a few relationships but none would be devastating were they known. The men left my life years ago, and married—happily, I guess. No, Steve, there's nothing I consider a threat. Does that answer your question?"

"It does, but I had to ask. To eliminate everything but Tommy before I focus on him." I pushed back my chair and got up. "Thanks so much for the evening—very considerate of you. I'll take your material and go through it tonight. When Tommy calls, I'll want to know."

She looked up at me. "No coffee? Brandy?"

"I really have to get to work. Rain check?"

"Of course." She rose and walked to the door. I picked up the heavy envelope and thanked her again for dinner.

As the taxi took me down Connecticut toward Georgetown I thought about Alison Revelstoke Bowman, and our conversational exchanges. She was lovely and lonely, vulnerable to a purposeful male, but also a client. With a husband.

Perhaps, I mused, when the Tommy episode was behind us and if we remained as compatible as we seemed to be I might review our relationship.

Then I remembered Hod's invitation to cruise the islands on his yacht. The two of us. Alison hadn't disliked the idea, or she wouldn't have relayed it. And she'd wanted my reaction. It was a provocative thought. One to examine more fully in days ahead.

FOUR

AFTER LEAVING ALISON Bowman's apartment I read the material she'd compiled, made notes, and turned in.

In the morning I spread everything across my conference table and briefed Mrs. Altman. "Establish a data base that can be enlarged, if necessary. Of all the senator's staff employees I'm interested in these four—Arnold Munger, her media man; Sally Pleven, executive secretary; Garth Anson, who administers the office and handles legislative liaison; and Joseph Gallegos, who responds to constituent mail."

"So Mrs. Stokes is really Senator Bowman."

"But her name's not to appear in our files."

"I understand."

"The common link among those four is that all came to the senator with letters of recommendation from the governor. She inherited the others from her predecessor or from other Senate offices—nonpolitical careerists."

I wasn't ready to enter Thomas Brooks's name because I felt it was probably an alias. Pat Moran might be able to clarify the matter. Continuing, I said, "I want Nexis and D and B reports on each of the four—their résumés may not be entirely accurate."

"I'll get right on it."

"One other thing." I paused to consider; no way to avoid it. "Harlan Bowman," I added. "You'll find his CV in that pile."

She looked at me in surprise. "We've never handled domestic disputes."

"I hope this isn't one, but let's find out."

"Full treatment, then—like the others."

"Right. And the policy hasn't changed."

"I'm glad to hear you say so."

At ten the temp lawyer came in. Burton Michaels had been with a medium-size D.C. law firm for nine years. Another year would have bought him tenure and a package of separation perks, but his firm merged with a larger one and Michaels was squeezed out. Tough spot for a forty-plus attorney with a mortgage to pay and family to support, so I was glad I could offer him remunerative work—not least to maintain his morale.

Michaels was low-key in voice and manner. I summarized the case he was to work on and showed him the extra office equipped with computer and printer. To spare him the embarrassment of asking, I told him what I would pay hourly, and asked if he preferred that or to be paid for the job. Hesitantly, he said, "Could I delay answering until I've sized up the case?"

"Of course."

"Thanks for the opportunity, Mr. Bentley, I appreciate it." He turned on power and booted up the computer. As he settled into the chair I left him to tackle what I lacked time to accomplish.

Walking back to my own office, I saw Pat Moran come in and said, "A welcome face indeed." He followed me into my office and closed the door. From a briefcase he extracted an envelope and laid it on my desk. I opened the envelope and took out a five-by-seven color print showing a young man sunning by a ship's pool.

"He's yer Thomas Brooks," Pat announced, "except that he was travelin' under false colors. True name Andrew Bostick of Baltimore, Maryland. I got it from the travel agency that booked him on the cruise. The agent didn't know Bostick was going to change his name for the cruise, couldn't speculate why."

"But we can," I remarked, and studied the photo. The face was handsome in a girlish sort of way; black curly hair, thin, weak mouth, no chest hair. Weight about one fifty, height maybe five nine. To me he didn't look masculine enough to be a stud, but seen through female eyes he probably was. "Rap sheet?" I asked.

Pat nodded. "Leased a car and vanished with it. Car recovered two months later in Las Vegas. Lessor didn't prosecute." He put on glasses to read from a pocket notebook. "Over the past two years Bostick persuaded two elderly ladies to invest in companies that didn't exist, had their checks made out to him personally. One lady declined to charge him with fraud but the other did. Unfortunately, she was in a hospital and couldn't attend the hearing. Charge dismissed."

"Lucky thief."

"Yeah, and there's more. He involved himself with the daughter of Governor Green and helped himself to some of her jewelry—diamond wristwatch, emerald necklace, and a gold bracelet. Sybil complained to her father, who reported the theft. Charges pending."

"So the governor has him by the balls."

"I'd say. Jewelry valued at about ninety thousand. Police recovered it from pawn shops in Baltimore and the District."

"Has he done time?"

"Not yet."

"Got an address for him?"

Pat consulted his notebook and wrote it on my desk pad. "Apartment's in a medium-low rent section that hasn't been gentrified."

"If he's not employed, how does he get by?"

"Maybe a doting mother," Pat suggested. "He's got a two-year-old green Audi he apparently owns."

"Yeah, I don't imagine he could manage long-term credit."

"Want him tailed?"

"Not yet. There are collateral aspects I'm checking on. I don't suppose the creep had any Chicago traces?"

He shook his head. "Not under those two names. Of course, there could be a third alias, or a fourth."

"Could be, but I'm satisfied with what we have. He misrepresented himself to a client, which is what I wanted to establish. Oh, what's known of the governor's daughter?"

"Sybil. Age thirty-four. Unmarried. Not a particularly attractive young woman. Lives apart from her father and has a job as an inner-city social worker. Said to have a history of mental problems. I don't know how she and Bostick got together."

"Not worth knowing. Thanks, Pat, for a job well done. I'll treasure the photo."

"That wrap it, laddy?"

"Fax me your bill."

"Will do." We shook hands and Pat grinned. "Next time, give me a hard one."

"How can I? You make everything seem easy."

"I love my work," Pat explained, and left, leaving me to synthesize his information.

Four of Alison's employees had gained sufficient favor with Governor Abel Green to warrant his recommending them for employment by the newly elected senator, a fact not necessarily damning. But include thief/con man/blackmailer Andrew Bostick, whose freedom depended on the governor's disposition, and I saw the elements of a conspiracy aimed at ousting the senator. As Alison and I had considered, the governor could appoint a puppet to her vacant seat, or occupy it himself. So Green had a personal interest in her disappearance.

And I wanted to know more about husband Harlan. He was floating out there, a kind of noncorporeal, ill-defined figure that even his wife apparently didn't pay much attention to. Still, I could theorize a possible interest on his part in extracting large sums of money from her, if not destroying her political career. Because a mistress could be a very expensive hobby, especially if the lady's upkeep required such durable mementos as jewelry. Against that theory was the senator's description of Harlan as the affluent owner of car dealerships, though I doubted that she had ever bothered to scrutinize his financial status. In Alison's genteel world it was "something one didn't do."

Well, I'd do it for her. And I reflected that the fifty thousand demanded by Bostick was only openers. Considering the senator's fortune it wasn't a troublesome sum, just a test by the blackmailer. If she paid he'd hit her again and again, and any promise by a blackmailer to turn over all the incriminating material—in this case, videotapes—was as solid as water. He might give her a sackful of tapes, but he'd always hold back copies for future use; that was the nature of the game. Smoke and mirrors.

That four of the senator's staffers knew Governor Green made me wonder if Harlan Bowman knew him beyond casual social and political contacts. The governor was the head of his state's political party as well as its chief executive official. As such, Green was in a position to buy or lease hundreds of vehicles for the state, a chop-licking bonanza for the fortunate dealer. If competitive bidding was mandatory, bids could be rigged. Or the business directed to Bowman by executive order. Was Bowman the lucky entrepreneur? Worth looking into.

A senatorial seat was said to cost an average of thirteen million dollars. Alison Revelstoke Bowman could afford the outlay but what about Abel Green? If he challenged her in the primary election, he'd have the heavy costs associated with an attempt to unseat an incumbent. And if successful he'd have to spend thirteen million more to have a realistic chance of success.

Governor Green enjoyed a solid trade union base. He had a hard-hat background and had manipulated it into high political office with the considerable help of organized labor and minority voters who responded to his populist image. Though aides and appointees had been convicted and jailed for corruption, Green had positioned himself above the scandals, declaring ignorance—and thus innocence—of their unlawful dealings. Publicly he had never been charged with felonious crimes. He was high in the national councils of his party, and esteemed by the media for wise manage‑ment of his state's affairs. To me it seemed obvious that he was, at least on his record, a potential candidate for national office.

The state's other senator came from the opposite party, a man in his late sixties who was automatically reelected by a largely rural constituency that abhorred the urban‑based Green. No opportu‑nity there for the governor unless the senator died, and he was known as a health‑food and fitness aficionado.

So if the governor were impatient he would have to target Al‑ison Bowman's seat. And if she had no vulnerability, creating one was the obvious, cost‑effective route. Not beyond the imagination of a politically attuned mind, I reflected. A few thousand spent on Bostick's cruise could be infinitely rewarding to his sponsor.

I didn't like the direction my thoughts were taking. Dealing with a low‑rent extortionist was how I initially evaluated Alison's problem, but taking on a governor—even indirectly—raised the stakes enormously. I wasn't going to back out; I'd given my word, and she needed help, factors I couldn't ignore and sleep peacefully.

Besides, an information search was underway, and the results could narrow the list of suspects and identify the malefactor behind Andrew Bostick.

When was her shipboard lover going to phone payment in‑structions? Weeks had passed without his calling. Far from meaning he wasn't going to follow through, I interpreted the delay as a nerve‑racking tactic calculated to soften her up until she was pliable and unresisting. Psychological warfare.

During the afternoon Mrs. Altman brought me printouts that expanded the basic employee information supplied by Alison.

Her executive secretary, Sally Pleven, had four charge ac‑counts canceled due to nonpayment of bills, and her car was ready for repo—until magically, a series of payments made on the same date restored her credit rating. The funds hadn't come from the Senate credit union, so their origin was unknown.

Press secretary Arnold Munger was a single parent raising two daughters unaided by a wife who had left the family in favor of a gypsy lifestyle touring the Southwest and Mexico on Arnold's credit cards, and Arnold had been able to meet the monthly nut until his wife's charge bills began rolling in. The combined expenses drained his bank account and left him in a negative financial position—until just after the previous Thanksgiving. Fresh funds suddenly enabled him to pay off credit cards, meet mortgage and car obligations, and emerge debt free. Amazing resurrection.

Office administrator Garth Anson, and constituent liaison Joseph Gallegos were current with their debts and appeared to lead untroubled lives. So it was Arnold and Sally I saw as probable moles providing information on their employer to their benefactor or benefactors.

They were the ones I intended to interview.

Leaving the enigma of husband Harlan Bowman to resolve.

I felt it was premature to confide my suspicions to Senator Bowman. She would be reluctant to believe there were traitors in her office, people she had chosen and paid and dealt with on a daily basis. Moreover, once the seed of suspicion was planted, her demeanor toward the suspects was likely to change, and I didn't want them to have the benefit of early warning. The crisp way to handle it was to confront them separately in an office apart from her senatorial suite. Once their guilt was confirmed, fire and expel them with no opportunity to cart off the senator's files.

As for husband Harlan, handling him would be infinitely more delicate, for there I would be intervening in a marital relationship. Still, before I went after Sally and Arnold I would have to get a fix on Harlan. If he was guiltless, so much the better. But if he was part of a conspiracy against his wife I didn't want him to be warned by her office help. Nor could I suggest to Alison, without damning proof, that Harlan had been at least partly responsible for the shipboard episode. Her immediate reaction would be disbelief; after all, he was her husband, her chosen mate. Admitting a bad choice would be a tough blow to her pride, and she'd face a decision to divorce or continue tolerating him. Not an easy choice.

Burton Michaels knocked on my door and came in carrying a sheaf of documents. "Got a moment, sir?"

"As much as you need."

He outlined the problem as he saw it and suggested two av-enues toward obtaining tax relief for the client. "I'd rather not take this into tax court," he said, "although I feel chances are good for a favorable decision. That would mean substantial delay for the client and additional expense. Alternatively, there's mediation. I'd look for abatement or at worst a compromise settlement."

"After consulting the client."

"Of course. I wouldn't want a compromise figure to exceed that of tax court representation, and I'd try for much less."

"Factoring in what the client stands to lose were the litigation unsuccessful."

He nodded. "How do you want me to proceed?"

"Work up figures for both tracks, take them to the client and see what he prefers."

He smiled, and gathered up the file. "You're showing a lot of confidence in a new employee. I appreciate it."

"It's your case from now on. Make appropriate decisions and keep me reasonably current." I paused. "You don't shrink from do-ing battle in the trenches with the IRS?"

His smile broadened. "It's my life's work, and I love it. And I like tax court representation too, because it deals with figures, not personalities."

"Your hours are your own," I told him. "We don't punch clocks around here. Just do the work."

"I will," he said, and left.

Toward five I took a call from Alison. "Steve," she began, "I have an eerie feeling that I'm being followed. I don't suppose it's one of your people?"

"Only suspects are tailed," I told her, "and you're not one, you're the client. But I can have you countersurveilled for a few days if that would make you feel better."

"It might, but I want to talk about it with you. Would you be free for cocktails? Six-thirty or so?"

"I would. And if dinner is contemplated I'll bring wine."

"That would be good of you."

"Actually, the time is right for a chat. There have been some developments I want to tell you about. Six-thirty, then."

This evening she was wearing a dress of white nubby silk, a single-strand pearl necklace, and white silk ballet slippers. I'd brought a bottle each of Beaujolais and Chardonnay, and seat them on the bar while I made a shaker of martinis. Alison watched with seeming interest, took her glass, and said, "I'm so glad you could come."

We carried our drinks to the coffee table, sat and looked at each other for a few moments. Finally she said, "When I left here this morning I noticed a man near the drive when I pulled out in traffic. I think I saw him again in the corridor outside the Senate Restaurant at lunch time. Steve, why on earth would anyone be following me?"

"No idea. Description?"

"Under six feet, narrow face, prominent nose. Wearing a tan raincoat and gray hat. Coincidence?"

I shrugged. "If you see him again let me know immediately. We'll find out who he is, the nature of his business." I sipped the mart and the chilled liquid set my teeth on edge before it warmed my mouth and throat. "I will," she said, "though I hope I'm not being followed." She sipped again and set her glass on the table. "You said there have been developments."

I nodded, drank and sat forward. "From the beginning of your ordeal it's been apparent that someone in your entourage helped set you up. Thomas Brooks joined the cruise for that purpose. His true name, by the way, is Andrew Bostick. He lives in Baltimore and has a substantial record of fraud and thievery."

She blushed as she looked away. "To think that I—"

"Don't think about it. The fact that you were targeted for seduction ought to diminish whatever guilt you still feel."

"And I feel plenty," she sighed, "aside from the threat to my political life."

"That's up to you. Anyway I'll want a private talk with some of your staffers fairly soon."

"Who, Steve?"

"I'm not ready to identify them. Just wanted you to know there's incriminatory information I've developed, and I think it will lead to the person responsible for setting Bostick on you. When the time is right I'll tell you."

"And I'll have to fire that employee."

"This person was paid to betray you. Having done so once, whoever it was wouldn't be reluctant a second time."

"God, I wish I'd never taken that damned cruise!"

"History, Ali. We're into damage control now."

"If we could only have that Tommy—I mean Andrew Bostick—arrested for extortion . . ." Her voice trailed off.

"Don't want that. Arrested, he tells the whole world about his affair with Madam Senator, so eliminate that thought from your mind. He can be handled in other ways. Quietly. By the way, have you got fifty thousand cash available?"

"She nodded. "In a shoebox in my closet."

"May need it to flash, but not hand over. And when he calls tell Bostick an intermediary will handle the transaction."

"You, Steve?"

I nodded. "Say you're afraid to see him alone, a cousin will pay him." From my pocket I took the shipboard photo and gave it to her. Alison gasped, "It's him! How on earth did you get it?"

"My investigator did. Don't worry, your name hasn't been mentioned, and won't be unless absolutely necessary." I drank from my glass, then pocketed the photo. "Hate to ask you, but under the circumstances, I feel I must." I took in a deep breath. "Your husband. I can get a report on his financial status, but I need some depth on your relationship. In effect you're separated, right?"

"For practical purposes."

"And it didn't pain you that he took a mistress?"

She looked down at her drink. "Briefly. It was a blow to my pride, then it came as a sort of relief."

"Does he know you know?"

"I never discussed it with him. As I told you he has his life and I have mine."

"And you're not seeing anyone, as the phrase has it?"

"Unfortunately, no. When I think about it I miss having a man to talk with, miss the physical part, but I'm used to that by now." She looked away. "Sublimating."

"What I'm trying to get at is whether you feel that Harlan would damage you in any way. Is the potential there?"

She thought for a while before replying. "I have to answer that with another question: why would he?"

"For money. For his freedom. Because he's forced to."

"Forced?"

"It's a tough word, but if someone had economic power over your husband and wanted his collaboration—well, he's already betrayed you by taking a mistress. It's not a long step to working against you."

In the kitchen the buzzer sounded. She got up, said, "Be right back," and went to the kitchen. When she returned, she said, "Rack of lamb roasting. That okay?"

"Very much okay. And we'll have the Beaujolais." I got up and went to the bar, uncorked and decanted the wine, noticing that the table was already set for two.

Ridgewell's had done themselves proud again. The trimmed chops were a faint pink, the rissolé potatoes and asparagus mouth-melting tender, and the rich hollandaise a cardiologist's dream. The slightly acidic taste of the wine caressed the tongue while accenting the varied flavors of the meal.

During dinner we talked generalities: places and resorts we liked, musical preferences, playwrights, Kennedy Center productions, and as Alison spoke I thought that this attractive, intelligent, achieving woman was a trophy catch for any serious man. And I wondered why husband Harlan had strayed so far from their marriage. Unquestionably my hostess possessed a magnetic aura that enhanced her persona and minimized the power of her wealth. I could easily overlook her misstep with Andrew Bostick, lay it to the beguiling diversions of a cruise and the apartness from the restriction of Washington. Besides, Bostick was a handsome and skilled exploiter of wealthy women.

I heard her say, "And you?"

"Hmm?"

She laughed lightly. "I was asking whether you're seeing someone, as the phrase has it."

"No," I replied. "No entanglements. Like you I'm absorbed in my work."

"All work and no play . . . except that you're not dull—far from it. And, thank God, you're not a politician. That's a big, big plus."

"No one ever suggested I run for any office. Besides, I haven't the talent to be a candidate, much less an officeholder."

"But lawyers seem to fit naturally into politics. They become lawmakers or judges."

"Those who have personal fortunes."

"You hold mine against me?" she said sharply.

"Of course not—just an observation. And you've used yours to advance the interests of your state—and the nation."

"I'm glad you feel that way, Steve. Because without the give and take of politics my life would be pretty barren." Pausing, she glanced away. "Especially without a husband to share it with." She rose and said, "Let's have coffee."

I went to the coffee table and presently she brought in a gadroon-edged tray with cups and a steaming coffee pot. "Liqueur?" I asked.

"Whatever you're having."

So I brought snifters and Hine to the table, and poured. As we sipped together I felt there was something on her mind. After a long silence she got up and put a CD in the player. When she came back I said, "Albéniz. Don't hear much of him on the radio."

"Edged out by gangsta muck. De Larrocha is the pianist."

"It's a fine recording."

She nodded. "If you have nothing more pressing, we could have a musical evening. I have a good selection of Spanish music."

"Let's hear it all," I said, and refilled our glasses.

Absorbed in music, we said little over the next two hours, and when the last selection ended, Ali said, "I really don't want the evening to end, Steve, I've enjoyed it so much. But—it's getting late, and I hardly know how to ask this—but would you like to stay over?"

I swallowed. "I'd love to," I said, and leaned over and kissed her warm lips. Her arms went around my shoulders, and in a little while she rose, took my hand, and led me to the bedroom. I untied my tie and was beginning to unbutton my shirt, when the telephone froze me with a strident ring.

She looked at me, fear in her eyes, and slowly picked up the receiver.

FIVE

———

"REMEMBER," I WHISPERED, "you're alone," and flicked on the speakerphone.

"Yes?" she said in a low voice.

"Alison," a male voice responded. "Glad I found you home. You've been waiting for my call?"

"Expecting it, Tommy, without pleasure."

He chuckled unpleasantly, and I saw the recorder tape turning. "Got the money?"

She glanced at me. I shook my head, and she said, "No."

"Get it tomorrow. Have it there when I call."

"Tommy, I need more time to get fifty thousand dollars together without causing, well, comment." She paused. "Unless you'll take a check."

"Check?" His laugh was mirthless. "And have you cancel it at your bank? No, babe, I'm not stupid."

"Indeed you're not. So you'll understand why getting all that money together isn't something I can do with a wave of my hand."

"You can't?" he sneered. "A U.S. senator can do anything."

"I need two days, Tommy."

"Day after tomorrow then, no excuses."

"There won't be any. Just you make damn sure I get what I'm paying for—all of it. Because once I pay you that's it, no more."

"Don't you tell me what to do, bitch," he snarled. "Screw this up, and I'll find another buyer—won't be hard, either. Any tabloid would make me a rich man, so keep that in mind." He chuckled nastily. "Meanwhile I enjoy watching that tape, babe . . . hate to part with it."

"But you will. For fifty thousand dollars."

"Cash. Two days, bitch. Get it together."

The line hummed dead. She replaced the receiver, hand trembling. Breathily she said, "Thank God you were here. Alone, I think I'd have come apart."

"Well, you didn't, you did just right." I removed the tape and replaced it with a new one, then checked Caller ID. Area code 410 meant Maryland, probably Baltimore, and undoubtedly a pay phone. I wrote down the full number for Pat Moran's possible use. A reverse phone book would pinpoint the phone's location.

Alison stood there looking at me uncertainly and I realized our moment of passion had passed. Taking her hand, I drew her from the bedroom and said, "Let's have a nightcap." I refilled our snifters and said, "To better times."

Hesitantly she drank. "Are you sure you don't mind?"

"There's a time for everything, Alison. Maybe after all this is over."

She nodded slowly. "But everything's on track?"

"Absolutely. And I'll be here for his next call."

"Two nights from now."

I nodded, and she moved against me. I could feel her body quivering. I kissed her forehead and she murmured unintelligibly.

"Night, Ali. Wonderful dinner." She pressed my hand and I left.

Home, I turned on my desk light and called Pat Moran's office. To his answering machine I read the phone number I'd copied from the ID gadget and suggested he check its location. "Probably Baltimore, and likely not far from that fellow's apartment. Next subject is Harlan Bowman, purportedly a well-to-do car dealer and husband of Senator Alison Bowman. If you still have that inside tax contact, maybe we could get a look at Harlan's recent returns. A client is concerned about his liquidity, and so am I. It's said on good authority that he's keeping a ladyfriend who could be draining his bank account. Got the picture? Call or come in when you have something. Erase this message when received."

After hanging up I got ready for bed. Initially I'd thought of asking Alison for copies of her joint tax filing, then realized they undoubtedly filed separately, he having business income, while her income derived largely from the Revelstoke estate. Alison was one of a few public officials who returned her Congressional salary to the Treasury. And could afford to.

The tape recording of "Tommy's" call was highly incriminatory and could be used against him. Not in a court of law, because Alison would have to be named as the target of his extortion. But letting him hear it would have a chilling effect. I'd consider that in the morning.

Meanwhile—I turned off the bedroom light and lay back—there was a major question out there and it needed to be resolved. And that was a possible connection between Governor Green and Harlan Bowman. Was it significant? Could be. Was the answer easy to come by? Hardly.

Something else to ponder in the morning.

Morning came with cloudy skies and rain, snarling District traffic as it always did, but the season was too far along for snow. Looking across Layfayette Park toward the White House, I recalled the night of Kennedy's inauguration when heavy snows stalled arriving limousines. Heaters and idling engines drained batteries and many partygoers had to hoof it through the snow and ice to the Executive Mansion. But even the chaotic beginning didn't dim the glitz and glamour of newly arrived Camelot.

At ten Mrs. Forsythe's heirs, Ashley and Bryan, came in. Neither looked pleased to be there, Ashley demanding, "What's all this about?"

"It's about your inheritance. As your mother's attorney and executor I don't want any post-mortem squabbling or litigation to invalidate her will. So here's how it is: equal shares. Fifty-fifty."

"Damn!" Ashley spat. "What about my kids?" She glared spitefully at her brother. "Bryan'll just piss it away."

"Spoken like a true lady," I remarked. "Ashley, you married against your mother's wishes, produced children. In that you were exercising free will options. You should feel fortunate your mother didn't eliminate you from her will. Think it over and reconcile yourself to fifty percent. An Oriental sage once opined that half is better than nothing." I turned to Bryan. "Any problem?"

He shook his head. "I have none and you won't get any from me. I'm grateful to my mother."

Ashley grunted. "Always the whining, crawling pissant. Do I have to see Bryan again?"

"Only when I read the will. And I hope that will be a lot of years from now. Your mother is a fine and generous woman, benefactress of more charities than you could count. She doesn't deserve a gimme attitude from you, so I strongly suggest you spare her." I got up from my chair. "If you think talking with your mother will change her mind, don't waste your time or her patience. She designated me to inform you and spare herself the unpleasantness of manifest ingratitude. Keep my office informed of your residences. That's it. Finito."

Bryan got up and shook hands with me. "Thanks, Mr. Bentley."

Ashley reached the door first, spun around and snapped, "Thanks for nothing." Went out. Bryan looked at me, shrugged, and followed his sister. I had the distinct feeling they weren't going to share the same taxi.

Burton Michaels asked me to check a portion of the work he'd completed and I spent half an hour at his desk before Mrs. Altman buzzed and suggested I take a call at my desk. When I got there she added, "Mrs. Stokes, and she sounds, well, very upset."

"Thanks." I pushed the line button and said, "Mrs. Stokes?"

"Yes, Steve, and I can't seem to stay out of trouble." Voice tense, pitch unnaturally high. "Have you seen this week's *Capitol*?"

"Sorry, no. Something in it to disturb you?"

Her laugh was short and strained. "Disturbed? I'm all of that. More accurately, I'm half out of my mind." She paused. "I'll read it to you—short but deadly: *'Beltway insiders are wondering which married female lawmaker enjoyed a holiday cruise in the company of a handsome, younger man. Fellow seagoers described the couple as being as happy as honeymooners. Who is she? Rumors abound.'* Steve, isn't that awful? What can I do?"

"Nothing."

"I feel like suing."

"I'm sure you do, but it's not an option. There's no basis for a libel action because what you just read me is basically the truth. If it wasn't, and you didn't mind having your name dragged through the mud, you'd have only a slim chance of prevailing. In practical terms, the media almost never lose a libel action, so all you can do is swallow hard, scoff at any linkage, and get on with your life and work. I know it's a tough prescription, Ali, but this is a time to put on a good face and be silent."

"At least the item didn't say senator."

"A good thing, too, and that reservation tells me the leaker didn't intend to destroy you—the purpose was to intimidate you."

"But who—?"

"Señor Bostick or his employer. They want your money, Ali, and that gossip item is supposed to soften you up, eliminate resistance."

"It's having that effect, I'll admit. Right now I just want to run away from the office, take a long drive—anywhere."

"Don't. Follow custom and routine. Leave at your normal time. Go home, enjoy a bubble bath and a good dinner. Watch a movie. Go to bed. Things will look a lot better in the morning."

"God, I hope so—and thanks for listening to me."

"Hold on through tomorrow night, Ali. I'll get that tape and your life will be normal again."

For a few moments she said nothing. Then, "It's not the money, you know, I don't care about paying the money."

"You won't have to. Now, try to calm down and I'll see you to- morrow evening."

"I'm counting on you—you know that."

"I do."

At noon I took Burton Michaels to lunch at the Lawyers Club and listened sympathetically while he described his reactions to being let go by his firm. Shock, disbelief, anger, resentment, and finally a feeling of hopelessness prevailed before he could pull him- self together and get on the job market. As we talked three lawyers came over to say hello to me, and I introduced them to Michaels. Two others came by to chat briefly with Michaels, and said they were glad he'd landed on his feet. When they left he said, "I hope word will get around I'm gainfully employed."

"It will, and could open new opportunities for you."

"That's why you brought me here, isn't it?"

"Plus the fact that the club serves a good lunch. Doesn't hurt to be seen where lawyers congregate. I don't deal in charity where business is concerned, Burton. You're doing good work for me or I wouldn't keep you on the job. Okay?"

"Thanks, Mr. Bentley. That's good for my morale."

After a drink and a shower at home I changed into black tie for a dinner at the Logos honoring retiring judge Seymour Gilstein of the District Court of Appeals. I had no professional dealings with the appellate court, but I'd known Sy when he was U.S. attorney for the District of Columbia, and found him fair and approachable. So I joined a table with five other attorneys, dined on Chesapeake Bay scallops and Maine lobster, enjoyed light wines, and listened to some predictable speeches. The president of the D.C. bar presented the judge with a gold-plated gavel and a set of golf clubs, after which

Gilstein reminisced somewhat lengthily, I thought, ending the evening on the short side of midnight.

As I taxied back to Georgetown I decided I'd suffered
through far less tolerable affairs and was satisfied I'd done the right
thing by attending.

Entering my house, I heard the summoning chirp of the answering machine in my office, and saw that there were two messages
on the machine. Both, it turned out, from Alison. The first had a
time imprint of 8:14 P.M. and said, "Steve, I hope you'll hear this in
the next few minutes because Tommy—Bostick, I mean—called to
say he wasn't responsible for what the magazine printed, and was
very sorry about it. He wanted to apologize in person and said he'd
give me back the videotape and explain things. He offered to come
to my apartment at ten and said he needed five thousand dollars to
get out of town. Five thousand now, and forget the rest. I said
I'd pay him five thousand for the tape and any copies, but he
couldn't come to my apartment, I'd meet him down in the parking
lot." She paused. "I need your advice, Steve, because this looks like a
golden opportunity to be finished with him forever, so I hope you'll
come here as soon as possible because I don't want to meet him
alone. Please call."

The next message was at 10:42 and her voice was close to hys-
teria. "Steve—oh God, I wish you'd been home because something
terrible has happened and I don't know what to do."

She answered my call on the first ring, and I said, "I just got in,
and—"

"Oh, Steve, please come right away. It's terribly urgent, and
you're the only one who can help."

"I'm on my way—can you tell me what it is?"

"He's—he's dead," she said, and hung up.

Dead? Christ, I thought. I pulled off my dinner jacket and tie,
and changed into slacks and a tweed jacket. The taxi dispatcher said
it would be a half-hour wait, so I got into my BMW and drove to
Alison's apartment building.

I rang her call button, the door opened almost immediately,
and I took the elevator to her floor. Her door was open, and I found

her weeping beside it. Wordlessly she came into my arms. I closed the door and said, "Bostick's dead? Where?"

"In his car, in the parking lot."

I pulled back to look at her face. "Did you kill him?"

"No—of course not," she said. "How could you think that of me?"

"You've been under strain, pressure. People react differently to stress than they otherwise would." I drew her to the sofa and told her to sit down. Then I poured scotch into two iced glasses, took a long pull from mine, and gave her the other. "Drink," I ordered, and as she did I said, "I went to a banquet and I wish I hadn't."

She swallowed, and dried her eyes and cheeks. "I did wrong, didn't I? You'll blame me for what happened."

"I'm not blaming anybody," I said as I sat beside her. "You felt you had to meet him, and under the circumstances I can't blame you. He said he'd be in the lot at ten o'clock, right?"

She nodded. "I expected him to ring from below and say he was here."

"Did he?"

"No. So I waited. And waited. And waited, my nerves getting tighter all the time. Steve, it was unbearable."

"I'm sure it was. What then?"

"At ten-thirty I decided to go down and see if Tommy—damn, Bostick—was playing some sick waiting game with me." Her hands clenched and unclenched. The cords in her throat stood out. I took her hands in mine and said, "So you went down to the parking lot."

She nodded. "Each resident has a numbered parking slot, and there are three for visitors." She paused. "One was occupied."

"By a green car?"

"Why, yes." She faced me. "How did you know?"

"Acquired knowledge. An Audi?"

She sucked in a deep breath. "Maybe, I don't know much about cars. But I went to it, and—the window was down and I could see a man in the driver's seat. I got the five thousand dollars ready to give him, called 'Tommy' as I approached, but he didn't answer." She swallowed. "I'd never seen a dead man before, but the position of his head, lying over on his shoulder in an unnatural way, gave me the creeps."

"I can imagine."

She swallowed again, licked dry lips. "Then I saw the blood." Turning, she buried her face in my shoulder and began to sob. I let her cry, drank from my glass, and waited for the spasm to end. Finally, she drew back and said, "I suppose I should call the police."

"Why? You didn't kill him. You found what the killer left, which is not a crime. But the fact that he's in the lot of your apartment building could cause unpleasant speculation."

"And I'd have to leave the Senate."

I shrugged. "Don't buy trouble. Okay, my car is parked next to his. I saw the corpse and he's very dead. One shot in the temple. Maybe more in the body but that's for the coroner to find. Show me the five thousand you didn't need."

Reaching across the coffee table she lifted a thick envelope and gave it to me. It was filled with hundred-dollar bills. I checked the serial numbers to make sure they weren't sequential, kept twenty bills and returned the rest. After pocketing them I drained my glass and got up. "To keep you out of this I'm going to have to alter the scene, understand?"

"Yes." She looked up me. "No police?"

"No police. If you have rubber kitchen gloves, give me a pair. And three or four bath towels that don't have a laundry mark. An old blanket would be useful, too."

She got up. "Anything else?"

"Destroy the tape in your answering machine."

"Yes, of course." She swallowed. "Will you be gone long?"

"Probably."

"Will you come back here?"

I shook my head. "Not tonight. After I leave, go to bed. Start forgetting this episode—all of it."

"Will you come for dinner tomorrow night? I mean, tonight?"

"Good idea—and you're not to worry. Now get me the things I need."

* * *

I left the building by the service entrance carrying a bulky plastic trash bag that I placed between my car and the Audi. I pulled on rubber gloves, opened the driver-side door and looked down at the dead man.

As Alison said, his head was positioned against his right shoulder and his eyes were extruded from the bullet's cranial expansion. A lock of dark hair slanted across his forehead and his lips were drawn back in the rictus of death. Before moving the body I draped towels over the passenger seat and noticed keys hanging from the ignition lock. I dropped another towel to cover Bostick's right side where gray-red matter from the wound had been sprayed. More of it clung to the inside of the right-hand door and window. Obviously, he had been shot from where I was standing. Either the killer had surprised him or Bostick recognized him and made no defensive move.

Opening the right-side door I began pulling the stiffening body into the passenger seat, taking care not to brush against the blood and brains. I seated it on protective towels and closed the door.

Breathing hard from the effort, I leaned against my car and looked around. From the avenue came the soft hum of late night traffic heading out toward Maryland. No movement or lights in the parking lot. A few side windows in the apartment building showed dim light behind drawn shades. So far so good.

While moving the body I'd noticed a crumpled paper bag on the floor, and stopped to check its contents. Three videocassettes. I transferred them to the trunk of my car and got into the Audi, wondering why the tapes hadn't been taken by the killer.

In the driver's seat, I opened Bostick's jacket and drew out his billfold. It contained a driver's license, forty-two dollars, and three credit cards. I pocketed the money and credit cards, and replaced the license before dropping the emptied billfold on the floor. Then I bent down the upper part of the body until it nearly touched his thighs, and draped Alison's old beach blanket over his back and head. In that position it was below window level.

Time to leave.

The engine started on the first try and I kept the headlights off until I was clear of the parking lot and turning onto Connecticut Avenue. Keeping well below the speed limit I drove north on Connecticut to pick up the Beltway. The route I chose was a lot longer than driving through the District, but had the advantage of no traffic lights and a higher speed limit.

Halfway around the Beltway and south of the District I turned onto Route 1 and followed it past Jefferson Memorial to Reagan Airport. In the second parking building I drove to the third level and picked a corner in the darkest area to park and move Bostick's body back into the driver's seat. The move was harder than before because rigor was advanced and the body seemed as unyielding as a statue and equally heavy.

I put bloody towels, gloves, and blanket in the trash bag, knotted the top and walked from the Audi to the stairs, carrying the bag.

On level 1 I found a large rubbish container and shoved the bag in it, then walked to the Metrorail Station and rode as far as Farragut Square. There I roused a taxi driver and had him take me out Connecticut Avenue to the apartment building I'd left an hour and a half before.

Pale moonlight showed dark, immobile cars. No visible lights in the building. As I got into my BMW I reflected that on the way to the airport I'd concentrated on driving safely and unobtrusively, not letting myself dwell on the nearby doubled-up corpse and its blood-soaked shroud. Or on the implications of what I'd done. Obstruction of justice could be charged, were I linked to the Audi and the dead man. Worst case: a murder charge that wouldn't be easy to beat—unless the true killer were found, or by some miracle confessed. Maybe I'd erred in leaving the trash bag in the parking building's container. But O.J. seemed to have jettisoned evidence in a container at L.A. airport and the missing black bag had never been found. Maybe I'd be as lucky.

I drove down Connecticut Avenue to Georgetown and parked at the far end of my drive. The house was on Q Street, a block from the house that had belonged to General Ballou and Francie. I saw it every day, and every day old memories returned. The general was buried in Arlington but I had no idea where Francie's remains had been buried. I'd avoided details of her fatal crash, didn't want to know how that beautiful, headstrong, vulnerable girl had perished. But I thought about it, probably too often.

After the general's death, his house had been sold by the Ballou estate. At the time I hadn't the money to buy it, and besides, it was far too large for my limited needs. So I'd settled on my present house, buying the owner's furniture to spare me the trouble of finding new furnishings. New mattresses and bedding were all I'd added to what was there.

I thought of the videotapes in my trunk and wondered again why they hadn't been taken by the killer. They were, after all, the reason Bostick had come to the parking lot, and so I had to assume they were linked to his death. But I could be wrong.

I pushed aside speculation, opened my trunk and got out the videocassette bag. He'd been prepared to exchange the tapes for Alison's five thousand dollars, or so it seemed. At least he'd brought them to the scene and kept that promise. Probably, I mused, the only decent thing he'd ever done.

After unlocking my front door I went inside and locked it after resetting the burglar alarm. Georgetown was a quiet, well-patrolled area with a low crime rate, but now and then burglaries made the papers and I thought it prudent to keep my home as inviolate as possible.

Walking to the kitchen, I realized I was a lot more tired than I'd thought. Adrenaline had pretty much metabolized and I was on energy reserves. I iced a glass, poured Johnnie Red and drank gratefully. Carrying my glass I went to the living room, turned on the VCR, and took the three tapes from their shabby bag.

I played the first tape long enough to see a naked couple copulating; the female was Senator Bowman, the man's face was hidden from the camera. I checked the other two tapes, and found them duplicates of the first. As I turned off the VCR and replaced the tapes in their bag I wondered if they were all that had been made, or if someone had another, or others. At least these three were out of circulation and no longer a threat to my client. Would she want them, or should I destroy them now? I decided she'd want the satisfaction of actually seeing the cassettes before disposing of them.

The phone rang twice. I answered before the machine could

cut in and heard Alison's voice. "Steve, are you all right? I've been terribly worried. How did things go?"

"Everything's okay," I told her. "I have the package and I'll bring it at dinner time. Now go to bed and stay there."

"Oh God, I'm so grateful," she said, "and relieved. Ever since he called I've lived a total nightmare."

"Well, the nightmare's over. Did you take care of your tape machine?"

"As soon as you left. I couldn't wait to get rid of it all."

"Good. We'll talk tonight. Now get some sleep—which is what I'm going to do."

"Thank you, thank you for everything." She paused, and her voice lowered. "Were you in love with Francie? My cousin Francie?"

"You asked that before. The answer is yes. Is that important?"

I heard a sigh before she spoke. "I find myself envying her, Steve, envying what she shared with you."

"It was very brief, and long ago. See you tonight."

"God bless you."

I finished my drink, built another and took it to the bathroom. There, under strong light, I examined my clothing. No visible blood, and only a bit of gray matter on my jacket's right elbow. I soaped it off and hung up the jacket, then took a long hot shower, as though water could purge away all that had happened that night.

Finally in bed, I found my mind pondering the mystery of tapes that should have been taken from Bostick's car but were left for me—or anyone—to find. The best answer my tired mind could devise was that the shooter wasn't looking for tapes, or if he'd found the bag didn't realize what it contained. The killer hadn't taken Bostick's money or billfold. Why not? Because he wasn't a robber. He'd gone there to kill the victim and had no other motive. My emptying the billfold of money and credit cards was only to es-tablish a presumption of robbery in police minds. Unless they con-ducted an in-depth investigation they'd report he was killed at the airport by an unknown robber, which was what I wanted their con-clusion to be.

In my mind I saw again the young, white face of Andrew Bostick, the powder grain tattooing around the entrance wound. The shot had been fired at close range, no more than two feet from his face. Wouldn't the approach of a stranger have alarmed him? But if the shooter was someone he knew, Bostick would have had no cause for alarm. Even in a dark parking lot.

Bostick, of course, knew who had employed him and targeted the senator. Maybe that employer wanted to shut his mouth forever. But then leave the incriminating tapes in full view? Stranger and stranger. My thoughts drifted off, swirling like dark smoke until they blotted everything from my mind.

SIX

BEFORE LEAVING FOR the office I erased my answering machine tape with its record of Alison's panic calls. Then I went out to the patio and burned Bostick's credit cards in the barbecue kettle. More obstruction of justice, but hell, I was used to it now.

As I drove to the office I listened to the AM news radio and heard nothing of a body found at the airport. Good news is no news, I told myself, so keep the good news coming.

This morning my office seemed normal and I felt good about that. No quarrelsome heirs, no distraught female senator, no dissatisfied clients scowling as I entered my sanctum. But I'd barely had time to view the White House as I liked to do because it gave me a sense of national solidity, when Pat Moran came on the line. He said he had some items of interest to convey. "Steve, I can be there in an hour, okay?"

"Sure, Pat, that's fine."

I had time to go through the morning mail: bills, charity solicitations, Bar Association dues along with an invitation to tax attorneys to foregather and consult on a ten-day cruise to Cancún. I gave the brochure a wry smile and dropped it in the circular file. Forevermore, cruises would be tainted with memories of Alison's misstep, plus I didn't enjoy forced conviviality with professional colleagues for anything like ten days. Among the mail was a postcard from Hod Gurney in Tortola, BWI, bearing a colorful tropical scene. The message in cramped schoolboy script reiterated his invitation to cruise with him—and Alison Bowman—as soon as we could come.

I put aside the postcard, reflecting that unlike the cruise to Cancún, Hod's proposal was a lot more intriguing. I understood, or thought I did, why he included Alison: she was a client of his firm, and he could deduct that portion of the cruise when she was aboard. Crafty Hod, I thought, and decided to show Alison his card at tonight's dinner.

After reading and signing three documents and placing four return calls, I took one from an IRS auditor, establishing a mutually satisfactory date to go over a client's questioned returns. Burton Michaels could handle it, I decided, and asked Mrs. Altman to give him the files. Then Pat Moran came in.

After closing the door, he sat across from me and opened his briefcase. "First item," he said, "is Harlan Bowman. Through my IRS contact I got copies of his last two tax filings. He's a high liver, m'boy, but he's living on the edge. One dealership franchise hasn't met sales quotas and is about to be taken from him. Also, he's taken out sizable loans using his stock of automobiles as collateral."

"That's a no-no," I remarked, "because the cars aren't his, they're only on consignment. What else?"

"Around Atlantic City casinos he's a well-known loser. I couldn't get figures, but I estimate his markers as exceeding two hundred thousand dollars."

"Doesn't sound like a stable, well-adjusted citizen."

Pat smiled. "On casino trips he usually has his bimbo with

him—name of Doris Conlon. He backs her wagers along with his own—on credit, of course. Credit check shows most of his cards maxed out. And he took out a mortgage on a Philadelphia condominium he shares with his wife, the senator." His eyes narrowed. "Thought you didn't do divorce work, Steve."

"Maybe I'm changing policy."

"It's scummy stuff, stay out of it."

"Guy's gotta make a living, Pat. There's such a thing as being overly selective."

"Yeah. Me, I usually take what comes in through the door but I draw the line at scumballs. Uh—mind if I smoke?"

"Your funeral."

Pat lighted a cigarette, inhaled, closed his eyes and sighed in satisfaction. "Speaking of scumballs, that Andrew Bostick is something else."

"How scummy?"

"Listen to this, Steve. I don't suppose you ever heard of a Baltimore dive called the Escapade?"

"No."

"It's a watering hole for leather freaks and rough trade guys. Down below, in what was once a regular basement, they have a big tub, like what the guineas stomp grapes in. Know what I mean?"

"I do."

"The tub is part sunk in the flooring. A guy with no clothes on sits in it and other guys stand around the tub and—well, they relieve themselves on him. How d'ya like that, Steve?"

"Not much."

"The guys pay for the pleasure of urinating on the Pit Boy, that bein' what he's called. They sort of rotate Pit Boys, but one of them can get a couple hundred bucks a night."

"And they get off on that?"

"Guess so. Haven't seen the spectacle myself, and don't want to, but my informant tells me Andrew Bostick's a favorite Pit Boy."

I stared at him. I'd lugged a dead Pit Boy halfway around the Beltway. My flesh began to crawl.

Pat said, "I guess that's how he pays his rent, buys gas and food. No other visible means of support. Not a model citizen, Steve."

"No." Seducing and compromising Alison would have been a welcome and profitable gig considering his nocturnal avocation. Pit Boy. Jesus!

"You want more on Bostick, *der Kinkmeister?*"

"That's plenty," I said, knowing I'd never repeat to Alison what he'd told me; she'd feel even more degraded and humiliated. "Anything else, Pat?"

"That's it," he said, returning papers to his briefcase, "but I'll say this—you have an interesting practice."

"Occasionally." We shook hands and he left.

For a while I considered the new information he'd brought me. Alison's husband was a gambler who owed big-time money, and what I knew of casino management told me they didn't wait forever for their pay. Harlan was probably too ashamed to ask his wife to cover his markers but that could change if he was faced with threats of death or physical injury. How much did Alison know? It was a question I ought to ask. I'd assumed Harlan was in bed with Governor Green, but his heavy debts turned my thinking in a different direction. The fifty thousand Bostick had demanded wouldn't clear Harlan's debts; the money would make a down payment, nothing more. Of course, I understood that fifty was only an initial demand, and more would be made. Were the three tapes I'd recovered the only ones remaining? Would Bostick have had access to all of them? It seemed unlikely. Still, his killer hadn't taken the tapes from his car, suggesting no connection between them and his killer. If Bostick's sponsor hadn't killed him—or ordered it done—where was the motive?

I realized that subconsciously I was attempting to fit Harlan Bowman into a circumstantial picture because no link between him and Andrew Bostick had surfaced. Yet someone with money had hired Bostick to compromise Senator Bowman. The 4X video was the big stick to threaten her, but now the agent—Bostick—was dead. Did that end her troubles?

And was she as innocent of murder as I'd instantly assumed?

She'd told me Bostick phoned to apologize for the *Capitol* item and offered to give back tapes for a quick getaway stake of five thousand dollars. In evidentiary terms that was an unsupported statement. But suppose she invited him to meet her in the parking lot, taken a gun with her and shot her betrayer, then called me and made me the clean-up man. It wasn't a scenario that pleased me, but Bostick hadn't tried to get away from whoever shot him, and the weapon was about .32 caliber. I judged that from the small size of the entrance wound and the dimensions of the exit wound, about the size of a plum. A .38 bullet would have blown out a cavity the size of an orange or larger, and not a lot of females used .38s because of the pistol's weight and kick. Among female shooters .32 or .25 was the preferred caliber. A general observation of no probative value.

Considering Alison as a killer made me uncomfortable, but in developing an overview of her blackmail and her blackmailer's murder it was a factor I couldn't ignore. What I couldn't find a logical answer to was why, if she'd killed Bostick, she hadn't taken the tapes, whose delivery was the purpose of the meeting. Leaving them in the hope I'd find them was far too risky an assumption, and it presumed her acting with icy cold resolve and monumental faith in my efficiency.

So barring hard evidence of her complicity I was prepared to eliminate Alison as a murder suspect.

Governor Green had leverage on Bostick, the threat of prosecution and prison. If Pit Boy was Green's lackey I reasoned that the governor had every reason to continue using him. Unless, of course, Bostick had unwisely blabbed his intention to implicate Green in the cruise seduction scheme. But was Bostick so moronic or naive as to challenge the powerful governor and risk prison? According to Alison, Bostick had asked for a getaway stake, meaning he didn't want to stay around the tri-state area where there was no future for him but trouble. I could understand Green's ordering a hit on his defecting agent to close his mouth forever. But there were those damned tapes. To Green their value was as an instrument to force Alison from office. So if they were found by police investigating the murder, subterranean whispering would identify Alison as Bostick's sex partner and perhaps implicate her as his killer. Killing Bostick would not only silence him and keep Green's name out of the affair, but once the nature of the tapes was known she'd have to re-sign, serving Green's interests and aspirations.

For wasn't that what the whole cruise conspiracy was all about? Getting Senator Bowman out of office and replacing her with Governor Green? That had to be the bottom line, the sum of all the related incidents, and I now saw Green as the figure respon-sible for it all.

I wasn't sure how much of my thinking I'd reveal to Alison over dinner, nor was I entirely confident that all the erotic tapes were accounted for. Only time would tell.

I had a working lunch at my desk, conferred with Burton Michaels, sifted through phone messages, and around three o'clock took a call from Pat Moran. Without preliminaries he said, "I know you don't monitor the police scanner, so I thought I'd let you know the Pit Boy is dead."

"Dead? How long?"

"Body found in his car at Reagan Airport, one of the parking garages maybe an hour ago. Shot in the head, the prelim report said. Robbery suspected. Parking ticket time showed he drove in late last night so he could have been killed any time afterward."

"I don't know if that's good news or bad, Pat. But at least he's out of the picture now, no longer a factor." I paused. "Plane ticket on him?"

"Maybe. Do you want to know?"

"Only mild interest, don't make a project of it."

"There'll probably be more details on the evening news."

"Probably. Thanks for calling."

"Okay. It'll likely turn out to be one of the many unsolved killings around our benighted area. I guess he'll only be missed by the Escapade crowd."

I grunted agreement and hung up. No reason for Alison to know the corpse had been discovered; I'd save that for later.

At five-thirty I left the office, drove home, and collected things to take to Alison. Then I had a stiff drink, showered, changed and set off for her apartment.

*　　*　　*

After greeting me with a peck on my cheek and a brief hug, Alison said, "they found Bostick's body at the airport."

"So I heard." I opened my litigation bag and produced two bottles of wine. She said, "I'll chill the white. And I'd love a martini—or two."

I made drinks, and at the coffee table returned the two thousand dollars I'd borrowed last night. "Thank you," she said. "Obviously you didn't need the money."

"I had a vague idea I might have to bribe someone—like a road cop—but that didn't happen." I took out the brown paper bag and showed her its contents. "Three tapes," I said, "and yours makes four."

She stared at the cassettes and swallowed. "What shall I do with them?"

"What Nixon should have done—destroy them." I gestured at the log fireplace.

"Yes, please. Light the fire, Steve."

While the tapes flared and melted, charred, and vanished in the flames we sipped our drinks and watched the conflagration. When the fire dipped low I refilled our glasses and noticed that Alison was still gazing at the fireplace. I sat beside her and said, "Hello."

"Oh, yes—sorry—I was thinking of those tapes and wondering if there were others." She sipped her drink. "What do you think?"

"I don't think it's something to worry about, Ali. We don't know what was in Bostick's mind when he called and offered to give them to you. It was certainly an unexpected development, but I'm afraid all gestures of contrition from a career con man have to be treated with suspicion."

Sitting back, she looked up at the high ceiling. "And I suppose the police will go through his apartment looking for clues to the killer."

"Routine."

"Yes, but if he hid another tape and it's found I'll be even more threatened than before."

"Maybe not." But I'd thought of that earlier and it disturbed me. "Can we try to be positive? Bostick is dead and four tapes no longer exist. I think that's a big improvement."

Her smile was brief and strained. "It is. Of course it is. And you risked so much for me. I'll—I'll never forget all you did."

"It would be better if you put the episode out of your mind and not fret the details." I got out Hod Gurney's card from Tortola and handed it to her. After reading it she said, "That would be nice, wouldn't it, Steve," and returned it to me.

"I haven't had a vacation in a long time," I remarked, "and cruising with Hod sounds like a glimpse of paradise. But it's really your call. At this point you don't need matrimonial problems."

"That's true—I can't predict what Harlan would do if he found out."

"Neither can I, but I've learned that he's heavily in debt to At-lantic City casinos, and one of his dealerships is about to be taken from him."

She stared at me. "You learned that and I, his wife, didn't even know?" She set down her glass. "What does it mean?"

"It means he needs money, Ali. If you wanted to you could probably buy him off for a quiet divorce. Use his vulnerability to your advantage. Oh, he's also taken out a mortgage on your Philadelphia place."

"He has? He didn't tell me, and I'd never have consented." She shook her head. "I didn't know this side of Harlan."

"The reason I looked into his finances was because of his rela-tionship with Governor Green."

"Abel? What kind of relationship?"

"Harlan's dealerships sell cars to the state, a lot of cars. Proba-bly a sweetheart deal with the possibility of kickbacks to the Gover-nor, directly or indirectly." I looked down at Hod's card. "I ought to say I'm sorry for turning up all this, but the truth is I'm not. I think you're entitled to know the true state of affairs, as is every wife. Looking into your husband's financial situation was a logical step because someone financed Bostick's cruise and seduction expenses, and told him to extort fifty thousand dollars from you. The fact that Harlan is in a deep financial hole suggested to me that he was look-ing for a big payoff. Through Bostick he could keep bleeding you for ever larger sums without the necessity of divorce. That's what I the-orized and it's still a reasonable theory. What's changed is Bostick's murder. Dead, he's out of the blackmail equation. And if there's some connection between him and Harlan I assume the police will find it and follow wherever it leads."

"And if he's in some way involved I'll suffer the publicity fall-out."

"In the worst case it will be a short-term embarrassment, not at all comparable to what those tapes contained."

For a while she was silent, hands opening and closing before she said, "Do you think Harlan was behind it all?"

"I have nothing solid to lead to that conclusion."

"Who, then?"

"Governor Green. He has motive, money, and he had hard leverage over Bostick. Do the governor's bidding or do jail time for stealing from his daughter."

She looked shocked. "Sybil? You mean she knew Bostick?"

"Intimately. Her jewelry was recovered, but her father had it in his power to have Bostick prosecuted. Harlan, as far as I know, had no such leverage over Bostick, if he even knew him."

"I can't imagine it."

The kitchen buzzer sounded. Alison said, "Dinner bell," and left for the kitchen. I uncorked Chablis and filled our wine glasses while Alison, wearing protective oven mitts, brought a covered casserole to the table. "Lobster Alfredo," she announced, and un-covered the dish, then brought in prepared salads.

The chunks of creamy crustacean were delicious, and the Chablis made a great complement to the wine sauce, I said so and she smiled. Over coffee I said, "I think that what you retained me for has been accomplished."

"But Steve, I still have my marital problem to resolve," she ob-jected.

"Not my field of expertise. Putting it bluntly, I don't handle domestic litigation."

"I see. But you could, well, advise me, couldn't you?"

"Not without treading on your attorney's turf." I paused be-fore saying, "I've identified two of your staffers with ties to Governor Green: Arnold Munger and Sally Pleven. It's likely that one or the other told Green—or someone—of your cruise plans enabling Bostick to book passage and meet you. I think you ought to be very circumspect around them for a month or so, then find reason to suggest they find other employment."

"Oh." She thought it over. "But suppose neither one was disloyal, acted against me?"

I shrugged. "In the interest of your Senate career I shouldn't think you'd want even potential spies on your payroll."

"That's true," she nodded.

"Moles, spies, informants could be even more damaging in a presidential campaign—feeding your speech drafts, travel itineraries, and contribution sources to the opposition, so—"

"But I'm not seriously thinking of trying for my party's nomination."

"That's today, Ali. But looking ahead you have to see how important a secure inner circle is to you or any high-profile political figure."

She looked away. "You're right, Steve. But I hate the thought of getting rid of workers I've come to know so well."

"Not well enough. Look, I'd planned to interview them, confront them with what I know, but the tapes no longer exist and Bostick is dead, so there's no point. Just let them go quietly, give each a bonus, if you feel that's appropriate, and write nice letters of recommendation, like the letters Green wrote on their behalf. Say you're downsizing your staff—that's commonplace these days—and say nothing more." I finished my coffee. "I'll miss seeing you, Ali."

"But it doesn't have to end so—so, totally, does it? I've come to depend so much on you." She gazed at me. "Is there any real reason we shouldn't be seen dining in public?"

"Can't think of any. Besides, I've felt the need to reciprocate, and I want to. Let's do it soon."

"Yes. Steve, do bring over the cognac and snifters—you'll share, won't you?

*   *   *

So we had after-dinner cognac and listened to an Andrés Segovia CD. The combination relaxed me, and after a while I felt Alison's hand creep over to cover mine. "The other night," she murmured, "we were interrupted—seems ever so long ago—but perhaps you'd like to stay over tonight." Before I could reply she said softly, "So many confusing things have happened I deeply need the reassurance you could bring me . . . Unless knowing about Bostick and me turns you off."

"Don't even think it," I told her, cupped her head in my hand and drew her lips to mine.

Her body trembled as her lips parted and the tip of her tongue teased mine. Then our arms circled each other, and like sleepwalkers we made our uncertain way to her bedroom.

There in the dark we stripped and joined together on the bed. Her ample breasts were firm, her loins velvet-soft, her buns unyielding. My lips and hands paid homage to this wonderful, unappreciated female, until passion surged over us in an irresistible wave that left us beached and languorous until another wave drew us back into a warm and depthless sea.

Later she stirred beside me, took my hand and held it to her lips. After kissing it she asked, "Is Harris Gurney married?"

"Yes, very much so."

"And would his wife be with us on the cruise?"

"We'd make it a stipulation." The thought of days and nights drifting through the Caribbean with this extraordinary woman excited me.

"For appearances' sake they could be chaperons."

"Of course. You're a client, Hod is discreet and would never do anything to bring discredit on you, dear. If we go, Mattie will definitely be there. Too, she's a creative hand in the galley."

Alison laughed. "How fortunate—because we do have to eat."

I kissed her full lips. "Occasionally. But we could make do on coconuts and bananas."

"Darling, so long as you were with me I wouldn't care if we never ate. I mean that."

"Brave words. We'll see how they stand up."

She sighed, pressed her body against me. "Then all we have to do is look at our calendars and tell Harris—I can't get used to calling him Hod. That's boy stuff, isn't it?"

"It is," I acknowledged. "By either name he's a good guy. Actually, Ali, he's a great guy."

"He must be. Because he brought me you."

"Mrs. Stokes," I said musingly. "How long ago that day seems."

"Doesn't it? And you became my white knight, rescuing a lady in distress. It's how I'll always think of you, dear."

I kissed her forehead. "You were the little girl in white pinafore, dimples, and brown eyes."

"And you made the bully go away." She kissed me. "My rescuer. No one else would have done all you did. Or could have."

Not being able to summon an adequate response, I said, "My only concern is your husband. I don't want him bringing a divorce action against you—now or ever."

"Then maybe I should have a legal separation?"

I shook my head. "That only prolongs the inevitable, gives people more time to gossip and spread rumors."

"Then what do you advise?"

"Take the problem to your usual attorney at Gurney and Steiner, suggest he call Harlan in for a conference. Have him tell your husband you want a quiet divorce. Before then you and your attorney should decide on monetary figures, a sum you'll pay him for an uncontested divorce." I nibbled her ear. "I imagine he'll want a pretty substantial figure, knowing the damage that could be done to your political career. On the other hand, your attorney will know he's in financial straits and if Harlan denies it he can be made to reveal his net worth and income, and that could be pretty sobering."

She sighed. "I've gone on so long not thinking about freedom that facing reality isn't comfortable." She swallowed. "Before I go back to my old thinking I'll see the attorney. Tomorrow."

I patted her rump affectionately. She said, "When I really want something I go after it. Steve, I don't care how much I have to pay. Money is a renewable resource but life is not. There's only so much of it to spend."

"Sage words," I remarked. "Would you be able to spend as much as two weeks away?"

"If you can."

"Tell me the dates and I'll call Hod."

"It's exciting just to think about, Steve. You won't back out?"

"Ridiculous idea." I kissed her nipples, felt them harden, and in a little while we were making love. It was so fresh and sponta-neous and new that it seemed like our first time.

And I deeply hoped it wouldn't be the last. Even though I re-alized I might be sleeping with a future president of the United States.

SEVEN

—

NEXT MORNING WE shared an early breakfast. Alison served scrambled eggs and warm croissants with marmalade and coffee, and we searched the *Post* for mention of Andrew Bostick.

Found it on page 18, one column wide and less than three inches long. It repeated basics already aired by radio, adding that Bostick had lived in downtown Baltimore, was believed to be unemployed, and left no known survivors. His murder was believed to have occurred during a robbery, no money having been found on the body. Police investigators invited calls from anyone who might have information on the robbery-murder.

I refolded the paper, drank coffee, and said, "So there it is.

We'd both like to know who killed him, but unless there's a confession I doubt we'll know anytime soon."

Alison nodded. "Now that I'm over my fright when I found the body I'll confess I don't really care who shot him. The creep had it coming."

"Maybe someone from his past," I mused. "Someone with a big-time grudge against him. Followed his car from his place to yours, shot him and disappeared. Ah—I don't suppose you have a handgun?"

"No, why? You don't think I—?" Her face clouded.

"Not at all, just asking." That much settled. I felt relieved. Unless Bostick had left notes with Alison's name in his apartment I could think of no discoverable link between them.

Alison said, "Have you any idea who could have placed that nasty item in *Capitol*?"

I thought it over, finally saying, "At first I figured Governor Green because he was one of a very few who might have known what went on during the cruise. But on reflection I couldn't define a motive." I studied her expression. "Have a candidate?"

"Afraid not," she shrugged. "But I wonder if my husband picked up on it."

"Suppose he read it—you're only one of dozens of lady lawmakers, Ali. Why would he decide it was you?"

"I don't know, but it still makes me uncomfortable. Guilty knowledge, I guess."

"Dinner tonight?"

"Love it."

"Pick you up—when—six?"

"Seven okay? I have a caucus I really need to attend."

"Seven it is. Informal dress."

She stirred her coffee before saying, "I have a country place not far from Leesburg, been in the family for eons. There's an unpretentious farmhouse, empty except when I go for an occasional weekend, a barn, and stables for horses I no longer keep . . . " She sighed. "I loved riding over the fields and down to a pond that's fed by a spring—even in the heat of summer it's icy cold. It's surrounded by a copse of birch and I could go skinny-dipping in private. But political obligations haven't given me time to enjoy the place as I'd like."

"And it's all there unattended?"

"Oh, I rent acreage to a farmer who works the land with his son-in-law. They raise corn and sorghum and all kinds of vegetables. And they harvest cherries and apples from the orchards. But between planting and harvest time I never see them. But then I haven't been there often the past two years."

"Sounds like a wonderful place to relax."

"It was. But Harlan doesn't care for the countryside, he's, well, urban by background and preference. So I got used to going there alone." She looked at me. "I have no right to monopolize your life, but perhaps you'd consider a weekend there with me."

"I've considered and accept. With anticipation."

She smiled. "This coming weekend—are you free?"

"Not any longer."

She smiled again. "Tonight I'll give you directions. Come Friday after office hours, I'll stock food and things so we won't have to go anywhere for anything."

"And I'll bring wine."

"Mmm. Lots of it." She glanced at the wall clock, sighed. "Gotta get going. There's shaving gear in the guest bath I keep for a husband who never comes." She got up, kissed my cheek and stroked it lightly. "Take care of yourself, Mr. Wonderful."

"I will," I promised, patted her rump and watched her walk away, the hem of the pink silk dressing gown swirling around her feet.

I opened the office earlier than usual, checked phone messages and e-mail, and made coffee for myself. Scanned the *Post* for developments in the Bostick case, found none, and turned to the day's agenda: one client conference before noon, two in the afternoon. Burton Michaels arrived, followed minutes later by Mrs. Altman, and now we were staffed and running.

Pat Moran faxed his bill for investigative services, I okayed payment and told Mrs. Altman to add it to the A. Stokes account.

"So far," she remarked, "you haven't billed anything. Don't you think it's about time?"

"Probably so. I'll think about it and come up with a figure." That couldn't include time relocating Bostick's body, nor the hours of bedroom embraces. The former was a chargeable offense, the latter priceless. An umbrella figure would cover legal advice and consultation. Six thousand was fair, I decided, plus Pat's fee. I made a note to that effect and decided on an informal billing since Alison wanted to keep her involvement anonymous.

At five I left for home, welcomed myself with a martini and changed from yesterday's clothing. At seven I buzzed Alison's apartment, and presently she joined me in the parking lot, wearing faded jeans and matching blouse. Before starting the engine I said, "How was the caucus?"

"Interminable, as they all are. Pure politics, nothing more."

"Pure?"

"That's wicked, Steve. Okay, *just* politics, okay?"

"Much better."

As I turned north on the avenue she asked, "Where are we going?"

"A place I'm sure you've never been."

"Why would you say that?"

"Well, it's not a haunt of the rich and famous; actually, it's patronized by frugal families and working stiffs, bikers and truckers who appreciate good food."

"Steve, not fair to sneer at me," she said tartly. "And by now you should know I love good food."

"You'll see a lot of shiny nylon jackets on the bowlers, and mechanics' overalls. Just to prepare you for the setting."

"I see. So you appraise me as a snob."

"Not at all. Just a lady who's been rather isolated from working America."

"And I don't much like that, either. Are you determined to quarrel? Is that how our relationship is developing?"

I laughed. "Lighten up, honey. I think our relationship—if that's the term—is developing marvelously, don't you?"

She snuggled against me. "If I didn't I wouldn't be here."

I steered through outgoing homeward-bound traffic on Georgia Avenue, down under the railroad bridge in Silver Spring, and turned into a small parking area beside an old two-story building whose neon sign read CRISFIELD'S.

We went in together and looked the length of the packed raw bar until an elderly woman with a sheaf of menus asked if we'd like a table. Alison said we would, and were shown to a small table in a far corner. Seated, Alison looked around at the Victorian furnishings, the old-fashioned white mosaic floor, the ancient player piano, and nodded approval. Taking my hand, she said, "I like it, Steve. What's the house specialty?"

"Seafood. Any kind, and freshly prepared. I usually have a dozen Chincoteagues washed down with a stein of beer, a plate of deep-fried shrimp with fries, more beer, salad, coffee, and lemon meringue pie."

"Wonderful—I'll have the same." She smiled teasingly. "That the diet menu?"

"Absolutely. Low cal, high cholesterol." A waitress appeared and wrote down our order. Alison asked, "Do you have wine?"

"Yes'm. White and red. Most folks want the white 'counta it goes better with seafood."

"Then I'll have white."

"Glass?" She looked at me. "Bottle," I told her, "and very cold. 'Counta the oysters."

"Thank you." She left and I said to Alison, "I never thought to ask about wine, so I've learned something. My girlfriends order beer or nothing."

"Hmm. I can see you with a bevy of large, muscular biker gals who drink boilermakers for breakfast."

"Wear chrome-studded black leather, *Wehrmacht* helmets and cavalry boots. So now that we've swapped lies and disposed of preliminaries, what's the divorce situation?"

Her expression sobered. "At noon I saw the firm's domestic

relations specialist and told him what I want done. His name is Chad Goodrich. He understands why I want no publicity. Gurney and Steiner always do my taxes, so the lawyer has access to what I'm worth. Then we decide a reasonable offer to Harlan."

"When's all this to take place?"

"He thought maybe the middle of next week. Then he'll have to contact Harlan and that's not always easy."

The waitress delivered a bottle of Napa Valley Chablis, uncorked it and set it in the worn ice bucket. "Back with glasses," she promised. And returned with two plates of oysters on crushed ice and a basket of French bread. The table already held a lazy Susan of sauces and spices, so after I'd poured wine we began on the oysters.

After swallowing six I said, "Invariably delicious," and Alison nodded agreement. After the shells were removed she said, "Do you have any feeling about the CIA?"

"Like what—good, bad?"

"Sort of. I'm on the intelligence subcommittee and sometimes I think I'm listening to aliens from another world. Do you have CIA friends?"

"I did but most of them left the Agency—retirement or disgust. The Agency has had some bad times, too many self-caused, but the people who work there are dedicated to our country and I hope most of them will stay."

"So do I. Not all committee members are pro-Agency; they're skeptical of its post–Cold War relevance. I'm a supporter, though, even if I feel some recent directors are substandard. Any thoughts on that?"

"Have to agree. CIA guys I met in Vietnam were pretty much okay, but none of us liked the Agency being dragged into the anti-narcotics struggle."

"I don't like it today, but someone has to do it."

"I suppose so, but that's a little like flooding the streets with infantry to maintain order. Let the cops do it, it's their job. And I've never felt that a Peace Corps background produced the ideal CIA director. Or someone devoted to the concept of nation-building.

Next they'll have Agency guys handing out food parcels in Upper Volta. That's not the career most Agency recruits were looking for when they signed up."

"Couldn't agree more. But I'm afraid mine is a minority view. At least in the committee, where I'm the obligatory female member."

"And probably the least biased."

"I like to think so. Anyway, the committee chairman noticed me for a meeting Friday, so that's where I'll be until I can break away and get out to the farm." She hesitated. "You *can* come, can't you?"

"Counting on it. Anything I can bring besides wine? Martini makings?"

"Good idea. Because I don't know what's hiding in the cupboards."

After the wine we had coffee in thick china mugs but Alison declined dessert. So I feasted alone on lemon meringue pie and paid for our meal, and we drove back to her apartment building.

In the elevator I said, "You mentioned our developing relationship—does that mean we're going steady like in high school?"

"I guess so, though I didn't attend a coed school. I went to St. Tim's—all-girl. Did I miss anything worthwhile?"

"Probably not. Unless you wanted to be a cheerleader."

"Not really. I played soccer and field hockey—pretty good too, if I do say so."

She unlocked the door and we went in. Almost automatically I brought cognac and snifters to the coffee table while Alison put on a Kenny G CD. As she sat beside me she said, "That was a wonderful dinner, Steve, I really enjoyed it. The place was warm and welcoming and I hope we'll go there again."

"Whenever you like." I touched my glass to hers, sipped and asked, "Did the divorce lawyer suggest a quiet, low-profile venue?"

"He mentioned Liechtenstein, if I wanted to pass waiting time in Europe, and said Belize and the Cayman Islands were possibilities." She took my hand. "Maybe I could combine that while cruising with Gurney."

"A twofer. Why not?"

"In about three weeks I can get free—Congressional recess. Confirm tomorrow?"

"Yes. Don't let Hod make other arrangements."

She kissed my cheek. "I think of you all the time, you're indispensable to me. My only fear is you have a wife hidden somewhere in the woodwork waiting to pounce on us."

"I thought we'd settled that."

"Uh-huh, but I need reassurance, being on the verge of a major life change."

"From time to time we all need reassurance."

"You? I don't believe it. You're one of the most self-assured men I've ever met. Steve"—she shook her head—"you must be joking."

"Believe it honey. I'm a worrier."

"I can certainly understand you worrying about my problems—but then I never thought they'd involve murder."

I took her hand. "That's over and done with. History can't be altered so the best course is to forget everything unpleasant."

She kissed my cheek. "I'm trying, I really am. And the good that's come out of it is finally deciding about Harlan. Even though I'm sure it wasn't your intention, you helped me make up my mind."

"I did?"

She nodded. "Unavoidably I contrasted my husband with you. Realized the possibilities of living an enjoyable life."

"Then I served a double purpose." I drew her lips to mine as she whispered, "I care for you very deeply, you must sense that."

"And it's obvious I care for you."

"You wouldn't believe how eager I am to go cruising with you." She drew back. "Turquoise seas, starlit nights—think we'll get on each other's nerves?"

"Not if I have anything to do with it." Rising, I drew her to her feet, kissed her deeply, and led her to the bedroom.

After making love, we fell asleep. A little after midnight the telephone rang. The sound wakened me, but Alison stirred only slightly and after half a dozen rings the call ended. The machine hadn't been activated, so I wondered who would be calling her so late at night, decided that since Bostick was dead it was probably her husband.

Hell with him. I turned over, nestled against the warmth of her body, and fell asleep.

Next day Alison phoned the promised dates, and I relayed them to Hod Gurney. He said he was delighted we were coming, and said Mattie was, too. "Ah, Steve, I guess you and our client are getting along well. Or shouldn't I ask?"

"Ask away. Answer is yes. Very well, and thanks for the invitation. I ought to add that she's consulting Chad Goodrich for the usual reason."

"Hm. Chad's a good man, be a real help to her. And I have to say that she's a wonderful woman. No pretensions."

"So I've found. See you soon, Hod, and best to Mattie. Oh, anything I can bring?"

"Just your young, charming selves."

Later Mrs. Altman showed me a check signed by Alison R. Bowman. "Full payment," she said. "Credit the Stokes account?"

I nodded. "For the time being it's best the senator not be a known client."

"Whatever you say, sir."

Friday after work I packed a small travel bag with weekend essentials and put it in the car trunk along with a case of wine—half Chablis and Chardonnay, also a quart of Bombay gin and a pint of dry vermouth. Plenty to last through Sunday afternoon.

I drove west to Wisconsin Avenue and stopped at a Georgetown butcher for lamb chops and sirloin steak, then over Key Bridge into Virginia. I didn't need Alison's directions to get to Leesburg because several times a year I had brunch at the venerable Laurel Brigade Inn on the town's main street. But I followed her sketch northwest from town into the fullness of white-fence country. Two and two-tenths miles on I came to her family retreat. The gate was open, and as I drove over the winding unsurfaced road I made out a Victorian-style house surrounded by tall elms. Two-story with gables, it had an open verandah on two ides with borders of flowering azaleas and other green shrubbery. I could see that the access road continued past the house toward a large unpainted barn and run-down stables. Plowed fields reached almost to the barn beside which a tractor with harrows stood idle.

As expected, Alison's sleek teal-green Jaguar was parked by the house, but just beyond it was another car—a white Mercedes roadster, top down. I braked and thought things over; was the Mercedes owner an expected visitor, or an unexpected drop-in? Would my arrival pose a problem for Alison? I turned off the engine and watched light-bluish mist rising from the fields. Sunlight was almost gone, breeze stirred the elms' upper branches. It was a peaceful setting. Suddenly the quiet was broken by a man's loud shouting from inside the house. I didn't like the sound of it, so I started the engine and was about to drive closer when the front door burst open and a man tore out. He got into the Mercedes, backed around and saw me. He drove toward me, braked and stared at me. His tanned face wore a slim mustache, and his back hair was curly and thick. I rolled down my window. "Hi."

"Who're you?" he snarled.

"Neighbor—down the road," I said pleasantly. "Is the senator in?"

"Yeah, she's in," he snapped. "Got business with her?"

I shook my head. "We don't see her often, thought I'd say hello. My wife—"

Abruptly he hit the pedal and his roadster spurted away, tires spraying gravel against my car. I turned to watch him careening from side to side, then lurch onto the highway without slowing.

I recognized him, of course, from a photo Pat Moran had supplied: Harlan Bowman. And now that I'd seen and heard him I knew him as a surly son of a bitch.

I parked beside Alison's Jaguar, mounted the porch and went in.

EIGHT

———

ALISON WAS STANDING just inside. Even in the dim light I could see her reddened eyes, the pink mark on her cheek. She dabbed a small handkerchief at her eyes and said tremulously, "You saw him."

"I saw him. Wanted to know who I was."

She pressed against me, circled me with her arms. "What did you say?"

"Told him I was a neighbor, asked if you were in the house." I kissed her forehead. "He said you were and shot off. Now let's bring in supplies."

I carried the case of wine while Alison brought in my travel bag, martini makings, and parcels of meat. Then I drove my car out of sight behind the barn and walked back. If Harlan hadn't noticed my license number I didn't want to give him another chance. Nor was it anyone's business that the senator had company.

Inside I said, "I prescribe a restorative drink. Where's the ice?"

She led me to the kitchen. I made a shaker of marts and while it chilled I put white wine in the refrigerator.

In the living room Alison turned on two Tiffany table lamps whose soft roseate glow enabled me to survey our surroundings while we drank. The furnishings were old but far from shabby. Walls held half a dozen oil portraits of men and women of an earlier era whose visages had frowns in common. A glass-front corner gun cabinet showed an assortment of shotguns and rifles. A locked bottom drawer probably stored ammunition and cleaning gear. Alison finished her drink and held out her glass for a refill. "I needed that," she said in apologetic tones, and drank again. Then she asked, "Did you hear what Harlan was saying?"

"Just the shouting before he ran out. I gather he was in a nasty mood."

"Very nasty."

I touched the side of her face. "It's almost disappeared."

"Thank God for that." Her gaze dropped and she said, "You're so discreet you haven't asked what he was shouting about."

"None of my business," I said, "but if telling me would make you feel better—"

"It will, definitely." She drew in a deep breath. "He wants money, a lot of money."

"For what?"

"Said he had debts, was under pressure to pay them."

"Ah," I said, "the casinos. But I'll bet he didn't identify them."

"No. And he doesn't yet know I'm planning to divorce him." She sipped from her glass and said reflectively, "Wonder what he'll do then?"

"Cave," I told her. "He must have been desperate to come and threaten you. Unwittingly he let you know you're in the driver's seat. That gives you and your attorney a real advantage."

"It does, doesn't it?" She smiled for the first time since my arrival. "Hadn't thought of that. Now I feel better about his coming."

"How did he know you were here?"

"Probably called my office—I always let Sally know how I can be reached. Can't blame her for telling my husband, after all, and it's better he did his shouting here than in my office."

"May I make a suggestion? Change the locks on your apartment door."

She nodded. "On Monday I'll tell the building superintendent." After a long sigh she said, "I'm so glad you're here Steve."

"Me, too. Let's put this incident behind us and do something about dinner."

While steaks broiled on the charcoal grill Alison baked potatoes and made a salad. The grill reminded me of burning Bostick's cards but I didn't mention it to my hostess.

We dined on a polished walnut table set with antique silverware, and after I'd refilled our glasses with Beaujolais she said, "Harlan wants eight hundred thousand dollars. Said if he doesn't get it he'll go to the tabloids with stuff I wouldn't want published."

"Is that an empty threat or are there things in your closet that concern you?"

"Only Bostick—and how could Harlan know about that unless he sent the bastard to do his dirty work?"

I shrugged. "My advice is to tell Harlan you'll talk to him through your lawyer and only through him. If he disregards that you can threaten him with charges of spousal abuse." I sipped from my glass. "Eight hundred thousand, eh? I'll bet he'd take half of that in exchange for an uncontested divorce."

"Really?"

"Another thing—if he did send Bostick to compromise you he can't pursue that line without getting linked to his murder."

She swallowed. "You think Harlan killed him?"

"Why not? He's as good a suspect as any."

"But why?"

"Who knows? The killer did us a favor, Ali, so I'm not keen on laying blame. Motives are strange things, believe me, and not always comprehensible to bystanders."

For a while she was silent before saying, "The thought haunts me there may be another copy of that damn tape and Harlan has it. Or can get it."

"Wouldn't he have said so to strengthen his demand?"

Her eyebrows arched. "One would think so, not knowing my husband. But when Harlan sets his mind to it he can be very clever—crafty is a better word. So I don't see him overlooking any stratagem that might help him get what he wants."

I drained my glass and set it down. "We've always hoped but never could be certain that all the tapes were destroyed."

She nodded. "And as you said we can't be sure until, God forbid, another blackmailer appears."

"Or until enough time elapses that we can be confident no other tape exists. More wine?"

"Thanks, no, I'm ready for coffee and brandy."

"So am I."

Seated on the old sofa with its embroidered antimacassars in place, we reviewed plans to sail with Hod and Mattie Gurney until Alison said, "Oh, how I pray Harlan doesn't do something to screw it up."

I took her hand. "The fact that he came here to bully you doesn't change anything or make him more important than he's been. I'm sure you were shocked to be slapped and abused by a man you once loved, but it's something that happens with dreadful frequency among couples." I glanced at the gun cabinet. "You said you don't have a handgun."

She stiffened. "You doubt me?"

"Not at all. I was just wondering if you can use those firearms—shotgun, rifle."

"Both. When I was quite young my father taught me, and often when General Ballou came here my father would let me shoot with them. It made me very proud, me, a mere girl competing with two grown men." She laughed. "Silly, wasn't I?"

"No, you had every right to take pride in your skill. And your father and uncle wouldn't have continued shooting with you if you hadn't been competent. Anyway, I'll check the pieces tomorrow, clean and oil as needed." I gazed at her. "Since then you haven't turned into an antigun freak?"

"By no means. I don't take contributions from the NRA or side with it publicly because I now how vicious the opposition can be. On the other hand, I don't support fanatics who insist on taking weapons of self-defense from the hands of law-abiding citizens. Am I being hypocritical?"

"You're being sensible, politics being what they are."

"Oh, Steve, you're never at a loss for reasonable answers. You'd make a great lawmaker if you could tolerate the aggravations."

"Nope, I'm contented out of the limelight."

"Then be my adviser."

"Covertly?"

"It that's what it takes. Deal?"

"Deal." I drew her close and kissed her lips. After a while she said, "I suppose we'll have separate quarters on the boat."

"Unquestionably. Mattie wouldn't have it otherwise. But when they're asleep we can always come on deck—to enjoy the moonlight, of course."

"Of course. You really are a wicked and resourceful man, and after the cruise is over I don't want to lose you."

"No reason for concern."

"Truly?"

"Truly," I echoed, because I didn't want to lose her either.

The house had no air conditioning and didn't need it; breeze through our open windows cooled the bedroom where we were sleeping. And if there was traffic noise on the highway, the house was too far away to hear it. A welcome change from Georgetown.

In the morning we made love again, slept a while, and when I woke I was alone. I found Alison in the kitchen mixing waffle batter and frying country ham. She poured coffee and we sat at the kitchen table enjoying it while breakfast cooked. After turning the ham Alison said, "I hope you don't miss a morning paper."

"I don't—there's never any good news."

"Isn't that the truth? I don't activate the telephone until sum-mer when I'm here more often. But if you need to make calls, my car has a cell phone."

"No calls."

"And I don't want to hear from anyone. At least not this weekend. Here I can be totally isolated from Washington and my office, and I treasure the privacy."

Breakfast was delicious. I ate twice as much as my hostess, re-plenishing vital forces, as it were, and after clearing the table I brought firearms and cleaning gear to the kitchen and set to work. One rifle was a .30-06 WWI Springfield, the other, a .30 caliber Winchester lever action. Despite cabinet storage both barrels and firing mechanism were dusty and the Winchester's barrel was fouled, not having been cleaned since last firing. I passed bronze brushes and solvent patches through the barrels until they gleamed when viewed against the kitchen light. Then I lightly oiled the re-ceivers and loaded cartridges into their magazines. Watching me while she did dishes, Alison asked, "Isn't it dangerous to have loaded guns around? My father and uncle always said so."

I wiped excess oil from the rifles and set them aside. "Since their day, there's a different school of thought. If you load a weapon you know it's loaded, no question about it. Also, it's ready for use. To fire you still have to work bolt or the lever to chamber a round so I don't see a danger factor."

"Unless there are children around."

"But you'd keep the gun cabinet locked."

"I would," she nodded and set plates in the sink drainer. "Morning and evening there are usually deer browsing in the or-chards, but I've never wanted to kill one. Could you?"

I smiled. "The Bambi syndrome? In the years when my father brought home a buck every fall I was too young to hunt with him, but I enjoyed venison steak and stew as did my mother."

I brought two shotguns to the table, an old Stevens single with ring sight, and a 12-gauge Remington semi-auto, both with worn bluing. Except for dust the barrels were clean, but I patched and oiled them and replaced them in the cabinet. That left two shotguns, an old Browning 20 semi-auto, and a Marlin superposed 12 gauge. All the firearms showed worn bluing but otherwise were in good shooting condition. After cleaning them I said, "I like pheasant shooting and I'll bet you have plenty of them around here."

"Yes, unless it's been a bad winter that kills them off. We could shoot pheasant in the fall."

Midmorning we walked to the spring-fed pond almost invisible within a grove of birches. A brace of pintails skittered across the surface taking wing and disappearing beyond the trees. Alison said, "They're coming north now and we'll see lots more when migration is really underway."

I kissed her cheek—the palm mark was almost invisible—and said, "If I lived here I'd never want to go in to town."

"It's how I feel every weekend. Maybe I'll just retire here and enjoy what I have. Anyway, I wanted you to see my bathing pond."

"It's great," I said, and we turned back toward the farmhouse. "Thanks for bringing me." Just then a doe that had been lying in the tall grass broke cover and bounded off into the birches. "Well," I said, "there's proof this is a secure sanctuary."

"They're never hunted here—the land has always been posted and I want to keep it that way." As we walked on she said, "You mentioned your father. Is he alive?"

I shook my head. "He had a college ROTC commission so when Korea broke out he shipped out and was killed over there."

"Oh, Steve, I'm so sorry."

"My mother never recovered from his death; she died two years later—heart attack the certificate said, but I know it was a broken heart."

Impulsively she hugged me. "That's a lot of tragedy for a young man, for anyone. But you survived—I admire that—and became a fine lawyer."

"Thanks to the GI Bill," I acknowledged. "My brush with the Ballous motivated me. I was an accountant then and totally subpar for someone like Francie. She and her father didn't have to say so because I felt it. So, I decided to better myself."

"Oh, don't be class-conscious, honey. If Francie had had minimum sense she'd have dragged you off to the nearest preacher."

I smiled. "Instead, I met you—the best possible outcome."

As we came around the barn, a light blue Toyota on the access road was nearing the house. "Expecting someone?" I asked.

"Unh-unh. Who could that be?"

The car stopped, dust rose from the rear wheels, and a woman got out.

She was a little taller than average, with bushy auburn hair, tight denim shorts, and shiny blue clogs. Above her bare midriff two unusually large mammaries were restrained by a purple halter top, and I noticed that her navel was pierced by a glinting ring. She came toward us, stopped a yard away, and put her hands on her hips. "Senator," she said, "I have to talk with you."

Now that her face was no longer shadowed I could see smudged mascara and eyeliner; purple lipstick accented full lips. She looked like a friction dancer in a topless joint.

After glancing at me Alison said, "If you'll call my office on Monday my staff will be glad to help you."

"No, you don't understand. It's personal, and I need to talk to you." Her words were urgent, but held a sort of defeated harmonic. "Alone," she added, after a glance at me.

"Well, I'll hear what you have to say, but my attorney will be present."

"Attorney?" Her eyes narrowed.

"Stokes," I said, giving the first name that came to mind. "Now, what—?"

She'd been chewing her lip, stopped and blurted, "Harlan was here yesterday, wasn't he?"

Alison's face tightened. "Not that it's any concern of yours, but what if he was?"

"I'm Doris Conlon," she said. "Mean anything to you?"

"Afraid not," Alison said coolly.

"I'm Harlan's girlfriend—or was."

"Oh. Shall we talk on the porch? The sun is getting hot."

Seated in wicker chairs around a glass-top rattan table, we looked at each other. Alison said, "This is quaint, isn't it? You know my name but I didn't know yours. What shall we talk about, Doris? Let's be frank. After all, we've slept with the same man."

Doris Conlon swallowed. "After he saw you Harlan started going crazy. He owes money in Atlantic City and he's afraid of being killed if he doesn't pay." She paused. "He tried to get money from you, he said."

Alison nodded. "Go on."

"Said if he killed you he'd inherit your fortune."

Time for me to join the conversation. "That's not how it works. No one can benefit from a crime."

She shrugged. "I guess I knew that but Harlan is smart enough to kill you, ma'am, and not be found out."

"I doubt that," I said. "So, how do things stand between you and the senator's husband?"

"He took back my jewelry—said he was going to sell it—and kicked me out." She swallowed again. "I mean, he's acting real crazy. Had me pack a bag and made me leave."

Alison asked, "What are you going to do?"

"Oh, I'll get work someplace—bar or waitress, maybe some, uh, exotic dancing—that's what attracted Harlan in the first place. But I thought, woman to woman, I had to warn you ma'am."

"And I appreciate it," Alison told her. "Mr. Stokes and I may have reason to get in touch with you, Doris. Where could we locate you?"

Doris drew in a deep breath. "Hadn't thought that far ahead, but I'll either get work in Baltimore or go back to Charleston—if the old heap will get me that far." Her eyes strayed to the old Toyota and I saw it had West Virginia plates, a busted front headlight, and a large dent in one fender. I said, "As the senator said, we appreciate your coming and sharing the situation with us." I got out my bill-fold. "To cover your time, and help with expenses, perhaps you'd ac-cept something from us. Also, I wouldn't drive at night with that headlight the way it is." I handed her all the money in my billfold—three hundred and twenty dollars. "When you get located please call the senator's office. Will you do that?"

She nodded, looked at the bills, folded them and tucked them in her cleavage. "This'll help a lot, thanks."

"Thank *you*," Alison said, and got up.

"Oh," Doris said as she pushed back her chair, "this is important. Please don't tell Harlan I came here—or what I told you."

"Of course not," Alison assured her. "We won't violate your confidence. And thanks again for coming."

"For once," Doris said, "I did the right thing. And you're a real lady, ma'am. You treated me with respect I guess I didn't deserve, and I won't forget it." She paused. "You're young and good-looking, so I'll never know why Harlan took up with me."

Alison's mouth opened and closed. Silence was better than any reply. I said, "Men don't always realize where their best interests lie—until it's too late."

"Ain't that the truth?" She straightened her shoulders and I walked her to her heap. Opened the door while she got in. "Good luck," I said. She started the engine, backed around and drove off to the highway. When I reached the verandah Alison was still watching the departing car. She took my hand and said, "Well—what a surprise that was! I need coffee or iced tea or something—how about you?"

"Uh-huh. You handled her just right, Ali."

As we walked to the kitchen she said, "What do you think of her?"

"I guess she could be classified as trailer park trash, but she's obviously got a good heart and a sense of right and wrong."

"Hm. Why do I have the feeling you knew her name?"

"Because it emerged when my investigator was checking Harlan's finances."

"But you didn't tell me."

"I didn't think it significant. You knew he was keeping someone, that was enough. If Doris stays in touch we'll have a useful witness should Harlan fight divorce."

"So I hope Harlan doesn't find her and give her trouble."

While coffee percolated we sat at the table and I said, "Be sure to tell Chad Goodrich everything Doris told us."

"I will."

"And I think it's time you changed your will, eliminating Harlan from inheriting." I looked around. "This place, for instance. He's already absorbed your Philadelphia condo, and I don't think you want Revelstoke land in his possession."

"Scary thought." She got up, poured coffee into two cups and brought them to the table. "I'll do it Monday."

"Good coffee. It occurs to me that if you have to sue Harlan for divorce—worst case—it won't affect your public image because the provable charge of adultery will gain sympathy for you."

"But we don't want it in court, do we? I mean, airing dirty laundry . . ." She left the thought unfinished.

"I said worst case, meaning last resort. After Goodrich lays out reality to your husband I doubt there'll be much fight left in him." I sipped again. "The situation is expanding and accelerating, Ali, like some alien growth. Doris's message calls for speed in resolving your marital situation. Get Goodrich to wrap it up next week. Then we can join Hod without the Harlan cloud hanging over us."

"That would be wonderful. See how I need your guidance?"

"You just think you do."

She stirred coffee with the tip of her finger. "After I'm no longer married, what about us, Steve? Have you thought of that?"

"I have," I admitted, "and reached no conclusion. Besides, you may have a major career decision to make, so at least for a while we shouldn't alter things."

"Meanwhile you'd be my official companion?"

"Something like that. After all, Queen Victoria had her Scotch gillie, and a rather famous lady senator from New England kept her acknowledged consort at her side."

"Oh, I know who you mean, but I didn't know she had a—a companion."

"It worked for them," I said, "and if we looked carefully through Congress I'm pretty sure we could come up with other examples."

She nodded. "Actually, I can think of several. Steve, I've done everything but ask you outright to marry me. Would that be so bad?"

"It would be wonderful," I said, and kissed her hand. "But we've each had a bad marriage, and now we have a chance to do things right."

"You're so lawyerly logical."

"If we're really in love, honey, it can only grow as we get to know each other more deeply. Then, when we absolutely can't stand to be apart that's the time to marry."

She sighed. "So, we'll wait, right? Remembering, that as the Good Book says, 'Tis better to marry than to burn.'"

"Who could forget?"

"But if Doris was truthful, there's Harlan's threat to kill me. How serious do you think it is?"

"Well, she said he'd been acting crazy, talking crazy, so I don't think we can brush it away. I mean, how sane is it to come here, slap you around and demand money? You know him, I don't. He's come once, maybe he'll come again, not knowing I'm here."

"And I'm so glad you are." She sighed heavily. "What can we do about it?"

"Arm ourselves," I said, and had her follow me to the gun cabinet. After unlocking it I took out the Marlin double and loaded it with two birdshot shells, then loaded the Remington semi-auto with four of the same. "We'll keep these by the bed," I told her, "and lock the first-floor doors and windows."

"No locks for the windows, I'm afraid."

"Then a prowler will make noise getting in." I'd never liked bolt-action rifles, so I took the Winchester lever upstairs along with the two shotguns. After stacking them bedside I said, "Seems like a miracle this place has never been looted or vandalized."

"Country people don't do that to each other."

"Your faith is touching, but what about city folk who come out here looking for opportunities to pillage?"

"I guess you're right," she said reluctantly. "There's a shop in Leesburg that's made keys for me—they install alarms and security devices."

"Good. Call them now, they can do a security review this afternoon, install on Monday."

"I'll have to call from the car."

"Meanwhile, the sun having crossed the zenith I'm declaring cocktail time."

I followed her downstairs, made drinks in the kitchen, and when she came back she said, "They'll be here in a little while."

"How little?"

"Couple of hours, I guess." Our glasses touched, and she said, "Why?"

"I was thinking of a nooner."

"A—? Oh." She blushed. "Well, why not?"

So we made love in the quiet bedroom, the only sounds those of birds calling and chirping in the nearby elms. And afterward as I lay beside her I reflected that generations of her forebears had rested and mated in this same bed, and I wondered if Francie Ballou had ever slept in it. Then I looked at Alison's smooth, lovely profile and told myself I was crazy to think of another woman—even a dead one—when I had this unique, incredible female to love, honor, and in time, obey.

A little earlier than expected the security boss and his apprentice arrived. I had them check the outside while Alison dressed, and then we toured the house together, the apprentice making clipboard notes of every feature his boss pointed out. Review over, we all had coffee in the kitchen while the alarm system was discussed and the bill totaled. "Oh, Senator, one other thing. Do you want a hookup with the police station?"

She looked at me and I said, "Runs on the telephone line, doesn't it?"

"It does."

"Phone won't be working until summer, so let's put that on hold."

"Whatever you say." He got up. "Thanks for the business, Senator. Monday afternoon everything will be in place."

"Thank you for coming so promptly." She saw them to the door and came back. "I should have done this long ago but I didn't feel the need."

"It would be fine with me if neither of us ever saw Harlan again."

Only it didn't turn out that way.

NINE

IN LATE AFTERNOON we followed the grassy borders of the plowed fields and saw the farmer and his son riding a mechanical seeder. I wondered what crop would be produced but saw no point in asking Alison, who was unfamiliar with matters of the soil. As we walked we startled two cock pheasants and a hen that exploded into brief winged flight then glided to far hiding places in the tall grass.

I'd made the mistake of wearing city shoes, so when we reached the pond I decided to treat my feet to the cooling water. It was cool, all right. I lowered my feet into the pond and in ten seconds they were blue. Quickly withdrawing, I massaged life into them while Alison giggled. "My God!" I gasped, "to bathe here you

have to belong to the Polar Bear Club. That water's just about freez-
ing."

Smothering laughter, she said, "Close to it, just under forty de-
grees. But in July and August it's a lifesaver. You'll see."

"Hm, not sure my heart could stand the shock." I peered into
the clear water and saw small fish darting to and fro. They looked
like fingerling bass except that bass were lovers of warm water.

We lay back on the grass and looked up at the sky through the
lacework of birch branches, and while we were motionless a whitetail doe and her spotted fawn appeared at the far edge of the pond
and very delicately began to drink. Ever alert, the doe looked up and
around from time to time, while her fawn kept drinking. Then, as
silently as they'd appeared, they vanished among the birches. "What
a lovely sight," Alison said softly. "Their only natural enemies are
foxes—and man."

"Where 'every prospect pleases, and only man is vile,'" I quoted.

"Why, Steve, you sound like an environmentalist."

"Do I? My mother said that occasionally, no political implications. Besides, rabid foxes can be pretty vile—and dangerous."

"How true. When I rode with the Warrenton Hunt several of
our hounds were bitten and died of rabies. I realized my hunter
could have been bitten, too, so I reconsidered fox hunting, and gave
up riding to hounds."

"Miss it?"

"The social part, but there are too many other things in my
life—time-consuming obligations. And Harlan didn't ride, so I
didn't give up much." She looked away. "Besides my PR adviser said
my constituents wouldn't like their congresswoman taking part in
blood sports."

"What about pheasant shooting?"

"That's different. If we don't bag them they'll be killed by
foxes, or a hard winter. And I love roast pheasant."

"Me, too. With apple-and-raisin stuffing."

"Mmm, I'm salivating."

So after a while we returned to the house, had lamb chops for
dinner, and went to bed around ten.

Alison slept beside me, her breathing soft and rhythmic, but I was restless, my mind trying to fit Doris Conlon's visit into the larger puzzle that surrounded the senator. I'd accepted Doris's story at face value, but another explanation occurred to me: Harlan could have sent her with his death threat as a means of terrifying Alison into meeting his demand. Doris certainly acted the role of a cast-off, frightened woman, but was it all a charade? And had she known Andrew Bostick? That was a far stretch, but if Bostick had acted for Harlan Bowman it was possible Doris had at least seen them together. And who killed Bostick? I wasn't eager to have the killer identified because Alison's name could surface. So my thoughts chased each other around my mind without reaching anything resembling conclusions, and they kept me from sleep.

Eventually I decided to go down to the kitchen for a soothing glass of milk, and as I crossed the open window I glanced out at the moonlit access road.

There, about a hundred yards away, someone stood looking at the dark house. My first thought was a stranded motorist looking for a telephone. Moonlight came from behind him so I couldn't see his face. If he wanted a telephone why wasn't he coming toward the house? He seemed indecisive, making up his mind. Quietly, I took a shotgun and decided to challenge him if he came closer. I went down the stairs, crossed the living room and opened the front door. Where the watcher had stood there was nothing but moonlit road. In the few seconds it had taken me to come downstairs he couldn't have come much closer to the house, and as I stood wondering what had happened to him I heard an engine start in the distance, then the car accelerated away. Baffling.

After a few moments I closed and locked the door and went to the kitchen, poured scotch in a glass and added milk. As I drank I tried to make sense of the nocturnal visitation. Maybe he'd come to burglarize the house, seen Alison's parked Jaguar, and decided not to risk it. Or he'd come to murder her and had had second thoughts. Whatever the reason, the incident had ended harmlessly. I drained my glass, felt the liquor warming my stomach, and went upstairs to bed.

As I replaced the shotgun the slight noise disturbed Alison, who sat up. "Steve? Are you all right?"

"Fine," I said, as I pulled up the covers. "Went down for a glass of milk. Everything's okay."

"Sure?"

"I'm sure." I kissed her cheek. "Go back to sleep."

She lay back and turned to me. "We had a wonderful day, darling. It's so good having you here." She yawned and turned over. I looked up at the dark ceiling. If I'd told her what I'd seen she'd have been frightened, and we'd have spent the rest of the night talking about it. Who? Why? And so on. I closed my eyes and, thanks to the scotch, sleep came.

Sunday was much like the day before, except that we drove in for brunch at the Laurel Brigade Inn. The setting was bright and airy, with well-dressed couples and after-church families enjoying the buffet's abundant offerings. No one took notice of Alison. We had wine with our meal, and got back to the farm about two. After a final walk to the pond we packed and got ready to leave. Alison said, "I'm sorry about leaving so early, but I have so much to do tomorrow I ought to start organizing things this afternoon."

"Of course. But if Harlan stops by the apartment don't let him in. Keep the door bolted until the locks are changed."

She nodded. "That reminds me, I should leave keys at the security shop in Leesburg so they can work here tomorrow. When will I see you again?"

"Call me." We kissed lingeringly, and while she was driving away I went down behind the barn and started my engine. As I steered toward the highway I recalled last night's anonymous visitor who, I now felt strongly, had been up to no good. Too bad I hadn't seen his car and license plate; with that Pat Moran could have gotten me a name.

Nothing beckoned me home, so I went to the office instead. The only telephone message was from Pat Moran. "Laddie," his voice greeted me, "I came by a snippet for you, nothing sensational, but interesting. No urgency, but if you want to satisfy your curiosity call my office when you hear this. Ta-ta."

I punched his office number and a clever electronic device

transferred the call to his home. When I heard him answer I said, "You piqued my curiosity, Pat, what's the story? Good news or bad?"

"Don't know it's either, Steve. What came to me over the counter is from a police report. After this Bostick weirdo was found dead at the airport the cops went through his apartment."

"Looking for stuff to steal?"

"Heh-heh. Only they were late on the scene. Someone had already gone through the place, gave it a thorough going-over, and left it in shambles."

"Anything taken?"

"A scene like that, how can you tell? Only Bosty, an' he ain't around to testify."

"Cops get any leads?"

"Well, they're kinda lookin' over his Escapade customers, speculating a revenge motive. Uh—prints to go on, but you haven't asked the obvious question."

I considered his bait. "So, how did the intruder get in?"

"That's it! Knew that razor-edge mind of yours was functioning even on a lazy Sunday afternoon." He paused, and thought I could hear the sound of a beer—or possibly water—trickling down his gullet. "No forced entry, so either the lock was picked or the perp had a key."

"Or one was taken from his car keys."

"Wasn't. So the cops figure the intruder was enough of a frequent visitor that he had a key of his own."

"Reasonable theory. Ought to narrow the suspect list. Makes sense that whoever shot Bostick ransacked his place afterward."

"Yeah. So let me ask you this—would a hoodlum robber take the time to do that?"

"Might—if he got nothing from the killing." I noticed perspiration on my palms. "Any money found on Bostick?"

"Not a thin dime, laddy, an' no plastics. The cops'll be lookin' for anyone who uses them. Or tries to."

"Hm. Considering the nature of Bostick's Escapade activities, it's possible he kept his door unlocked—all comers welcome."

"Sure. A hustler who got a final hustle himself."

I nodded. "It's hard to mourn the death of a world-class scum-bag, so I'm not going to try."

"Me neither, I got no problem with that. Okay, so much for the dead kinko. How come you're at the office today?"

"Got bored around home with no NFL game to watch."

"Yeah, long time until that first kickoff. Go hustle us some clients, Steve, I need the work."

"Me, too, and thanks for the tidbits." Hanging up, I wiped palms and forehead with a handkerchief. For all I knew the cops had found an extra videotape in Bostick's warren—or the killer had, and that was a lot worse. Sitting back, I gazed out toward the White House, my mind not focusing until I recalled the mystery man on the road last night. Was he Bostick's killer? Had he gone through Bostick's place and come up with a tape to renew the blackmailing? Was that why he'd appeared at Alison's farm? Had second thoughts standing there, and decided against trying?

Too many questions, and the only significant answer would surface when and if Alison was called by someone claiming to have a compromising tape.

The killer must have been startled to learn his victim's body was found at the airport. If he'd killed Bostick in Alison's parking lot to suggest a relationship between them, he now knew she had friends resolved to keep scandal from her door. And he'd be wary.

Pat hadn't said, and I hadn't asked, if the cops found anything with Alison's name or phone number. I was reasonably satisfied they hadn't because enough time had passed for the cops to ask the senator discreetly if she knew the murdered man. And Pat's rumor net hadn't produced anything, so that was a sizable plus.

Looking around my office, I reflected on how much my life had changed since the first time Alison had entered it. As she'd said, it was a highly personal matter—blackmail and extortion al-ways is—but divorce became involved, and even though the black-mailer had done us the extraordinary favor of getting himself killed, his shadow lingered everywhere. I didn't think the police were going to extend themselves looking for his murderer; unless some drugged-out idiot confessed to it the Bostick case would be filed away and forgotten as new violent crimes took precedence—and around Washington and Baltimore there was no shortage of them to investigate.

By dining at the Laurel Brigade we'd taken a chance of her being recognized, but even if she had been, who was to say she wasn't with her husband? So even if it wasn't prudent to be seen together inside the Beltway, there were plenty of dining spots like Crisfield's where we could enjoy each other's company without fingers being pointed.

I poured a glass of sherry and carried a heavy section of the tax code to my desk. Made notes relating to a client's claimed business deductions that had been disallowed by the IRS, and otherwise made myself professionally useful. Just after six the desk phone rang, and when I answered Alison said, "What are you, a worka-holic?"

"Unh-unh, workaholics don't live long enough to enjoy the fruits of their labors. How's your work going?"

"Pretty well—problem is, I miss you."

"And I miss you."

"What a wonderful weekend, Steve, I'm just sorry it couldn't go on and on." She paused. "I tell myself it's a sample of better things to come."

"We'll nurture the thought. Uh—haven't heard from Harlan, have you?"

"No, and I hope not to. Ever. I left a message for Chad Goodrich to speed things up. I don't care how much it costs me, I just want to be rid of the man."

"Let Chad navigate you through the rocks and shoals. I'm confident he'll arrange things to your beneficial interest."

"Lawyer talk, honey. You mean he'll do it on the cheap."

I smiled. "That's what I mean. Gotta remember who I'm talk-ing to."

"It would help," she purred, "because I have far-reaching plans for the future. And they include not waking up beside a lawyer; I want to wake up beside a lover—you."

"That's totally agreeable, Senator."

She sighed. "Unfortunately, this is going to be a complicated week. Tuesday I leave for two days in Atlanta—a public health conference—back sometime Wednesday night. Uh—would you wait up for me?"

"Do better than that, I'll meet your plane."

"That would be very nice, and I look forward to it. Thursday morning the intelligence Oversight subcommittee meets for a CIA briefing on North Korea's nuclear missile and biological warfare programs, and I must be there."

"Sounds interesting."

"But I won't be able to tell you anything that's said."

"I understand. You have Astral clearance, and I don't."

"*Steve*—you're not even supposed to know Astral exists!"

"Promise not to mention it again."

"But who told you?"

"Deep Throat."

"Oh, Steve, you're meddling in national security and you don't even care."

"Call me irresponsible."

"And other endearments—but you're working and I should be. Just wanted to be sure you got back safely." Her voice lowered. "Because I love you." Click, and the line hummed dead.

This was one determined woman, I mused, and her pace was faster than I liked. Whatever she felt for me had to be a combination of gratitude and sexual attraction, because I no longer believed in love at first sight. We were adults, and adults were supposed to be cautions and wise, not adolescents infatuated with the thrills of instant romance. I'd lived a long time without a wife, and while Alison was by far the most compelling candidate who'd come along I wasn't convinced our lives could mesh successfully. Not that I worried about being called Mr. Senator, it had to do with lifestyles we'd adopted. Mine was that of a sedentary attorney, while Alison was younger and happy as an active politician immersed in national affairs. She'd worked hard to win her Senate seat, and she'd work equally hard to be reelected. Then there was a possible presidential campaign. Could I handle the stress of inevitable separations? Until I was sure, it was best to restrain my enthusiasm even if I couldn't check hers.

I realized that Alison had the female nesting compulsion, and

because she hadn't had much of a nest with Harlan she was probably determined to build a new one that was both comfortable and
durable. I'd passed whatever subliminal screening her mind imposed, in large part, I supposed, because Francie had spoken well of
me, and despite our social and financial disparity. Over years of representing wealthy clients I'd noticed that they were less conscious
of their fortunes than those who weren't similarly blessed. Like me.

But I'd never been money-driven. I wanted to live comfortably and was willing to work and deliver for value received. Like any
small businessman I had monthly house and office bills to meet, a
conservative stock portfolio, and not much else. I liked it that way.

The planned cruise would be an unstated testing period for
us both. How would we react to cramped quarters and the monot-
ony of a long sail? Alison was accustomed to space and constant activity. Maybe she'd adapt to the quieter life, maybe not. The cruise
could help reveal what we ought to know about each other before a
marriage plunge.

Finishing my sherry, I got back to work and kept at it until
seven-thirty, then had a quiet dinner at the University Club and
drove on home. I turned into my drive and noticed a black Lincoln
Town Car parked at the curb. When I walked back it was still there
and the driver was getting out of it. He came around the front of
the car and stopped on the sidewalk facing me, a man of average
height wearing a chauffeur's cap and gray whipcord uniform. "Mr.
Bentley?"

"Yes."

"If you'll get in, there's someone who wants to talk with you."

"No street conferences. My office opens at nine." I started
past him but he sidestepped and blocked my way. Just then a tinted
rear window rolled down and I saw the white mane and rugged
face of Governor Abel Green. His gravelly voice said, "I'd appreciate a few moments of your time, Mr. Bentley—on a matter of mutual interest."

He opened the door and I got in.

TEN

———

BEFORE THE DOME light went out I glimpsed the face of a young woman seated on the facing jump seat. Green said, "My daughter, Sybil. I thought you might be more at ease if she were with me."

"Evening," I said to her and she said, "Hello." Her face resembled her father's too closely to be attractive, and the way her hands folded in her lap suggested habitual submissiveness. Her gaze settled on me in a way I didn't like.

Green cleared his throat. "I chose this unconventional way of meeting you because the press watches me pretty closely, and I didn't want troublesome questions arising."

"About what, Governor?"

"The fact that I was seen visiting a tax attorney. Rumor and speculation are an unpleasant aspect of public life, and it might be thought that I was in some sort of financial difficulty. Fodder for my political enemies."

I nodded. "And the matter of mutual interest?"

"The future of Senator Bowman, your client."

I glanced at Sybil Green's impassive face and wondered if she was wearing any of the jewelry that had been taken by Andrew Bostick. To her father I said, "What about the senator's political future?"

"First, you'll acknowledge that Alison is a client of yours?"

"On the contrary, Governor, any relationship I might or might not have with Senator Bowman is in the category of lawyer–client confidentiality. So I'm neither acknowledging nor denying your suggestion."

"Let's be frank, Mr. Bentley. In addition to being governor I'm also de facto head of the political party of which she is a prominent—very prominent—figure. Accordingly, her political well-being is of some concern to me."

"I appreciate your frankness, Governor, but before you became governor you were state's attorney general, and before that a lawyer. So you have to be well aware of the delicacy that attends confidential relationships between a lawyer and his client."

"I do, sir, and I'm not asking you to violate that relationship, if indeed one exists as regards the senator. Now, as you may know the senator's marriage is troubled. I know her husband—perhaps too well—and find him difficult to deal with on occasion. I assume that Alison has found him equally difficult to live with, at least they hardly make a pretense of being a happily married couple. Further, I have learned that Harlan Bowman is in deep financial trouble, brought on by himself, I should add, and I would not want his problems to sully the outstanding reputation of his wife." He sat back and ran an index finger across his chin.

"So?"

"I would like to think that in you I have an ally in preserving the senator's reputation."

I grunted. "Governor, I try to protect all my clients within the limits of the law. Were the senator a client I would do the same for her—without being asked. As for the marital situation you outline I don't handle domestic litigation. My practice is limited to taxation and financial advice and I intend to keep it that way."

"So, for the sake of argument, were the senator a client of yours, you would be advising her in areas not involving domestic disputes."

"For the sake of argument. Is there anything else?"

"One moment, sir. Most lawyers better themselves by enlarging their practice. As governor it is not infrequently within my power to direct state legal business in certain directions—bond issues, for example, highway construction contracts, selecting the chair of regulatory committees—no impropriety involved."

I smiled. "Of course not."

He nodded. "I'll go further in explaining my particular interest in the senator's future. At our party's nominating convention I hope to see my way clear to placing Alison's name before the delegates as candidate for the presidency of the United States."

I stared at him and swallowed.

"Accordingly," he continued, "I would make a very strong effort to see that nothing untoward occurs to prejudice the candidacy."

"I see."

"The time is right for a woman president, Mr. Bentley, and I believe Alison to be the ideal candidate. The country is sick of males who bring scandal and controversy to the highest office of the land, and the people are willing to vote for a qualified female. Although Alison is young in years she is politically seasoned, and backed by influential interest groups that would be of immense value in raising contributions and getting voters to the polls." He paused and fashioned a deprecatory smile. "You know how those things go."

To Sybil I said, "What's your view, Miss Green?"

With a slight shrug she said, "The same as my father's."

Governor Green said, "I expect you to keep confidential my expectations for the state's junior senator."

"No problem," I said, and reached for the door handle.

Green said, "Thank you for your time, Mr. Bentley. Is there anything you care to add?"

"It's been interesting," I said, and got out. The door closed and the big car moved silently away. For a few moments I watched it go, and then I went up the walk and unlocked my front door. Inside, I half-filled a tumbler with scotch, added ice and had a long swallow. As I went upstairs to my bedroom I wondered about the real purpose of Green's visit. Alison downplayed presidential ambitions, but as I considered Green's words I had to agree that she would be an outstanding candidate. But, *cui bono?* What was in it for him?

For one thing, Alison would have to resign from the Senate in order to run, freeing the seat for Green's occupancy. Second, as perhaps her most prominent supporter Green would enjoy special access to her White House and be in a position to fulfill his own ambitions, whatever they were. Yet it seemed to me that Green had formulated a long-range strategy that gave small hope of foreseeable success. Was the governor really that patient? He had nourished a reputation as a hurry-up, let's-move-along guy, short-fused and intolerant of delay. What a change.

How had he learned that Alison was a client? Viewing me as able to influence her, Green had come directly to me—no whispering intermediaries—and in effect told me the state's coffers would open for me if I kept her free of trouble. What trouble did he have in mind? Bostick's erotic tape? Harlan's gambling debts and backstairs mistress? A senatorial divorce?

Conversely, had Green opened golden vistas for me in order to suggest what could happen if I did not become his "ally"? Unquestionably the governor was a devious bastard, fully capable, I felt, of dispatching Bostick to compromise her.

I gulped the rest of my drink and wished I had the bottle at bedside. Now I had an ethical problem: should I tell Alison about the governor's nocturnal visit? If so, how much should I tell her? Everything, including Green's stated advocacy of her presidential candidacy? That might be the most startling news she'd received since becoming senator.

Fortunately I didn't have to make an immediate decision. First I had to decide how much of Green's spiel I believed. Beyond that, I was worried over his information sources. She'd once mentioned that she thought she was being followed, but there hadn't been a second sighting, and I'd dismissed the first as coincidence. Besides, why trouble with hit-or-miss foot surveillance when there were moles in her office? Past time to get rid of them.

Where was Harlan in all this? Green had spoken negatively of him, but what better way to dissemble a close conspiratorial relationship? Who was the nocturnal watcher in the farm road? Harlan? Unlikely. He had keys to the house if he wanted to enter. Some minion of Green's was more plausible. Harlan wanted Alison's money, Green wanted her Senate seat; their interests converged on her.

As I undressed I considered a likely motive for Green's visit— the man wanted to evaluate me, take my measure. As an experienced man of affairs he would want to understand the opposition and maneuver accordingly. Was that why Green had included daughter Sybil in our tête-à-tête—to get feminine input on his target? She'd come off as a clone of her father's, without independent thought. For a conniver like Bostick she'd have been a willing victim, and I suspected that Green would hold it over her for the rest of their lives.

Well, I couldn't resolve anything tonight. I was tired from a long day, stressed by Green's unexpected appearance and ambiguous message. Being Alison's sometime attorney had turned into a kaleidoscope of high-level intrigue and intractable personal problems that were overwhelming me. Against an enemy like Abel Green she needed a lot more protection than Steven Bentley, Esq.; she needed a mixed regiment of CIA and FBI agents to shield her and guide her to the promised land.

Thank God tomorrow was another day.

ELEVEN

MONDAY NOON I took Burton Michaels to lunch at the Lawyer's Club to give him a little exposure to colleagues who might be looking for someone of his abilities and experience. Two lawyers stopped at our table to exchange pleasantries and curse the new tax code.

Back at the office I hadn't heard from Alison regarding evening plans, and decided not to phone her because I hadn't yet reached a decision on how much to tell her about Governor Green's visitation. Tomorrow and Wednesday she'd be in Atlanta, and when I met her Wednesday night I'd have made up my mind about Green. I wanted to hear how things were going between Chad Goodrich and her husband, but that could wait, too.

Another postcard arrived from Hod Gurney saying he'd meet us at St. Thomas and begin our cruise from there. I had only to give him day and time of arrival. Easy, I thought, will do.

Two successive client consultations took me through four o'-clock, Burton Michaels returned from a successful meeting with an IRS auditor, and Mrs. Altman advised me that Pat Moran was on the phone. "Counselor," he began, "name of Doris Conlon mean anything to you?"

I tensed, cleared my throat, and said, "Should it?"

"Well, she turned up as the, uh, paid companion of Harlan Bowman—ring a bell?"

"Does now, so?"

"She turned up again—dead."

I could feel my pulse accelerate. "Natural causes?"

"Not unless a slug qualifies as lead poisoning—these strange times I guess even that's possible."

I wet dry lips. "So Harlan's bimbo no longer figures as a tax de-ductible dependent. Where'd she bite the bullet, as the saying goes? Their love nest?"

"Unh-unh. Downtown motel in Baltimore, not the classiest part of town. Checked in Saturday evening with one bag and a duster Toyota. Cops say she worked that night at a strip joint, took the afternoon shift yesterday. No one saw her come back—that kind of place—and the body wasn't found until a maid went in around noon today."

"Was she done in by persons unknown or did she manage it herself?"

"Cops are wondering the same. I haven't seen the actual crime scene report, but it seems the body was in a chair, fully dressed, re-volver on the carpet near her right hand, entry wound in or near the heart."

"Any suspects?"

"Dunno. But the case detectives figure it was supposed to look like suicide. But some handwriting found in her purse told them she was probably a left-hander. That's point one. Point two is the statistical improbability of killing herself with a shot in the heart. Most folk don't really know where the heart is located, and it ain't easy to point a gun muzzle accurately and fire—it's awkward—so they poke the barrel in their mouth or against the temple."

"So it will be interesting if the paraffin test shows powder traces on the right hand."

"Yeah, and it wasn't even a contact wound—shot fired from maybe a yard away." He cleared his throat. "Not a classical suicide scene—more like a bad attempt. Vince Foster come to mind?"

"Sort of. So the poor woman was murdered."

"Looks like. When they find a motive they'll find a suspect—pardon me, an *alleged* suspect. One other thing—the revolver was thirty-two caliber, an old Iver Johnson. Two shots fired from it, but only one into poor Doris. Don't know if I passed this along to you in the case of the Pit Boy, but a thirty-two bullet killed him."

"Interesting. Wonder if the cops will try to make a connection."

"Doubt it—different jurisdictions. But one trail is going to lead to Harlan Bowman's doorstep. Like, she was a known beneficiary of his hospitality, who suddenly goes stripping in Baltimore and ends up dead in a transient room with one suitcase and an empty purse. Implication, she left Harlan who followed her and killed her."

"Not good news for his wife, the senator."

"Not if his name doesn't surface."

I thought it over. "Parse that for me, Pat."

"Well, the guy's upper class, got influence and money. Unless his prints are on the gun the cops'll probably find some homeless creepo to frame. Addict needing money for crack. Hell, the guy might even confess."

"Why?"

"Plea bargain for twenty, get ten, and be on the street in five. Five years in a warm cell with a mattress, good food, and TV would look pretty attractive to a street bum."

"Pat, you make more sense than half the people I know."

"Life on the street, laddie. Want me to follow up on Dorie?"

"Not unless Harlan is arrested."

"Have a good evening." The phone cut off but Pat's disturbing news had my mind spinning. Doris's murder could expose the

Bowmans' marital discord and feature Alison in the tabloid press—
just what she, I, and possibly Governor Green, wanted to avoid.
Poor Doris Conlon, a wasted life and a tragic ending. Two days ago
she had performed a courageous and generous act in coming to Alison. Was that why she had been killed? To prevent her testifying
against Harlan Bowman? I could sort that out later, but now I had
to prepare Alison.

She answered her personal phone on the second ring, and I
said, "Call me from a pay phone, this is urgent. No talk, just make
the call."

Five minutes later my phone rang, "Steve? You've got me terribly frightened. What is it?"

"In case anyone's watching, put a smile on your face while you
listen." I drew in a deep breath. "Okay, Doris Conlon was murdered—shot to death, body found in a fleabag Baltimore motel. Details can wait, but I'm concerned your husband's name is going to
surface as her keeper."

"*Oh God!*"

"Easy. At the moment, as I understand it, the police have no
suspects, and it appears an effort was made to make the scene look
like suicide. Now, how far did Chad Goodrich get with Harlan?"

"He said—oh, Steve, I can't think straight."

"Calm down. Did Chad talk with Harlan?"

"No. He said he left a message on his answering machine."

"Good. If it ever becomes necessary Chad can testify you discussed divorce with him well before Doris was killed. That would
show good sense on your part, and—"

"But Steve, don't I have to show support for him? Stand by
my man?"

"I wouldn't advise it. There could be speculation that you demanded Harlan break off with his mistress, and he did it the extreme way. I think your posture should be that you and your
husband have been leading essentially separate lives for some time;
you inferred he had a companion but knew nothing about her, not
even her name."

"That's true." Her voice was firmer. "So what should I do
now?"

"Nothing. Await developments. If the police want to question you, be cooperative, but have an attorney with you. Let everything come as a big surprise to you. There's no reason Harlan's
misadventures should drag you down, so don't let them. If Harlan
has an alibi he's free and clear, and I'm not at all suggesting he killed
Doris. All I've really said is the police will view him as a suspect because of their, ah, romantic relationship, until he clears himself."

"But who would do such an awful thing?"

I sighed. "Oh, a burglar or some crackhead looking for money
to make a buy. Or some john who thought she stiffed him at the strip
joint. Those girls work for drink percentages. If a guy found a nine-
hundred-dollar bottle of champagne—for which read sparkling
cider—on his bill he could get pretty upset. So what I'm saying is
there are a lot of possible suspects and what you have to do is stay
loose."

"I—I understand. Will we talk later—tonight?"

"Your place?"

"If you don't mind. I'll need at least two hours before I can
leave here, so can you come at eight?"

"Eight it is." I hung up and looked around my office. Not just
one murder but two were now associated, however tangentially,
with my client. Both, I couldn't help reflecting, were the aftermath
of Alison's bad decisions: marrying Harlan Bowman and parting
her thighs for Andrew Bostick. What was done was done, no going
back in time, no erasing the blackboard. The question was how to
extract her from this latest imbroglio.

I got to her apartment at eight-fifteen. She was wearing a flowing
hostess gown, and her hair smelled fresh when we kissed. There was
an ice bucket on the bar so I poured two healthy measures of scotch
and added splashes of Evian. As we drank I saw no trembly hands
and decided she had a grip on herself. When we were seated she
said, "Dear, thanks so much for coming—and calling me. In government circles that's called a heads-up. Fortunately, so far I haven't
been contacted by police or anyone."

"Harlan?"

She shook her head. "I hope he won't, but I suppose he will." She drank deeply. "Do you think her murder will be in the *Post* or on radio?"

"Probably not. Washingtonians don't have much interest in what goes on in Baltimore."

"Until some public figure is involved. Still, I can't help but be worried."

"Save that for later."

"All right. You said you'd give me the grungy details in person."

"Right. Aside from a careless mise-en-scène I've heard that she was shot from several feet away, gun found by her right hand though she was apparently left-handed. The revolver was an old thirty-two caliber from which two shots had been fired."

"How do they know that?"

"Two empty shells in the cylinder." I swallowed a hearty slug before saying, "Bostick was shot with a small-caliber handgun, possibly the same weapon, but that's only my speculation."

"Can't the owner be traced through the gun's serial number?"

"Too old for that, unless it was resold by a gun shop that registered the piece. That's been required only in recent years, but the revolver could have been stolen from the original purchaser and passed hand to hand over the years. That's a blind alley. Fingerprints on the weapon are unlikely, given that the shooter went to a certain amount of trouble to frame a suicide scene. Doris's prints would have to be on the weapon, and may be. Freshen your drink?"

"Please."

I mixed a pair with less scotch and more water and sat beside her as she said, "So you think Bostick was killed with the same gun?"

"I think it's possible. Can't be proved unless both slugs can be microscopically compared. Soft lead bullets spread and mushroom on impact making comparison very difficult." I hesitated, thinking of another factor. "For the sake of argument, let's say the police find Bostick was killed with the same handgun. It could be theorized that Doris shot him and killed herself in remorse—except that she didn't kill herself. And a connection would have to be established between her and Bostick."

"Is there one?"

I shrugged. "He might have stolen stuff from her the way he stole jewelry from Sybil Green."

"Sybil—? The governor's daughter?"

I nodded. "The jewelry was recovered and Bostick wasn't prosecuted, but Green had it in his power to send Bostick away for a long stretch. That's the leverage he had over Bostick."

"Good Lord! Why didn't you tell me before?"

"Because I'm paid to filter information, decide what's important for you to know. I decided the Green–Bostick connection wasn't relevant."

"But it is—makes me suspect that Abel had Bostick compromise me."

"I've thought so, too, but there was nothing resembling proof, then Bostick turned up dead." I breathed deeply. "All right, that leads to last night when Governor Green and his daughter showed up at my house."

"No! Why?"

"Not sure. Here's what he said." Then, as well as I could I reconstructed the conversation and watched her face. "What really rocked me was Green's solicitude for your political well-being, then his saying he hoped to see his way clear to placing your name before the party convention as nominee for the presidency."

She looked stunned. "He—said that?"

"He did. Indirectly offered me big-fee state business if he could count on me as an 'ally' in protecting you from untoward occurrences."

She sank back against the cushions. "What did you say?"

"That I had an obligation to protect all clients within the limits of the law."

Her face tightened. "*Are* you Abel's 'ally'?"

"No way." I drank from my rapidly emptying glass. "But since he raised the subject, *do* you have presidential ambitions?"

She considered before replying. "It's one of the main areas I wanted to ponder privately during the cruise, but—well, you know what happened."

"And, with the cruise behind you?"

She breathed deeply. "In theory I'd love to win the world's most exclusive prize, but could I even get the nomination? That's step one. Then there's the challenge of all those months on the road, speeches, debates—I'm not sure I have the stamina to survive it all. Of course I think about the honor, the power, of reaching the apogee of political life." She paused. "Apparently Abel Green has given it deeper thought than I have. What do you make of his confiding in you?"

"Initially I thought he'd come to appraise me, decide if I were friend, enemy or useful tool. And I had to wonder how he learned you were my client, and more. Then I decided there had to be some deeper significance—his mentioning your troubled marriage and his distaste for Harlan—"

Quickly she sat forward. "Distaste?" She laughed hollowly. "They're thick as thieves."

"So what do you make of it?"

"The whole thing is baffling. And I don't at all like his bringing up my marriage. As though it's his business."

"Seems he's taking proprietary attitude toward you and everything that affects or could affect your political health."

Her mouth twisted. "Because he wants me to be President."

"Of course. He didn't mention supplanting you in the Senate."

"But that has to be his basic motivation."

"Can't think of another. So you don't want to be President? That's supposed to be the goal of every red-blooded American boy. What's wrong with you?"

"I'm not a boy." She smiled.

"True. And you're blue-blooded."

"Don't be class-conscious," she chided.

"Okay." I'd managed to get her smiling and I admired her resilience.

After finishing her drink she asked, "How hungry are you?"

"Middling."

"Not much in the freezer, I'm afraid—I just haven't been thinking domestically. We could go out but I'm wondering about us being seen together—I mean, the Harlan thing."

"Then let's send out. Great Chinese restaurant by the zoo, and it delivers."

"Almond chicken?"

"Pork lo mein?"

"Wonton soup?"

"And fortune cookies."

"You open mine—I'm afraid what it might say."

Lin Fong delivered a sumptuous repast—all the above dishes plus fried rice—and we ate at the coffee table, sharing a cold bottle of rosé. I showed her Hod Gurney's offer to meet us at St. Thomas and she suggested we buy separate tickets for the flight. I said, "That would preserve appearances, but for heaven's sake don't let your staff know your plans. Until you get rid of Arnold and Sally."

"I called them in separately and gave them the rest of the week to leave. They were shocked, but I put it in the context of downsizing to save taxpayer money. They realized it was unalterable."

"Ought to minimize leaks." I carried plates and food cartons to the kitchen, scraped the former and compacted the later. Alison added glasses and cutlery to the dishwasher and said, "I hope you'll stay over. Doris's murder is making me edgy."

"That the only reason?"

"Course not." She kissed me. "I've got a thing for you."

"Likewise, honey. And tomorrow you'll be in Atlanta."

"Two days. May I call you tomorrow night?"

"I'll be unhappy if you don't."

Her office phone rang. She answered after the third ring and flicked on the speakerphone. I heard the caller say, "Senator? Chad Goodrich, have you got a few minutes?"

"Of course."

"Apologies for the late hour, but there's a development you should know about."

"The time is no problem. This concerns my husband?"

"It does, yes. He just left my office. We talked for an hour and he didn't seem surprised that you want a divorce."

"I should think not, it's been far too long in coming."

"I understand. Well, Senator, I laid out the parameters—un-contested divorce in a venue of your choice, sealed papers, no pub-licity. Irreconcilable differences the rationale."

Alison looked at me and I nodded. She said, "Go on."

"His initial demand was two million dollars. I said that was entirely unreasonable given his young age and potential earning ability. I pointed out that, unlike California, there was no commu-nity property law in the District, the contiguous states, or Pennsyl-vania. I added that my firm had handled your financial reporting for years and knew your financial circumstances. Knowing that he is ex-periencing financial difficulties gave me a powerful, negotiating lever. So I offered three hundred thousand, he said eight was his minimum figure, and after more back and forth he agreed to bow out of your life for four hundred thousand. The one difficulty was his demand for instant payment of the entire sum. I said I would have to get your assent to any payment, and told him I would advise you to pay half when he signed the necessary documents, one hun-dred thousand when the divorce was finalized, and the final hun-dred thousand six months afterward, contingent on his meeting your requirement for his silence."

"That sounds very good, Mr. Goodrich."

"I had drawn up a draft agreement complete but for the amounts specified. I filled them in and your husband initialed them and signed his agreement, which I witnessed. Because of the hour, there was no office notary available, but his signature and yours can be notarized on Friday."

"I'll be in Washington on Thursday."

"Then, if you'll come by the office for a few minutes . . ."

"Yes." She hesitated. "And Harlan?"

"Your husband said he'd be away until Friday and come in then for formal signing and your check. Is that agreeable?"

She breathed deeply. "It is. Thank you. Uh—do I have to see him?"

"No. The oaths can be administered separately."

"Wonderful. I guess the last question is divorce venue. Where do you suggest?"

"Well, as I told you, there are a number of possibilities, but one advantage of the Caymans is that the parties don't have to appear in person. My firm has a correspondent there who can handle the entire proceeding. The documents can be expressed there for submission to the court."

I gave Alison a thumbs-up. She smiled and said, "Thank you so much, Mr. Goodrich. You've accomplished everything I wanted done."

"No thanks necessary, Senator. See you Thursday."

Alison clicked off the phone and turned to me. "I feel so relieved . . . and what you told me about Harlan's financial problems saved me a great deal of money."

"He's still getting a lot of money for signing a couple of papers—but only twenty percent of what he wanted. I'd say your lawyer is a first-class negotiator."

We strolled back to the living room and Alison said, "I'd really love a nightcap."

So I poured cognac and sat beside her. After sipping I said, "Can't help wondering if Harlan's going out of town has anything to do with Doris's murder."

"That is a possibility, isn't it? To avoid police questioning, you mean."

I nodded. "If he's innocent that's a rather foolish thing to do. If he's guilty . . . well, he'll probably go far, far away." I sipped thoughtfully. "Or he might be going to Atlantic City to assure the casinos he'll soon be able to pay his debts. That would relieve pressure on him and cancel the threats of bodily harm."

"That's probably it. But I feel so sorry for Doris. Adultery shouldn't be punished by death—I mean, as far as I know she only lived with Harlan, she wasn't a criminal."

"But someone had reason to kill her. I hope your husband didn't do it, and the police will find out some robber did if for her money."

"Poor thing," Alison sighed. "Seeing her face makes me wish she hadn't come to the farm—then she'd be only an anonymous victim."

"Well, sooner or later it'll all sort out. If I hear anything I'll phone you in Atlanta. Where are you staying?"

"The Peachtree. Call me in any case, will you? For my morale."

TWELVE

———

IN THE MORNING I was conferring with a client whose tax problems arose from the construction of thirty-two public housing units. Before occupancy they had been judged substandard; the District of Columbia refused to pay the final increment, and wanted Rico Manfredi to return what had already been paid. Manfredi had a lawyer handling that part of his problem; what he wanted from me was advice on whether he could claim anticipated loss as a tax deduction. I didn't care for Mr. Manfredi, classifying him as a shady operator who worked within the interstices of HUD regulations and wanted to be paid much for producing little. I said, "Since you're contesting the District's demand you can look forward to a long period in court. For your problem I ought to get an IRS ruling and there's time to do that."

He scratched at a gray-black mustache and scanned me with beady eyes. "How much will that cost me?"

"Hard to estimate. If the IRS is cooperative, not a lot of money. If IRS takes a negative position, more."

"Bottom line, Mr. Bentley?"

"We could cap the cost at four thousand."

He nodded. "That's manageable."

"And I'll need a retainer to represent you."

"How much is that?" he grumbled.

"A thousand. Give the check to my secretary and she'll issue a receipt."

He grimaced. "I was hoping you'd do this on contingency."

"That's a dirty word around here. No, I'm not a contingency lawyer—anyway, you're not anticipating money; all I can do is try to save you from paying more."

He thought it over. I shuffled papers on my desk before saying. "You don't need to decide now. But if you want to retain me it's a thousand down. Otherwise the consultation is two hundred."

"Jeez, so much?"

"Prime office rentals aren't cheap—you're in the business, you ought to know."

Mrs. Altman knocked on the door and came in. She handed me a note that read *Governor Green on line 2.* I nodded and said, "Mr. Manfredi will give you a check." He looked at me, at Mrs. Altman, and stood up. "I'll think it over."

To Mrs. Altman I said, "Consultation fee." And to Manfredi, "If you want me to face off with the IRS I'll need your attorney's cooperation."

"Sure, no problem." We shook hands and he went out, followed by my secretary. I picked up my telephone, punched in line 2 and said, "Bentley here. What can I do for you, Governor?"

"Maybe help me with a small problem."

"How small, sir?"

"Well, I've been trying to reach the senator but her office says she's out of town. That true?"

"I'm not her keeper, Governor. I don't know. But if it's an urgent matter perhaps you could get in touch with her attorneys of record—Gurney and Steiner."

"You think they might know how to contact her?"

"No idea." I didn't want to prolong the conversation, and I didn't mind a small lie to someone who had no business knowing where Alison was or was not. Green's presumed agents, Pleven and Munger, were still in her office, but no longer of tactical help to Governor Green. As the silence spread between us it occurred to me that they might have prevailed on Green to plead for their jobs. "Sorry I can't help you," I said in tones suggesting my part of the exchange was over.

"Wait up, will you?" he said irritably. "All I'm trying to do is alert her to a situation that seems to involve her husband, and the senator by extension."

I grunted. "He's extended his gambling debts?"

"Well, it's more serious than that."

"Oh? What could be more serious than death from a casino hit man? I can't think of anything worse."

He sighed. "Bentley, I sense you're trifling with me. Now, we've already discussed the state of the senator's marriage—a shambles, to put it bluntly."

"Your description."

"Believe me. Now, you'll agree that many fools who lose the respect of their spouses seek approval and affection in other quarters, validation of their manliness, as it were."

"Well, I've certainly heard it said. And Harlan is one of these insecure clowns?"

"In addition to his other shortcomings. I don't know how much the senator knew about Harlan's mistress but I'm afraid she's going to hear plenty now."

"You mean her husband is going to confess and ask for forgiveness?"

Green snorted. "Too late for that, Bentley. She's dead, murdered in a cheap hotel room, and before long it's going to be known that Harlan was her generous friend."

"I see what you're getting at. But if Harlan was a generous keeper, why would the lady be in a cheap hotel room dead or alive?"

"God knows. Harlan didn't elaborate. Said they parted company last Saturday, and Monday's Baltimore *Sun* carried the news. He sounded upset but not guilty, and for now I want to believe him."

"Of course. It's a long span between lovers' quarrel and murder."

"Exactly. But I'm concerned about the senator's name being brought in, subject to negative publicity."

"Feel that's inevitable?"

"Maybe not—I have some influential friends in Baltimore who might be able to keep the lid on until the police find Doris's killer."

"Doris?"

"Doris Conlon—a cheapie bar dancer from West Virginia. Harlan was infatuated with her, kept her in style, spent a lot of money on her, money he didn't have."

"Old story."

"Yes, but that doesn't mitigate the damage it could cause the senator. I mean being mentioned even tangentially in a murder case is bad news for a political figure."

"For anyone. But it could elicit sympathy for the senator, I mean being married to a disreputable fellow who strayed from the marital bed."

"Yeah, but I don't want to deal with what's far off. Actually, Harlan phoned me in quite a good mood."

"Isn't that a bit strange?"

"Well, any sorrow or concern he felt was overridden by a lucrative divorce agreement he'd just concluded with the senator's attorney. He didn't say how much was involved, but I gathered it would pull him out of the money hole and something left over."

"Lucky fellow. Of course, a lot of that could go for attorney's fees if he's indicted for murder."

Green gave an unkind chuckle. "Ain't that the truth? In one

hand, out the other. Fortunately, Harlan doesn't owe me any money. I know men, and I would never lend Harlan a rusty dime." There was an extended silence before the governor said, "The purpose of my call, basically, was to contact the senator and alert her to the murder situation so she could prepare for possible questioning. So in the event she gets in touch with you I'd be obliged if you'd tell her what I've told you, okay?"

"That's fine," I replied. "Count on me—only I can't think of a reason she'd be calling me. In any case, Governor, I'm sure she'll appreciate your effort."

"You understand why I couldn't leave the message with her office."

"Absolutely. So let's hope the police identify a perp other than her husband, and soon."

"We're of a mind on that. Meanwhile, I'll be in touch with a friend or two about the direction the investigation may take." He paused. "Thanks for your time."

"It's a pleasure to exchange ideas with an active mind like yours, Governor. Any time."

"Thanks, I'll remember that."

We broke off at the same time and a few moments later Mrs. Altman came in, a check fluttering between her fingers. "Two hundred dollars," she told me.

"Hasten it to the bank before the wrongdoer changes his mind."

She eyed me. "I thought he might pay a retainer fee."

"I was afraid he might. No, I don't want Manfredi as a client. Let us take the money and run." She smiled frostily and left on her banking errand.

In the quiet office I reflected on the governor's call and sensed he was continuing to probe my relationship with Senator Bowman. His expressed concern for her political future and Doris's murder possibly staining her skirts would be more credible if he had anything tangible to gain from keeping her skirts unsullied. No doubt, like many politicians, he habitually operated on parallel tracks of which one was calculated to be a winner.

He'd said Harlan had called him, sounding neither upset or

remorseful over Doris's death though joyful over the windfall he expected from the divorce agreement. Odd that Harlan should have
phoned the governor for any reason that could withstand public
scrutiny, for there were probably darker motives for the call. Their
relationship was a puzzler unless their bonding was that of thieves,
something I could understand.

Green hadn't mentioned Harlan being away until Friday.
At least Green hadn't informed me if he did know. An easy explanation was Harlan's desire to avoid police questioning, unless he
had a rock-hard alibi for the period in which Doris had been killed.
In that case, produce it for the cops, let them check it out, and
breathe easy.

I didn't minimize Green's ability to keep the police from sur-
facing Harlan's name nor his power to influence the direction of
their investigation. In the political arena there were always favors
owed, and some were repaid directly or indirectly from the public
treasury. For others a promotion or a transfer would suffice. Green's
deck was a full one and he knew exactly how to play his cards.

I was planning to call Alison that night and decided not to
mention Green's call. I couldn't come up with a clear reason for it
and the ambiguity would only upset her.

After Mrs. Altman returned from the bank she brought a
client file to my desk and reminded me that the client was due in fifteen minutes. I scanned the file, made notes on a legal pad, and got
back to work.

It was after eleven when the hotel switchboard connected me to Alison's room, and I heard her answering voice. "It's Steve," I said.
"How's your morale?"

"Better now, much better. It's been a not very exciting day.
These conferences with panels of experts never are, but they're part
of my job and I *am* interested in public health."

"I'm lighting a cigar," I told her. "That make me a naughty
boy?"

"Not that alone, but it's part of your rebel persona."

"You want perfection? Look elsewhere."

"I have, dear, and what I came up with was you. How was your day?"

"Routine. But I banked two hundred dollars."

"So much?" She laughed. "You *have* been busy."

I told her about sleazy Rico Manfredi and how desperately I didn't want him as a client. She thought that was pretty funny, and unusual for a lawyer. "But then, you're sort of a maverick lawyer."

"If you say so. But, aren't you glad I am?"

"Grateful beyond words. I suppose you're in bed watching TV and enjoying a nightcap."

"I'd enjoy it more if this bimbo I met in a singles bar would stop tugging my arm and spilling precious brandy."

"Hmm. Does she have a name?"

"Probably, but it's a secret from me."

"And you like it that way."

"Ships that pass in the night . . ." I intoned, "and I've made it clear breakfast is not included."

"That shows character. Now that you've tried and failed to upset me you can tell me what you've really been up to all day."

"The truth would anesthetize you, so I try to spice it up, present a dashing, romantic image."

"Rogue. Exclusively for me?"

"You have my heart in the palm of your hand."

"Wish I believed you, honey."

"Tonight I'm Mr. Candor—not Cantor, Candor."

"I get it. Anything else to pique me with?"

"There is. I've been pondering Harlan's apparently inevitable publicity problem and I think you ought to tell Chad Goodrich about it."

"I should?"

"He's entitled to know whatever could prevent the divorce from going smoothly. You don't want him reading about it later."

"No, you're right. Um, how's the cigar going?"

"Ashes dropping everywhere. The bimbo's had enough, she's getting dressed."

"Good for her. No self-respecting woman goes to bed with a guy who smokes cigars while making love."

"So she told me. But, seriously, you ought to call Goodrich tomorrow."

"Tomorrow? Too much to do—honestly. Would you do it for me?"

"I would—as part of our ever-expanding lawyer–client relationship."

"Dear man. And you'll meet me at Dulles?"

"Natural disasters aside. Eleven-fifteen, Delta."

"Can't wait."

As I replaced the receiver I realized that I missed her more than I had thought possible.

Next morning Chad Goodrich and I played telephone tag until Mrs. Altman finally put him through.

"Sorry about the back-and-forth, Mr. Bentley. Is this about our mutual client?"

"It is. When we spoke last night she asked me to fill you in on a development that may have some impact on the divorce."

"I'm all ears."

So I told him about the murder of Doris Conlon, her relationship with Harlan Bowman, and my concern that his being identified as Doris's keeper might adversely affect the senator's public image.

"Mm, yes it could. Has he been named a suspect?"

"Not as far as I know. Most of what I'm telling you came from a Baltimore *Sun* story—not naming Harlan. I might add that the senator has for some time been aware that her husband had an illicit amatory interest, though not the lady's name."

"But you knew it?"

"The name surfaced when I was having Harlan's financial situation looked into. The investigator recalled it and brought the *Sun* story to my attention."

"I'd better start reading the *Sun*." He paused. "Monday night when the husband left my office he seemed happy as a cow in corn. Wonder if he knew about the murder?"

"I guess only he can say."

"He's supposed to show up on Friday to sign the divorce

agreement. Now I'm worried he's on the lam—any thoughts on that?"

"No, but it strikes me as strange that with big bucks nearly in his grasp he'd delay picking it up."

Goodrich grunted. "You know him?"

"Glimpsed him only. We've never spoken."

"He's a piece of work. I'll say that. A grasping, avaricious, amoral fellow. Can't understand how the senator tolerated him all those years."

I thought it over. "Probably easier to ignore him than confront him—and she had plenty of Congressional demands on her time."

"Yeah, I understand that. She's coming in tomorrow to sign the formal agreement and write the first check for hubby." He paused. "Well, thanks for the information. I certainly hope nothing develops to block or postpone the divorce."

"Me, too."

"Appreciate your call, sir."

It was after ten when I drove away from the house and crossed Key Bridge to Virginia. Clear night, plenty of stars, and a silver moon crescent that looked like Diana's bow. Between Rosslyn and Arlington I noticed a flasher sparkling my rearview mirror, checked my speed, and confirmed that I was well below the limit. Other cars were passing me but the flashing light persisted until it was almost tailgating. Slowing, I pulled onto the verge and braked. The car followed and stopped. I turned off the radio and rolled down the window, looked back and saw two men walking toward me. One was tall and husky, the other short and wide as a barrel. Both wore street clothes. The tall one stopped beside me and barked, "Out. Hand over the keys."

"What's the problem, officer?" I gave him the ignition keys and got out slowly.

"Hands on the roof, feet back."

I felt a gun barrel against my spine while the short guy patted me down. "License, registration, and proof of insurance," he snapped.

"In my wallet."

"Hear that, Charley?" the short one jeered. "Wallet, he sez, not billfold like ordinary folks." His hand came around and filched the wallet from my inside coat pocket. He handed it to his partner who scanned the contents with a mini-Maglite. I asked, "How about some ID, fellows?"

"You want ID?" A karate chop against my neck almost dropped me. "That's what you get, wiseass."

When colored lights stopped blurring my vision I glanced around and saw them counting my cash. "Okay," I said, "keep it, no harm done." Charley spun me around so my back was against my car, and held up a small transparent bag filled with white powder. "Whaddya think this is?"

"Dentifrice," I suggested. "Not mine."

"I pulled it outta your billfold, and Red's a witness."

A shakedown, I thought, or worse. "That's bad, isn't it? I could do time."

"You got it, wiseass, like five years."

Red rasped, "He oughta know, he's an officer of the court."

Charley snorted, "I hate mouthpieces. Bloodsuckers. Snotty bastards like you." While he was talking I'd let my arms drop slowly to my sides, Charley tossed me my wallet but I let it drop between my feet. I bent over and came up fast, grabbed his right wrist with my left hand and kneed his crotch. Hard. He yelped, reached for his injured balls and I broke the revolver from his hand. Red watched in horror. I stepped back and waved the .38 at them. "Off the highway, lads," I ordered, "and down the slope."

"Fuck you," Charley gasped.

Waiting until an eight-wheeler rumbled by, I fired a shot between his feet, turned the revolver on Red. "Replacement knees are all the rage, but I hear they're not as good as what you were born with." I pointed the barrel at his right knee. "Wanna find out?"

"Jesus, no!" He backed down the slope, and I shoved Charley after him. I pulled the flasher dome from their car top and ripped out the wires, tossed the dome into the underbrush. Now we could conduct business unseen.

"Red, if you've got a piece on you, take it out very carefully and toss it to me."

"I—I got none," he stammered.

"If I pat you down and find one I'll kill you," I said flatly, "and Charley will get the blame. Understand?"

"Give it to him, Red," Charley wheezed, still cupping his aching testicles. "This motherfucker is serious."

"Damn right I am." I fired a shot into the ground between them. Red bent over, lifted his pants leg and pulled out a two-shot derringer. "Thanks," I said, and threw the backup piece far into the brush. "How about you, Charley? Got an ankle peashooter?"

In a pain-filled voice, he rasped, "No."

"Next," I said, "I'll have your wallets—just to paw through the way you did mine. Toss them here."

I picked them up and pocketed both. "Now my keys."

Charley flipped them at me and I caught them in midair.

"Now you can lie on your backs and enjoy the moonlight. That's Sirius over there. Mars just off the horizon." A landing plane screamed overhead and I wondered if I was going to be late meeting Alison. I watched them get down and when both were prone, I snapped, "Stay there." Then I moved to their Mercury and pulled out the keys. They watched as I threw them into the dark brush beyond the highway. Then I smashed the revolver butt against the windshield. A fragment broke off as the entire windshield ruptured into concentric circles like a spiderweb. Red whined, "Aintcha gonna give back my billfold?"

"Possibly," I said, "after I examined it and checked your names through NCIC. I'll bet you've both got rap sheets a yard long."

"Cocksucker," Charley mouthed, and I fired a shot near his head. Red began to blubber. "That's for bad language," I told them. "Let's have no more of it." Then I laughed. "You must have thought you were in Miami where every tourist is a shakedown target for phony cops. Funny how things turned out."

"Keep thinking it's funny," Charley grated, "until next time."

"If there's a next time," I said, "I'll be less charitable. You'll learn what it feels like having a hot slug in your belly."

Red moaned unintelligibly. Standing above Charley's head, I

pointed his .38 between his eyes. "That sugar bag you showed me— let's have it."

"Whatcha want it for?"

"To snort, asshole. Slow and easy." I watched his free hand slide into a pocket. It came out with the plant-bag. I took it and walked to their car, opened the bag, dumped powder across the seats and dropped the bag on the floor. I hoped it was coke. Then I wiped prints from Charley's .38 and slid it under the front seat, but not so far back it couldn't be found.

Finally, in my car, I started the engine and drove away. No moving figures behind, just the old Merc dark on the shoulder. I wondered how the lads would explain it all to the highway cops— real ones. The least they could expect was a ticket for illegal parking. At worst a narcotics charge.

As I drove into Dulles Airport I recalled transporting Bo- stick's corpse to Reagan. Gradually adrenaline drained from my bloodstream and my vision cleared. But the side of my neck felt as though it had been slammed with a baseball bat. Powerful guy, Charley; I was glad I hadn't had to grapple with him.

I found Alison collecting baggage from the carousel. Her face lighted when she saw me, but we didn't kiss, just squeezed hands while the skycap loaded his carrier.

On the way into town she snuggled against me and mur- mured, "I'm so glad you're here." Her head pressed against my neck until I winced. "Oh, honey, I hurt you?"

"Old crick in my neck," I explained. "From when I used to be a girl-watcher."

She nibbled my ear. "And when was that, dear?"

"Early puberty. I gave it up when I started shaving. Now, to get back on track, I told Chad Goodrich all he needed to know."

"What did he say?"

"He's concerned Harlan may be in hiding."

"Hmm. Then he must have something to hide."

"That would be the police take on it. They get very hostile to people who aren't around to answer questions. But Harlan is too smart to become a fugitive. He could be looking for an affordable lawyer."

"Is there such a thing?"

I carried two bags into her apartment and left them in the bedroom. Alison stepped out of her shoes and said, "I could really go for some chilled wine. Look in the fridge, will you?"

When I carried bottle and glasses back to the bedroom she was in the shower. Through the steamed dimple-glass door I could see her moving body. After the highway episode I needed a shower myself. I found aspirin in the medicine cabinet and gulped four tabs to quell neck pain, then got out of the steam while she dried and toweled her hair. Emerging, she took a glass from me and drank cold wine. I did the same and refilled our glasses. She said, "I really needed that. Why don't you get into something comfortable?"

So I showered, wrapped a towel around my hips, and entered the dark bedroom. Alison was in bed, and soon all the stress and aggravations of that long day melted in her welcoming arms.

THIRTEEN

IN THE MORNING I emptied the contents of my attackers' wallets on my office desk. According to their driving licenses Charley was Charles Joseph Winkowski of Suitland. Red's name was Jacob Adam Stonefield, resident of the District of Columbia. I recovered the bills they'd taken from my wallet and pocketed fifty-five dollars of theirs. Little enough recompense for my time and trouble, I reflected. Business cards were from the Janus investigative agency. *Call anytime* was printed below an Egyptian eye logo, and a D.C. phone number beside it. There were a rent receipt, cards from various strip joints in and out of the Beltway, and phone calling cards. The only credit card was a Visa bearing another name—I suspected it was stolen.

After faxing their licenses and Janus cards to Pat Moran's office, I added *Call me,* and shredded the accumulation. Twenty minutes later Pat phoned to ask what I wanted done with the subjects. "I'd like them wasted," I told him, "but failing that, a police rundown." Then I told him how they'd pulled me over and given me grief before I got my act together.

"Listen, Steve, taking away a gun from a perp is damn risky. You're too old for that sorta crap."

"They got me mad."

"Still got the piece?"

"No."

"Find a concealed weapons permit?"

"No. And no PI licenses, either. Scumball shakedown artists both of them."

"Sounds like. Figure you were a random target?"

"If I'd lingered to interrogate them I might have found out. But they're just the type unscrupulous characters hired to do dirty work. Like intimidating me, telling me to do this or that. They could have tailed me from Georgetown. I didn't notice the car following until the roof flasher went on."

"Yeah, there was a guy like that who worked the Beltway. He'd pull over lone women drivers and rape them in the bushes. Had a long run until the cops sent out decoys—one of them nailed him."

"The Beltway Rapist. Roof flasher and bullhorn, but that was then, this is now. Find out if the Janus agency exists, will you? And the principals."

"I'll call later today."

An hour later Alison phoned from Chad Goodrich's office. "I've signed everything," she said, "and now it's up to Harlan." Her voice lowered. "Wonderful homecoming last night. I should take trips more often."

"Don't think of it. When you're away I wander around like a stray cat. Uh—are we together tonight?"

"Maybe around eleven," she said, regret in her voice. "There's

a state dinner at the White House for some sub-Saharan dictator
and I have to be there. Some of my constituents could take offense
if I wasn't, and political enemies would say I snubbed an important
African leader."

"Maybe you ought to try out the Lincoln Bedroom—get accustomed to sleeping at Sixteen Hundred."

"Oh, Steve, what do I have to do to convince you I have no
such ambitions?"

"Tell Abel Green to lay off."

"That wouldn't be wise. I'd like his support when I run for reelection. Anyway, the idea is just too unlikely."

"Whatever you say."

"I'll call when I leave the White House."

"I'll be waiting."

Pat didn't phone, but sent several faxes. Two were criminal rap
sheets, the third a bankruptcy declaration by Janus, Inc., culled from
the newspaper's announcements section of a year ago.

Corporal Winkowski had received an undesirable discharge
from the Corps of Engineers at Fort Belvoir; later he'd been fined
for issuing a bad check to a liquor store. More recently he'd been apprehended trying to sneak merchandise out of a Sears store, case nol
prossed on payment of a fifty-dollar fine.

His partner in crime, Private Stonefield, had been given a dis-
honorable discharge after court-martial for stealing government
property from the PX at Aberdeen Proving Ground. A charge of
sexual assault by a female trainee was dismissed when the trainee
was transferred to Fort Hood, Texas. After discharge Stonefield
was charged with grand theft auto but the charge was vacated
when the arresting officer failed to show up at trial.

Low-class petty thieves and burglars. No wonder they'd
turned to highway robbery, if that was their sole intent.

According to Pat's report Winkowski and Stonefield had co-
owned the bankrupt Janus investigative agency—no surprise there.
The phone number on their business card fed to an answering service, again no surprise. Real sleazeballs but potentially dangerous.

Unavoidably I wondered if those two dud missiles had been pointed at me by a third party who wished me harm. A reasonable question, but who could that person be? Ostensibly Governor Green was cultivating me as an ally, and what motive did Harlan Bowman have for hiring the hapless pair? No real reason for him to resent my sleeping with his wife—he hadn't tilled the marital garden for many months, and had his own sleeping companion until very recently. Besides, he was walking away from marriage with a huge payoff. No, Harlan didn't fit the equation.

Somehow, the murders of Bostick and Doris were linked, and as I thought about last night's highway thugs I decided that Charley Winkowski was entirely capable of shooting both, for a motivating fee. But if Charley had collected for two hits, how come he was working the highway with only beer money in his jeans? The average hired gun would take off for Acapulco or Vegas to enjoy his blood money with broads, brandy, and baccarat.

Mrs. Altman's voice on the intercom interrupted my thoughts. "Sir, a Captain Stepinak—that's phonetic—would like to speak with you."

"Captain of what?"

"Said Virginia Highway Patrol. Shall I—?"

"Give me a minute."

"Line three."

Uh-oh, I thought, this is the aftermath of last night's encounter. Charley and Red had seen my name on my driving license, if they hadn't known it before. Well, be pleasant, Bentley, and fully cooperative like the White House always is. I picked up the receiver and punched the button. "Captain Stepinak? How can I help you? If you're seeking an attorney, my practice is limited to tax matters, but—"

"No, sir, fortunately I'm not looking for a lawyer. But there was a highway incident last night that raised some questions and I'm hoping you'll be able to assist our investigation."

"Of course—what sort of incident?"

"Very odd. One of our patrol troopers noticed a darkened car parked on the shoulder and stopped to investigate."

"Where was that, Captain?"

"About two miles east of Dulles Airport. Ah, were you on the road last night?"

"I was. Meeting an incoming passenger on a Delta flight."

"And what time was that flight due to arrive?"

"Eleven-fifteen. Miraculously it landed on time."

"Yeah, that *is* a miracle." He chuckled before asking, "Could the arriving passenger confirm your account?"

"If necessary. But I'm not going to name her at present because the lady is married—you get my meaning?"

"Yes, sir, I do, and I don't think it's going to be necessary. Now, roughly about the time you were meeting your passenger the same patrol trooper picked up two men who were illegally walking along the highway toward Arlington. Uh—I'm ahead of my story, because the trooper who looked into the dark parked car had a K-9 with him. The windshield was cracked, suggesting the driver might have suffered a head injury, so the K-9, Sadie by name, sniffed around and hopped into the car. A controlled substance was spilled around, and Sadie sniffed out a handgun under the seat. The trooper radioed his findings and was told to resume patrolling. That's when he came across the pair on the highway. He asked if they had left a car on the shoulder, and they admitted they had. So in view of Sadie's findings the trooper called for backup and both men were taken into custody."

"Good work," I said enthusiastically. "But how does my name come in? Why are you calling me?"

"Well, that takes a bit of explaining, sir. The two suspects claimed a car with your District license plate forced their vehicle off the highway, said the driver held them at gunpoint, robbed them, and smashed their windshield after stealing the ignition keys."

I managed a short laugh. "Pretty fanciful, Captain."

"We thought so. Can you clarify any part of it? For instance, how the pair came by your license number?"

"Well . . . as I proceeded toward the airport I noticed a car just off the road so I slowed, planning to offer assistance if required. My slowdown gave anyone opportunity to read my plate."

"Right."

"The car looked empty—abandoned, I thought—and seeing no one about, I drove on to the airport."

"I see. Did you notice if the windshield was broken?"

"No. Captain. Both cars were facing the same direction, and I had no reason to look back, that being the only way I could have seen the windshield." I paused. "Besides, as I recall, that portion of the road was pretty dark. My car was moving and I wasn't looking for details on an off-highway car. In fact, I don't remember what kind it was. The incident seemed unimportant—until now."

"Well, thank you for your time, sir. You've been very forth-coming and helpful."

"That's quite all right. The whole thing sounds, well, bizarre. I mean, why would two fellows with drugs and weapons in their ve-hicle come up with a story like that?"

"Our guess is they needed a way to explain how the gun and drugs came to be in their car. The best they could come up with was your license plate."

"Inventive," I remarked. "Have a good day, Captain."

"You too, sir." The inflection told me he had more to say so I said, "Go on, Captain."

He uttered a deprecatory laugh. "This *is* a strange one, and being a lawyer you'll appreciate the situation." He paused. "Looking at the case it seems bass-ackward."

"How so, Captain?"

"We got perps in custody—now we got to figure out the crime." We both chuckled at that, and broke the connection. As I wiped stress moisture from my forehead, I reflected that I hadn't heard "bass-ackward" said by a grown-up since a Lyndon Johnson press conference—and that was a while ago.

Having lied, apparently successfully, to Captain Stepinak, I thought how foresighted the two thugs were not to mention my name. If they had, it would have brought them more grief than they already had, even if specific charges hadn't yet been filed. And I wondered if my car had been a random selection or whether they'd tailed me on orders.

If they'd been working for a principal they'd now look to him for a lawyer, so it would be interesting to find out if a private, non-Legal Aid lawyer represented them. And who was paying him or her.

That night I was home, doing catch-up work, when Alison called on her cell phone. She was just leaving the White House and would be at the apartment in twenty minutes or so. "I'll be there," I replied. "How was the affair of state?"

"Generally boring. The guest of honor came in full regional regalia plus about ten pounds of gold around his neck and wrist. He's generally regarded as a cannibal, you know, said to roast his enemies, eat their hearts and livers as delicacies. Ughh."

"I think that's been widely known."

"He didn't bring any of his wives and took up with me as the lone unattached female. After dinner he edged me into a corner and said he'd like to fly me to his country. I could stay as long as I liked, and when I left he'd give me a box of gold and diamonds."

I laughed. "When do you leave?"

"Bastard! That was an offer I could easily refuse. I explained I had a husband who would object mightily, even if that's not exactly true, and he asked me to think it over. Then one of the President's aides interrupted to say the Prez and the secretary of state wanted to confer with him in the drawing room. So he bowed, kissed my hand, and walked away."

"Nick of time, eh? You live dangerously."

"Don't I though? I missed you terribly."

"I'm leaving now."

Turning into the apartment parking lot, I saw her Jaguar already in its reserved space. That was fine. *Bueno.* But I tensed when I saw a white Mercedes roadster in a guest slot. I slowed to look over the scene before pulling into a guest space one slot beyond the Mercedes. Seeing my car arrive, Alison got out of hers and began walking toward me. The Mercedes door opened and a man stepped out. I'd only glimpsed him once, but it wasn't difficult to recognize Harlan Bowman—the somewhat missing Harlan Bowman. He was wearing a dark rumpled suit, dark shirt and no tie. Without even a glance at my car or me, he began striding toward his wife. Seeing him, she broke her pace, then resumed it. Harlan intercepted her and I got out of my car. He reached for her wrist but she jerked it quickly away and stepped past him. She'd seen me now, and her pace quickened. Harlan caught up with her, snarling, "Bitch! You changed the door lock."

She stopped, and faced him with a cold smile. "So you tried getting in."

Angrily he said, "Why'd you do that? We're still married."

"To keep bastards like you from going where they're not wanted."

He struck her then, the blow rocking her against the fender of a parked car. "Give me the key," he said loudly and turned to see me approaching. "Beat it," he snapped. "This is a family discussion."

"If you're feeling muscular, try me." I stepped between him and Alison.

His eyes widened. "I've seen you—saw you at the farm." He turned back to Alison, who was holding her left cheek. "This your constant companion? My replacement?"

"Maybe," I said. "Any business of yours?"

"Damn right it is."

"You're wrong," Alison said in a hard voice. "What are you doing here?"

He glanced at her, at me and back to her. "I need to stay for a while."

"Not possible," she said flatly. "The marriage is over."

"Not until I sign the papers—if I do."

"Or until I sign the check for you—if I do."

He looked down, mouth moving silently. He said, "I need a place to stay."

"Rent one," she told him. "I'm not going to harbor a fugitive."

"Fugitive?" He sounded puzzled.

"Don't try that old innocent act. The police have been asking about you. The theory is you shot your sweetie."

"That's . . . that's ridiculous," he blurted. "They can't pin it on me."

"Well, Harlan," I said, "it's like this. The cops have a dead woman you've been living with. They look at you and think motive and opportunity. So they want to hear your side of the case."

He shivered. "She left me. Doris left me," he said in a voice of disbelief, "but I didn't kill her." He turned to Alison. "You've got to believe me, help me. You owe me that much."

She removed her hand from her cheek. "I owe you nothing. In fact, I'm not sure I'll go ahead with the divorce. I could save a good deal of expense by waiting, seeing how things turn out for you. I don't want a two-hundred-thousand-dollar payment to be construed as getaway money."

He turned to me, hands clenching and unclenching. I said, "This is where you throw a punch at me, I knock you down and kick the shit out of you. That's the sequence, Harlan. I've now seen you hit your wife on two occasions. That's spousal abuse in any court and I'd love to testify against you."

He took a step back. "Got it all figured out, you two," he sneered.

"Right. Just waiting for you to show up. Maybe Abel Green would like to hide you, but I tend to doubt that. He won't want to buck the Atlantic City boys who are looking for you. So your best bet—in fact, your only hope—is to go back to Baltimore and answer cop questions. They'll appreciate your volunteering, as it were—might not even stick you in a cell."

"Oh Christ," he said despairingly, then sucked in a deep breath. "The publicity won't be good for you, Alison."

"I can ride it out," she said calmly. "Even get public sympathy for being married to an utter scumball who is also a murderer."

"But I didn't kill her," he shrieked. "I don't know who did."

I shrugged. "Maybe not. But the suit's tailored for your frame. Go see the cops, sooner than later, with or without a lawyer. Make it easy on yourself." I reached out and clamped my right hand around his throat, thumbed the pressure point and heard him squeal.

Alison cried, "Don't, Steve. Don't hurt him."

Dropping my hand, I grinned at Harlan. "Unmerited solicitude. Remember that when hatching plots against your wife."

"Yes," Alison said coolly, "and remember this—I don't want
you around me, don't want to see you. Anything you might want to
convey, do it through Mr. Goodrich. Do you understand that, Harlan?"

Without replying, he spun around and began walking toward
his car. "Don't be surprised," I called, "if the cops ask you about another murder." I took Alison's arm and tucked it under mine. Harlan stopped and looked back at me. "What murder?"

"That would be telling, wouldn't it? Just let the polygraph do
its work, don't buck it."

He cursed me sotto voce, yanked the roadster's door open and
got in. We stood clear while he backed around, tires screaming. As
he turned onto Connecticut Avenue I noticed a car that was
parked at the curb in front of the apartment building. As the Mercedes headed north the parked car's lights went on and it pulled
away from the curb. The windows were tinted, and we were too far
away to make out the driver's face, but I had no doubt the car was
following Harlan.

I said so to Alison, and she said she thought so, too.

Arm in arm, we left the parking lot and went into her building. As we waited for the elevator she said, "I'm so fortunate you
were there when I needed you. It's becoming almost habitual."

"That's an exaggeration." I kissed the pink mark on her cheek.
then I held back the elevator door while she stepped in. She
punched the floor button and circled me with her arms. "Who do
you think is following Harlan?"

"Who knows?" I said. "He's got more enemies than Fidel Cas-
tro. Let's not do his worrying for him."

Her hands framed my face, and her tongue traced my lips before parting them. I unlocked the door with her new key but her
hand kept mine from the switch. "No light," she breathed, "we can
find each other in the dark." Then I heard the whisper of her zipper
as she peeled off her evening gown.

We didn't wait to get to the bedroom but made love on a

Navajo throw rug, the long cushioned sofa, and finally an armless chair.

Like a couple of horny teens.

In the calm aftermath, Alison sleeping beside me, I mused that although lovemaking couldn't resolve our problems it was a soothing relief from them.

Night vision enabled me to scan the outlines of her body: the aristocratic Revelstoke profile, high cheekbones, the soft contours of chin and throat leading down to sloping breasts, flat belly and tapering thighs, all attributes genetically shared with her cousin, Francine. Alison's quiet, regular breathing was having a hypnotic effect on me. Time flashed backward and for a moment it seemed Francie was once more beside me. But that was only the persistence of memory, and I knew I would never see my dead love again. But perhaps, I thought, her spirit had guided Alison, whom I was now required to preserve and protect.

Almost unthinkingly I had accepted the mission, but after two murders and a murky cloud of intrigue around us I had to wonder what more I would have to do to force light into dark and dangerous places.

FOURTEEN

IN MY MIND Harlan Bowman remained an enigma, acting like a manic deprived of lithium and giving an overall impression of involvement in the Conlon killing. So I phoned Pat Moran and asked him to find out whether Harlan had shown up at Baltimore police headquarters, or whether the cops were expecting him to do so. Pat said he'd get on it and let me know.

This was also the day Harlan was scheduled to sign the divorce agreement and collect Alison's check. Were I Harlan, I mused, I'd get the check, then see the Baltimore cops, but a call to the office of Chad Goodrich informed me that Harlan hadn't yet appeared. Even if Harlan was going to avoid police inquiries and leave for sheltering climes he would need Alison's money. So his delay in seeing Goodrich made me wonder.

Then I recalled seeing the car follow Harlan's Mercedes from the parking lot, and wondered if it had caught up and what ensued. Given Harlan's debts to the Atlantic City mob it was easy to cast the follower as an enforcer dispatched to collect from Harlan or leave him in grievous pain. That was the way things were in the gamblers' world, and I had no problem with it. All I wanted from Harlan was his signature on the divorce agreement and even if both wrists were in casts he ought to be able to scrawl his name.

Mrs. Altman informed me that Rico Manfredi had returned and given her a thousand-dollar retainer check. Now he would like a word with me. I said I'd see him, and presently my new client came in. We didn't shake hands and he seated himself and gazed across the desk at me. "Okay," he said, "we on the same track now?"

"Probably. After you left the other day it occurred to me that a good strategy would be to have your lawyer file suit against the District for full payment plus damages and attorney's fees."

"It would? Tell me why."

"Your lawyer may disagree, but I feel it would lend weight to my discussions with the IRS. On the one hand we're asking the IRS for a deduction ruling if the District doesn't pay, while on the other letting the IRS know taxable money is in prospect if the District comes through."

"Mmm," he said after a few moments' reflection. "I like it."

"Okay, I'll need your lawyer's name so we can share the files."

"Sal Bonfaccio," he told me, "office on K Street." He stood up. "Four thousand cap?"

"That was an estimate prior to reviewing the case files. A lot depends on the IRS's reasonableness, or lack thereof."

"But you'll let me know?"

"I'll let you know."

He left then, and I had Burton Michaels come in. I explained Manfredi's problem, outlined the discussion just concluded, and gave him Bonfaccio's name. Michaels frowned. "Not the most ethical lawyer in town, Steve."

"That's Manfredi's problem. All we want from Sal is a copy of the file, and I want you to handle the case."

"Sure, glad to." He was smiling now. The work meant additional money for him. "I'll do a good job."

"I'm confident you will."

As he was leaving, my private phone rang and I heard Pat Moran say, "No trace of Harlan at police headquarters. They're hot to talk with him and beginning to think he may have blown town."

"I think he's still around, reviewing the odds before deciding what to do." I paused. "For your information only, I had a brief unexpected contact with him last night after which he took off for parts unknown."

"But you don't want the cops to know that."

"I'm hoping he'll go to the cops on his own and spare his wife embarrassment if he's brought in."

"Gotcha. I should add the police have no suspects for the Conlon killing. They can write it off as a crackhead robbery-murder, but not until after they talk with Harlan. Anyway, it's not a high priority case for them."

"Thanks, Pat." I broke the connection, and as I thought it over I speculated that Harlan was staying out of sight in hopes that Governor Green would put in the fix even though Green had told me Harlan hadn't asked for help or money. But that was only Green's word, and their phone exchange could have been quite different.

Late in the day Alison phoned me, saying she was distressed because Harlan hadn't signed the agreement.

"Or picked up your check?"

"No. But forget the check, I want his signature above all."

"Of course. And I can't understand his not collecting money he's desperate for."

"Nor can I." She paused. "Steve, you don't think—I mean there was that car following him last night . . ."

"Well, maybe it wasn't following him, just coincidence it pulled away when he did."

"Maybe," she said, "but it certainly looked strange. Also, I wanted to let you know I have a committee meeting that will keep me from leaving for the farm until later. Suppose you get there when you can and I'll join you as soon as possible. Is that okay?"

"Sure. I'll chill wine and mix drinks, enjoy a peaceful sunset in the country."

"You *are* wonderful. I'm anticipating another marvelous weekend."

"So am I."

"Oh—one other thing. I was going to stop at the security shop for the new keys and alarm system instructions, but would you do it?"

"Of course."

"Love you."

Replacing the receiver, I looked at my watch. To do all I had to do I'd better get going. So I wished Mrs. Altman and Burton pleasant weekends and said I'd see them Monday. Burton told me he'd collected Manfredi's case file from Bonfaccio and said he was staying at the office long enough to copy it—the lawyer wanted it back on Monday. "Also, he asked if I'd suggested Manfredi sue the District and I said no, knew nothing about it. So he said it was a good idea, and I could visualize him adding up new billing hours."

"You've got him in the palm of your hand."

At home, I put shaving gear and walking shoes in a bag, added gin and vermouth bottles, and drove over the river into Virginia.

In Leesburg I reached the security shop just before closing, picked up the new door keys, and listened carefully to the owner's instructions regarding arming and disarming the alarm system. He gave me a brochure containing the same instructions and a bill for his services. I assured him the senator would pay promptly, and drove on to the farm.

It was dusk when I got there, a light golden haze covering the western fields, and I parked by the front entrance and got out my travel bag.

At the door I punched sequential numbers into the shielded electronic lock and saw the red alarm light vanish. Then I inserted a key in the door, opened it and went in. The air was dead, so I kept the door open and opened the rear door to let breeze circulate through the house. There was cold wine in the refrigerator, and plenty of cubes in the ice bin. I poured a glass of Chablis and sipped it, wondering if I should thaw steaks or wait until Alison arrived. Then I went up to the bathroom and left my shaving gear on the counter before changing into ankle-high trail shoes.

In the kitchen again, I got two T-bones from the freezer and set them out to thaw. Checked salad vegetables, and saw the cooler had kept them fresh. Poured another glass of wine, and decided to move my BMW out of sight from the highway, parking where I'd left it the weekend before.

Recent rain had left the soil damp, and as I started back for the house I noticed tire tracks leading toward the barn. At first I thought a farm truck had made them, but the tracks would have been farther apart, the shallow ruts deeper and wider. So a car had made them.

My gaze followed the double trail to the barn door. It was closed, but when I walked past it less than a week ago it had been partly open. Of course, the leasing farmer might have put a car inside the barn, but I was curious enough to walk to the barn door and unlatch it.

The old wood frame sagged and groaned as I tugged it open, and what I saw inside made my neck hairs prickle. For there in the gloom was a white Mercedes roadster, top in place so I couldn't see if anyone was inside. Cautiously, I went around to the driver's window and looked in. Empty. I didn't like that because I figured Harlan was waiting nearby to ambush Alison when she arrived.

Only how did he know she was coming? He was an impatient fellow, and I couldn't see him hanging around for hours, maybe a day, unless his plan was to murder his wife and inherit the immense largess of her will. That much made sense. Now I had to search for the bastard and prevent him from harming Alison. No wonder, I thought, he hadn't gone to the Baltimore police—he could do that after his wife was dead.

Shit!

I had to assume he was armed with some sort of weapon, so

for self-preservation I ought to arm myself before beginning the search. So thinking, I walked back toward the open door and began to close it when something caught my eye.

Where the trunk lid closed above the license plate I saw a small section of fabric pinched in the closure. I pulled at it, but it didn't yield, so I opened the car door and got out the car keys. One of them fitted the trunk lock. I turned it and the spring-loaded lid lifted and bounced. Now I could see what the blue fabric was attached to—the pants leg of a man's body.

For a few moments I stared at it, heart pounding, throat dry, as I studied the contorted body of Harlan Bowman. I reached deep into the truck to press Harlan's carotid, and as expected no blood was pumping through it.

What I could see of his face was unnaturally pale, and I thought that he had bled a lot. I tried to move the rear leg but the joint was stiff with the rigor of death. He had been killed and stuffed in the trunk of his car like a sack of grain. Only this sack wore a blue suit and lay rigidly in fetal posture, knees shoved up to his chest to fit him in.

My first thought was the irony of Harlan dead in the trunk of his beloved Mercedes. My next thought was the absolute necessity of keeping Alison—now his widow—from the scene. She hadn't killed her husband, knew nothing of the how and why of his death, yet his being found on her property would cause publicity, suspicion, and speculation enough to damage her irremediably.

Almost reflexively, I knew what I had to do.

FIFTEEN

——

MUCH OF LOUDON County is white-fence country whose grazing meadows for horses and cattle are separated by midrange housing developments, mini–shopping centers, and fast food drive-thrus. I left it all as I turned the Mercedes onto the Dulles Airport access road and turned on the headlights. The dial showed that I was well below posted speed, and when the airport's unique architecture showed against the nearly dark skyline I breathed deeply in relief.

Before leaving the farmhouse I'd posted a note to Alison saying a client emergency had come up and I'd be back as soon as I could. That was basically true, although I didn't specify that she was the client, and the emergency involved her dead husband. While I was away she could crisp salad greens, sip wine, set the table, and otherwise occupy herself. I hoped her committee meeting would last a long time; there was even a chance I could get back before she arrived, but I wasn't counting on it.

The open parking areas sodiums hadn't gone on, but I parked the Mercedes in a far corner between two cars already parked. Before getting out I wiped fingerprints from the keys, steering wheel and clutch knob, the inside windowsill, and finally the outside door latch. For good measure I polished the trunk lock area in case I'd inadvertently touched there when I opened the lid. Then I stood back and looked over the roadster. It was a sporty car, one I wouldn't mind having, but its owner had met an unexpected death and the car had become his coffin.

From the lot I walked to the front of the airport and got into the nearest taxi. In mangled English the driver told me the fare to Leesburg was twenty-six dollars. I said okay, and we drove out of the airport and headed back along the access road.

As long as I was at the wheel of the Mercedes I had suppressed memories and similarities of a late night drive I'd made with an earlier corpse—Andrew Bostick. That was a hairy trip because the corpse had been beside me, so transporting a corpse in a car trunk was by contrast an easier run. So now for the first time since leaving the farm I allowed myself to think about Harlan's murder. He could have been killed elsewhere and driven to the farm by the killer. Or had Harlan gone there alone, alive, and been killed on the premises? By whom? Inevitably I thought of the anonymous car that had followed him from Alison's apartment building. The next question was why.

After finding his body I hadn't looked for cause of death, but I assumed it wasn't due to natural causes. His throat showed no knife slash or marks of strangulation, and what I could see of his face and skull revealed no gunshot wounds. A bullet or dagger in the heart was a likely explanation, but in a day or so the county coroner would make public his findings, and I could wait for that.

Off on the horizon the lemon-colored moon was beginning to rise. It was fatter now than when I'd last observed it, more like a boomerang than a hunter's stylized bow. By month's end it would be a full pale circle, and I wondered where I would be—and Alison.

Traffic was light, so we reached the center of Leesburg earlier than I expected. The Bangladesh driver thanked me for the three tens, and drove back out of town. I walked down West Market Street toward the Laurel Brigade Inn, and hailed a taxi that had just dropped off diners. From there, another ten minutes to the farm, and as we drove in I was hugely relieved that Alison's Jaguar wasn't parked at the side. Nor were there more inside lights than when I'd left the house. My car was in the barn, door closed in case the killer cruised by. No point in showing him the Mercedes was no longer there.

Whoever he was.

Inside, I took down my note to Alison and crumpled it into the compactor. She need never know that I'd come, gone, and returned. Inevitably she would be asked about her husband's death in the standard formula: what did she know and when did she know it? As a fairly accomplished liar I felt I could beat a polygraph, but it was far better that Alison could recite only the truth as she knew it. Her surprise would be authentic.

No wonder Harlan hadn't shown up to sign and collect at Goodrich's office; he was too dead for that, probably since late last night. By the time airport parking security got around to checking the white Mercedes before impounding it, rigor mortis would have passed off, the corpse would be supple, and the tightly sealed trunk would keep the putrid stench inside. So the body might not be found for two or three days and, by then the medical examiner would be unable to establish a probable time of death.

I dropped cubes into a glass and drowned them with scotch, added a splash of sweet well water and took a long pull. Next, I mixed a shaker of martinis and set it in the freezer. The steaks were thawing well, so I turned them over and marinated them with teriyaki. Still, Alison hadn't come.

I filled the barbecue grill with charcoal and got the fire going, left the patio and built myself another tranquilizing drink.

Half an hour later, when gray ash covered all the glowing

coals, I heard a horn honk outside. Before leaving the kitchen I filled a martini glass and carried it out to the front porch.

Alison hurried toward me, called, "Are you furious, honey?"

"For what?" I handed her the glass.

"I'm so damn late. I was furious at the committee chairman for drawing things out, but there was no way I could leave before he closed the meeting."

She drank thirstily, spilling little driblets on her blouse, brushed them away and said, "When I didn't see your car I thought you weren't here, or you'd come and left in a snit." She smiled and laughed. "I really should have more faith in you, darling, and I actu-ally do. Then I saw lights inside and knew you were really here."

"With dinner underway." I took her arm and we went back into the house. She saw the marinating steaks and said, "You *have* been busy. What can I do?"

"Salad, in due course."

She finished her drink and held out her glass for a refill. "Where's your car?"

"In the bar, away from prying eyes."

"Of course, I should have thought of that." She sighed. "It's been a hectic day, Steve. All my usual work plus the committee meeting, worrying over Harlan and the divorce papers, and saying goodbye to Sally and Arnold . . . made that short, believe me."

"I believe you."

"And your day?"

"I was thinking about Harlan, too, learned he hadn't taken my advice and checked in with the Baltimore cops."

Her face sobered. "Do you think he's gone away? I mean, fled somewhere?"

"Without your money? Not a chance."

"Well, that's what I think, too, so maybe he'll go to Chad's of-fice on Monday. It's not much longer to wait, is it?" She kissed my cheek, then my lips. I drew her close against me and said, "Not long at all.

*　　*　　*

The steaks' charred outsides sealed in the pink juices, and the tart salad and Beaujolais were great complements to the tender beef. We lingered over wine, then Alison made coffee, and we were taking our cups to the living room coffee table when we heard a car turn in from the highway and come up the drive. We looked at each other, I unlocked the gun cabinet and opened the door before going to the porch. A police car braked near Alison's and a trooper got out. As he strode toward me he said, "This Senator Bowman's place?"

"It is," she said from behind me. "What can I do for you, officer?"

In more deferential tones he said, "I recognize you, ma'am, and I apologize for the intrusion."

"We were just having coffee—will you have some, officer?"

"Thanks, another time." He looked at me until Alison said, "This is my lawyer, Mr. Bentley."

"How do you do, sir. I'm Sergeant Bottscher." Briefly we shook hands, and he said, "I really apologize for interrupting your dinner, but I've been sent to follow up on an anonymous phone call."

"Anonymous?" I asked. "Phone call? About what, Sergeant?"

"Oh, these things come in all the time—usually neighbors with a grudge."

Alison said, "As far as I know none of my neighbors has a grudge against me."

"I should think not, ma'am, but with your permission I'd like to do my job and leave you in peace."

"Of course—what is your job? The phone call?"

He nodded. "Caller said—and please don't hold it against me, Senator—said there was a white Mercedes car in your barn with a dead man in it."

Alison laughed. "That's really weird, Sergeant. My husband has a white Mercedes but he never comes here—we're separated, you see, in the process of divorce." She paused. "I'd appreciate you not mentioning that in your report."

He glanced at me. "I understand. But if you don't mind I'd like to check your barn—unless you want a search warrant."

"Of course not," she said firmly. "Just go to the barn and look inside. Go wherever you like, take as long as you like." Shaking her head she turned to me. "How very odd."

"Very, I agreed. Bottscher touched the brim of his hat and left the porch. We watched him walk to the barn and pull the door open. The beam of his flashlight played inside for a few moments then he closed the door and came back to us. Apologetically he said, "Thanks, ma'am. I didn't expect to find no Mercedes there, and I didn't, but I had to look-see for the report."

"I understand. And no dead man."

"None I could see, ma'am, so thanks for your courtesy, and I'll be going now." He touched his hat again and strode to his car. We saw him back around and leave the way he'd come. Then we returned to the coffee table before Alison asked, "Know anything about that, Steve?"

I shrugged. "For a moment I hoped alien magic had transmuted my BMW into a white Mercedes but, alas, it didn't happen."

"Who on earth would come up with such a wild ides? And then make the police come here."

"Lot of freaky folks out there, honey. It's over, let's not dwell on it, okay?"

She snuggled against me. "You forgot the brandy."

"So I did. Shall we take the bottle upstairs?"

"We shall." And after cups of brandy-laced coffee, we did.

While Alison was showering I went downstairs, locked both doors, armed the alarm system, and left lights in living room and kitchen. Just in case the anonymous caller—Harlan's killer—stopped by to up the farm's body count.

After we made love Alison dropped off to sleep, but my mind was still churning with flashbacks to Harlan Bowman yelling at his wife in the parking lot, then Harlan Bowman dead in the trunk of his car, body awkwardly jammed into the limited space. And I realized that if I hadn't glimpsed that cuff fabric where the closing trunk lid had caught it, Mercedes and corpse would have remained in the barn, and Sergeant Bottscher's inspection would have had a different outcome. Sheer chance, or great peripheral vision? I didn't care.

Restlessly, I turned on my side and saw the moon glowing well above the tree-fringed horizon. Who was the anonymous caller who had tipped the police? Why wait so many hours after Harlan was dead? Obvious answer: he wanted Alison on hand when discovery was made.

A strong indication that car and body were located on Alison's property to give her maximum embarrassment, if not to implicate her. Now my mind turned back to a week ago when I'd spotted the man in the road watching the farmhouse. Had the nocturnal intruder been plotting even then to secrete Harlan's body on the farm? Extending the logic: the watcher was the killer and the caller—and before that the driver who tailed Harlan from the parking lot.

In retrospect I wished I had braced the watcher, or at least taken down the license number of his car—the car I heard drive away from the farm. I had a gun in my hands, why hadn't I gone out and confronted him? As I reconstructed my thinking, I hadn't wanted avoidable trouble and had wanted to avoid waking Alison. Then, while I was considering a course of action he'd turned and walked away. End of incident, I'd thought, but now it seemed to be the beginning of something else. A baffling new phase I wasn't prepared to deal with.

Paramount was keeping Alison's persona unsullied. As her lawyer I had responsibility for that, never mind that I was also lover and prospective husband with a heavy personal stake in her well-being and future. The murders of three persons connected directly or indirectly to Alison told me that she was the ultimate target. Had all three crimes been committed by the same person? Probable but not conclusive. Doris Conlon, I mused, could have been a target of opportunity, killed by a robber who followed her from the strip joint. But there was her longtime involvement with Alison's husband. I doubted Harlan had killed her because I couldn't think of a motive beyond vengeful rage. So either she had been purposefully killed by a third party whose motive was to embarrass the senator, or the random robbery theory had to prevail. The Baltimore cops were going to have to settle for that, Harlan Bowman being unavailable for interview.

Let's take it from the top, I told myself: My understanding was that Governor Green coveted Alison's Senate seat and wanted it before her term expired. With her dead or morally disqualified he appoints himself to the vacancy and runs later as an incumbent to easy reelection. Yet I had nothing resembling hard evidence that Green craved the Senate enough to have three people killed. Bostick, we knew, was under Green's thumb while alive and had followed someone's orders to compromise Alison during the holiday cruise. He'd been killed before he could name his principal—if he'd intended to reveal the plotter—but he hadn't said so to Alison. Then he was dead, killed within a few yards of her apartment, and I'd done the clean-up job.

To me Green alleged an unsatisfactory relationship with Harlan Bowman and that might or might not be true. Undoubtedly Harlan could have given chapter and verse to whatever kickback schemes he was involved in with the governor. His knowledge of shady dealings would pose a threat to Green's aspirations for national prominence. And I didn't doubt that Doris Conlon had acquired information on their dealings. She might even have known who dispatched Bostick to seduce her lover's wife. The videotape operation had been nullified by Bostick's defection with the duplicates, so why not nullify Harlan by killing him in circumstances that would in some minds implicate Alison? *Cui bono?* Governor Green was the theoretical beneficiary of all three murders. Not that he was the actual triggerman—as governor he would have plenty of early-release killers available to do assigned hits for a few hundred each.

Yet the governor had taken the trouble of going to my house and telling me he wanted Alison nominated for the presidency. Why was I important in his calculus? Was he to be believed? He'd invoked my help (unnecessarily) in keeping Alison's reputation free of scandal and so far I'd done that. There was no way Green could know I'd relocated two bodies and I had no plans to tell him—or the police. Unavoidably Alison knew I'd removed Bostick's corpse and car, but so far she didn't even know her husband was dead, much less that I'd left his body at another airport. The killer must have wondered who moved Bostick, and why Harlan's corpse and roadster hadn't been found by Sergeant Bottscher where planted.

I was tired, depleted of adrenaline, stressed from the drive to Dulles and the strain of dissembling to Alison. A few more half-formed thoughts and my mind surrendered. I turned toward Alison and joined her in sleep.

Saturday we drove to a Warrenton horse show, where Alison took a keen interest in a number of mounts in the for-sale riding enclosure, telling me she was considering keeping horses again and did I think it was a good idea. "It's a splendid idea," I told her, "so long as no photographer captures you in hard hat and hacking coat with the Fauquier Hunt. Your political enemies would charge you with upper-class elitism and callous disregard for the homeless and those in need."

"Hm, that's true," she said reluctantly, "but we could ride on my property as I used to."

I nodded. "Something for the future, an idea for the back burner, hon. But that roan mare you liked *is* a beauty."

We moved over to the jollification tent for champagne cocktails and hors d'oeuvres, and several of her hunting friends stopped to say hello and be introduced to me as her attorney.

I liked the atmosphere of casual enjoyments among people of similar cultural backgrounds and tastes. It was the first time I'd seen Alison in a social situation and it was obvious she was relaxed and entirely comfortable away from press corps and politicians. She remembered everyone's names, asked about their children and travels and summer plans and was congenial to all. Small wonder, I thought, that she had won her first Congressional seat almost by acclamation.

This was Alison's natural environment, I knew, even though she had adapted to the partisan bickering, deal-making, and confrontational atmosphere of the United States Senate. Her character was such that she needed to mingle with social equals to mitigate the harsh demands of political life, a career she had chosen under the rubric of *noblesse oblige*. And as I watched her make her gracious way among the fancy I admired her more than ever.

The moment was one for both of us to remember. It meant

much more to me because I was aware of the impending storm that would break around her when Harlan's murder hit front pages. There was no way I could prepare her for it, but I had no doubt of her ability to ride it out.

After a dressage exhibition by teenage riders, Alison complimented each one, and we left for late lunch at Middleburg's old Red Fox Inn, where several of her friends were drinking and dining.

After lamb chops, artichoke salad, and lemon pie we had coffee and drove back to the farm. From outside, the farmhouse looked unchanged, but I visually checked the barn door before we went in. After I reset the alarm system we went up to the bedroom, and slept through the afternoon.

Toward four we took a bottle of wine to the pool and kept it chilled in the water, sharing the bottle from time to time. Alison took off her shoes and dangled her toes in the water. I said I'd wait until midsummer. She smiled, offered me the bottle, and while I drank, said, "Did you like my friends?"

"Very much. Even more, I liked seeing you at ease and happy."

"They liked you, Steve. I overheard some of them buzzing about you—so handsome, they were saying, and wondering about our relationship."

"It's strong and healthy—did you tell them that?"

Her cheeks colored faintly. "I wanted to, but how could I? I guess their seeing us at the inn answered most questions."

"Do you mind?"

She shook her head. "Not at all. Until you came into my life I now realize I had no life at all. So if they see a happier, better adjusted Alison that's all to the good. Besides, they're not gossipmongers. Out here in the hunt country affairs go on—sometimes for years—and nothing ever appears in the press."

"So your friends don't think it odd that you're spending time with me and not your husband?"

"They've long known we're estranged, and I sort of felt they were relieved that Harlan wasn't there. Most of them are really good people, honey, and we'll have friends among them. Good friends. You'll see."

Reflectively I said, "After divorce I turned into a sort of hermit, which I was until I met you. For me it's an enormous change."

"But you can handle it."

"I can certainly try."

Then to my surprise she pulled off her denim shirt, wriggled out of her jeans, and dropped into the pool. She shot up gasping and shaking her head like a wet poodle. "*Oh!*" she cried, "I didn't know it was so *cold!* I'm practically paralyzed." But she swam freestyle to the far side, ducked and dolphined back underwater. I could see the curving outlines of her body, the taut buns and smoothly tapering thighs, and for a moment I watched in awe that this miraculous female was choosing me as her mate. Then she popped up from the water, grasped my hand and stood dripping and shivering, until I drew her shirt around her body.

When shivering stopped I handed her the bottle; she tilted and drank deeply. I urged her to finish it off, and she did so, saying she was warmer now, and perhaps we ought to go back and do something about dinner.

As we walked hand in hand, I realized that my resistance to marriage was dissolving. We could make adjustments to each other's careers, I told myself, and it would work out as long as I didn't meddle in her political life, and she didn't try to practice law. The important thing was to focus on each other, nourish love, and never go to bed angry. We'd each had a bad marriage and now fate was giving us a second chance.

And after those musings I saw them as premature because she would have to extricate herself from the backwash of Harlan's murder and allow a conventional interval to pass before marrying again. Unless, of course, we married quietly in the Caribbean, Hod and Mattie our witnesses.

While Alison showered, I chilled more Chablis and checked the freezer for dinner entrees. Neither of us had brought anything, I settled on a family-size container of lasagna. That meant red e, so I decanted a bottle of Beaujolais and set it aside to breathe e dinner.

When Alison came down she was wearing a fluffy bathrobe hatching slippers. She gave me a kiss and said she was still trying to get warm after the icy pool. In the freezer the shaker held enough dividend martinis for a pair of drinks, and after pouring them we went out to the patio and watched sunset paint the fields pink-gold.

"I think," I said, "we ought to firm up plans for getting to St. Thomas. When can you conveniently leave?"

"Ten days suit you? That's when recess begins."

"Ten days is fine. I'll make our flight reservations, but you gotta get your own ticket."

She smiled. "For appearances' sake."

And as we spoke I wondered if we'd actually cruise with Hod. Alison might feel that Harlan's murder put an end to our vacation plans, and she should stay around for her husband's funeral while acting the bereaved widow. But that was to be resolved in the future.

I expected car and corpse to be found and identified as early as tomorrow, no later than Monday. The FBI would have jurisdiction, Dulles Airport being federal property, and I wondered how hard their agents would lean on a U.S. senator who was not a suspect but a widow. They would want to know when she had last seen her husband, and if I got the chance I would advise her to tell the truth without embroidery. Mention of the possibly tailing car would likely excite agent interest and properly channel their investigation away from Alison.

When it was dark outside we came in and Alison set the table. I microwaved the lasagna to steaming warmth while Alison put together a salad. The wine was poured and we ate without much conversation. I didn't ask what preoccupied her thoughts because I couldn't tell her mine. And so, after cleaning up the kitchen we headed for bed.

As before, I locked doors and armed the alarm system for the night. Then, lying beside Alison I said, "I think the alarm signal ought to be connected to the police station. That will take care of intruders when we're not here. Less worry for you."

Sleepily she said, "You're worried about something?"

"Mainly Harlan."

"Why? By next weekend he'll be gone."

"Let's hope. Meanwhile, I don't like the thought of him break-ing in and vandalizing the place. Maybe setting fire to it. You know better than I how unpredictable he is."

"All right, honey, will arrange it with the security people?"

"On Monday."

SIXTEEN

SUNDAY MORNING I drove Alison's car to Leesburg and bought newspapers. We shared them over breakfast and continued reading in the living room. I found nothing about Harlan Bowman, and felt relieved. The longer it took to discover his murder the better for his widow and her peace of mind. Ahead of her lay long days of distraction and aggravation, so the relaxation we were enjoying stored energy against the storm to come.

In midafternoon we decided to close up the house and head back to town before the inbound rush began. Alison was putting bed linens in the washer and I was collecting shaving gear when I heard a car pull into the access road.

Looking out of the bedroom window, I saw a dark gray four-door Ford. It was unremarkable except for a foot-long radio antenna projecting from the roof.

That made it either CIA or FBI.

The car stopped by Alison's Jaguar and two men got out. They disappeared under the porch roof, and I went down to meet them. The doorbell rang and I took a few moments to walk the distance. The snub chain was in place, so I opened the door as far as the chain allowed, and looked over the visitors. One wore a gray suit with a white shirt and tie. His hair was close-trimmed and his black shoes polished. His partner was shorter and bulkier than J. Edgar would have liked, and his hair was speckled with gray—or was it dandruff? "Yes?" I said politely.

"FBI," the tall man said. "Special Agent Smithers, and my partner Special Agent Dorfuss." Without being asked both displayed their laminated credentials. I scanned them and asked, "What can I do for you gentlemen?"

"Is Senator Bowman in?"

I nodded.

"Are you a friend of the family, sir?" Dorfuss asked.

"Yes, and the senator's attorney. My name is Bentley." I produced my D.C. Bar card for the agents. "Perhaps I could—" I began, but Smithers shook his head. "It's the senator we need a word with."

"I'll tell her."

Leaving the door still only partly open, I found Alison at the washer and told her about the visitors. Her eyes and expression showed alarm, but she dried her hands and walked with me through the living room. At the door she said, "I'm Senator Bowman. How can I help you?"

The agents exchanged glances before Smithers said, "I have very bad news for you, Senator. Your husband is dead."

"Oh God!" Her eyes closed and she slumped against me. I opened the door and the agents came in. Still standing, Smithers said, "Senator, I understand the shock you're feeling, but I have to ask when you last saw your husband?"

Steadying herself, she breathed deeply and turned to me. "Thursday night, I believe—yes, Thursday night."

I said. "We both saw him then, by the senator's apartment."

"What time?" Dorfuss had his notepad in hand. Alison seemed to be having trouble breathing. She looked at me helplessly so I said, "About eight o'clock."

"Thank you, sir," Dorfuss said dryly, "but we prefer the senator answering."

"Then as her lawyer I suggest you interview her another time, after she's able to compose herself."

Smithers scratched the side of his face. I led Alison to the sofa and helped her sit. Smithers said, "We really prefer conducting the interview at this time."

"I'm sure you do, but I've given you a reasonable alternative. Otherwise I will instruct my client to say nothing at all. Tomorrow, at her home or office, she will be fully cooperative."

Dorfuss cleared his throat, looked at Alison, then at his partner. I asked, "What manner of death? Traffic accident?"

"No," he said in a low voice, "Mr. Bowman was murdered."

That brought a shriek from Alison. Her reaction persuaded the agents to deal with me. "How and where?" I asked, "if you don't mind."

Dorfuss grimaced before saying, "His body was found in the trunk of his car parked at Dulles Airport—that's FBI jurisdiction."

"I know. Murdered how?"

"Stab wound in the chest. The body was in pretty poor—"

I held up one hand. "Let's step outside."

We regrouped on the porch out of earshot of Alison, and I said, "Consideration and courtesy shown the senator could be beneficial to both of you. Now, you were saying the body was in poor condition?"

"Terrible," Dorfuss said. "Hot in that trunk, you know."

"I can imagine." I looked inside and saw Alison seated where we left her, face taut. "The murder, the car trunk and so on fits in with a strange incident the other night. I think it would be useful for you to know about it now—and of course the senator can comment later." I paused. "Friday night the senator and I were finishing dinner when a state trooper came to the door, said he was following up an anonymous lead."

Dorfuss said, "What time Friday night, sir?"

"Between eight and nine I guess. Sergeant Bottscher will have the precise time in his report." I spelled Bottscher for them.

Smithers asked. "What was the anonymous lead?"

"Well, the trooper told of an anonymous phone call that said there was a dead man in a white Mercedes vehicle in the senator's barn." I pointed at it. "The trooper asked if he could check it out, and the senator agreed. No search warrant involved."

"What did the trooper find—if anything?"

"He looked in the barn, saw my car where I had parked it to keep tree sap from marring the finish, and apologized for disturbing the senator. Now you say the car and dead man were found at Dulles Airport." I shook my head. "Someone's cruel joke."

"It's probably more than that, sir," said Smithers, and turned to his partner. "Get on Sergeant Bottscher right away, take his statement."

"Right." He looked at me. "Can I use the phone?"

"Not connected," I replied, and Smithers frowned. "We checked that out before coming here, remember?"

"Right," said Dorfuss. "I'll call from the car." He went down the porch steps and Smithers sighed. "Good help is hard to find," he said quietly, then in a normal voice, "Is there anything you care to add?"

"There is." I summarized Thursday night's encounter with Harlan in the apartment parking lot, keeping it low key without details, and said the senator and I had been concerned after we noticed a car apparently following Harlan's.

"What direction?"

"Let's see—that would be north. Looked like a dark two-door, but that's the extent of my observation."

"And the senator would recall the incident?"

"Absolutely." I looked back into the living room and saw that Alison was no longer there. Smithers cleared his throat. "Can you tell me the subject of the parking lot discussion?"

I hesitated before saying, "This gets a little tricky, but I'll say what I can without violating my client's confidence. And I'll ask you to be discreet as to what you pass along."

He nodded. "We have no wish or reason to embarrass the senator."

I took a deep breath. "The background is for perhaps five years the senator and her husband have been estranged. Recently she decided to extricate herself from a marital situation she found intolerable, and consulted a domestic relations attorney to that end."

"May I have his name, sir?"

"Chad Goodrich. The firm is Gurney and Steiner, her long-time attorneys."

He wrote rapidly on his pad before asking. "That your firm?"

"No, I have a private practice limited to taxation matters. Financial advice."

"And the senator has been consulting you in that area?"

I nodded. "Her attorney negotiated a divorce arrangement with Harlan Bowman that was to take effect immediately on his signing. Financial considerations involved were beneficial to her husband."

"I see. I assume the matter is now moot due to her husband's death."

"I'd say so. Due to her political career and position the senator desired a very quiet termination of her unsatisfactory marriage." I paused. "I don't feel at liberty to disclose more about the arrangement, which, after all, has no relevance to Mr. Bowman's death. All I can add is that terms were negotiated between the senator, attorney Goodrich, and her late husband. I was not party to them."

"So *if* more information *was* required I'd have to get it from Mr. Goodrich."

"With the senator's assent."

"I understand." He made a note and looked up. "In retrospect, sir, do you attach significance to the fact that Mr. Bowman's car was followed on Thursday night?"

"Apparently followed."

"Right."

"But in view of Bowman's murder I think it could be significant."

"So do I. Now, before Mr. Bowman drove away did he indicate where he might be going?"

I shook my head.

"Nothing about a flight from Dulles Airport?"

"No. And if he'd been going there his departure direction would have been opposite to the one he took."

"Exactly. Well, maybe the contents of his car or clothing will cast some light on why he was at Dulles."

I said nothing. Dorfuss joined us, beckoned Smithers aside and spoke just above a whisper. Smithers nodded and came back to me. "The trooper sergeant is off duty today, fishing somewhere, but we expect to interview him tomorrow. I'm hoping there is a tape of the anonymous call."

"Yes, that could be helpful."

The door opened and Alison came out. She had repaired eye makeup but her complexion was still pale. "I've taken a tranquilizer, so I think I can manage your questions." She gave me a bleak smile. "Fire away, gentlemen."

"Ma'am," Smithers said in deferential tones, "your lawyer has supplied most of what we need to pursue the investigation. Whatever verifications we might want from you can be obtained later on."

"I appreciate that," she said, "but I'm mainly concerned about sensational publicity. Steve, did you mention the divorce?"

"I did."

Smithers said, "I certainly understand your desire to avoid publicity, but of course the press will learn of your husband's murder. Your pending divorce will not be leaked by my office."

"Thank you," she said quietly.

"One final area, ma'am. Did your husband have family?"

She nodded. "Parents in Omaha. I never met them . . . where is my husband's body?"

"Violent death requires autopsy—sorry, ma'am. The body can be claimed later at the D.C. morgue."

To Alison I said, "I'll try to get in touch with his parents, see if they have burial preference."

"Yes, of course they must be consulted." Her lips trembled. "I'll pay for whatever's involved." She shook her head. "Poor Harlan." She turned back into the house.

I said, "I'll notify Chad Goodrich of Bowman's death, tell him to expect a visit from you."

"Thank you, sir, but that may not be necessary—not for a while at least." He closed his note pad. "Can you think of any reason for that anonymous phone call?"

"Maybe the killer wanted to implicate the senator in some tangential way. Or maybe just alarm and harass her. By the time the call was made Mr. Bowman must have been dead, but only the caller knew that." I paused. "Very strange."

"Yes. Between you and me we don't have much to go on in the way of clues—mainly the apparently following car. But Forensics may come up with more."

"Hope so," I said, "and the sooner the better. We don't want the senator to become a tabloid target."

"No, sir, by no means."

I gave him my card. "Don't hesitate to get in touch with me."

"Thank you, sir." He put the card in his wallet and handed me one of his Bureau cards. To his partner he said, "Can't do more here, let's get back to the dungeon."

The three of us shook hands, and when they were getting into their car I left the porch and found Alison upstairs on the bed. "I can't believe he's dead," she said. "Murdered."

"I think we need a drink." I brought up two glasses of cognac. Sipping, she made a face, but drank more before saying, "I guess you were able to satisfy them."

"For now, but I'm afraid this is only the beginning. I think you have to realize there's a substantial PR problem, so I suggest you have Gurney and Steiner hire a firm to field questions until media interest dies. My thought is for you to stay in seclusion, so cruising with Hod Gurney will be ideal. And understandable."

Wordlessly she nodded. After a while she said, "I guess I won't go to the office tomorrow."

"No. Stay home and talk to your lawyers, let them handle things with the Bureau and the press."

She smiled wanly. "I've become a troublesome client for all my lawyers." She pressed my hand. "Including you."

"Don't be concerned about it."

She sighed. "How did I do with the agents?"

"Admirably."

"I'm so grateful you were able to assume the burden, answer questions. I reacted badly, I know, but it was quite an emotional shock and I wasn't prepared for it."

"I understand."

Abruptly her tone changed. "Who killed him, Steve? Why?"

"My guess is the mob he owed money to."

"But he would have had divorce money to pay his debts if only they'd waited another day or so."

"They're not patient people. Maybe the killer didn't give Harlan a chance to talk, just carried out the hit."

She nodded thoughtfully. "And what's really odd is that call to the state police saying Harlan and his Mercedes were in the barn." Reflexively she glanced in its direction. "I just don't understand."

"As I told the agents, I could only surmise it was a way of bringing you to police attention." I stroked her hair. "They'll talk to Sergeant Bottscher, find out if the anonymous call was taped. Bottscher can confirm the car wasn't on your property, and that's helpful. It won't take a genius to figure two men had to be involved—driving the Mercedes to Dulles, and returning in their other car. The killer alone couldn't have done it."

"I hadn't thought of that but you're right. Even so, it won't be easy to avoid suspicion."

"Not easy, no, but it won't last."

"I wonder when the story will break?"

"Maybe tonight, more likely tomorrow."

"But reporters listen to police radio transmissions, don't they?"

"Yes, but this is different. They can't easily or legally intercept FBI communications. Frequencies are secret for one thing, usually beyond range of a Radio Shack scanner, so it comes down to when the Bureau decides to issue a statement about the murder."

"God I wish they didn't have to."

"Unfortunately, they must." I kissed her cheek. "Feel up to driving home?"

She swallowed. "Not really, but I will."

"Or I could drive you in my car, leave yours here."

"That would be better."

An hour later I left Alison at her apartment, having assured her I'd make all the necessary notifications. Then I drove home, made coffee, and at my desk made a list of all I had to do before the story broke.

I reached Chad Goodrich at his home—he'd just returned from a day's Bay sailing with wife and child—and told him of Harlan's demise. When he recovered from that I told him I was speaking for the senator and wanted his firm to assign an experienced criminal defense attorney to work for Alison with a public relations firm his office was going to hire. After he'd absorbed the message he said, "I appreciate the heads-up, gives us a little time to put things in place."

"Very little. Fortunately, the FBI is in charge of the investigation, so the leakage will be minimal, if any."

"God," he said abruptly, "no wonder the husband didn't come in Friday, he was already dead."

"So it seems. Time of death is always going to be speculative due to postmortem changes because of the sun-heated car trunk."

"I guess. Anything else I should know?"

"I've given you what there is," I told him, and supplied names of the special agents who had interviewed us. "They realize this is a politically delicate case and will probably treat the senator with consideration."

"I think I'd better phone Mr. Steiner tonight, don't you?"

"I do. He'll designate a defense attorney, won't he? I just want to make sure that all Bureau and press inquiries filter through him. He'll tell the PR people what to say and when. The less contact the senator has with the media or the Bureau the better. For now she's a grieving widow in seclusion."

"I understand."

"Keep that draft divorce agreement available, the one Harlan initialed, along with Alison's check and the conformed agreement she signed. I'm pretty sure the investigators will want to see it all."

"Without the senator's permission?"

"Only with the senator's permission—through the defense at-torney, and no copying to be made. She's not a suspect, after all, nor a target of the inquiry, so the divorce material isn't subject to sub-poena."

"I wondered about that. Thanks for the tip."

"We're working for the same client, Chad, and I'll be glad to butt out as soon as your firm takes charge." I paused, wondering what I might have omitted. "There's Harlan's parents to be noti-fied. The senator never met them but said they live in Omaha. She'll honor their wishes regarding burial."

"I'll take care of it."

"The senator is resting in her apartment, won't be at her office for a while."

"That's understandable. You've told us what to do, so I doubt the firm will need to disturb her."

"Try me first."

"I'll pass the word."

By Monday noon the law firm's response team was in place. Arthur Jensen was the designated defense attorney although we weren't calling him that, and a Ms. Sean Elkins from the firm of Elkins, Farr and Bryan had moved into Jensen's office to take up her duties.

None too soon, because a midday radio report announced the murder of Senator Bowman's husband, whose body had been found in the trunk of his car at Dulles International Airport. At-torney Jensen vetted a press release that was faxed by Elkins to twenty media outlets. It said the senator was shocked by the mur-der of her husband, was grieving for him, and was in seclusion.

After that, queries flooded in. Working together, Jensen and Elkins answered as many as they could, and referred callers to the FBI's Washington field office, which was responsible for the inves-tigation. Five o'clock TV news showed stock footage of Senator Bowman plus cuts of Dulles Airport, and promised a full account at eleven. At seven I joined Alison in her apartment, brought veal scal-lopini from Mauricio's, and encouraged her not to watch TV or listen to local radio. I sensed her feeling guilty over Harlan's death, so I argued that she had no responsibility for the murder, and none for their estrangement. "Anyway," I said, "it won't be long before it gets out that Baltimore cops wanted to question him about Doris's death, and he'll be seen as less a victim than a bad guy who might have killed his mistress. That takes the spotlight from you."

"I can't wait," she said earnestly. "Barely a day has gone by and I'm feeling claustrophobic. How long before I should go back to my office?"

"Let Jensen and Elkins decide. Have you talked with your office?"

"No."

"Better you don't. If you say anything at all to your staff, and the media learn of it they'll put their own spin on it, maybe fabricate a conversation that never took place. Talking to your staff gains you nothing."

"I understand."

I told her Chad Goodrich had notified Harlan's folks in Omaha, and their preference was to have him buried there in the family plot. She nodded without saying anything. I confirmed that the farm telephone was being activated so a signal would run to the Leesburg police station from the house alarm system. Again she nodded and I realized her thoughts were elsewhere. Finally she said, "Has the FBI come up with any clues?"

"If so, they're not saying. Arthur Jensen is the contact point. He'll be informed before the media."

"I've been thinking we might be able to join Harris Gurney a few days earlier."

"Maybe. It's something for Jensen to decide. He'll want to be sure the Bureau isn't planning to reinterview you and finds you're cruising the Caribbean. But in principle it would be a wonderful refuge for you."

"You'd come with me, wouldn't you?"

"My inclination is you go first, I join you later."

She smiled wryly. "For appearances' sake?"

"In your profession appearances are at least as important as substance. Regardless of your dysfunctional marriage you don't want to be seen enjoying life in the tropics before your husband is cold in his grave."

"No, I guess not. But I truly, deeply want to get the hell away from here."

"Is there likely to be a memorial service for Harlan?"

"I won't ask for one, and I can't think of anyone who might— Doris Conlon being *hors de combat*, " she added.

"That eliminates one delay-causing obstacle. Like the veal?"

"I would if I were hungrier, but I appreciate your bringing it." She had only toyed with her plate of meat and pasta. "I might warm it later." She looked away. "The man's death is having more effect on me than his life did. And that was bad enough."

"I'm sure. Oh, Governor Green's office called with expressions of sympathy. You don't need to respond, and in fact I prefer you not talk with him at all until after the cruise. Potentially he can do you a lot of damage while you're vulnerable."

"I know he has a lot of power."

After leaving the table we watched a new Showtime TV movie, and when it ended I said I thought I ought to go to my place.

"Really? I've counted on you staying here."

"Tomorrow the Washington press corps will be baying outside, and I don't want to embarrass you by being seen leaving."

She shrugged. "I'll miss you tonight."

"And I'll miss you beside me. I'll call tomorrow."

So we said good night and I drove out of the parking lot after checking the street for possible surveillors. I didn't want the serial killer on my tail.

At home there was a phone message from Arthur Jensen asking me to call him. I poured a measure of Ballantine's and a few ounces of Saratoga spring water. As I drank I thought about Arthur Jensen, Alison's new defender. He was a seasoned criminal defense lawyer who served the Department of Justice for three years in its Organized Crime section. He might have become attorney general but for an unexpected change in administration, after which he joined Gurney and Steiner. To his surprise and that of everyone else in the Washington Bar, a three-judge panel selected him as a Special Counsel to investigate and prosecute Congressional bribe-taking,

which was both flagrant and widespread at the time. Of eleven in-
dictees Jensen won nine convictions; one upstate congresswoman
copped a plea, and a congressman from south Texas shot himself before trial. His reputation was that of a fair, meticulous, and determined attorney, and I was very glad that he had been assigned to
shield and assist Alison.

Returning his call, I said, "Steven Bentley, Mr. Jensen. What
can I do for you?"

His voice was rough baritone with an edge of irritation. "We
haven't met, Mr. Bentley, but you have a good reputation around
the firm."

"Nice to hear."

"Yes. I was startled to learn that the senator's late husband
was a marginal suspect in the murder of his former mistress. I'm
wondering why I had to hear it from the FBI."

"Doris Conlon." I drank from my glass and set it down. "I was
distracted by other things involving the senator and simply neglected to mention the situation to Chad Goodrich. Sorry, my
fault."

After a pause he said. "Well, I guess it's no immediate problem, but the woman's murder adds a line of thinking. For instance,
if a boyfriend or lover decided Harlan Bowman shot her he'd be a
likely suspect for Bowman's killing."

"I'm with you."

"But the Baltimore police haven't identified anyone who
might have been so close to Conlon as to generate a revenge motive."

"Maybe they'll work a little harder on the case now that Bowman is also dead. Gives them two lines of inquiry."

"So it does," he agreed.

"Is the Bureau investigation going anywhere?"

"If so they're keeping it sub rosa." He cleared his throat. "That
whole business about the Mercedes allegedly being in the senator's
barn with her husband's corpse in the trunk is the most baffling aspect of the murder. Do you have any thoughts about it?"

"Only what I gave to the special agents yesterday, and the
trooper sergeant before that."

"Bottscher," he said.

"The agents were to talk with him today. They were interested in the possibility of a taped call from the anonymous tipster, and of course they wanted to confirm what the senator and I told Bottscher, and what he didn't find in the barn; the time he came to the farm, and so forth. Before Bowman's body was found, the anonymous call seemed a minor harassment of the senator, but in retrospect there was probably more behind it."

"I think you're right, but I can't find a rationale."

"It's an enigma. Now, on a different subject, Hod Gurney and Mattie invited the senator and me to cruise with them during Congressional recess."

"Right—Hod's in the Caribbean somewhere. Sounds like a great vacation."

"I mention it because I think it's appropriate for you to advise the senator when she could leave and seclude herself with the Gurneys. She's anxious to."

"Hm. Well, that would be after the Washington Field Office no longer needs to interview her."

"And after her husband's burial in Omaha."

"That, too. Well, I'll talk with the Bureau tomorrow, try to wrap up the interview ASAP."

"And let me know, will you? I'm on the guest list, too."

"Lucky guy." He paused. "If it's not too personal, I'm curious about your representation of the senator; my firm has represented her for years."

"Not personal at all. Goes back to a period when Hod was handling legal affairs for General Ballou and his daughter. Your firm hadn't yet expanded, so Hod asked me to take on some financial work for the general. I did so, and everyone involved seemed satisfied." I paused. "The general was Senator Bowman's uncle. His daughter, Francine, spoke well of me to cousin Alison, so when the senator was seeking specialized tax advice she remembered me."

"That *is* complicated." He chuckled. "Can't hardly charge you with poaching a client. Anyway, I appreciate the background. I was in the Marine Corps after the general retired but he remained a legend."

"Deservedly," I remarked, "and as I told Chad Goodrich I'm bowing out now that your firm is in charge of the senator's problems."

"Okay. But before long we ought to lunch and discuss the ins and outs of the situation."

"Call me when you're free," I told him, and the call ended.

At my desk I drank scotch and reviewed what Jensen had had to say. He was point man now, and I was really relieved he was serving as Alison's legal shield. He'd been in Justice long enough that Bureau agents weren't going to intimidate him or try any end runs; he knew all the tricks and had a few of his own, as his successful Congressional prosecutions had shown.

When I placed a radio call to Hod's boat, the *Mattie*, I'd forgotten the time was a couple of hours later than D.C. Accordingly Hod was grumpy until I explained the purpose of my call—summarizing Alison's problems arising from the clueless murder of her husband.

"Good Lord," he exclaimed, and I could visualize him rubbing his eyes, "what's being done about it?"

I told him Arthur Jensen and a PR specialist were representing the senator's interests, and he muttered approvingly, "Good man, Arthur."

"I know, or you wouldn't have taken him on. Next item is Alison's understandable desire to get away from Washington and join you for seclusion. She's had a preliminary FBI interview and Arthur is going to prod the Bureau to speed anything outstanding. When he gives the green light she'll fly down—by the way, where are you?"

"Anguilla," he said. "We can meet her at San Juan, better plane connections. You too, right?"

"Well, I think I ought to delay a bit for appearances' sake."

"Yeah, I suppose that's in order." He paused. "Changes things a bit."

"So that's the present situation and I thought you ought to know about it."

"Absolutely."

"Fill you in when I get there."

"Look forward to it, and thanks for the call. Tell our client she's welcome anytime."

"Will do. Night, Hod."

"Good night, Steve."

I finished my drink and went to bed, glad I'd thought to call him.

At night my alarm system was silent throughout the house. But in my bedroom a light blinked and a low intermittent buzzing sounded, similar to a pager. I wasn't yet fully asleep when the light flashed and I heard the warning buzz. It got me out of bed quickly and silently, and from the drawer of the night table where I piled books and magazines, I got out my 9mm Beretta pistol.

Listening before moving, I thought I heard soft footsteps below. They weren't coming up the staircase, seemed to be moving around as though searching for something—probably valuables. Barefoot, I went to the head of the stairs and looked down. Nothing visible in the living room, but I saw a flash of light in the kitchen and started down, heart pumping.

I was nearly on the living room floor when I heard the metallic grating of something opening and closing. Light glinted and went off. I got to the kitchen quickly and saw the rear door open and close. I switched on the overhead lights—mistake—and started after the intruder, but I was blinded by the kitchen light and saw only a running figure rounding the side of the house. I followed as far as my car in the drive, and saw the intruder racing down Q Street toward Wisconsin Avenue. I wasn't going to shoot at him, he was too far away, and the target was moving and indistinct. And just then I heard a car engine start and accelerate. Tires screeched, then the night fell silent as before. Shit, I thought as I retraced my steps into the kitchen.

On the way out I hadn't noticed glass on the floor, but now I saw an oval section that had been cut from the door pane nearest the inside lock and door handle. On it was a wad of putty with a long string. The burglar had cut the glass and lowered it inside without the usual noise of breakage. That hadn't interrupted the alarm circuit; opening the door inward had done it.

I sat at the kitchen table and looked around. Surely the thief hadn't made careful entry to steal pots, pans, and cutlery, and as far as I knew he hadn't gone elsewhere in the house. Why had he come? What had he taken?

I remembered the odd sound of an appliance opening and closing. Toaster oven? Refrigerator? Microwave? Freezer? No, they all had rubber seals. Kitchen drawers? They were on silent rollers. Looking around, I could see nothing missing. As I sat there bafflement rose, along with anger over having my home violated. In the morning, a glazier could replace the ruined pane, but I sensed a vulnerability I'd never felt before.

Perfunctorily I went through drawers, refrigerator, and freezer, but not even ice cream had been robbed. Then, as I turned around to switch off the light I noticed my built-in trash compactor. Its vertical, tilting side hadn't been tightly closed by the worn spring. I always had to give it an extra shove before activation, and couldn't remember not having done so after my last deposit of trash.

Using a kitchen towel, I pulled back the handle and looked inside, sifted through meat wrappings, pastry boxes, and discarded *TV Guides*, and was about to ridicule myself, when my hand plunged deeper and touched metal.

I scuffed trash aside and saw it.

A six-inch hunting knife whose blade and haft were clotted with blood.

After a deep breath I nudged the lid shut and reached for the phone.

SEVENTEEN

———

BEFORE ARTHUR JENSEN arrived I made a pot of coffee and now we were seated at the kitchen table with our cups. Time: 2:16 A.M. He said, "You don't use cream either."

"Gave it up years ago."

"Me, too."

"Helps with the flab but coffee sure kills sleep." He drank again and refilled his cup. "I happen to need this." Simultaneously we both gazed at the open compactor, then Jensen gestured at the glass oval on the floor. "You said you didn't touch anything."

I shook my head. "I'm not in the crime field but I know from TV movies to leave a scene undisturbed. No, I didn't touch anything, except to open the kitchen door to go after the thug."

"There could be prints on the putty unless the guy wore plastic gloves." He looked at his wristwatch. "This break-in is a new element, Steve. If that's the knife that killed Bowman, why in hell would it have been planted here?"

"No idea. I figured the car-in-the-barn episode was calculated to implicate the senator in some way. Now I seem to be a secondary target."

"Yeah. When I talked to the WFO night supervisor he wasn't interested in your problem until I mentioned Senator Bowman and her husband's murder. Then he got eager to cooperate."

He looked at his watch again and frowned. "Taking their time getting here. Maybe they'll pick up a detective from the Georgetown precinct, housebreaking normally being a local affair."

"I know. Can't have local noses out of joint."

"And expect cooperation next time around." He squinted at the bloodied knife. "Sure you didn't touch it?"

"Maybe a knuckle scrape. Care for a splash of brandy to fortify the joe?"

He smiled. "How come a dogface spouts jarhead lingo?"

"Association," I said, "in mess lines that didn't discriminate."

"Yeah, I'm not sorry I missed that one. Korea did it all for me. Dugout Doug and that damned Pusan caper." He sighed. "Buddies I'll never see again. Used to think about them all the time, but they've almost drifted from memory. Way of the world, huh?"

"Unfortunately."

The doorbell rang and I went to answer it. Two FBI special agents and a G'town detective. They introduced themselves and I led the way to the kitchen. The detective photographed the door, floor glass, and compactor, focusing closely on the knife. I poured coffee for all three and set a fresh pot to percolate. All of us looked pretty tousled and un-shaved, but hell, it was close to three.

The senior special agent said, "Mind taking it from the top, Mr. Bentley?"

"Glad to."

"I note your lawyer's present. You called him first?"

"Because of what the knife implied I thought he'd better inform the Bureau—he's had more experience with you gentlemen."

They looked at him respectfully and Jensen returned a vague smile. The senior agent said, "Mind if we tape this, sir?"

"I'd prefer it," I said, and Jensen nodded. So I repeated what I'd told Jensen—I described my in-house movements, my brief, failed effort to overtake the intruder, and my inability to describe his face or clothing. The detective said, "What makes you think it was a male?"

I shrugged. "I guess statistically most burglars are males."

"But no feminine traits?"

"Unless foot-speed is one." They all smiled, and we went out and down the drive so I could point out where the housebreaker had fled. After we got back inside, the detective said, "Since nothing was stolen, sir, I won't write this up as a burglary, just a break-in, okay?"

Jensen said, "Whatever's appropriate." The detective thanked us for cooperating and took his leave. To the Bureau team Jensen said, "Without offering unsolicited comment, my thought is to keep this incident under wraps until we learn something about the motivation."

"Agree with that, sir," the senior agent said. "We'll take the knife with us as potential evidence, have the blood compared with samples from Mr. Bowman's autopsy."

Jensen said, "Assuming there's a complete match, what do we have?"

"Can't say, sir," the agent replied. "I'm only substituting until Smithers and Dorfuss get back on duty in the morning. You could talk with them."

"I may," Jensen said, "and I assume you'll have door, glass, and compactor dusted for prints."

"The case agents are responsible for that."

I said, "After they're finished I'll have the pane replaced."

"Good point," Jensen nodded. "For tonight, close the gap with duct tape."

The agents got up and the senior said, "The fingerprint team will call before coming in the morning. How early can they come?"

"As early as possible," I responded, "since I have my own job to go to."

Jensen laughed. "Modest fellow. Our host is a low-profile behind-the-scenes operator. You know the term power broker?"

The agents nodded and Jensen gestured at me. "In the flesh," he said, and after more handshakes they left the house. Closing the door, I said, "Why give me such a grandiose and fraudulent character?"

"Never hurts to let the other guys think you have influence. They'll pass the word around."

I liked his manner, his way of dealing with people who could be difficult. No wonder Gurney and Steiner had taken to him. He looked at his watch and shook his head. "Late for me, Steve. Any other monster problems I can resolve?"

"You can answer a question: I don't think I should tell the senator about the knife, do you?"

"Not a word. Until the shiv becomes meaningful it was never here."

Walking him to the door, I said, "Unless the intruder planned to tell the world the death knife was in my house, the break-in was meaningless."

"Anonymous tip—why not? Local cops would come with a search warrant and eventually find the weapon. That wouldn't be good for you or the senator."

"Not good at all."

"Particularly since I gather you and she are each other's sole alibi for the approximate period when Harlan was probably killed."

"When would that have been?"

"Any time from late last Thursday night to early Friday morning."

I nodded. "We were together."

"At her apartment?"

I nodded again.

"Let's hope that doesn't come out."

I grunted. "We weren't murdering her husband, Arthur, we were sleeping together. Otherwise we'd have arranged separate backstopped alibis."

Stifling a yawn, he glanced at his wristwatch and said, "Sometimes no alibi is the best one. I'm going home and try for some sleep before daylight, and I recommend you do the same."

"Plan to."

"Just let the crime scene guys in, you don't have to bother with them."

I nodded, and opened the front door. "Thanks for coming," I said. "Next lunch is on me."

After he left I reset the alarm system and went back to bed and slept until nine, when the Bureau team called and asked permission to come.

There were three of them, and the first round of coffee went pretty fast so I perked more. A young lab tech asked, "When you saw the knife was anything wrapped around it?"

"No, it was just lying there under scattered trash. Why?"

"Because there are no prints on it, just smudges like from being handled with a glove." He paused. "Didn't see any discarded gloves, did you? Rubber, cotton?"

"None. But you could check along the drive and under my car."

"Done that," another tech said, "so I guess the guy had it wrapped with some kind of cloth, maybe a handkerchief."

"Sounds reasonable." I got up from the table. "Gotta shave and get going. Help yourselves to coffee, and close the door on the way out."

"Will do, sir, and thanks for your cooperation."

From the bedroom I phoned my office and told Mrs. Altman to expect me around ten-thirty. I was leaving the shower when the phone rang, and Alison said, "Have you seen the morning paper?"

"No. Why?"

"Local section—Harlan's murder is very big."

"You shouldn't read the papers, honey. Do without for a few more days. Likewise radio and TV."

"I know, I know, but I feel I ought to know what's being said about me."

"Not good for morale," I told her. "By the way, I talked to Hod last night, filled him in, and he said you should come whenever you can get away. The boat's in Anguilla now and he offered to meet you at San Juan—direct flight for you."

"That's so considerate of him."

"He's that kind of guy."

"The big question is when I can get away—you can't believe how anxious I am."

"Arthur Jensen may have word for you today. Meanwhile, you could have the body claimed from the mortuary and tell Don-nerwetter Funeral Parlor to ship it to Omaha."

"Yes. But Harlan always said he preferred cremation."

"Then follow his wishes." I paused. "Do you have a copy of his will?"

"Uh—never thought of it, but I don't recall him mentioning one."

"Aside from Harlan's wish to be cremated the will could be significant in other ways."

"Oh?"

"Like, if he willed you the dealership franchises. They could be worth a lot of money. Contents of the condo, so on."

"I see. Well, how can I cope with all that?"

"Simple. Ask Arthur Jensen to have the firm locate and eval-uate Harlan's assets. He probably had a commercial lawyer to handle his dealership matters and he should be able to provide consider-able information."

She was silent for a while. "I'll do as you say, Steve. But it oc-curs to me that with my late husband so desperate for cash his assets can't be worth much. I assume things were attached with liens."

"That's probably so, but the franchises might well be worth saving if only to sell later."

"Now you're talking about things of which I have no under-standing at all. Can you guide me through the maze?"

"Yes, I've handled similar things before. But I'm hoping a will will surface. If Harlan died intestate all sorts of claims could pop up—new liens, undisclosed debts, and so on."

"Undisclosed debts," she echoed. "That could be what he owed the gamblers."

"Owed but legally uncollectable. And the mob certainly isn't going to pressure a United States senator to pay gambling debts not her own."

"I guess not," she said slowly, "but so many strange things have been happening."

In that moment I felt an impulse to tell her the apparent murder weapon had been found in my kitchen, but that would only upset her more. Better wait until we were cruising the Caribbean, if then. And as I dried and dressed I reflected that the knife's appearance was upsetting to me. But if an anonymous call was to have directed police to my home I'd probably wrecked the plan by discovering the intruder and finding the knife.

What would be next?

Around eleven Burton Michaels came into my office, set a case file on my desk, and said, "That Rico Manfredi is a real crook."

"So I surmised. But we work for crooks, too, so long as our work is legal."

"Of course. It's just that I can't work up much empathy for a guy who builds substandard housing for poor folks and tries to collect for good work."

"Way of the world, eh? Maybe Rico neglected to bribe the right housing officials."

He smiled. "Could be. Even Sal Bonfaccio seems embarrassed by our mutual client. How far do you want to take this?"

"No further than an IRS opinion. How ready are you?"

"Couple more days, okay?"

"Fine with me. Your case."

After Michaels left, my private phone rang, and I heard the cheery voice of Lauri Nathanson, a young lawyer I'd taken to Bermuda a couple of years ago before she married a regional television mogul. "Steve! Darling man! Obviously you haven't heard the news."

"What news?"

"My divorce, silly. Final decree right here in the District—and I took Sam for a bundle. I mean a *real* bundle."

"Hm. So you can abandon divorce practice?"

"Hardly. Now I can put hard-won experience to the benefit of female clients. I'll be the most wanted practitioner for miles around. Phone's been ringing off the hook since Friday."

"Congratulations, Lauri."

"Well, thanks, darling. I wanted you to be the first to know I'm once again available. And to prove it, I'm prepared to reciprocate that heavenly week in Bermuda. Where would you like to go—Paris? Madrid? Geneva?"

"All three, sweetie, but I'm booked until summer."

"Summer's fine—better climate in Europe, right? But don't put me off until then. I'll be expecting a splendid dinner with you and a series of exquisite lunches. Steve, I'm so thrilled to be free!"

"Appreciate the news, Lauri, and I'll be calling."

"Do so, love. Bye." She rang off and I sat back smiling. Lauri's joy over freedom from the trammels of marriage was out of character. She was a remorseless little sinner, bothered less by adulterous behavior than by smoking in a taxi, but I'd managed to resist her occasional overtures to illicit pleasure. Lauri couldn't be more than thirty-two, a blond, bouncy young binzel with an almost insatiable sexual appetite. And now with more money than she knew what to do with. Lauri Nathanson. After trouncing old Sam Wharton in court, and probably debilitating him in bed, she was headed for a career of marrying and collecting heavily from foolish older men. I couldn't be a target because I wasn't old or wealthy. What she got from me was great sex, or so she said. But it would be a long time before I phoned Lauri for dinner, lunch, or even drinks. What I had with Alison was far too good to risk with Lauri.

Mrs. Altman produced a story from last week's paper that set Lauri's divorce take at $3.75 million. Wharton was worth a lot more, but he could have figured his health was priceless and Lauri's exit payoff a guarantee of longevity.

Nearly four million, I mused. With only a small part of it she could take us around the world for the next year. But I preferred a quiet Caribbean cruise with Alison. Hands down.

*   *   *

I lunched at the Logos with Dr. Perry VanAlstine, a potential client, and his wife. He was a scientist who'd developed a recondite process to enhance superchips through recrystallization in super-cold. Whatever it was, he'd patented the process and was preparing to sell manufacturing rights for many millions down, and more to follow.

He had unkempt gray hair and dressed like an old man, though he was barely sixty, with a starched white collar almost as wide as Herbert Hoover's, a Logos Club tie, and starched cuffs with engraved gold links. His face was as lined and gaunt as Jeff Davis's after Richmond. His head sported a rich crop of nose and ear hair, and it occurred to me that the doctor might belong to a cult that forswore their trimming. He favored double gin martinis with a twist, as did his wife, Gretta, with the exception of a stuffed olive in place of the twist. Of all the women present she was the only one wearing a hat, and a flowered one, at that. The artificial flowers and twigs were so profuse as to resemble the woodsy nest from which a thrush might be peeking, and after two doubles down her gullet the hat clung at a rakish angle. Her gaze seldom strayed from her husband, whom she regarded with a mix of admiration, awe, and resentment.

VanAlstine cleared his throat, beckoned to a waiter and pointed at his nearly empty glass. Then, bony fingers laced, he turned to me. "As you likely know," he began in a mellow voice, "I spent many years in government service—after MIT."

I hadn't known, but I nodded.

"That servile experience inculcated in me an extreme distaste for governments—"

"And government bureaucracies," Gretta added.

"Quite so. A revulsion, to be frank, and Livermore was no exception."

"No exception at all," his wife confirmed. Her cheeks were flushed, and I noticed a trickle of perspiration beginning at her throat inching down into the cleavage of her more than ample bosom. She lifted her drink and tossed it off in a surprisingly quick movement so that it was empty and waiting when the waiter delivered her husband's fresh martini. "Please," she said throatily, "do me, too." The waiter took her meaning and her empty glass. She set elbows on table, and cradled her chin on joined fingers. "Go on, Perry," she encouraged, "don't let me interrupt you." And winked slyly at me. Good God, I thought, but faced VanAlstine, who said, "My point being, that as I appear to be on the verge of very substantial riches it is my intense desire to share as little as possible with the rulers of our country."

"Share nothing would be better," Gretta said stonily.

"Much better," her husband agreed. "Accordingly, Mr. Bentley, I have decided to seek your advice in the matter and if I find it sound, to be guided thereafter."

In a neutral voice Gretta said, "That's how it is, Steve." She smiled and I saw her eyes were wide and glistening. They seemed to be waiting for a response from me so I cleared my throat and sat forward. "Actually, only the Internal Revenue Service will determine if my advice is sound, but based on considerable precedent, I predict that tax predators will feed poorly from your table."

The couple exchanged pleased glances. Her fresh drink arrived and as she lifted it she murmured, "Chin-chin."

VanAlstine touched the rim of his glass to hers. "Chin-chin," he repeated, and I realized the formula was precious to them. Possibly conceived at Livermore. Gretta dabbed at her lips with a cocktail napkin and stared at me. "Well?"

I said, "I'm sympathetic to your desire to retain as many of the fruits of your labors as is legally possible under—"

"*Legally?*" Gretta shot. "Don't give a damn for legally."

"Well, not entirely, my dear," her husband mollified. "Don't want to end up in durance vile, do we?"

She grinned and cocked her head, and the birds' nest tilted even more alarmingly. I said, "Options to choose from depend on the schedule of payments you will receive. For instance, a lump sum payment now could be disadvantageous if—"

Gretta ran her wrist across her forehead. "Wha' about overseas bank accounts? For'n investments?"

"They exist," I told her. "What about them?"

VanAlstine said, "We have in mind sequestering funds against old age and misfortune but I don't want to get crossways with the law."

Gretta laughed shortly. "Screw the law. We're already in old age. Right, Mr. Bentley?"

"Well, yes and no. As an officer of the court I have to stand against tax evasion. But there is no law whatsoever against tax avoidance."

Her face lighted like high noon in Yuma. "Hear that? Avoid, don't evade."

VanAlstine chuckled. "Sounds like a CPA slogan."

"At least a rule of thumb. But to cut to the heart of the matter, my office would have to examine all contracts involved in the sale or lease of your patents and determine your fixed and potential royalty receipts before competent advice could be rendered and a suitable program devised."

VanAlstine nodded. His wife twirled her glass between thumb and forefinger and said, "I'm like David Copperfield."

Okay, I thought, I'm the straight guy. "How is that, Mrs. VanAlstine?"

"Makes things disappear," she said triumphantly, and her husband smiled in approval. "Quick wit, Gretta. Don't know what I'd have done without her all those years."

"Me neither," she replied levelly, "and it was one goddam hell of a long time. You in the effing lab twelve hours a day, and me washing clothes, cooking and trying to find a life for myself beyond subscription magazines an' all the damn contests." She shook her head. "No more of that. No more company cafeterias either. Now we got it, I want to live, Daddy, live a lot and long. No expense too great."

Her husband nodded supportively. "That is exactly how things are going to be, honey. From now on we do things your way. House, travel, whatever."

She blew him an alcoholic kiss. I said, "Folks, how will we leave it?"

VanAlstine said, "What is your preference?"

"Considering luncheon as a preliminary and informal get-together, I suggest you make an office appointment to bring in all the contracts you may have signed. With figures at hand I should be able to tailor a program to meet your desires, if not your expectations."

"What'n hell's he mean?" Gretta asked suspiciously.

"What I think, my dear, is that Mr. Bentley believes he can accomplish pretty much what we want. That right, Bentley?"

"That's right, Doctor."

"See?" he turned to his wife. "Told you it'd work out. Now
let's do something about lunch."

A vigilant waiter brought over parchment menus and stayed
with us while the VanAlstines ordered, changed, altered, reversed
and finally settled on salads, entrees, and side dishes. By the time he
turned to me the waiter was fatigued. I said "Mixed grill and endive
salad. Ask the sommelier his recommendation."

The VanAlstines regarded me with interest, and when the
sommelier attended us he suggested a bottle of Pinot Noir, and one
of Montrachet. I said that would suit us admirably, and Gretta said,
"Daddy, we better learn about wines and such. Right, Steve?"

"Not necessary at all. Never go wrong consulting the wine
steward."

VanAlstine nodded. "Sounds like good advice. Uh, 'nother
cocktail, Bentley?"

"Not now," I said, and smiled. "Gotta have a clear head dealing with folks like you."

"Bullshit," Gretta said, loudly enough to attract the attention
of nearby diners. "I din learn fancy French words at Blacksburg
State Teachers, but learnt to rekanize bullshit." She smiled amiably,
and clawed at her husband's hand. "This is a no-bullshit guy an' I
love the pants off him."

The sommelier returned with two bottles, followed by a
waiter with an ice bucket stand. When he offered me the corks I
gestured at the doctor, who sniffed perfunctorily and said, "Great.
Hope the wine's as good. Ha-ha."

The doctor had a robust appetite, but his spouse toyed list-
lessly with her poached rockfish while disappearing several glasses
of wine. Between us, we arranged a proximate meeting in my office,
when he would bring all pertinent documents.

As we talked, Gretta's head dropped lower and lower, until
her husband drew it back and straightened her hat. She smiled happily, leaned sideways and began toppling from her chair. I kept her

from falling, and while I was righting her torso I realized she was rubbing her breasts across my arm. The doctor seemed amused, so I smiled back. The maitre d' came over and offered to be of assistance, but VanAlstine said, "Take care of it myself, used to it by now. Just call a cab, please." And when the maitre d' left VanAlstine said, "Don't take these things seriously, Bentley. Gretta's had a hard life with me, and now she's loosening up a bit. Can't blame her. But I do wish she wouldn't try to drink it all at once."

VanAlstine couldn't manage her alone, so two waiters helped Gretta from her chair. She tossed me a crooked smile, punched at her hat, and allowed herself to be led away. The doctor signed the luncheon check and after he departed, I lingered for coffee before returning to the office.

While I was dictating a record of the meeting, it came to me that Gretta had been awkwardly angling for a little jump—maybe in the guest rooms upstairs—but dat ol' debbil gin had disabled her, and for that I was grateful. Note: confer with client or with client *and* wife, never wife alone. Mandatory.

I hadn't heard from Pat Moran for a while so I wasn't surprised to hear his voice on the private line. "Well, well, me bhoy," he began, "wait long enough and things sort themselves out."

"Meaning what?"

"Meaning Harlan managed to evade the Baltimore cops."

"Yeah. Any other suspects for Doris's killing?"

"None I heard of, but the big question is who killed the senator's husband—and with a knife, yet. So messy."

"I guess the perp will be caught in time."

"A long time is my guess. You heard anything?"

"No, and I'm a world-class listener."

"So you are—give you that. So, what now?"

"What now about what?"

"About anything involving your varied interests."

"What a way to put it. My interests, such as they are, aren't that varied or numerous. And while we're talking murder, what's the status of Andrew Bostick's case?"

"Resting peacefully—victim and case both. No clues, no nada. Case fully inactive."

"Doesn't seem fair, Pat. I mean the man was murdered so someone ought to care."

"That's what happens to Pit Boys. Here today, drowned to-morrow. I shed no tears for the likes of him."

"See a priest today, get compassion."

"Compassion I'm long out of. Besides, it's a shitty world."

"That it is. Anything else?"

"Just making sure you're okay."

"Why wouldn't I be?"

"Well, you're connected with all three corpses, Steve, not di-rectly, but closer than me. So it figures maybe the Apache sign is on you, too."

"Geronimo," I said, and hung up. I thought of my unusual lun-cheon companions, and decided that Lauri Nathanson would have made a perfect fourth. I suspected that her acquaintance with the scientific community was limited, and the VanAlstines would have given her a hilarious glimpse to alter all preconceptions. They were practically daguerreotypes but I intended to cater to the doctor. Han-dling financial affairs to his and Gretta's liking would provide for a retirement more luxurious than anything I'd ever contemplated.

For that, I could even tolerate the bibulous former hausfrau rubbing her ruby nips on my arm. What a couple.

Mrs. Altman took the tape from my recorder and said, "I feel so sorry for Senator Bowman, all the publicity about her husband's murder. It must be devastating."

"Well," I said, "nothing lasts forever, and the Bureau may come up with the killer."

"But when?" she sighed.

Alone, I phoned Alison and learned that her administrative assis-tant, Garth Anson, was with her working on Senate business. "And he brought really countless sympathy cards and condolence mes-sages to be acknowledged eventually. I didn't know so many people cared."

"Outpourings from the heart," I remarked, "and they should make you feel better."

"Except that I feel like a hypocrite."

"Don't. Just be the grieving widow people expect."

"I'm trying." She paused. "Oh, Arthur Jensen will be here later with those Bureau agents."

"Good. I'm sure he will stipulate that this is their one and only chance at you, and you'll be free of them afterward."

"That's what he indicated. He also told me his firm is searching for any will Harlan may have made."

"Good. What about burial?"

"I have to go to the mortuary to identify the body and release it to Donnerwetter. Harlan's parents don't object to cremation and ask only that his ashes be sent them in a nice urn—and of course I'll have that done. Arthur will go to the mortuary with me and I'll call you later."

"Please do. Are we going to break bread together?"

"Yes. Ridgewell's is delivering a week's dinners so there'll be something in the larder. Bye."

I went home while the glazier replaced the door pane, had a drink and went back to the office. A message from Mrs. VanAlstine greeted me, requesting I call their suite at the Madison, their local pied-à-terre. I gave some hard thought to the message, not wanting to slide into a one-on-one situation with her, but not wishing to affront her either. Considering all she'd drunk at the Logos and her assisted departure from the club, I figured she ought to be suffering a gigantic hangover, but you could never tell about drunks. I also doubted she wanted to tender apologies for the incident, that not being the alcoholic's way. So I asked Mrs. Altman to phone Gretta, say I wasn't returning to the office and would phone her tomorrow. While she was doing that I had Burton Michaels come in for a briefing on Dr. VanAlstine's prospective wealth, and suggested a Lexis search for tax-saving precedents.

He nodded. "What's the urgency?"

"None, really. The doctor is to make an appointment and

bring in relevant docs. I don't know if he's agreed to outright sale or lease of his process and of course that makes a huge difference."

He nodded, "I'll have the search include leasing as well as capital sale. Is there a VanAlstine file?"

"Meager, but you can build on it. And at all costs avoid his wife. She likes to drink, and gets chummy in the glow. Just so you know."

He smiled broadly. "Appreciate it."

After he left, Mrs. Altman came in to say Gretta VanAlstine seemed very upset that she couldn't talk with me. "Also she sounded . . . tipsy."

"Probably was. We'll make it an office rule that any time she calls I'm not in. My business is with her husband."

She gave me a sardonic glance. "I understand."

"Dr. VanAlstine gets red carpet treatment, his wife gets a barred door."

"Very prudent, I'm sure."

I got to Alison's apartment a little after eight. By then her AA had left, as had Arthur Jensen and the Bureau bravos. I mixed a shaker of martinis, and Alison said a seafood dinner was ready to be waved. "Bureau guys treat you right?" I asked.

"Surprisingly deferential, probably because Arthur followed every word. Basically, I repeated what I'd told them Sunday afternoon. Agent Smithers said Sergeant Bottscher confirmed details of his visit to the farm and provided a copy of his contact report. After that the agents left and Arthur told me I was free to leave town."

"You might check first with Sean Elkins."

"Good. When are you going?"

"I thought I'd wait two days—for appearances' sake." She smiled thinly. "Always doing things for appearances' sake, aren't we?"

"Only when necessary. I checked six-o'clock TV and there was nothing about Harlan or you—big improvement."

"And a relief." She sipped from her glass. "When can you join me?"

"Well, not knowing your plans I haven't made any of my own. But I'm about to take on a major client with big-time money, and I should formalize the relationship before leaving."

"Meaning?"

"I'll try for a Saturday flight. That should put me on board by moonrise."

"So I'll have only a few days without you—I was afraid it might be longer." She pressed my hand. "Garth Anson said he hadn't heard any negative comments about me so I may go to the office tomorrow, put in an appearance."

"You might check first with Sean Elkins."

"Good idea. I'm paying for her advice, why not use it?"

"Yes. And don't tell your staff where you're going. You and I know, and so do the Gurneys. Four's enough."

"Arthur?"

"I'll tell him after you leave." I refilled our glasses, and Alison asked, "Have you heard anything about who killed poor Doris Conlon?"

"Nothing. Unless some crackhead confesses the case will stay open—and gather dust."

She looked away. "Do you think Harlan killed her?"

"I have no idea," I said truthfully. "He might have had opportunity but where was the motive? The chance she might make hostile statements at a divorce hearing isn't enough. By then your husband had agreed on a settlement without trial. Doris told us he'd kicked her out, but he said she'd abandoned him. Where's the truth? Does it matter now? They're both dead—murdered."

She thought it over. "Surely you don't want murderers to get away with their crime."

"I don't, but it happens. In the District fewer than a third of murders are ever solved—by which I mean a perp indicted and brought to trial. Other cities less, some more." An idea occurred to me. "PR-wise, and for your own peace of mind, why not post a reward for the conviction of your husband's killer? Fifty thousand for information leading to an arrest, another fifty on conviction. That oughta bring information out of the woodwork."

She sat forward, eyes wide. "What a wonderful idea! How would I go about it?"

"Let Sean handle details, assuming Arthur agrees."

"Why would he not? It's brilliant, Steve. But who would hold the money and award it?"

"Gurney and Steiner. Don't know why I didn't think of it before . . . Anyway, posting a reward would publicize your concern for your late husband, stimulate a flow of information, and provide a form of closure. After which you seclude yourself, having done all within your power to bring the murderer to justice."

"Win-win," she mused, "with the possibility of Harlan being avenged."

"Exactly."

Impulsively she kissed me. "You wouldn't believe how much I value you. I've said that before, haven't I?"

"And I love hearing you say it."

That ended the concerns of the day. We enjoyed a rich seafood casserole with French bread and Chablis. Took cognac to the bedroom and shared it before making love.

One day I'm going to learn to think things through before speaking out. Posting a reward, I'd thought, would be broadly beneficial to Alison. But I hadn't considered the kind of trouble it was going to bring.

EIGHTEEN

———

AFTER EARLY BREAKFAST with Alison I left for home and office. She was to arrange reward details with lawyer Jensen and PR adviser Sean Elkins, then get a plane ticket to San Juan under an assumed name.

About ten-thirty Dr. VanAlstine phoned that he was free to come in. Would one o'clock be convenient? I said it was, and alerted Burton Michaels to be available. Consciously I was reneging on my promise to phone Gretta VanAlstine, assuming she'd show with her husband at one.

My concern dissolved when the client arrived alone, with his scuffed briefcase. After being introduced to Burton Michaels he said, "Gretta's not feeling well today, but sends her regards to you."

"Thoughtful of her," I responded. "And I reciprocate her message." We went into the conference room and VanAlstine opened his briefcase on the table. From it he extracted a dozen legal-length documents bearing the imprimatur of InfoComp, a leading U.S. manufacturer of computer hard- and software. I said, "I think we'd better copy these so you can keep the originals in a safe place."

"Until now I've kept them in the hotel vault—that okay?"

"Temporarily. But a bank deposit box would be more secure and permanent."

"Unfortunately, I don't have a bank in Washington."

"Then I could file your originals in our office vault until you make other arrangements."

"I'm sure that would be satisfactory."

"We'll study everything with great care," I told him, "but what's the corporate offer?"

"Thirty million to purchase the VanAlstine process."

"Lease option?"

He nodded. "Fifteen million down and a royalty of thirteen percent of each item manufactured."

Michaels asked, "Manufactured or sold?"

"Manufactured," VanAlstine said with a sleek smile. "I wasn't born yesterday."

I said, "Doctor, we're not knowledgeable about the computer industry, but someone should be able to estimate the potential demand for your product."

"That's right."

"Then there is no problem with my retaining a consultant in the field to work up figures? It's essential to have them as a basis for choosing between sale and lease."

He nodded. "Of course. Worth it in the long run."

Michaels, who was scanning the documents said, "According to this, InfoComp's offer is limited to the next fifteen days."

"Yes, they want to get going."

I sat back and gazed at him. "Fifteen days isn't much to accomplish all you want done, so I have this suggestion: in the specified period we will recommend either lease or sale, and as to advice concerning how, when, and where your funds are received, that can be postponed."

He frowned. "You mean I can't get the money right away?"

"Realistically, you shouldn't, considering the confiscatory tax that would be imposed. Far better to have the funds held by a financial institution that does that service for the securities industry and shields you from constructive receipt. Your funds would be secure while decisions are made."

He thought it over. "Gretta will be disappointed, and I don't like disappointing her." He grimaced. "Very well, I consent to what you propose. After all, the whole purpose of retaining you was to save money legally. I'd be a fool to ignore your advice."

"Apropos," I said, "a retainer at this time is customary."

His bushy white eyebrows went up. "You mean you don't bill me afterward?"

"I've indicated the work we have to accomplish in order to serve you properly, and it all costs money. Consultant's fees, banking services, collateral expenses. I'll accept ten thousand now to get things started, and we're working against a fifteen-day time limit. The retainer will be a down payment against future costs as they occur."

He looked down at his scarred briefcase. "Good Lord, I had no idea it was all going to be so expensive. Ten thousand . . ."

"On the bright side, Doctor, payments to the office are business-related and tax-deductible."

"Mm. I take your point," he said grudgingly. "And what are future costs likely to be?"

I shook my head. "If you'd like to set a top figure I'll inform you when it's reached and you can then decide how to proceed."

"I see. Ten thousand . . ." the words sounded like a mantra. "Wouldn't, um, consider reducing it?"

"No, Doctor."

He hesitated. "Or perhaps accepting a percentage of my expectations in lieu of fee?"

I smiled. "Millions tomorrow, nothing today? Sorry, Doctor. As professionals you and I are worthy of our hire. The amount of legal work in prospect is quite considerable and it's customary for clients to underwrite the expense." I reached over and gathered up his sheaf of documents. "You're welcome to seek other counsel," I told him.

He held up one hand, face registering dismay. "Oh, no, not at all—it's just that I'm not used to dealing with lawyers, you see, and I—" He dug into his briefcase and brought out a checkbook. "How do I make it out?"

"My secretary will fill in the payee. Burton, bring a client agreement for the doctor."

Michaels came back with the standard form, I penned in blank spaces and dated it. Dr. VanAlstine read the agreement carefully, nodded to himself, and signed with a flourish. "How soon will I be hearing from you?"

"Before the time limit expires. Burton will have everything copied now, and I'll keep originals in the office vault."

VanAlstine watched Michaels leave with his precious papers, and when we were alone, he said, "I wish Gretta had been here for this important moment."

"Yes, hope she feels better soon."

He moistened his lips. "She wanted to apologize to you for yesterday's incident—"

"Not necessary," I interjected.

"But I do so in her place."

"Generous of you, Doctor, and I appreciate the courtesy."

He swallowed. "You'll get right to work?"

"Of course." Providing the check's good, I thought.

Michaels returned with originals and copies, gave the latter to our new client and said, "Pleasure to meet you, Doctor."

"Thank you." To both of us he said, "I feel immensely relieved. I've unloaded a heavy burden."

"That you have," I agreed, "and now we'll carry it."

We parted at the door, and after it closed Michaels said, "I have to admire the way you handled him."

"Closing is often the hardest phase of acquiring a client. At least we've got a down payment on our labors. Locate the best available computer consultant and bring him on board. You know what we need from him."

"I do."

"And I'm depending on you to handle all the preliminary work."

He smiled. "The more hours I bill the better for me."

I looked at my watch. "The meter's running."

I was making a Things to Do list for Dr. VanAlstine, when Mrs. Alt-man notified me that Governor Green was on line 1. Picking up the receiver, I said, "Yes, Governor?"

"Mr. Bentley. I must congratulate you for what I'm now read-ing."

"And what is that, sir?"

"Why, the reward offer just posted by Senator Bowman."

"Oh? I'm not familiar with it," I lied. "Reward for what?"

"Information and conviction of Harlan's killers. It is a magnif-icent stroke, personally and politically, and you must forgive me if I don't entirely credit your denial."

"Be that as it may, Governor, let's assume the reward idea was generated by the people who represent her interests, Arthur Jensen of Gurney and Steiner, and Sean Elkins, the PR whiz."

"Oh. Actually, I didn't know either was involved with the senator."

"Not only involved, but the current source of all information concerning her activities."

There was a long silence before he said, "That's a very inter-esting development. Quite inspired on her part—or theirs. I'll be in-terested to see how the reward offer plays on the evening news."

"So will I, now that you have informed me."

"I foresee great political benefits for her—very much in con-cert with the plans I mentioned to you."

"I understand," I said, noncommittally, "and I appreciate your call."

"We'll talk again, sir," he said, and as I replaced the receiver I thought, Not if I can avoid it.

Toward day's end Mrs. Altman came in to report a call from Mrs. VanAlstine. "I followed your instructions, sir, said you were in tax court and not expected back."

"Thank you . . . How did she sound?"

"Disappointed."

"Tipsy?"

She nodded. "That, too."

"Not my business, but the doctor ought to give her a couple of months at the Betty Ford—she needs it and he can afford it."

"Quite," she said, and left.

Briefly I thought that I ought to feel sorry for the VanAlstines, but she was enjoying her lifestyle, as alcoholics do, and her husband seemed adjusted to it, or at least tolerant of it—so what was to feel sorry about? With all those millions to enjoy the VanAlstines were sitting on top of the world. A couple to be envied not pitied.

I was home changing for the evening when Alison called. She said she was getting stir-crazy and would I consider dining out?

"Of course. Where?"

"I love Crisfield's. Let's meet there. I have a couple of errands to run, so is eight-thirty okay?"

"Perfect."

But half an hour later, while I was pouring a second scotch, the phone rang and I heard Alison's breathy, shaky voice. *"I'm scared to death. Someone just shot at me."*

NINETEEN

———

"ARE YOU HURT?"

"No."

"Where are you?"

"Driving—using the car phone."

Oh Christ, I thought. "What happened?"

"I came down to my car in the parking lot and opened the door—" She broke off, and I could hear choking sounds. "Easy," I said, "take it easy. What then?"

"Heard this sharp sound, like a bottle breaking, only I knew it wasn't that because a bullet hit the car door." She began whimpering, finally saying, "I was paralyzed with fright, but I forced myself into the car and drove away as fast as I could."

"Good thinking."

"Reaction—fled from danger."

"You saw no one?"

"No, the lot was dark and the shot came from the far end."

"Was the shooter in or out of a car?"

"I—I don't know." She paused. "Steve, I'm driving aimlessly. Shall I meet you at Crisfield's like we—?"

"No, come to my place, you'll be safe here."

"Yes, I know I will. I should be there in ten, fifteen minutes."

I swallowed my scotch in two gulps and looked around. Jesus, shooting a U.S. senator . . . to kill or frighten? Who held the gun? The usual suspect—Harlan—was dead, no longer a player. The midnight watcher in the dark road? Bostick's killer? The parking lot site suggested it. But why? My thoughts whirled. Who would benefit from Alison's death? The only name I could think of was Abel Green, impatient to take over the Senate seat. Not that he'd fired the shot, but the governor could easily have hired thugs like Winkowski and Stone to do her in. Or held leverage over them as he had over Andrew Bostick. As my thoughts decelerated I wandered into the kitchen and made a large shaker of martinis—99.9 percent Bombay gin, the balance dry vermouth. Ice cubes, stir slightly and pour a tasting sample. Mmmm. Taste buds came alive. I smacked my lips and finished the sample before going out to the street to wait for Alison.

Seven minutes and her Jag slid into the curbside space. I opened her door and helped her out. She clasped me in her arms, body trembling. I kissed her cheek, lips, and forehead, guided her up the walk and into my house. She sat beside the coffee table and looked up at me, eyes wide, face unnaturally pale. I poured martinis in two jumbo glasses and we sipped together. After a protracted sigh, she said, "Nothing's ever tasted so good." She drank again. "Am I a silly female for being so scared?"

"Hell, no. Think I wasn't scared in Nam? Every time a street kid tossed a firecracker I'd jump out of my boots."

"Liar," she said, but with a faint smile. "And in the jungle? In combat?"

"Much, much worse." I waved a hand. "Don't remind me."

"You're something," she said teasingly. "My hero."

"So I'm Batman, the Shadow and Flash Gordon. Tell me where the bullet hit."

Her face tightened. "The door, just missed me."

"Okay," I said. "I'm going to take a look at it. Keys?"

"In the car, I didn't think to bring them."

"Two minutes," I said, and went out to her Jaguar. The bullet impact point was almost in the center of the door panel, about three feet above street level. Had it struck her the slug would have hit her knee or lower thigh. I opened the door and looked for an exit hole. None. The slug was still inside the door frame. I put the keys under the floor mat and closed the door.

Back in the living room I reached for the telephone and Alison asked, "Calling police?"

I shook my head. "You're so damn honest and ethical you instinctively turn to the cops. Think it through, honey. A bullet hole in a senator's car is big news, especially in the wake of Harlan's murder. Now if you want to spill the episode to the cops—"

"All right, dear, point taken."

I punched the number of Pat Moran's office, left my name and number on his answering machine, and said, "Call me. This is urgent."

"Who'd you call?" she asked.

"My investigator, Pat Moran, a fine and faithful gentleman of Irish descent. Okay?"

"Okay, but—"

"I'm going to give him some instructions. Finish your drink and I'll fill your glass. Mine, too."

After sipping her refill she said, "I might as well tell you I've lost my appetite. No Crisfield's, not even Dominique could tempt me." She shivered. "Who would want to kill me? Why?"

"Wish I knew. But from where the bullet struck I can tell you your life wasn't in danger."

"Really?"

"Really." I smiled. "Disappointed?"

She smiled back. "A little, I guess. But if the shot wasn't meant to kill me—"

"The shooter was either a poor marksman, or a very good one. Meanwhile, to avoid anything resembling repetition I want you to leave town tomorrow."

"*Tomorrow?*"

"Pack a small bag and take a cab to the airport. I'm serious."

"Well," she said uncertainly, "if you really think I should . . ."

"How much warning do you need? Think it over—three murders directly or indirectly connected to you, now a shot coming at you out of the dark, and you want to hang around?"

"Oh no, not when you put it that way."

"No other way to put it. Someone wants the state's junior senator disgraced or dead."

She drew in a deep breath. "So it seems. And you—what are you going to do?"

"I don't know, but I'll feel a lot easier if you're safe with the Gurneys. Agreed? I'll fix it with Hod. He'll meet your flight at Muñoz Marin or have you met, and take good care of you."

"Until you come."

I nodded just as the phone rang. Pat Moran. I said, "Listen up, you old son of Erin, put on your shoes and shirt and come to my place. I mean now."

"Seriously? What needs doin'?"

"Parked in front of my place is a Jaguar with Senate plates, also a bullet hole in the left front door panel."

"Holy Mary!"

"And all the saints. I want you to get the Jag to a body shop tomorrow, have the hole repaired and the panel repainted. But before that, take a careful look inside the door for the slug."

"Right. And if there's a slug to be found?"

"Use your cop contacts for comparison with the slugs that killed Bostick and Doris Conlon."

"Hm. I see what you're getting at."

"If there's a match with one or both, tell me, not the cops, okay?"

"Never a word, laddie."

"Keys under the floor mat. Just take the Jag and do what has to be done."

"Sure. Me wife'll shuttle me to your place." He cleared his throat, but before he could speak, I said, "Obviously you're on double time, Pat, and cop gratuities are extra."

"Always the generous client. Uh—and when the door's okay?"

"Call me."

"On me way."

I hung up, exhaled, and Alison said, "That's that, huh?"

"That's that. Now, phone American and get a morning flight reservation. When you have flight number and San Juan arrival time I'll call Hod."

She smiled engagingly. "You're so wonderfully organized, darling. I could never be married to a disorganized man."

"I take that as a big-time compliment."

"So intended." She moved against me, touched my cheek and kissed where her fingers had been. "Are you going to tell Arthur Jensen about—?"

"Of course. Arthur, not Sean. And you could phone a message for your staff saying you've left town for a while, back after recess. Now call the airline."

About an hour later I warmed croissants and made a cheese and mushroom omelet for a late supper. We didn't hear Pat come for her car, but when I next looked outside it was gone.

With a sly smile Alison said, "How am I ever to get home tonight?"

"You're not. Tonight we christen the Dolley Madison bedroom."

"The Dolley—? Where is that?"

"Directly overhead. Second floor, right."

"Oh. Who named it the Dolley Madison bedroom?"

"I did."

"And it's never been christened before?"

"Never," I lied. "Kept pristine for you, dear." I kissed her lips and now they were warm, her color natural. Fear was behind her.

And mine hadn't yet begun.

TWENTY

———

NEXT DAY WHILE Burton Michaels dealt with our computer consultant, Walter Embry, I received two clients, advised one to keep better financial records, and briefed the other for a forth-coming IRS audit. Toward two o'clock I took a call from Alison at San Juan's airport. "Smooth flight," she told me. "Mr. Gurney sent a car and driver to take me to the marina and we're about to leave."

"Very glad you called."

"As you ordered me." She laughed briefly. "Oh, honey, it's so good to be out of Washington, but I'm also away from you, and I'm not used to that."

"Neither am I. But you'll have a fine time with our friends."

"It'll be even finer when you join us. And when is that likely to be?"

"Unless something of consequence erupts I'm planning to fly down in two days."

"Wonderful! Oh, the driver has my bag, so it's time to go. Love you, honey."

"Miss you," I replied, and heard the line go dead. She was in safe hands now, I reflected with relief, and on the far periphery of actions and events that could threaten her life or career.

Michaels brought in Embry for a brief discussion, and then Pat Moran was on the line. "Laddie, the slug was where you said, but after slamming through the panel and hitting a steel crosspiece it looked like a mushroom. No rifling marks to compare with other slugs." He paused. "Sorry."

"It was only an off chance, Pat. How long will panel repair take?"

"Shop foreman said couple days. Need it sooner?"

"No hurry, the owner's out of town."

"Good, they'll do a better job."

"Pat, not a better job, a perfect job, okay?"

"Sure, sure. I was plannin' to keep it in my garage until you tell me otherwise."

"Good man," I said, "and thanks for the super service."

My next call was from Lauri Nathanson inviting me to dine à deux at her Watergate condo. I declined on the false excuse of prior commitment, but suggested we have a drink at the Lawyers Club around five.

"Super," she said. "I'm heading for the fitness club so make it five-thirty, okay?"

"Okay."

"You'll note my trim figure and ruddy cheeks—the new total health Lauri."

"Meaning no more pallid, slack-jawed Lauri with the big tochis?"

"Beast! What I mean exactly—though I was never that." She paused. "Steve, would you take me as a client?"

"Why not?"

"Well, I thought you might have reservations, considering our past involvement."

"Of which I have naught but the most pleasant and stimulating memories. I have no problem if you don't."

"Good. I may never again get a windfall like my recent award, so I want to shelter it from tax predators and have it grow. You'll help me with that?"

"I can certainly try."

"You *are* a love. Five-thirty."

Well, I mused, cocktails with Lauri would lighten a couple of otherwise dull hours, plus the prospect of being fiduciary guardian of her sudden wealth. Business and pleasure combined.

Toward day's end Burton Michaels came in to summarize the consultant's preliminary findings. "He's leaning toward VanAlstine leasing his process for a period of ten years. The doc hasn't patented the supercold process—which is wise since competitors, particularly the Japanese, would be able to jump in and duplicate the process from patent specifications. Embry figures there will be technical advances within two to five years making VanAlstine's process obsolete. But he says ten years to keep residuals coming from Info-Comp."

"Makes sense," I responded. "So let's establish VanAlstine on a ten-year basis for tax purposes. My thought is to have payments go to a Delaware corporation from which they can be transferred to banking safe-havens elsewhere in the world."

He nodded agreement. "I can get over to Wilmington tomorrow, start the paperwork moving. Okay?"

"Fine." I looked at my watch. "Before you go tell VanAlstine what we propose and ask if he wants to name the corporation and who the principals are to be—aside from him and his wife."

"I'll call him now."

Anticipating her tardy arrival, I waited at the bar until Lauri showed, eighteen minutes late. Her blond hair was fashionably layered, giving her pixie face a partly cute, partly no-nonsense look. She wore a tailored tan silk blouse, matching pants, and running shoes.

The immense diamond on her right hand caught every light in the room as she dragged me to a table. "Steve, honey, I am *so* sorry about being late, but then that's to be expected of me, isn't it? Sort of, I mean?"

The waiter's arrival spared me from fabricating an answer. She asked for a champagne cocktail—French champagne, not domestic—and I said I'd have the same. Tossing her head, she said, "What a relief to be with a male who doesn't move by walker. Hon, you don't know what I *endured* with Sam."

"True. But let's agree you're amply rewarded."

She smiled slyly. "We could say that—but, God, it's good to be free, have only myself to worry about." She sighed. "I spent an hour at the Rolls showroom and I've almost decided on a gorgeous Seraph with light blue leather. It's a goddam dream, Steve, but I have this one problem about buying it."

"Lease it, then."

"Not what I mean, silly. I mean, I just can't see myself behind the wheel driving myself here and there, looking for parking places—you know the aggravation."

"I do."

The waiter brought our drinks, and while they were still fizzing, Lauri dipped a finger in hers and traced it across my lips. "Good?"

"Nectar." Our glasses touched and we drank. "You were explaining the Rolls problem."

"Yes. Sam always had a driver, of course, slept in the carriage house. But I don't have servants' quarters at my condo. I lust for the Rolls, but what to do about a driver?"

"Ask the Rolls agency. They can probably recommend someone reliable to work reasonable hours for you."

She pouted. "But I don't want to be bothered with his social security, retirement, tax withholding, and so on."

"You've got a fertile mind, Lauri, you'll figure something out."

She shrugged. "Guess so." She drank and rotated the tulip glass. "What's with you, handsome? Keeping company?"

"Sort of."

"Marriage in mind?"

"Could be."

She leaned forward on her elbows. "You don't have to be eva-sive with me."

"It's not that, Lauri, the lady's married and we can't predict the future."

"Ah, that explains it." She sat back and drank again. "Sounds sort of hopeless, but fun while it lasts."

I nodded. "Who handled your divorce?"

"Marty Gerson. She's almost as good as I am."

"C'mon, nobody is."

She smiled happily. "Anyone better in the tax field than you?"

"Dozens," I conceded. "But they don't work as hard."

She beckoned the waiter for refills and asked, "How am I looking?"

"Spectacular."

"Thanks, I work at it, believe me. Diet, exercise, pure thoughts. . . ." She giggled. "Sure you can't cancel your date and hook up with me tonight?"

"No way, exciting as the prospect sounds. When were you thinking of unloading your tax problems on me?"

"Pretty soon. You'll need court papers from Marty but she's out of town—in Bonaire with a new boyfriend. I'll call you when she gets back."

"Suppose she stays forever?"

"Unh-unh, it's a trial run."

I smiled. "And if he passes muster she'll put him on retainer."

"Something like that." She was turning her hand to display and admire the diamond. "Marty's no fool. Her folks made her marry in the faith but it was a bummer and she's taking time to find just the right guy—not necessarily Jewish."

"That certainly broadens the field."

"It does." She swallowed the last few drops of her drink.

I said, "Interesting, what you tell me. Marty's an active femi-nist—or feminist activist—and I heard she was a bi-gal."

"That was one of her main problems with Joel. He was not what you'd call a highly sexed male so she compensated by seeing a gal she'd gone with for years. Joel got all pissed off and denunciatory. The idiot refused to see he'd driven Marty from his bed to hers. Marty really prefers guys, but she needs one who can produce seriatim."

"See what you mean." I wondered if the general subject was one she and her friends explored during long luncheons. Probably.

Refills arrived. Lauri lifted her glass, watched bubbles rise, and drank deeply. "Since your ladyfriend is married you ought to be able to do Europe with me this summer. Yes?"

"It's at the forefront of my thoughts," I lied. "Something comes up, I'll tell you. You do the same."

"Fair enough." She sipped and said, "I gave you my private phone number, didn't I?"

"And it's in my private Rolodex." I asked the waiter for our check, signed, and said, "I'm glad you called, Lauri. I'll be thinking about you."

"Leaving so soon?" She squeezed my hand tightly. "Let's have another, these cocktails are addictive."

I bussed her forehead. "Besides, I'm heading for the corner optometrist."

"What?"

"I'm half-blinded by your rock."

"Oh, you. Get outta here." She mouthed a kiss and I left.

Home, I made a short scotch and checked the office phone for messages. The blinking light converted into the voice of Arthur Jensen, who said, "It's about seven, Steve, and I'm wondering what's happened to our client. I'm at the office and suggest dinner if you have no plans. Call me."

When I reached Arthur I said, "I'm all in favor of dinner. It'll be on me because I've neglected calling you as I promised our client I would."

"Great." His voice sounded less nettled than on the message replay. "She's not in town, I take it."

"We'll go into that. Where do we meet?"

"Why don't you choose among the Palm, Jean-Pierre, and the Olde Ebbitt Grill."

"The Ebitt. It's not far from your office, and I can usually find parking."

"The Ebbitt, okay. Sort of a risky part of town after dark, but what isn't? Eight o'clock?"

"I'll be there."

Arthur's cautionary words about downtown D.C. persuaded me to pack my Beretta in a comfortably fitting spine holster.

Driving through Georgetown, across the Rock Creek bridge and into Washington took six minutes. Finding a place to park my BMW consumed eight more, but it was less subject to stripping and vandalism because of the nearby streetlight. Except for hotels and theaters after-dark Washington was pretty deserted. As I walked into the Grill I glanced around and saw furtive shadows near alley entrances. As the night deepened their numbers would increase. And this was our nation's capital.

The Ebbitt's Victorian interior was dark and pleasantly smoky. Arthur Jensen had a booth near the bar and was already working on a drink. Seeing me, he got up and shook my hand warmly. "What's your poison, Steve?"

"Scotch and water, Johnnie Red."

Overhearing me, the waiter nodded and walked to the service bar. I sat down and opened the menu but didn't read it. "Our client," I said, "is sailing with Hod and Mattie Gurney."

"Well, good. That's a relief. But weren't you planning to be with them?"

"Soon," I said. "A major client appeared and I have to appease him before leaving. But I suggested the senator leave today because of an apparent attempt on her life a couple of nights ago."

His features stiffened. My drink arrived and I sipped before saying, "This is for your ears only, Arthur, Sean's excluded."

"Go on."

I told him about the shot that had narrowly missed Alison, the body work underway, the condition of the lead slug, and my strong recommendation that she join the Gurneys a few days earlier than planned. Listening, he nodded thoughtfully. "No idea who fired the shot, or why?"

"It was dark in the parking lot, she heard the gun fire, heard the slug hit her car. Drove away as fast as she could and eventually called me." I grunted. "Her impulse was to call the police but I pointed out the trail was cold, and publicity about being a target could tarnish her image."

"Quite right." He finished his drink and ordered another. "If more evidence were needed this certainly proves she has an enemy, or enemies. Of course the shot may not have been intended to kill or wound her. So—"

"I'd say intimidation, but to what purpose?"

"Exactly. And the senator has no clue?"

"None she's shared with me. However, in political circles it's rumored her seat is coveted by Governor Green."

"He'd have two years to wait in the normal course of events."

"Unless she resigned and Green appointed himself to fill the vacancy."

His eyebrows lifted. "Never thought of that. And if she were killed he could jump in immediately. Gain seniority."

I said nothing.

"Don't suppose you have anything to inculpate Green in these strange episodes?"

"Nothing tangible." I wasn't going to bring up Andrew Bostick's thievery and unsolved murder because that would have led to revealing her sexual escapade on the holiday cruise. Or Green's two contacts with me, because Arthur had no present need to know.

"Let's order," he said, "I'm hungry."

We started off with escargots, I ordered rack of lamb with hollandaise asparagus and baked potato; Arthur asked for a rare filet mignon, and we agreed on a bottle of Burgundy. That accomplished, we had another round of drinks and exchanged impressions of Alison's forebears, the legendary Revelstokes, and the unsolved murder of Harlan Bowman.

"Concerning Harlan," I said, "his sweetie predeceased him by a couple of days—shot in a cheap Baltimore motel."

"Oh? I didn't know about that. Is the senator even tangentially involved?"

"Only to this extent: a day or so before her murder Doris Conlon came to the farm and said Harlan had kicked her out and taken back the gewgaws he'd given her while they were resident lovers."

"Why'd she do that?"

"Said she wanted to apologize to the senator and implied she'd be a willing witness if the senator divorced Harlan."

"Did that make sense?"

"Nothing else did."

"Then she was dead. Police working the case?"

"Not much to work on. The setup was supposed to suggest suicide, but with no witnesses or discernible motive, the cops tend to theorize some random crackhead robbed and killed her."

"Yeah, much easier that way." He speared a snail. "Was the senator interviewed?"

"Not to my knowledge."

"So she got a break." He broke a roll before saying, "Think Harlan did Doris in?"

"Unless he was insanely vengeful, where's the motive? He was getting what he wanted from the divorce settlement. There would be no trial so Doris couldn't injure him. Of course, anyone who was antsy over what she could reveal of his dealings with Governor Green and the Atlantic City mob might want to silence her preemptively. But that's a very remote possibility."

"I'd say."

Our entrees arrived, and we tucked in enthusiastically.

Gradually, conversation drifted from Alison to the state of the D.C. Bar, the lethargic judiciary and stone-deaf court of appeals; lawyers who'd been sanctioned or disbarred; the bankruptcy of District finances despite confiscatory taxation; the chaotic condition of District public schools, and the strange deaths of several public figures.

We declined dessert, settling for coffee and brandy, and by then only a dozen customers remained. As I signed the check Arthur said, "Great dinner, Steve. Appreciate it."

"Glad you suggested it. With Alison away time's sort of heavy on my hands."

"You two serious?"

"Well, we're doing some serious thinking."

He smiled. "Spoken like a gentleman. I hope we'll do this again. Soon."

"Me, too. Give you a lift home?"

"Thanks, but I'll grab a taxi. I live in Spring Valley."

"Nice section."

"It is. Uh, as we talked I began wondering if you'd consider an offer from my firm?"

"That's very flattering, Arthur, but I'm still contented being my own boss." I paused. "Five years ago Hod Gurney invited me to join. I declined but told him that if I joined any firm it would be yours. That's still my position, but I appreciate the compliment. By the way, if you have anything you want taken to Hod I'll be glad to courier it."

"I'll bear it in mind."

We got into my car and I drove Arthur to the Willard's taxi stand, where we said good night. From there I continued on over into Georgetown and home to Q street.

I pulled into the drive and parked at the far end just short of the garage. I got out, closed the car door, and started walking back when a dark figure hurled itself at me and slammed me against the rear of my car. The impact knocked breath from my lungs but I tried to kick him away.

Too late.

I glimpsed the raised club, heard it whistle downward before crashing against my skull. Pain overwhelmed me, dissolved into streaking, flashing lights as I plunged into a bottomless abyss.

TWENTY-ONE

PAIN SIGNALED MY return to consciousness. My head was a coconut smashed by an ax. Pain flashed downward with each throbbing pulse. Motion. Jolting motion. I was in a moving car lying across the rear footwell, knees nearly touching my chest. I tried to move, found my wrists bound. Smelled vomit. Pooled under my cheek. Stench nauseating.

Turning my head, I could look up through the rear window. No streetlights visible, no sound of nearby traffic. Wherever I was the area was deserted.

A man was at the wheel, no passenger, just the two of us. Suddenly I realized I was in my own car, shanghaied by my attacker. I could see only his right shoulder and arm. I forced myself to breathe deeply and that brought on more pain. Gritting my teeth, I sucked in more air; oxygen would get my brain working again. Breathe, Bentley, breathe, use what's left of your mind.

A streetlight flashed past, first I'd seen. Country road. Some-where. Breathe. Think. Memory was returning in chunks like river ice cracking apart. I'd packed my piece before leaving for dinner. Was it—? I pressed down against the flooring, felt the hard resis-tance of the spine holster. Wriggled again, felt the pistol grip's hard-ness. I breathed a prayer of thanks, turned back on my side and began plucking at wrist cords. Too tight. What now?

Quietly, slowly I drew up my legs and began working my wrists around one shoe. Made it. Now the other as the rope chafed my wrist bones, dug into flesh.

Sweating, pain ignored, I brought my hands to my chest, then higher. A brief streetlight flash showed the knot. Gnawing loos-ened it until I could get a finger in and work the knot apart. Hands free, I dug back under my coat and pulled out my Beretta. Now I was on equal terms with my kidnapper. Better than equal. I got as comfortable as I could. Waited.

What was his plan? Where were we going? The road got bumpier. Who was he? Why the attack, the rural ride? I wiped dry-ing vomit from mouth and chin, saw my wristwatch dial: 11:14. Un-conscious forty-odd minutes. I rubbed my wrists, felt the stickiness of blood. I itched to point the muzzle at the seatback, and fire through it into his body, but a dead driver at the wheel was a recipe for disaster. Wait. Grit your teeth. Wait.

Another five minutes and the car turned left, slowed down a rough incline, drove a few more yards and stopped. Turned off the engine. I saw his head move as he opened the door and began get-ting out. The squat body—Christ, Red Stonefield! Half of the pair that grabbed me on the road to Dulles. Where was Charley Winkowski?

Red jerked open the rear door and was reaching in to grab me when he saw the Beretta in my hand. He tried to slam the door shut but I kicked the door panel and he backed quickly away. He was clawing for a handgun when I snapped, "Hold it," and got stiffly out, keeping him covered. "Shit," he muttered, "oh, shit, that damn Charley. I shouldna let him talk me into it."

"Into what?" I pulled out the car keys, walked around and unlocked the trunk lid. "Any of what?" I asked. The spring-loaded trunk lid bounced open and Red stared at the interior. "You know," he said hoarsely, "the senator, the stripper—shit like that."

"And killing me, right? Heavy shit."

He seemed fascinated by the empty trunk. "You gonna put me there?"

"You should be so lucky," I grunted, pulled out the L-shaped tire iron and went toward him. "On your knees, Red. If you want to pray that's okay with me."

"Pray?" He got down slowly, breath wheezing in his throat. "Pray you don't kill me?"

"Pray it's quick and painless. We're here for killing—right?"

His mouth twisted, his lips went slack, and I thought he was going to blubber. He didn't look at me, he stared at the ground. Through the pulse pounding in my ears I heard running water and looked around.

Behind me was the embankment we'd come down. From it stretched a flat zone of rushes and stunted trees that reached to the river. The Potomac. Now I could orient myself. I'd been driven out Canal Road toward Great Falls Park. Clouds partly masked the moon but I didn't need a lot of light. I walked past Red and slapped the back of his skull with the tire iron. A choked moan and he dropped forward. I tapped the base of his spine with the iron and he yelled and twisted away. That exposed his knees and I hit the nearest kneecap. He yelled more loudly and grabbed the injured knee. The iron struck his wrist and he yelped as the wrist dropped free. "Not so loud, Red," I cautioned, "neighbors might hear. Face down, and if you move I'll shoot."

Bending over, I frisked him, found a Saturday Night Special in one trouser pocket, a spring cosh in the other. No ankle gun. I tossed his weapons into my car and sat on the fender. "You were going to kill, let's not argue about it. That gives me every right to kill you. But I'll give you a chance you weren't giving me."

"Yeah? What chance?"

"Information for your life. Lie or clam up and you'll hurt."

"Whatcha wanna know?"

"Who paid you scumballs to tail me last week? Who's paying you to kill me?"

For a while, he said nothing. Breeze from the river rustled the rushes. In the strange cloud-filtered light they looked like spears and arrows of an ancient army. "Speak up," I said harshly, "can't hear you."

His face turned toward me. "Harlan Bowman paid for the tail."

"Why? He tell you why?"

"You been messin' with his woman."

"He had that right. You kill Andy Bostick?"

"Who? Andy who?"

"Bostick. The Pit Boy."

"Never hearda him."

"Next question: who's paying for tonight's caper?"

"Nobody. Charley and me wanted to get back for what you done to us." He glanced up toward the road, just long enough to let me sense he was expecting an arrival. I slid down from the fender, got his cheapie revolver from the seat and ejected six .38 shells. Set the piece on the fender. "Bowman didn't pay so you knifed him?"

"No, hell no, he paid. Cash."

"How much?"

"Hundred each."

"I like your rates," I said. "Now, what about Doris Conlon?"

"The stripper? Yeah, Charley done her."

"For Bowman?"

"Yeah. She coulda caused him big trouble."

"You were there?"

"I drove, waited outside the motel. Charley was supposed to leave it like suicide."

"Swell job," I muttered, "a blind man could see through it." I gestured at the empty revolver. "You took a shot at the senator."

"Huh? Not me."

"No? Charley?"

"Don't think so, didn't say."

I walked to his feet, slammed the tire iron against a shoe sole. Red howled and flexed the leg so he could reach the foot but I rapped the knee and he yelled again. "Lie and you die," I snarled. "The senator wasn't hit so no big deal, I just want to know."

"No, man, Jesus, stop hurting me," he pleaded.

"Who killed Bowman?"

"Dunno," he choked, massaging his knee. For a few moments I watched the hired killer, revolted by his casual cold-bloodedness. "When's Charley coming?"

"Huh?"

"You heard me. He'd want to be here for the fun, so when is he meeting you? What time?"

When he said nothing I tapped the injured knee. "If I don't kill you I can cripple you for life. What time, Red?"

"Midnight—don't hit me no more."

"Why wasn't he with you at my place?"

"We had a bet."

"What kind of bet?"

"I said I could take you alone, get you here."

"And you did. How much was the bet?"

"Fifty bucks."

"Big money."

"Yeah. An' he was with his girlfriend."

"So he's coming to check on the arrangement?"

"He don't take nothing for granted, less'n he sees it."

"Careful fellow," I said disgustedly. "Then the two of you would haul my body to the river. Right?"

"Yeah, you're a pretty heavy guy. Jus' gettin' you in the car like to broke my back."

"What a shame," I said. "Okay, when we hear his car we'll trade places. You'll be standing with your twenty-buck shooter like you had me covered. I'll be lying down and I'll have you both covered. Just to even things a bit I'll put a cartridge in the cylinder. You won't know how many clicks it takes to fire and neither will I—but life's a gamble."

"Russian roulette. Why?"

"Adds a little suspense. Of course, if you point at me and pull the trigger I'll blow you away. Clear?"

"You're crazy," he said as I dropped a cartridge into the cylinder. I snapped it in place and spun it before setting the piece on the fender. His gamble was one chance in six. Fair odds for a killer.

Time: 11:51. Nine minutes to Charley—if he was prompt. Clouds eased past the moon's gray face. I looked down at Red Stonefield and wondered why I didn't zap him now instead of waiting for Big Charley. But time and place were right to bag them both, an opportunity that might never again come. If I left now I'd have Charley to deal with later in less favorable circumstances. Charley killed poor Doris Conlon and deserved to die. As his driver, Stonefield was guilty of felony murder and God knows what other dark crimes. He, too, had to be stopped.

Overhead, the distant whisper of a jet making for Reagan Airport. I looked up, trying to make out its running lights, but it was too far away. Careless on my part because my brief inattention made Red suddenly brave. From his knees he launched his body at me, arms thrusting, hands clawing, grunting as he grabbed my left ankle. I kicked his face, then clipped his head with my Beretta. Moaning, he dropped flat. I stepped aside and rapped the base of his spine with the tire iron. He screamed, arched his back and vomited. I snapped, "As you were, Private Stonefield. Try anything else and I'll pop your skull. I said, move."

Groaning, he crawled backward. "Far enough," I told him. "You were ugly before, but all that puke is disgusting. What'll Charley think?" I eased back on the fender, glanced at my watch and listened for the sound of a car but all I could hear was the river running by. The river that was to have taken my body and dropped it over the falls. Red was scouring his face with his coat sleeve. I laughed at him. "If a couple guys can't have fun on a great night like this, why're we here?"

"Fuck you," he spat.

"Not tonight, not ever. Where's your partner in crime?"

No response. As I stared at him I felt an overwhelming urge to kill him and have done with it. But then the charade I planned for Charley's benefit wouldn't play—and Red wouldn't be able to take his one-in-six chance to kill me. I said, "You weigh what, two hundred, two twenty? Bet I can drag you to the river without Charley's help, so I'll tell you this: one of you's not going to leave here alive. Feeling lucky, Red?"

He shook his head.

"Right answer. You're a lifetime loser." My watch showed midnight. Charley still balling his broad? No, even sex wouldn't keep him from the scene he expected to find here at the river's edge; he'd pay Red fifty for doing all the work. Or maybe not.

I reached into the BMW and put on the low lights so Charley could spot them from the road. Listened.

Then, faint as the hum of a distant bee came the sound of a car. My muscles tightened. I jacked a shell into the Beretta chamber and thumbed off the safety. "Time to trade places," I said. "You up, me down. When Charley gets here it's best you say nothing, just let him see you've got me covered."

Slowly, painfully he got to his feet, came toward me until I tossed him the revolver. He looked at it and his face twisted.

"Your chance to live," I said and walked past him to the edge of the car's light. Then I sat down. Red was still studying his revolver. I said, "If you haven't spotted the bullet it's too late."

The car sound was louder. A cold haze seemed to have settled around us. I pointed the Beretta at Red, held his chest in my sights, longed to press the trigger. Then my gaze lifted and I saw a dim glow on Canal Road. Heart pounding, I licked my lips. "When he gets here," I said, "you don't move. I'll do the talking."

"Yeah, you're a great talker, you prick," he retorted. "What's gonna happen?"

"Take it easy, you'll find out." From the road above the car lights were brighter, engine sound louder. I eased back on my elbows, pistol against my thigh. Night chill seemed to grip my bones. Why was I doing this? This was crazy. I had a life to live, a sailboat to board, a woman to love . . .

The oncoming car slowed, then turned off the road and its headlights fanned above us. Then it rumbled down and stopped beside my BMW, the lights still on.

Red's shoulders jerked. "Cover me," I said, and then Charley was out of his car, pistol in hand. To Red he said, "Damn if you didn't do it. Owe you fifty."

"Don't pay him," I called. "He ratted on you, spilled about Doris, said he'd testify you killed her."

"Lies," Red yelled, "don't believe him," and swiveled the revolver to point at Charley, who stopped in his tracks and stared at his partner. "You draw on me. *Me?* You snitched me out? Why, you—" His pistol lifted menacingly. "I'll show you—" Red's revolver clicked on an empty chamber. Charley fired, the round missed, Red pulled his trigger again and the revolver bucked in his hand. Hit, Charley fell backward as finger reflex fired another round. Impact dropped Red to his knees, clawing at the spurting wound in his throat. Then his hand fell away and he sprawled forward.

I got up and looked over at Charley. He was still alive but his shirt seemed drenched with red paint, and hoarse mushy sounds came spasmodically from his throat. I knelt beside him and said, "Make your last breaths count for something. There's a widow who needs to know how her husband died and why he was killed." I paused and saw his gaze fixed on me. "Who killed Harlan Bowman, Charley? You? Red?"

His head moved slowly, negatively. "Don' know," he managed to gasp, the effort coating his lips with dark foam. He coughed and one hand crept toward his dropped pistol. I moved the pistol away. "The truth, Charley," I said but he seemed not to hear me. Bending close to his face, I asked, "Bostick the Pit Boy. Did you kill him?"

His eyes were blank, without depth, and I knew what that meant.

"Bostick?" he whispered.

"Yeah, Andy Bostick." I pressed the right carotid behind his jaw, barely felt a pulse. His body shuddered as a red stream poured from his mouth. He was coughing and wheezing as he drowned in his own blood. I wanted him alive to answer me, but the decision wasn't mine, and as I watched his eyes they rolled back and he was gone.

Shaken, I got up. Two men down and I hadn't had to fire a shot. Gripping my pistol I thumbed on the safety and walked to my car, gripped the door while my body shook. No moon now and I'd seen enough. My face was cold with perspiration. I glanced at the death scene illumined by Charley's headlights, went to his car and clicked them off. Then I got into my BMW and started the engine. As I gripped the wheel I noticed my bloody wrists, dark stains on shirt cuffs. The stench of my own vomit rose from behind me. I turned on the air conditioning and rolled down my window to gulp fresh air. Then I backed around and drove up the incline to the road. Headed back toward Washington.

I drove unsteadily, mind not focused on the road but on what I'd just lived through. I slowed to thirty, made it past the university and took the bridge turnoff onto M Street. Its bright lights pained my eyes. I turned north to Q Street and followed it to my drive.

For a while I sat there, weak and disoriented as I remembered Red's sudden attack, and then I got out of the car and walked to the front of my house, Beretta in hand.

Inside, I headed for the bar, poured a tumbler of scotch and downed it in two long pulls that left me coughing and dizzy with head pain. Upstairs I swallowed three pain pills (Not to Be Taken with Alcohol) and got into a hot tub.

After a few minutes the warmth relaxed my body and the pills began working. Pain went away, I felt drowsy, closed my eyes and fell asleep.

When I woke it was four o'clock and the water around me was cold. Chilled, I put on a terry cloth bathrobe and got into bed. Slept as soundly as though I hadn't come near death or caused the deaths of two murderous thugs who deserved to die.

TWENTY-TWO

WHEN I WOKE again it was afternoon—1:37—and I was hungry. I was also in pain from my battered skull, so I popped another pair of Percodans, cleaned and bandaged the wrist abrasions, and settled down at the kitchen table with a cup of fresh coffee fortified with rum. I supplemented it with toaster waffles and syrup, and gradually began feeling human. After a while I phoned the office and asked Mrs. Altman if any pressing business was scheduled the rest of the day.

She cited a four o'clock consultation and reminded me that Burton Michaels was in Wilmington establishing VanAlstine's corporate shield. "Also," she continued, "Mrs. VanAlstine wanted you to lunch with her in their Madison suite but I said you were out of town and unavailable."

"She's a persistent baggage," I remarked, "and I appreciate you fending her off."

"Part of my job," she said, "and have you seen the morning paper?"

"Haven't got around to it. Anything special?"

"It concerns Senator Bowman. Governor Green announced formation of an exploratory committee to advance the senator's nomination for the presidency."

So Green had accelerated his plan. Was that good or bad for Alison?

"Mr. Bentley? Are you there? Mr. Bentley?"

"Here and in a state of shock," I said. "Anything else?"

"The committee is being chaired by the governor's daughter, Sybil. They appeared together on noon TV to make the announcement and answer media questions." She paused. "What do you think of that?"

"I think the senator would make an excellent president. God knows she can't do worse than the last few we've had."

"You can say *that* again. Will you keep the four o'clock appointment?"

"Definitely." With another Percodan to steady me.

"Oh, I should have mentioned Arthur Jensen's call. He'd like to speak with you at your convenience."

"Did he say about what?"

"No, sir."

"Give me his number, please, I'm too lazy to look it up." Actually, my vision wasn't focusing well and anyway, I hated the directory's minuscule print.

Arthur said, "Glad you called back. What do you think about Green's announcement concerning the senator?"

"I'm just out of bed," I told him, "haven't had a chance to lucubrate."

"You had no advance notice?"

"Not from the senator."

"Hmm. Sean Elkins wants to know if there's any chance of getting a statement from the senator."

"Not immediately but since she'll have to respond eventually I suggest Sean draft up a brief statement saying the senator is surprised and flattered by the Green's initiative, which was taken without her knowledge. On her return from mourning seclusion the senator will respond more fully concerning the possibility of a national candidacy. Meanwhile, she intends to meet her senatorial responsibilities as the voters have every right to expect."

"Hell, that's the statement right there. Mind repeating it to Sean?"

"If she'll consider it merely a draft suggestion. I can phone Alison for approval."

"I'll put Sean on."

So I repeated my thoughts to the public relations specialist, and asked her to fax me a copy of the proposed press release. "Of course, Mr. Bentley," she said. "I had no idea the senator was entertaining the idea of a run, but that's Washington, isn't it?"

"Definitely. And I'm far from sure she's receptive to the idea."

"Oh?" She sounded disappointed. "And Governor Green is such a powerful political figure. Has his daughter Sybil been politically active before?"

"Probably in her father's campaigns but I really don't know."

"Well, what's important is the senator. I really would like to get the senator's statement on TV and in the news mags, so after she approves the release I'll cover the field."

"I'll be in touch," I said and hung up.

Even were Alison to approve it, formation of an exploratory committee wouldn't require her to resign her Senate seat. The committee could solicit contributions and conduct voter polls without her approval. Friends of Eisenhower had done it and pressured him into making the run. It was axiomatic that if the votes were there, the money would be there too. Clearly, Sean Elkins would love to be part of a Bowman presidential campaign, but I was uneasy about it. Abel Green's interest had surfaced but I still wondered what lay behind it. By endorsing Alison so far in advance of the nominating convention the governor had broken party tradition and discouraged other potential candidates. Heavy-handed action by Green that a lot of party loyalists were bound to resent. Still, he was a skilled maneuverer, a shark familiar with every rock, current, and shoal within his feeding zone.

As I dressed I began wondering if Green had had Harlan Bowman removed from the equation because he would have been an undesirable consort for a presidential candidate. Given Green's intimate knowledge of Bowman it was a possibility, even if remote. On the other hand, why have Bowman's corpse left where its location would inevitably raise uncharitable questions about his wife? The two theories were incompatible.

After leaving the house I drove to Slick's Kleen-Kar Emporium to have the rear carpets cleansed of vomit and the interior treated with new-car scent. A wash was also in order, but in view of the time I left the BMW and taxied to the office.

Sean Elkin's fax was on my desk. I read it and thought the response appropriately noncommittal. I phoned Sean and said I'd try getting the senator's okay before day's end. She thanked me, and I dialed Pat Moran's office. His secretary said she would try to reach his beeper and have him phone me. Was the matter urgent? Not especially, I told her, but I wanted to see him before I left town.

Head pain was returning, so I swallowed another Percodan before receiving my four o'clock client. We were discussing an estate and inheritance tax problem when Mrs. Altman came in and placed a note before me. *Gov. Green on line 3.* "Tell him I'll get back to him," I said, and continued with my client.

Before calling the governor I placed a radiophone call to Hod's boat, and heard his voice four minutes later. After an exchange of pleasantries I asked if they were aware of Governor Green's announcement. He said they hadn't heard a word and did I want to talk with Alison? I did, and presently her voice said, "Steve? Everything okay?"

"Personally, yes, but Abel Green's gotten ahead of the loop and put you in a minor bind." I described his endorsement announcement, heard her mutter disapprovingly, and said, "Let me read you a response Sean's prepared for the media. It won't be issued unless you approve."

"I'm listening."

After I'd read the release she was silent for a few moments before saying, "Can't hurt, can it? And it gives me time to think about the implications. Do you approve?"

"I do."

"Then so do I. Now, to a far more important matter. When are you coming?"

"I can be in St. Thomas tomorrow. If that's convenient for Hod."

"I'll put him on."

Hod said, "We're just off St. Croix, Steve. Make St. Thomas easy tomorrow. I'll dock at Charlotte Amalie and wait for you."

"Good. Bring you anything?"

"No, we can get supplies while we're waiting for you. We're all anxious to see you. Here's Alison."

She said, "I'm having a marvelous time and it'll be even better with you aboard."

"Honey, can't wait to get there. Regards to Mattie."

I asked Mrs. Altman to get me a seat on a morning flight to St. Thomas, said I'd be gone about a week, and to keep my whereabouts quiet. She said she understood. I called Sean Elkins, okayed the press release, then took a call from Pat Moran.

He said he was driving south on the Baltimore–Washington Parkway and could be at my office in half an hour if that's what I wanted. "That's what I want, because it's too hot for the airwaves."

"See you shortly."

While Mrs. Altman was talking with the travel agency I placed a call to Governor Green. After a short wait I heard his hearty voice saying, "I haven't been able to contact the senator, but I thought you might."

"Sorry, Governor, no recent contact."

"Then you don't know her reaction to my announcement?"

"No, but I'd assume she'd basically welcome it. Have you talked with her personal representatives—Arthur Jensen and Sean Elkins?"

"No, I haven't, but I'll do that now."

"Anyway, she'll be impressed by your daughter's heading the committee."

"You like that, huh?"

"Brilliant," I said. "Congratulations to you both."

That charade concluded, I noticed Burton Michaels waiting and took his report on the day at Wilmington. "Got all the papers here," he said. "Just need VanAlstine's notarized signature. The corporate name is Pergret—Perry plus Gretta."

"Got it. Tell you what—see if the fortunate couple can sign today. If so, take Mrs. Altman along to notarize everything."

"I'll do it," he said, and looked at his watch. I said, "I'm leaving town for about a week, so you're in charge of the office. If anything really urgent comes up Mrs. Altman can get in touch with me. Okay?"

"Sure." He sucked in a deep breath. "I appreciate your confidence, and I'll do my best."

"I know you will. Now make that call to the Madison."

I was straightening my desk when Pat Moran sauntered in, closed the door and sat down. "I'm listening," he said with a broad grin. I went to the cellarette and poured two glasses of Solera and gave him one. "After five," I said, "so this is legal."

"Wouldn't have it any other way. Now, what's too hot for the airwaves?"

"Remember Harlan Bowman's discarded mistress?"

"Doris Conlon, sure." He sat forward, interested.

"And the two hooligans who braced me on the highway?"

"Yeah. What were their names? I disremember."

"Winkowski and Stonefield."

He nodded. "Ran their rap sheets for you. What about them?"

"I encountered them last night, never mind the circumstances, and Stonefield blabbed, said Big Charley killed Doris, hit paid for by Bowman."

"Be damned!"

I downed the rest of my sherry. "Stonefield claimed he was wheelman, waited outside the motel while Winkowski shot her. Charley took offense at that, shot Stonefield who shot back. Bottom line: two bodies between Canal Road and the river. They been found yet?"

He shook his head slowly, said, "Not so's I heard," and drained his glass. "I guess you were there."

"Sal's in the whorehouse, Pa's in jail, and I'm the one to tell the tale."

"Ain't you the one? I'm supposed to do something with the information?"

I shrugged. "Not sure anything useful can be done with it. Doris was killed with the gun found with her body so there's no point in comparison firings with the dead thugs' guns. You could phone an anonymous tip but the cops could never prove their culpability."

"And Bowman, the guy who hired them, is likewise cold meat." He shook his head.

"They got a hundred each," I added.

"They worked cheap," he remarked and held out his empty glass. Burton Michaels knocked on the door and looked in. "On our way," he said. "Have a good trip," and closed the door.

Pat said, "Leaving town?"

"For a while."

He smiled. "I see you got wrist bandages."

"You're observant. Beyond that, no comment."

"I understand. Tomorrow I'm supposed to get the Jag back from the body shop. I keep it out of sight until instructed otherwise."

"That's the drill."

"Any idea who punctured the panel?"

"My hunch is the same guy who shot Bostick, but that remains a mystery."

"What do you think of the governor boosting Senator Bowman for president?"

"I think he has his reasons. Did it without getting the senator's okay."

"Think she has a chance?"

"To become president? Sure, why not? Question is, does she want it."

"What's your hunch?"

"Too early to tell."

"At least she won't have to drag around that husband—dead weight. Uh—no pun intended."

"Liar. I haven't seen a bill lately."

"We'll remedy that now." He brought out billing sheets and gave them to me. I said, "After I eliminate padding I'll have Mrs. Altman cut you a check. Mail it tomorrow."

"Appreciate it." He hesitated before saying, "Since there's a chance the senator might go national, there's more baggage she ought to cut loose from."

"Oh? Like what?"

"Like Sybil Green." He seemed reluctant to go on, finally saying, "Oh, hell, might as well out with it." He sucked in a deep breath. "As you know, while I was checking into Bostick the name of Sybil emerged, so I decided to check her background as well—figuring there might be an explanation of how and why she got involved with the Pit Boy."

"Was there?"

"Sort of." He swallowed. "The lady has what used to be called a checkered past. Examples of aberrant behavior from first grade on; biting and kicking classmates, poking them—and teachers—with pencils and pens. In high school, she cut a girl classmate, but Dad's influence got it hushed up. In college she tried to run over a girl she thought was stealing a boyfriend. Again, Dad stepped in and cooled things off. But not before the Reisterstown cops had her examined by a shrink."

"Who found—what?"

"Sociopathic tendencies, paranoia. Voluntary institutionalization." He shrugged. "Nothing for the past couple of years. Downtime. When she got involved with Bostick. Maybe she'll never again harm someone, but the senator's future enemies would love to publicize Sybil's past and suggest the senator approved of all those things: and was soft on crime."

I nodded. "All that is good to know, Pat. By helping her dad politically maybe she's hit the sawdust trail to righteousness."

He stood up. "Maybe. Don't count on it. Have a nice vacation, Steve. By the look of you you need it."

"I do," I agreed. We shook hands and he left the office.

I was reviewing Pat's charges, when I saw a messenger enter the outer office. A girl wearing a cop-style cap and military-style uniform. Curls peeped under the cap. "Mr. Bentley?"

"Yep."

"Tickets for you, please sign." She gave me an airline envelope, and held the clipboard for my signature. "Much obliged," I said, and tipped her five dollars. "Oh," she said, "that isn't necessary, really." She blushed. An attractive, good-looking kid.

"Haven't heard that in years," I said, "so here's another five for restoring my faith in human nature."

Her blush was even deeper but she tucked the bill in a pocket with the other. "Thank you, sir. You're very generous."

"I appreciate prompt courteous service. Good night, miss."

"Good night, and have a nice trip."

After she left I closed up the office and took a taxi to Slick's, where I recovered my shiny, new-smelling car. From there I drove home, took a Percodan and turned on the local TV news.

Sho' nuf, there was photo coverage of the double death scene taken from a helicopter: Charley's car, two bodies invisible under plastic sheets. The reporter said the bodies had been spotted around noon by a traffic chopper and the police called in. Initial determination was that the two men had killed each other and the reporter hinted at a possible suicide pact. No names had yet been attached to the victims, since several different identification documents were found on each. The final shot showed the bodies being loaded in a fire-and-rescue van for delivery to the D.C. morgue. Next segment: a molester apprehended outside an elementary school . . . I built myself a drink, feeling very damn lucky I'd survived the night. Presently a Capitol Hill TV reporter reprised Governor Green's announcement and showed a still photo of Senator Bowman while the reporter read her comments on the endorsement. Then I flicked off the TV and considered inviting Lauri Nathanson to dinner on neutral turf.

She didn't answer her condo phone, so I left the invitation on her machine, assuming she was out for the evening. After that I walked down to M Street and had dinner at Chez Grand-Mère, a small inexpensive French restaurant, walked back home, and packed a bag for the morning flight.

The prospect of being with Alison again erased my moodiness, and after setting the alarm I got into bed and enjoyed eight hours untroubled sleep.

TWENTY-THREE

DURING THE SAN Juan stopover I didn't leave the plane. Heat waves rose from the tarmac and I was content to stay in the air-conditioned cabin and sip my second colada of the day. The sweet rum mix was a lot tastier than the Percodans I'd been gobbling for two days, and suppressed skull pain equally well.

A few minutes after takeoff I spotted St. Thomas in the distance, and as we neared it the island looked like a green jewel in a warm tourmaline sea. Against its bone-white sands the lazy Caribbean rollers were wisps of cotton, and as the plane dropped lower I could see the spine of mountains topped by Signal Hill, the rusty tracery of roads cut through heavy jungle, and the pink and white buildings of Charlotte Amalie sprawling to the west of the landing strip.

Ten years ago I'd come to help millionaire entrepreneur Vernon "Sonny" Tyner establish his Coco Isle development by taking advantage of the Virgin Islands special tax exemptions. On that trip I'd stayed at the Lodge, Sonny and Allegra's ten-room guesthouse and found myself in the middle of a domestic dispute arising from Sonny's infatuation with a light-skinned calypso dancer, Reba Royce. I remembered her sultry beauty and her murder, for which Sonny had been charged. He hadn't done it, of course, but it cost me some pain and a lot of hangovers from drinking Cruzan shinny at the Normandie, the Gate, and other gathering places where I circulated among Cha Chas and gathered enough information to nail the killer and free Sonny. While doing all that I'd become attracted to a red-haired Irish beauty named Kelly Martin but she'd gone off with a wealthy yachtsman who made her an offer she couldn't refuse—marriage. Then Sonny and Allegra reconciled (Reba no longer a disruptive factor) and departed for a long second honeymoon in Europe. Soon their lodge was sold and demolished to make way for a fifty-room hotel run by a Spanish hotel chain.

A few months after I got back to Washington a letter from Chamonix told me the Tyner reconciliation hadn't lasted—Allegra had found a special guy and gone off to live with him in Provence. Sonny didn't sound too upset, and when last heard from his address was a P.O. box in Estoril near Lisbon. Construction on his Coco Isle development had been leveled by a hurricane, but Sonny collected project insurance and sold the land and foundations to a Japanese consortium eager for a foothold in the U.S. Virgins.

So, I reflected, I had some experience of St. Thomas and a number of its denizens, not all good, not all bad, but I wasn't going to visit the Gate or the Normandie even if they'd survived the hurricanes. Too many memories. I'd let Kelly slip away because I wasn't ready for marriage, and later when I was I made a poor selection.

As the plane dropped into the landing pattern I could see Frenchtown and the West India docks, a string of cruise ships, and a scattering of sailboats offshore. When we touched down, the jet brakes reversed thunderously, and the plane slowed and veered toward the arrival gate.

Hod and Alison were waiting behind the barrier, he in shorts, tank top, and deck shoes. In his early sixties, Hod had a spare sinewy frame topped with a pleasant face tending to roundness. His remaining hair was short and gray, brushed forward. Alison wore an island-made sugar-sack top, sailing cap, bleached denim shorts, and rope-soled alpargatas. We hugged and exchanged a discreet kiss before I shook Hod's deeply tanned hand. He grabbed at my bag but I said "unh-unh," and carried it to a waiting cab. Hod sat in front, Alison beside me. We held hands, and she said, "Mattie's at the boat inventorying stores and sort of guarding everything."

Hod nodded. "Normal amount of waterfront thievery, but the real hazard is pirates. All the Coast Guard does is warn owners not to hire unknowns as crew. Every year some pretty grisly things happen."

"Sounds like Washington. You have weapons aboard?"

He shrugged. "Shotgun and rifle, the rifle's for sharks. No handguns—Mattie's averse to firearms."

"Basically," Alison said, "I am, too, but I can certainly recognize necessary exceptions."

"Can I quote you to the NRA?"

"Devil," she said. "You *would* bring that up."

Hod said, "How much of a stir did the governor's endorsement of Alison create?"

"Local stations covered it and I didn't check the networks."

"Maybe it will all die away," Alison suggested.

"Maybe."

Then we were pulling in to Yacht Haven, where we got out and walked along the pier to where the *Mattie* was tied up. "Looks the same, Hod," I said admiringly as I scanned the sixty-eight-foot length of his broad-beamed shallow-draft auxiliary ketch. "But those big diagonal blue stripes won't be welcomed at the Corinthian."

"True. But they're distinctive enough to maybe deter pirates—or so I thought when I had them painted on."

"Makes sense," I acknowledged, "safety first." And then Mattie Gurney emerged from the cabin. "Hi, Steve," she called, and stepped on deck where I joined her for a hug and a kiss. Like her husband she was wearing a tank top, shorts, and deck shoes. Also, like Hod, she was tanned walnut brown, and her short hair showed sun-bleached highlights. "Steve, we've been having hell's own time with this lady's pining for you."

"Oh, Mattie, don't talk nonsense." Alison blushed furiously.

I said, "Been doing some pining myself."

"So much you slashed your wrists?"

"No comment," I replied. "Anything to drink aboard this derelict?"

"Only champagne," Mattie replied, "and it's plenty cold. C'mon down and we'll break out a bumper or two. Drink to capacity because it's tax free."

We filed down the steps into the main cabin, and there in the galley sink stood a bucket filled with ice and two large bottles of Veuve Cliquot. In the center of the cabin was a polished teak table with drop leaves. On either side, long transoms with sailcloth-covered cushions, convertible into bunks.

Mattie got chilled tulip glasses from the refrigerator while Hod popped a bottle, filled our glasses. Hod said, "Let's have a toast among friends."

"Honey, not one of your salacious ones," Mattie warned. "There's a lady present."

"Okay, okay, let's drink to Senator Bowman's successful candidacy for the presidency of the United States."

"And," added Mattie, "to loved ones left behind."

After sipping, Alison said, "I haven't any."

I said, "Nor I. So we'll also drink to the health and success of all Gurney children."

"Hear, hear." Hod grinned. "The ever tactful Bentley." He added more bubbly to our glasses, closed the cabin door and turned on the air conditioning. Almost at once, a cool breeze smote the back of my head. At approximately the spot where Red Stonefield had coshed me that unfortunate night. Mattie said, "Steve, we had lunch at the Red Cock Inn, but I brought sandwiches for you. Hungry?"

"Not yet, thanks, I sort of destroyed my appetite with a plastic airlines snack. Yech."

Taking my hand, Alison said, "I'm so glad you're here."

"Me, too," I replied, thinking, And glad to be alive. "These boat bums been treating you right?"

"Like royalty," she said, "and I guess that's because they regard you so highly."

Mattie said, "Nonsense. This tramp lawyer couldn't come aboard without your recommendation, Ali, and it's time he knew it." Then her face broke into a smile and she hugged Alison. "We think the two of you are just great. Hod, pop that other cork, will you? We'll finish that bottle and cast off, okay?"

Our glasses once again brimming, I said, "Mattie, if you haven't told Alison how the two of you came to be married, I wish you would. Not only a great story, but a recipe for a long, happy marriage."

Alison shook her head. "Haven't heard it, but now I'm eager."

Mattie set down her glass. "Okay, here goes. Fresh out of college—Goucher—I found work as secretary to Saul Steiner. I didn't like the salary and I certainly didn't like the hours, and I soon realized that to get ahead in Washington I needed more than a bachelor's degree in English literature. I liked the problem-solving aspect of the law—not the litigation—and thought I could do as well as some of the associates in Steiner's office. So I told my boss I was going to George Washington Law School as a night student and he could forget my working late—for which I wasn't paid, anyway." She picked up her glass, drank, and continued. "Toward the middle of my third year this fellow here joined Steiner's firm." She looked lovingly at her husband. "He was mature but not too mature, and serious, but not overly so if you get my meaning."

Alison said, "Sounds like this other fellow here." Her elbow jabbed me.

"Possibly." Mattie smiled. "Occasionally Hod and I had a quick dinner together and sometimes he'd walk me to class. But I spent weekends studying, time out only for church services, and finally I got my law degree. Saul hired me as an associate before I passed the Bars, and there I was, on an equal footing with these male associates—for all the good it did me." She gave her husband a dark glance. "Except that now I could go out evenings and Hod and I began dating."

Hod, who had been listening in silence, said, "It gets romantic now."

"By some definitions," Mattie said dryly, "if romantic means being grabbed in taxis and having to struggle free."

Hod smiled. "Gave me a hard time, folks, very hard."

"Even in the office he'd brush against me, grab a feel when he could, sneak a kiss and smear my lipstick."

Alison began laughing. "Assaulting your virtue."

"Exactly. Didn't take me much time as a lawyer to realize I was working under a glass ceiling, promotions limited, no chance at a partnership. So I told Saul I'd had enough, thanks and goodbye. He said he was sorry I was dissatisfied, but I'd divined the situation and he hoped I would be happier elsewhere."

Hod said, "Saul's never been a sensitive soul."

"What an understatement," Mattie said thinly. "So there I was cleaning out my desk, taking down my framed law degree, and sobbing like a fool when who walks by but Mr. Harris Gurney. He gives me a big handkerchief and tries to talk me into staying, but I was angry, Alison, pissed off at the world, and particularly at his law firm. I told him I was tired of fighting him off and if he wanted to stop playing grabass he could damn well marry me." She chuckled at the memory. "I spoke plainly in those days."

"Very plainly," her husband said, "even bluntly."

Alison asked, "So what happened then?"

"Hod seemed staggered. He left the office, I continued packing, and ten minutes later he came back and asked me to marry him." She paused. "As I've learned, he doesn't make impulsive decisions. Later he confessed he hadn't seriously considered marriage, but my plain speaking focused his attention."

"Sure did," Hod confirmed. "A week later we were married in Baltimore, and had our honeymoon in New York."

"Yes," she said, "a three-day theater weekend. I moved into his apartment, and when I found I was pregnant we bought our first house. Long story, good ending."

"A very good ending," Alison remarked, "and I'm glad you told me."

Mattie looked at the bulkhead chronometer. "All stores aboard, Captain," she said, "and with our crew complete it's time to get underway."

"Hearing and obeying," Hod responded, drained his glass and went up on deck. The rest of us followed and I noticed how efficiently Mattie disconnected the auxiliary power and water lines before casting off from the pier. Auxiliary engine running, Hod backed out and circled around for open water. Alison sat in the cockpit beside him and when course was set she took over the wheel, gaze on the compass gimbal.

In the cabin, Mattie was washing our glasses. "We're heading for St. Croix, put in for the night at Christiansted and move on tomorrow. Very leisurely, Steve, no one's in any hurry to get anywhere." She pointed forward. "Hod and I have the master cabin, Alison's to starboard, and you're across the passageway to port. I stowed your bag there. Open bar. I cook one hot meal a day, the rest is catch as catch can. Take off your jacket, get comfortable."

I did as bidden and went up on deck. To Alison, Hod said, "Keep her nose on the mark while Steve and I hoist some sail." Nodding, she said, "I love this, love all of it."

"Well," I remarked, "your great-great-grandfather was a notable sailor, so you've inherited his genes."

"I hope so," she said, "because now I want my own boat."

Hod and I put up jib, mainsail, and foresail and he showed Alison how to catch the prevailing breeze before cutting the auxiliary engine. Suddenly the boat was quiet, only the slap of canvas and the gentle swoosh of water against the hull. This was deepwater sailing as I remembered it. I sat on deck facing aft just forward of the cockpit, and watched Alison intent on the compass reading. We were sailing south, sun to starboard, wind from two points off the fantail. It blew her hair back from her forehead and she looked clear-eyed, young, and very vulnerable. In that moment I thought of all the complications knowing her had brought into my life, and all of them were erased from my mind. Because, I told myself, if I hadn't done what I did for her, who would have?

From beside Alison, Hod said, "I thought we'd continue down the Leewards, skipping here and there, maybe going as far as Grenada."

"Well," I said, "you know the islands, skipper, we're in your hands."

"I've got Loran and radios to the point I hardly need a chart. And there's an emergency beacon I can activate if we ever get in deep trouble."

Alison said, "I guess I'll have to learn about all that."

"Absolutely," I said, "if I'm to go sailing with you."

"This is such a beautiful boat, I wonder if I could find one like it."

"Similar, yes," Hod told her, "for about a million dollars. This ketch was built of Burma teak to Art Crimmins's specifications and named the *Traveler*. Art was the first of the extended cruise charter skippers and really established the business, which is why there's so much comfort built into the design." He looked at me. "Art built a second *Traveler* but it was stolen in Nassau and stopped months later off Cape Cod. The smugglers opened the seacocks so the Coast Guard wouldn't find the drugs it was loaded with, and the boat sank in a hundred fathoms. Still there." He shook his head. "Art built a third *Traveler* in Hong Kong, sailed it for a couple of years and sold it when he retired. So I was lucky to buy this boat, the original. I love it."

"So does the first mate," Mattie said, coming on deck. "With the children gone we don't really need the Washington house and I'm quite contented at sea. We have everything we need, specifically each other." She bent over and kissed Hod's bald spot. "You dear man," she added affectionately, then told him she'd supervise Alison while he took a break.

I followed Hod into the cabin where we shared a bottle of chilled Evian. He asked, "Any information on her husband's killer?"

"No, but the reward should encourage tipsters." I added more water to my glass. "Very confidentially I want to pass along information acquired privately the past few days. Your ears only, okay?"

"Okay."

"Last week a couple of thugs pulled me over on the road to

Dulles—I was meeting Alison's flight from Atlanta. Fortunately, I got the best of them and ruined their car. Three nights ago, one of them attacked me in my drive, tied me up and took me out Canal Road to a spot by the river. By the time his partner arrived, at midnight, I'd equalized the situation and provoked them into an argument during which they shot and killed each other."

"Good God!"

"Yeah. Before that I pressured my kidnapper into revealing they'd been hired by Harlan Bowman to rough me up on the highway, and he'd paid them to kill his ex-sweetie Doris Conlon. A hundred dollars each, blood money."

Hod shook his head. "I never cared for Harlan, but it's hard to see him as a murderer. Did his thugs kill him, too?"

"I don't think so, they had no reason to."

"Does Alison know this?"

I shook my head. "And I don't intend to tell her. She's gone through enough."

"Who else knows? Arthur Jensen?"

"No one except you. With both men dead there's no way of proving they killed Doris for Harlan. Just another unsolved murder."

"I see," he said thoughtfully. "So I guess that's how your wrists got to be bandaged."

"Scraped off some flesh shedding ropes. How does Alison feel about a presidential candidacy?"

"Sort of flattered by Green's endorsement, but apparently not very interested. How do you feel about it?"

"Whatever Alison wants is okay with me."

"Wouldn't interfere with any possible plans you might have concerning her?"

"Day at a time," I said. "I think she's a terrific lady but I'm not sure we could make a go of marriage. Particularly if she were to spend, say, a year and a half on the candidate road."

"She loves you, Steve. I'm sure she wants to marry you."

"She say that?"

"Not in so many words, but Mattie has a good sense of things, and told me." He looked away. "Francie Ballou's shadow still haunt-ing you?"

"Maybe," I said, "but that was really long ago. She's dead, the general's dead. . . ." I spread my hands. "Nothing left."

"Want my advice?"

"Of course."

"Then marry Alison, let the future take care of itself. As you say, she's a wonderful woman, and she deserves a guy like you."

I smiled. "Compliment appreciated."

"I don't give out many—I'm serious. You'd make a great couple. Don't let short-term concerns interfere with long-term hap-piness."

Alison came down the steps and said, "Interrupting some-thing? You guys look oh-so-serious."

"That's because we're discussing the one subject of para-mount interest to all true intellectuals." I looked at Hod, who grinned.

"And what is that, please?"

"Girls," I said. "In all their varied forms and guises."

"Oh, pooh." She picked up the water bottle and poured a glass for herself. I said, "Did you tell our hosts about the shot in the dark?"

"I did."

Hod said, "That's a strange one. No idea who fired at her?"

"None," I acknowledged, "but the door panel's been repaired. We have to settle for that."

Alison yawned. "Think I'll nap for a while, any objections?"

"None," Hod said, and I remarked that I was getting hungry and the sandwiches would be welcome. With maybe a bottle of Tuborg to wash them down.

So passed the afternoon, and as the sun lowered we made landfall on St. Croix dead ahead. Hod got on the radiophone and called the port captain for dockage space, frowned, and said, "Then we'll tie up to a buoy. A-six? About sunset. Thank you, Captain."

Mattie said, "That's okay, skipper, we'll dine ashore."

After tying up we took a harbor boat to the landing, and had a fresh seafood dinner in a portside tin-roofed shack near the old windmill recommended by another yachtsman. Two bottles of cold Chilean Riesling added to our enjoyment, and after stretching our legs on a walk outside the ancient fort, we headed back to the boat.

After coffee and Courvoisier on the fantail our hosts excused themselves in favor of bed, and Alison and I were alone in the starry night. She kissed my cheek and murmured, "You've been ignoring me ever since you arrived."

"Not so. Didn't want to give Hod and Mattie the right impression of our relationship." I drew her to me and kissed her lips long and meaningfully. "I've wanted you so," she whispered, "and my only question is, your place or mine."

"Choose."

"Mine."

So half an hour later when all was quiet below decks we entered her cabin and closed the door, undressed in the dark and made love in the narrow bunk. Afterward, she said, "If we can manage this every night I won't feel so nonessential to your life."

"Then tomorrow night, come visit me."

"I feel so wonderful, Steve, so complete. I don't want this to ever end."

"What about your career?"

"The nomination? It'll never happen."

"But if it does?"

"Would it make a big difference to you—about us?"

"I don't know," I said truthfully. "If it comes, it comes. We'll consider it then."

"I don't want it to be a problem between us."

"We won't let it," I told her. "Now go to sleep."

Hours later I tiptoed to my cabin across the passageway, and woke to the smell of bacon frying in the galley.

After a leisurely breakfast we got underway heading east by southeast toward Saba, a tiny island in the Dutch Antilles. A hundred and thirty miles distant, Hod informed us, so we'd sail all night if that was agreeable, taking turns at the wheel. Alison said, "You'd really trust me to stay on course?"

"Why not?" Mattie asked, "You're now a qualified watch

stander," and Alison looked doubtfully at me. I said, "You're getting the best possible seafaring education."

"Well, if you think I can manage . . ."

"Of course you can," Hod said reassuringly.

"But if the wind freshens?"

"Break me out and I'll change sail setting. Don't worry about it."

So the day and night passed uneventfully, and before dawn we tied up at one of the permanent offshore buoys. Slept through the morning, and took the skiff ashore after lunch. From the narrow shoreline we took a hiking trail up the steep mountainside through dense tropical vegetation: ferns, giant elephant ears, lianas, banana and mango trees, and wild orchids. We paused to sample small sweet bananas before reaching the top of Mount Scenery, and rested there before descending by another trail.

Snorkelers and scuba divers were working from other boats in our area. One swam over to us, offered a large snapper in exchange for a bucket of ice. Mattie cleaned and stowed it in the refrigerator for the night's dinner. Strolling near the bow with me, Alison said, "This is a wonderfully simple life. Can't say I never imagined it, but the experience is something else." She sighed. "If I could have a month of this every year I'd never burn out."

"In reality you're pretty much your own boss, and you don't have to come this far from Washington. Keep a boat at Fort Lauderdale and take a long weekend around the Bahamas."

"You'd be with me?"

"Only if asked."

"I don't want to be with anyone but you."

TWENTY-FOUR

FROM ONE ISLAND to the next our routine was pretty much the same. Tie up or anchor, spend time ashore hiking or shopping, make love at night. After Saba we cruised to St. Kitts, then Nevis and Antigua, each island with its own history, identity, and special attractions. We reached Antigua's capital town St. John's, after dark and found the port closed. Hod steered a few miles north to Runaway Bay, a long sheltered harbor, where we dropped the hook for the night. Coming in, we spotted two powerboats, one rigged for game fishing, the other apparently nothing more than a pleasure craft; each was at least a hundred yards from the *Mattie*.

"They're close enough," Hod remarked. "I'm not in the mood to lay out sugar and beer."

"They won't bother us," said Mattie, "I'm sure. Anyway, I'm too tired to cook a real meal so you're getting soup and sandwiches."

"Perfect," Alison said, "if you'll let me make the sandwiches."

So we ate on the fantail, clustered around the cockpit, listening to island music on the FM radio. Both powerboats left harbor, and after a while Hod said, "For your historical information Lord Horatio Nelson hove in to what became known as English Harbour, British naval headquarters in this part of the world. That was some two hundred years ago, and natives say they see Nelson's ghost stalking the old fortifications around Shirley Heights. On special nights, of course." He smiled conspiratorially.

"What special nights?" Alison asked.

"Every night the moon is green." He stretched and yawned. "If we're going to exert ourselves walking around town tomorrow I suggest we get a good night's sleep. It's a long haul to Montserrat, our next port of call."

"Mattie, you go along now," Alison ordered. "I'll do what little clean-up there is."

"Well, if you really don't mind . . ."

"Insist on it," she said firmly. "Good night to you both. Sleep well."

They went below and from the cockpit I turned off running and mast lights. Now it was dark all around except for occasional streaks of phosphorescence in the water. The boat tugged gently at its cable as the tide began to turn. Silence prevailed except for the occasional sounds of Alison in the galley. Comfortable domestic sounds. I stretched back on the transom and looked up at the clear sky dominated by an almost full moon rising.

I must have dozed, because when I woke the cabin lights were out and the galley silent; Alison must have turned in. Well, I'd be along soon, I thought, but then I heard a bumping sound amidships, port side. Could be driftwood pushed by the tide, I told myself, but when I heard it again my muscles tensed.

Peeking above the cockpit coaming, I saw a man in swim trunks climbing over the gunwale, a machete clamped between his teeth. Gripping a stanchion, he pulled himself onto the deck and looked around. Both Hod's firearms were below deck, so I had nothing to fend him off with. Then I saw the short, stout marlin rod Hod kept on the cockpit bulkhead. I gripped it as the intruder took his machete in hand. To reach the cabin door he had to walk just forward of the cockpit and as he started he must have seen the rod's motion. Six feet away he froze, looked down at me, and expelled air in a breathy grunt. Moonlight showed the whites of his eyes as he slashed the machete at me. I jumped backward onto the cushion where I'd been lying and swung the rod at his head. He ducked and I missed. Again he slashed at me. I jabbed the rod in his gut, he bent over howling, and I whipped the hard bamboo against his right arm hoping to dislodge the machete. But he jerked upright and came at me again, stabbing the machete. With all my strength I slammed the rod across his face. Blood gushed from his smashed nose, he dropped to his knees, eyes rolling wildly, and sprawled on his back. Lay still.

Shakily, I grabbed the machete just as I saw a second man climb on deck. He took in the scene, face registering shock and disbelief, then he jerked a pistol from his trunks and pointed it at me. Before he could pull the trigger I threw the rod at him and when he jumped aside I flung the machete point first at his middle. He fired but the bullet went skyward. The pistol clattered on deck as he clenched the machete with both hands to draw it from his belly. He groaned, staggered backward and toppled over the side. I picked up his pistol and looked over. He'd fallen into the dory that brought them, body bowed backward across a wooden seat. I couldn't see the machete but I could see blood spurting from his belly. Abruptly it stopped and I realized he was dead, spine snapped by the fall.

I felt cold, rigid, but I forced myself to kick the first pirate's ribs. No reaction. I knelt beside him, pressed the carotid and felt nothing. Turning his head, I saw his nose had been flattened by the rod blow, forcing bone slivers into his brain.

I got up and looked around. Their boat was twenty or thirty yards off the stern. They'd come that close under power and I'd never heard them.

Cabin lights went on, Hod emerged from the cabin doorway and saw me. "I heard a shot," he said. "Everything okay? Or wasn't it a shot?"

"It was, and everything's far from okay."

He looked down, saw the body and gasped. "Pirates," I told him in a tight voice. "Other's in the dory." I gestured to port. Hod stepped around the body and looked over the side. "Good God, two of them!"

"Two," I repeated, "and if we're found with them we'll never leave Antigua."

Leaning against the mainmast, he breathed deeply. "You're right. Any ideas?"

"Try this. Dump this fellow in the dory and I'll row them to their boat over there. Stow them out of sight in the cabin and I'll swim back here."

In the moonlight his features were strained; he looked years older. "Then," he said huskily, "we'd better haul out of here."

"At flank speed," I added. "Island police can take their duties too damn seriously if money's involved."

"Yeah, every hand out, every hand against us." He turned from me. "No need for the ladies to know, you agree?"

I nodded. "What they don't know can't hurt any of us. Besides we don't want their psyches traumatized."

"How delicately you put it." His lips relaxed into a partial smile. "You're a cool cat, Steve. Never appreciated it until now."

I ignored the compliment and said, "There's the political fallout too. The tabloids would love to link our client to violence and murder. Even the suggestion would destroy her career."

"Unfortunately so."

"Okay, there's work to do." I pointed at the body. "Grab his shoulders, I'll take the feet."

So we dragged and lifted and flung him into the dory like a sack of grain. He landed on his evil partner and lay motionless. I stripped to my shorts, climbed down the side, unsnubbed the dory, and began rowing to their boat.

It was hard work fighting the current, and their powerboat was drifting slowly away, as they'd used only a drogue to keep it in position. The anchor cable was flemished on the foredeck.

Finally I made the dory fast to the boat's stern and began shoving their deadweight bodies aboard. They were slim, well-muscled

predators in their thirties, and they looked enough alike to be broth-
ers. When the slit belly gushed blood over me I fought off nausea
and levered both bodies down into the cabin. Then I eased back
on the railing and sucked deep breaths until my heart stopped
pistoning.

At the console I pressed the starter button and the engine
caught. I walked to the stern and freed the drogue line, watched it
vanish below like a long, white sea snake. I turned on the boat's running lights, and when the current swung the bow toward open
water I clutched forward, setting the throttle at 700 rpms by the
tachometer, enough speed to hold it steady for two or three miles. It
would run while fuel lasted or until it beached itself. By then, the
Mattie would be far away.

I dove over the stern and swam back to the *Mattie*, aided by
the current. The water was almost body temperature and when I
climbed on deck the blood had washed away. "Let's get out of
here," I said, and together we raised anchor, set jib and mizzen, and
began moving south to the harbor entrance. Hod had the helm, so I
went below and filled two glasses with dark rum, no ice. The raw
taste made me grimace but I downed half a glass before handing
Hod his bracer. He'd brought up a bathrobe and I put it on to ward
off chill from the freshening breeze.

After a long pull of rum he said, "Damn it, Steve, you should
have roused me, not done it all yourself."

"Don't grumble about it, Hod. There wasn't time."

"Well, there's time now. Tell me about it."

Small waves slapped the hull. Wind rippled and slapped the
canvas. We were running free and out of danger. I relaxed in the
cockpit beside him and said, "Once, Hod. I'll tell you once and never
again. From tonight on the subject is taboo. It happened, it's over
with and we're all alive." I finished my rum and described the action
sequence. No questions from Hod. But he said, "I really owe you,
Steve. For saving my life. Mattie's and Alison's."

"Hod, I wasn't exclusively saving your lives, I was concentrat-
ing on saving my own, that's the truth of it."

He shrugged. "You went up against two armed men with
nothing but that fishing rod."

"The bastard jumped me and the rod was handy. I'm grateful it was there."

"Yeah. I'm going to keep it as a lucky piece. And stash a real weapon topside."

"As far as the ladies are concerned, we decided on an early start to Montserrat. That's our cover story."

"Thank God those pirates didn't get below with their damned weapons." He shook his head. "Now we know firsthand these waters aren't always peaceful." He said something else, but his voice seemed to be coming from far away, fading into silence. By then my eyes were closed. I stretched out on the transom and drifted off while Harris Gurney, Esquire, guided us through the night.

TWENTY-FIVE

WE PUT IN at Montserrat only long enough to take on potable water and recharge batteries. The air was still laden with dust and corrosive ash from volcanic eruption and not many natives were visible around the port. Hundreds had been evacuated during the worst of the eruption. No steel band music greeted us, and there was little joy to be seen on the faces of those who stayed.

From there we called at Guadeloupe and Dominica and decided to skip the French island of Martinique in favor of British St. Lucia. Hod calculated a twelve-hour run with favoring winds, so we decided to share three-hour watches until landfall.

Halfway through second watch, Mattie at the helm, Hod took

a radio call and looked over at where Alison and I were playing backgammon. "For you," he told her. "Arthur Jensen."

With a questioning glance at me she got up and took the receiver. "Yes, Arthur," she said, "this must be important." And then listened in silence. Finally she said, "Thank you. I'll let you know what we decide." and replaced the receiver. "Well," she said to us, "Arthur wants me to come back to Washington. He said there was a significant development concerning Harlan's murder, and I ought to be there."

Hod asked, "Did he say what it is?"

She shook her head. "Said it was too sensitive for radio transmission."

"Did he connect it to the reward offer?"

"No." She looked at me. "What do you think?"

"I trust Arthur's judgment."

Hod said, "So do I." He went to the chart table and checked our course, beckoned us over. Pointing, he said, "Castries, the capital, is on the northwest of the island, but the Vieux Port airport is at the south end. I suggest we put in at Castries, spend the evening at La Toc, a really superior resort, and let the hotel's travel service make your flight arrangements." He glanced at me. "I'm assuming you're leaving with Alison."

I nodded. "We've been enjoying your hospitality nearly two weeks, Hod, and we pretty much agreed St. Lucia would end the cruise for us."

"Alternatively," Hod said, "we could put in at Vieux Fort and be near the airport. But then you wouldn't see La Toc and enjoy it's cuisine—which I look forward to."

"Then we'll have a party," Alison announced. "My treat."

In late afternoon Alison and I cleared ship and took a jitney up to the hotel. We signed for adjoining rooms, and while a courteous native bellboy was taking Alison to hers I made arrangements with the maitre d' for our festive table. And before the travel office closed I got tickets to Washington, with a connection at Miami, leaving St.

Lucia on the morning flight. The agent said, "A hotel car will take you to the airport. It leaves here at eight-thirty. Trip to Hewanorra takes about an hour."

"To where?"

The agent smiled. "Hewanorra is the airport's official name. The hotel dining room serves breakfast beginning at seven."

I thanked him, took our tickets and let the bellboy show me to my room. Inside, I unpacked and hung my travel suit in the bathroom, expecting shower steam to unwrinkle it after two weeks' cramped stowage.

The hot shower was luxurious after the boat's bathing limitations. I shaved, dried off, and stretched out on the large comfortable bed. Knocking on the connecting door roused me, and when I opened it there was Alison in a fluffy hotel bathrobe, champagne bucket and glasses in hand. Kissing her I said, "Back to civilization," and popped the cork.

"Yes, but I'm going to miss the *Mattie*. I've never had such a wonderful, relaxing time. I really want a boat, Steve." We drank together, and she said, "I want to do something for Hod and Mattie, any suggestions?"

"They won't expect anything," I told her, "but they'd appreciate a gesture." I paused. "We've drunk up most of their champagne. How about sending a couple of cases to the boat?"

"Great idea. Will you arrange it?"

"Gladly."

We didn't make love then, there wasn't time because the Gurneys were joining us at seven for cocktails on the poolside patio. But we fooled around some, kissing and nuzzling while enjoying our Piper-Heidsieck. Then it was time to dress and meet our dinner guests.

Alison went to the patio table while I enlisted the concierge in delivering two cases of Heidsieck to the boat. The four of us had champagne cocktails, enjoying the tropical view and the sunset breeze until the maitre d' informed us our table was ready.

I'd ordered crown roast of lamb with assorted vegetables, beginning with shrimp cocktails and bouillabaisse. Between courses we danced to a small, unobtrusive orchestra. Dancing with me, Mattie said, "This is great, Steve. I'm going to make Hod take more overnights in port. The boat's fine but enough is enough. Here I can expand, mingle with actual people."

"We're so grateful for all you've done for us, the two of you."

"Believe me, you've been marvelous shipmates. So, let's cruise again next year. Okay?"

I nodded. "Assuming Alison can get away."

"Why couldn't she? Oh, you mean the political thing—the nomination."

"Yeah."

"I gather you're not enthusiastic."

"You pried it out of me—I'm not."

"Uh-oh, shoal waters. With Hod I don't have to be tactful so I've sort of forgotten how. 'Nuf said." She squeezed me, the music ended and we returned to our table.

Alison danced much more smoothly than Mattie, flawlessly following my sometimes uncertain lead, cheek against mine, and when I complimented her she said, "This is the first time we've danced together, and I love it."

"Around Washington there aren't many opportunities, mainly club Saturday nights and private parties. And we haven't had a club night together."

"Soon we'll be able to be in public wherever we want to go. I'd feel even more of a hypocrite if I extended mourning, so I'm officially ending it. Does that please you?"

"Of course it does." I nuzzled her temple. "Maybe we'll learn Harlan's killer has been arrested."

"Oh, I hope so. Not that he was a great guy but he didn't deserve to die so wretchedly." In a dark corner she nibbled my ear lobe. "I want to be alone with you, but that means the evening's end, and I don't want it to end."

"They're older folk," I said, "and probably tired from sailing so they can't last much longer. Why don't I order cognac and cappuccino?"

"Mm. Think they've enjoyed the party?"

"Every minute of it."

"And the good part is we'll see them back in Washington. Our circle of friends begins with them."

*   *   *

So after a leisurely intake of cognac—the Gurneys declining coffee in favor of sound sleep—the evening came to a close. And as we walked out to the jitney stand Hod took me aside. "It gnaws at me, Steve."

"What does?"

"Wondering why those pirates decided to take over *my* boat."

"Because it's big and beautiful, I suppose. And reeks of money. Few if any like it in these waters, Hod. The pair looked us over and saw opportunity." I paused because I sensed he was having a kind of flashback that made him uncomfortable.

"They'd have killed us, you know, all of us," I reminded him. "Be grateful the ladies weren't involved."

"Yeah," he nodded. "I can imagine Mattie waking up at night screaming."

"Just pretend it didn't happen."

"I'll never forget your courage, Steve. Count on me for anything."

"Goes both ways," I replied. "You've given us a wonderful interlude from Washington. Can't thank you enough."

"And don't forget my marital advice." He patted my shoulder. "She's unique."

"And I know it." Then I kissed Mattie, Hod embraced Alison, and we watched them get into the jitney for the ride down to the port.

Alison undressed in her room and came into mine, where we made love in the tropic breeze, soft Caribbean moonlight filtering through the louvered blinds. We shared room service breakfast, and then it was time to leave for the airport, forty miles away.

In Miami we changed planes for the flight to Dulles, where Arthur Jensen met us with a limousine. Facing us from the jump seat, he said, "What I withheld during my call is sensitive information. The Organized Crime section of Justice gave it to me because I'm still remembered there. Stipulating that it can't be made public for the present, and probably not for the foreseeable future."

Alison frowned. "It concerns Harlan's murder?"

Jensen nodded. "There's a former mobster in protective custody, witness protection program, actually. While working out a deal for leniency he told interrogators of a contract hit on the husband of a senator. Meaning Harlan Bowman, of course."

"The mob?" Alison blurted. "But why?"

"The informant said Harlan owed big money around Atlantic City, and kept stalling the casinos despite being warned of the consequences. So the hoods in charge decided to wipe out the debt by erasing the debtor."

"How dreadful!" Alison exclaimed.

Jensen shrugged.

I said, "If the informant didn't kill Harlan, who did?"

"He named a hit man unfavorably known to the department—one Willie Coto—but it's only his word. Unsupported, it wouldn't secure a conviction."

"I understand," Alison said slowly, "but why can't the truth be told?"

"Because publicizing the fact that the informant is in federal custody would damage cases Justice is working on, based on his information."

She turned to me. "It's very complicated. Do you understand?"

"I think so. Arthur, did the informant supply details of the hit?"

"He said the body was left in Harlan's car—in the senator's barn. There's a problem with that because car and body, as you know, were discovered at Dulles."

Alison said, "My barn? That's absurd."

"Did he mention the murder weapon?" I asked.

"No. But you and I know where it was found."

"Where was that?" Alison asked.

Jensen looked at me, I nodded, and he said, "In Steve's kitchen."

"Good Lord." She turned to me. "You never told me. Why was the knife left there?"

Jensen said, "To throw suspicion on Steve, I guess. Anyway, Steve called in the police and I was present when the knife was collected. We agreed not to tell you about it."

"Why not?" she said irritably. "Isn't the widow entitled to know?"

"Good point," Jensen said. "Want to answer, Steve?"

"Two things. First, I didn't want you to be upset. Second, the knife couldn't be tied to the murder until blood tests were run."

"Confirmed a couple of days later," Jensen supplied.

"So all I could tell you was that a bloody knife had been left in my kitchen. Raising troubling questions with no answers."

Alison sighed. "I guess you did right, both of you. But are you always going to shield me from unpleasantness?"

"I've considered it one of my functions," I said, "and persuaded Arthur to that view."

Jensen opened his jacket, took out a law firm envelope and gave it to Alison. "The reward check," he told her. "Not needed now."

Her forehead wrinkled. "Isn't the mob informant entitled to it?"

Arthur shook his head. "He didn't come forward independently and name Willie Coto—that was extracted from him as part of the plea-bargaining interrogation. Besides, Justice regulations prevent him from profiting from his knowledge of crimes. And the reward criteria included indictment for the murder—which as I've explained isn't going to happen. At least not based on the informant's assertion alone."

To Alison I said, "It's also possible the informant did the killing and named Coto to shift blame."

"So," Alison said, "it's possible we'll never know the truth."

"At least you know why your husband was murdered."

"For whatever satisfaction there is."

"On the plus side," Jensen said, "you're spared having it publicly known that your husband was a heavy gambler who welshed on his debts—politically a negative."

"That's true. My opponents could charge I allowed Harlan to

be killed by refusing to pay his debts." She turned to me. "I hadn't really expected all this on returning, and I wish I were back on the boat where everything was clean and uncomplicated."

I had no response to that so I picked up the car phone and dialed Pat Moran's number. After his wife answered I identified myself and said I wanted Pat to deliver the Jaguar to the owner's parking area. I supplied street address and parking slot number. She said she'd get word to Pat at first opportunity.

After I hung up, Jensen spoke to Alison. "Sean Elkins is eager to huddle with you about the growing political interest in your possible candidacy. Governor Green and his daughter have been bugging her for your reaction and future plans."

"At the moment I have none, but I suppose I'll have to say something in public. Either disavow the exploratory committee or endorse it. I'll ask Ms. Elkins to help with that, maybe arrange a low-key press conference."

Jensen said, "She's bright and creative and I trust her judgment. Now, Senator, I don't feel you need my full-time services any longer, so if you agree, I'll return to the conventional practice of law."

"Of course, Arthur, but I want to be able to call on you for advice about any loose ends. Is that agreeable?"

"Entirely," he replied.

"And let me say how greatly I value and appreciate what you've done for me." She smiled briefly. "Though I guess I'll never know everything. For instance, who killed poor Doris Conlon, or had her killed. Was she a mob victim, too?"

I looked out at the spring greenery, said nothing. Arthur Jensen shrugged. Presently we crossed the river bridge into downtown traffic. Jensen said, "If you don't mind I'll get off at my office. The driver will take you wherever you want to go."

"Of course," Alison said, "and I'm grateful you met us."

"Steve," Jensen said, "I'm sure we'll be talking." The limo stopped at Jensen's K Street office building and I gave the driver my Q street address. I carried our bags into the house, toed away a scattering of letters and bills, and kissed Alison. "I'll drive you home," I told her, "see you safely to the door."

"I'm in no hurry," she said, "and I'd really like a shower. But before that, please show me where the murder knife was found."

In the kitchen I pulled out the trash compactor, then pointed at the replaced window pane. Alison shook her head. "To think you were alone with the killer."

"Sort of, except that I had my buddy, Signor Beretta, in hand."

She smiled. "You make jokes of everything serious. I guess that's your way of staying stable."

"I guess," I said, "when reality is too unpleasant to deal with."

She kissed me and said, "It's cocktail time, honey. I'll take mine in the shower."

So I made a large shaker of martinis, took it upstairs with glasses, and poured drinks at the bathroom counter. Alison's hand emerged from the shower, grasped a glass, and withdrew. In the bedroom I got out of my rumpled clothes and prepared to follow Alison into the shower. But the dimpled door slid back and her hand beckoned me in. "More cozy like this," she murmured, and moved her warm, wet body against mine.

We stayed in Georgetown for dinner at the 1789 House, by the university. Dined expansively, though not in La Toc's high style, after which Alison said she wasn't up to facing her apartment that night and preferred staying with me.

After early breakfast I drove her to the apartment, where we found the refurbished Jaguar parked in her slot. As I carried her bag to the entrance she said, "I'll always wonder who fired that shot at me, who could hate me that much."

"It happened and it's behind us. Call Sean and your office and prepare to rejoin the flow of Washington political life."

"Whatever you say, bwana. When do we meet again?"

"Tonight too soon?"

"Tonight is just right." She kissed me and went in.

From there I drove to my office where Burton Michaels was already at work. He greeted me warmly and said nothing untoward had occurred in my absence, although the VanAlstines were becoming rather difficult clients. "Not the principal, just the wife. She finds fault with almost everything and asks rather foolish questions. Of course she's not always entirely sober."

"Dogs bark but the caravan moves on," I quoted, and heard Mrs. Altman come in. Her welcoming smile told me she was pleased by my return, though she said, "I've a box full of matters for your attention. I disposed of what I could but the rest is up to you."

"With your inestimable help we'll vanquish the beast. Especially if you'll hold all calls for the next two hours."

"And I've had to postpone meetings with three clients pending your return. Shall I schedule them for tomorrow?"

"Please. Otherwise . . . ?"

"Otherwise, there is a great deal of media interest in Senator Bowman's political future. Of course you may know more about that than the media do."

"I know nothing," I said, "so let's get to work."

In midafternoon I took a call from Sybil Green, who said, "I've talked with the senator about ways to handle exploratory committee funding, and she strongly suggested I take it up with you."

"I'm agreeable," I replied. "We certainly don't want her pilloried for unethical conduct. Are you in the area?"

"About ten minutes away. Have you time now?"

"I'll make time," I told her, "because I've been wanting to talk with you."

She arrived in fifteen minutes, not ten minutes. I'd never viewed her standing or in full light, and now saw a tall, gangly young woman with equine features that expensive makeup and grooming couldn't disguise. She wore a somewhat masculine gray-black pants suit and carried a saddle-leather shoulder bag. I offered a chair, and as she sat she placed the bag on the floor beside her. She crossed her legs and I said, "This is an occasion I've anticipated."

"Oh? Why so, Mr. Bentley?"

"Because, Ms. Green, it's time we talked about the late Andrew Bostick."

TWENTY-SIX

———

HER FEATURES TIGHTENED. "Andrew Bostick? I hardly knew him."

"But you knew him."

"I said so."

"And not casually."

Looking around, she frowned. "Whatever the brief relationship might have been I don't see that its any business of yours."

"Well, yes and no," I replied. "You're here because I represent Senator Bowman."

"Yes, but not—"

"And in that context whatever affects her or threatens her becomes my business."

She reached for her shoulder strap. "I don't think I like the trend of this conversation. I don't think I'll stay."

"Before you depart you ought to consider this, Sybil. You'll hear what I have to say or I'll say it all to your father the governor."

Her lips pursed. She said nothing but stayed in her chair. The grip on her bag strap relaxed. For a few moments we looked at each other, then her gaze left mine. "My father knew about Andrew."

"Because Andy took your jewelry. But before that the two of you had enjoyed many blissful moments in his apartment."

She said, "I got the jewelry back."

"Because your father threatened him with prison."

Her eyes narrowed. "How do you know all that?"

"An investigator I hired went through Andy's place soon after he was murdered, found a good many traces of you."

Her eyes widened. Continuing, I said, "It wasn't a gentlemanly thing to do, but then Andy was far from Chesterfield's definition of a gentleman. He violated the code by keeping a journal listing by date each and every time the two of you made the beast with two backs. Worse, he commented on your sexual development from the time of your near-virginity to your growing avidity for his embraces. With particulars of the positions and erotic activities that really got you off. Not all of them—shall I say—conventional in the generally accepted sense."

Her face turned toward the window. Choking sounds came from her throat. "He had no right to do that, no right at all."

"So you didn't know about it until afterward. And you didn't know what kind of creature he was." I got up and poured sherry for myself at the cellarette. "You?" I asked, but she shook her head. After sipping, I said, "Andy was handy with a camera, too. A video camera. You never saw it because of the clever way it was concealed above the bed. Many of your most rapturous moments were captured—not for posterity, it wasn't a family-type tape, more likely for blackmail."

"Where is it?" she said loudly. "I want it. Give it to me."

"Did I say I have it? Relax, Sybil. If you're blackmailed it won't be by me." I drank more sherry. "We both know what happens to blackmailers, don't we?"

"I don't know your meaning."

"I think you do. For Andy your encounters were a practice run. He perfected the technique of covert photography on a certain cruise boat not awfully long ago."

Her expression was sullen, hands opening and closing. This was a high-strung nervous filly whose breaking point was probably not far off. I said, "I never had a chance to ask Andy who paid him for that reprehensible caper because he was suddenly dead. But I guess he told you about it, maybe boasted how easily he'd seduced the target."

"I didn't pay him to do anything."

"Probably not. Had to be someone with a lot more money and an overwhelming desire to enter the national political scene. Your goal was less grandiose: you wanted Andy to stay your man and you wanted the intimate tape he probably gloated about."

"He did. He was awful, a beast." Tears welled in her eyes. "I paid him what money I had but he wouldn't give me the tape, threatened to show it to my father." She dabbed at her eyes with a man-size handkerchief, and blurted, "I'll take some of whatever you're drinking."

So I filled a sherry glass and handed it to her. Without looking at me she took it and drank half in one gulp. When she seemed less disturbed I said, "After Andy was dead you ransacked his apartment looking for the tape—you didn't know about the journal."

"No."

"Your father could have gotten the tape from Andy."

"But then he'd have known what was on it." She drank more sherry, and her face contorted. "Daddy still thinks of me as his little girl, unsullied, pure as snow."

"That's always been a problem, hasn't it?"

"He didn't want me to grow up, didn't want me to date anyone he didn't approve of."

"Possessive."

"Like I was a possession he didn't want exposed to others—men in particular." She sniffled and finished her sherry.

I breathed deeply. "Moving on, there came a time, when you

learned about his holiday cruise, his shipboard romance with an attractive, somewhat older married woman. You were worried, deeply concerned, because the last thing you wanted was to lose him to another woman. Andy was what you had and you were even more possessive of him than your father is of you. The thought was intolerable. You knew he was in touch with this woman and one night he told you he was going to see her. He may have explained he planned to apologize for betraying her, but that could have been interpreted as a way of ingratiating himself, solidifying the romance. And you reacted badly."

Her expression was fixed. Lips barely moving she said, "It was a bad time."

"Maybe you thought or hoped he was only taunting you, testing your devotion, so to establish the truth you followed him. That was one night he didn't show at the Escapade where he acted as a urinal for sado-leather rough tradesters. A Pit Boy."

Her hands covered her face and her shoulders heaved. After a while she choked, "I wish he'd gone there, but he didn't."

"For once he'd told you the truth. He drove in to the District and you followed him. When he turned in at an apartment building you recognized, you drove in, too. He must have been startled to see you because he was expecting the other woman in a few moments. I believe you begged him to leave, not see her, give her up and settle for you, for whatever you thought you had together. But Andy was single-minded, intent on repairing a wrong and doing probably the only decent thing he'd ever done in his life. Told you to leave, you were ruining everything, and you went blind with rage." I picked up her shoulder bag, pressed it between my palms and felt the outline of a revolver. "Got a permit?" I asked conversationally and dropped the bag to the floor. "What's it like to kill the only man in the world you love?"

Her gaze was hard. "I admit nothing, and you can't prove anything."

"But something happened."

"I don't remember. I must have blacked out."

"Uh-huh. Tell me about it, Sybil."

"Nothing much to tell. I found I was on the road to Baltimore."

"Very convenient," I said. "Especially when you learned he wasn't found where you left him."

She nodded. "It made no sense. So I began to wonder who shot Andrew."

"That's good, very good. A useful recollection, Sybil. Also it's wishful thinking."

"You say."

"How much does your father know?"

Her eyes were like pale blue ice. "Why would he know anything?"

"Because it involves you."

She looked away. "Andrew was a thief."

"Not a compelling reason to kill him."

Her gaze returned to me. "You moved him, drove the car away."

"Why me? Why not your father?"

"Leave my father out of it."

"Can't. He's integral to the chain of events. In addition to Andy four others are dead."

Her hand went to her mouth. "I didn't kill them!"

"Didn't say you did. They were victims of unintended consequences. What started with blackmailing a vulnerable woman involved other persons, other interests, but all connected one way or another to the woman Andy blackmailed."

Her fingers were fidgeting with the shoulder bag clasp. "Stop it," I said, "and don't open the bag in here—unless you want a ballistics test on your revolver."

She lowered the bag to the floor. "I don't want that," she said plaintively. "May I go now?" Her tone was submissive, like that of a reprimanded child.

"I'll tell you when you can go, Sybil. But maybe you'd like the governor to join us." I looked at my watch. "I'm in no hurry if you want to call him." I gestured at the desk phone but she shook her head. "Very well," I said, "we'll continue our chat, see where it leads."

"I need to go to the bathroom."

"Just hold it," I snapped, "because I want no interruption."

Her face and gaze lifted. "You sound like my father."

"I'm not your father and wouldn't want to be. Now, while I may be able to understand your disillusionment with Andy, your deep resentment over the loss of his affection, I don't understand why you tried to shoot the woman he betrayed."

Stonily she said, "You can't prove that."

"We have the slug fired at her. A test firing of your revolver might be revealing. Would it, Sybil?"

When she said nothing, I went on. "The target never loved Andy or cared for him. She didn't love him with a passion as you did, she loathed him passionately. If Andy thought otherwise he was delusional." I stared at her. "Like you. And if you still want to blame someone, take a look at your father."

Her face lowered. "He used Andy?"

"And he's using you. What's behind this exploratory committee you came here to discuss?"

"Why not ask my father?" she said defiantly. "I've said all I'm going to say. Now, I want that tape. And Andy's journal. Give them to me."

"Or what—shoot me, too? Get real, Sybil."

"They're my property."

"Just because you may be featured gives you no claim to them."

"You could be breaking the law, you know."

"Oh? How so?"

"Possessing obscene materials."

"Hadn't thought of that. Of course, the other side of the coin is taking part in obscene acts for the camera."

Her expression became sly, calculating. She looked around the office before saying. "Give me what's really mine and I'll do you. Right here. Now."

The offer was so unexpected I groped for words while she said, "You'd like that, wouldn't you, Steve?"

"Who wouldn't? But this isn't the Oval Office, Sybil. We'll take it up again when things are sorted out, okay?"

She shrugged. "If that's how you want it. Now I really need to go, before I—"

"All right. We're finished for now. But take this message to your father: we have things of pith and substance to discuss, matters of significance potentially affecting him."

She rose, hoisted the heavy bag to her shoulder, and said, "I'll tell him."

"When he calls I'll set time and place for the meet." I paused. "Here's a thought for the day: anyone taking a shot at me better make it good because the shooter won't live for a second try. Now get out of here."

She strode to the door but before turning the knob she looked back at me. "You can't prove anything," she said disdainfully. "It's all smoke and mirrors."

"Don't you wish it were?" I asked, but spoke to a closing door.

For a few moments I stared after her, thinking of all that had transpired. My hands began trembling, but I steadied them and went to the chair where she'd been sitting. I checked the varnished seat, relieved she'd spent no golden pennies, and built myself a major scotch at the cellarette. The telephone rang but I ignored its summons. I didn't want to respond to anyone, answer questions, make forced observations. My thoughts were in fixed focus on the Greens. In his way, I mused, the father was as bad as the daughter, though maybe not as crazy.

I wanted his reaction to the scenario I'd laid out for his daughter, though by challenging him I realized I was entering a zone of heightened danger.

I sat at my desk, drinking therapeutic scotch, letting the telephone ring. When it stopped, I reached over and picked up the minirecorder. It was smaller than a deck of cards and she hadn't noticed it among my desk papers or heard its silent running. I flicked it to Rewind and pocketed the microcassette.

The recording of our exchanges could be useful in uncertain times ahead.

TWENTY-SEVEN

THAT NIGHT I met Alison at Harvey's for dinner. After we were seated and drinks ordered she asked, "How did things go with Sybil Green?"

"I told her I wasn't familiar with Federal Election Commission regulations and gave her the names of several lawyers who practice the specialty." After our martinis arrived I sipped and said, "It's a recondite area with changes cropping up from year to year."

"She didn't tell me you declined."

"Well, it was late in the day. Anyway, to avoid having it appear that you're endorsing her activities you ought to have minimal personal contact with her—like none."

"Oh? You don't like Sybil, do you?"

"No. But to be impartial I don't like her father, either. If you feel you have to talk with her do it by phone. But I suggest you turn contact over to Sean Elkins."

She nodded. "How shall I handle that?"

"Hire Sean to take over all public relations matters for you. She should be moving out of Jensen's office today and back to her own. There she has electronic equipment to contact the media in your behalf."

"Tomorrow night she has me booked on an NBC program. Subject, political fundraising."

"Good. I'll watch from the farm. It's Friday night, so I thought I'd stock supplies for the weekend." I paused. "We're weekending there, aren't we?"

"Of course, it's just that I'm having difficulty with calendar days. Cruising, they didn't matter." She smiled apologetically. "I'll be fairly late at the studio."

"Then come out Saturday. I don't want you driving country roads at night."

"I'll give you keys and the alarm numbers."

I finished my drink and told the waiter we were ready to order. Alison asked for deviled Chesapeake crab and I chose oysters Rockefeller with a bottle Chablis. After the waiter left, I said, "I sense you're feeling more positive about the possible nomination."

"I am. If it doesn't come to me I'll at least have had a lot of national television exposure." She smiled. "But to make things more difficult for the party I won't accept nomination for the vice-presidency."

"A title without a job. So it's Numero Uno or nothing."

"Think I'm presumptuous?"

"You have to do what you're comfortable with."

"That's what I told myself. I don't want a cabinet job either." She finished her drink. "That puts me in a pretty good bargaining position."

"It does. And three weeks ago you were cool to the idea of a presidential run."

"Well, I've thought things over since then. On our cruise. Without distractions." She paused. "It's an interesting idea."

"That could develop."

"So please don't be harsh or critical with Sybil. After she lost her mother she was institutionalized for a couple of years, Sheppard-Pratt, I think it was."

"Recall the diagnosis?"

She shrugged. "Schizophrenia, I believe—but that's a catchall diagnosis. Anyway, as you've seen she's not an attractive young woman, rather suppressed, like other children of dominant parents. And with mental problems she hasn't had a very happy life."

"Too bad."

"I think Abel got her into this exploratory committee to give her something significant to do. He's very protective of his daughter and I admire him for that."

"Is it a good idea having a kook chairing your committee?"

"Steve, she's not a kook as you put it, just a young woman with past mental problems. If the work overwhelms her she'll leave, but a demanding job could be the saving of her if she can handle it."

"We'll hope for a good outcome," I said as the waiter brought our entrees.

After dinner we drove to Alison's place, put on music and danced in the living room. At ten-thirty we went to bed, made love, and slept side by side until the alarm woke us at seven.

When I reached my office Dr. VanAlstine was waiting for me. He greeted me warmly before saying they were leaving Washington and going back home. "Just me, really," he said. "Gretta will be at the Betty Ford clinic for a while. It wasn't easy but I managed to prevail on her to take the cure."

"Great idea," I remarked. "The place has done wonders for a good many notables. Then the two of you can really enjoy the fruits of your labors."

"That was part of my argument. Anyway, I wanted to thank you and Burton for steering me so competently through so many problems I was unaware of before consulting you."

"It's never easy to safeguard riches," I said, "and you're fortu-nate InfoComp has been so cooperative."

"Why shouldn't they be? They'll make millions from my process."

"And their payments to you express their corporate grati-tude. We'll be in frequent touch for several months until everything settles down and becomes routine."

"And I may pop in here from time to time. We'll lunch at the Logos again." He grinned. "On me."

"Always glad to confer with you, Doctor," I said and walked him to the elevator, glad he'd persuaded his wife to enroll for pro-fessional help. A really odd couple. But with his consent I'd arranged to have my retainer transferred monthly from his bank to mine. As I explained, it would obviate the inconvenience of sending a check from wherever he and Gretta might be traveling. A sub-stantial sum, it would cover overhead nicely, with a few thousand to spare.

So, while I was in an upbeat frame of mind, a call came from Governor Green.

"Bentley," Green said in a military voice, "my daughter tells me you suggested a private meeting."

"It would be to our mutual advantage, Governor, and the op-erative word is private."

"What do you have in mind?"

"If you're free this evening or later on we could get together at Alison's country retreat, her farm. The two of us."

"The senator?"

"Doing a TV show in town. You know the farm?"

"I've been there but maybe you should give me directions."

After he'd copied them down and repeated them, he said, "Sybil also says you treated her badly in your office."

"Depends on one's point of view, Governor. We'll discuss it tonight."

"We certainly will. Sybil's psyche is rather frail, and I won't have anyone beating up on her."

"As I said, we'll discuss it. Seven o'clock?"

"Not knowing the country roads, I'll say seven-thirty."

"I'll be there," I said, and broke off. My right hand was trembling, heart pounding. A long drink would help, but I needed sharp faculties to plan all I had to do. For a start I phoned Pat Moran.

At ten I received one client, at eleven another, and at one-thirty the third of those Mrs. Altman had postponed during my absence. I turned the second client's problems over to Burton Michaels, and began work on the other two before leaving the office at four. Ridgewell's supplied me with four frozen gourmet dinners, and I bought wine, fresh fruits, and vegetables at Constantino's on Wisconsin Avenue. I stopped home long enough to change clothing and pack shaving gear, my Beretta, tape recorders and a portable black and white TV. Then I crossed the river via Key Bridge and drove toward Leesburg.

I turned in at the farm and unloaded the car, then walked to the barn and pulled open the door. Before opening the house door with Alison's keys, I punched numbers into the sequential alarm system and saw the On light blink out.

I carried clothing and shaving gear upstairs, and came down to stow Ridgewell's meals in the freezer, vegetables in the cooler bin. Then I granted myself the luxury of a double shot of Red Label over ice. Drink in hand I moved around the living room looking for a place to conceal one of the tape recorders, and heard a car pull in from the main road and scatter gravel as it came toward the house. From the porch I waved Pat Moran toward the barn and went down to meet him. He had a hard-sided suitcase and one of aluminum that I carried to the house. "Nice spread here," he remarked. "Got anything resembling a beer?"

"Tuborg do?"

"Does a kitten like milk?" He set the suitcase on the living room coffee table, and while he was loading a miniature surveillance videocam I got a Tuborg from the fridge and added more Johnnie Red to my glass. Pat drank out of the bottle and opened the aluminum case. From it he extracted two tape recorders and several blank cassettes, conventional size. He handed me a third cassette, and said, "I transferred your microcassette recording to this one," then fitted it on one of his tape recorders. Pressed the Play button and I heard my voice saying, "*This is an occasion I've anticipated.*"

Sybil: "*Oh? Why so, Mr. Bentley?*"

Me: "*Because, Ms. Green, it's time we talked about the late Andrew Bostick.*"

"That's enough," I told him. "Let's get on with it."

Pat rewound the copy. "Ready for replay," he said, and returned the microcassette original. I went over to an antique milk-glass pitcher on the mantel and dropped it in for safekeeping. Pat prowled the room for a while and settled on a bookshelf where he set a minirecorder between two old books. "Three-hour tape do it?" he asked.

"Should. We'll see."

From there he went to the adjoining dining room and positioned the miniature videocam in a dried-flower table centerpiece. The half-inch wide-angle lens took in three-quarters of the living room. He bent a flower stem away from the lens and stepped back to admire his work. "Spy stuff, huh?" He swigged at his beer.

"So they say."

"I'm going to plant a small remote mike down here so I can listen upstairs to what's going on."

"Good idea. I may need reinforcements."

"The final touch," he said, "is the decoy recorder. Keep it sort of visible on the mantel so if your guest spots it he'll assume that's all there is." He chuckled. "Got that technique from spy books. Like how the KGB mikes Moscow hotel rooms. The target spots one poorly hidden mike and rips it out, never realizing there are three others well concealed."

"A fellow can learn a lot from books," I remarked. "No doubt about it. Ready for another beer?"

"Sure am. Hot day. Unseasonable." He began inserting his remote mike in the back-throat of an antlered deer head on the wall. I twisted off the bottle cap and gave him the Tuborg.

"You carrying iron?" he asked.

I flipped up the back of my coat to show him the holstered Beretta next to my spine. Where Red hadn't found it.

"I'd say we're well prepared, laddie."

We sat on the sofa, and for a while sipped our drinks in silence. Finally Pat said, "That's quite a conversation you had with Miss Green. But she avoided actually admitting she shot her boyfriend. Came close to it, though. Then the blackout." He blew a raspberry mockingly. "Oh Judge, dear Judge, I just don't know what happened after that." He grunted. "Oldest dodge in history. Now tell me about Andy's sex journal—you found it in his place?"

"No. As far as I know one doesn't exist. But he was the kind of creep who might have kept one, and Sybil had few illusions about him. After all, she knew about his Pit Boy nights and tolerated them." I drank from my glass.

"And the videotape you told her about?"

"Fabricated, But she knew he'd videotaped my client so she could easily believe he'd done it to her as well." I drained my glass. "As you found out, Pat, Sybil is a head case. She was in an institution for a couple of years diagnosed schizophrenic but I think it's more like paranoid sociopath. That's my diagnosis, plus a lot of bottled-up rage."

"Rage? Who's she mad at?"

"Pop. Years of dominating suppression. Resentful at him and the world because she's an unattractive woman." I got up to remake my drink. "Yesterday she brought a revolver to my office."

"Jesus!"

"I told the governor the two of us would meet so I hope Sybil doesn't come along for the ride. "Hungry?"

"Unh-unh, stopped at Burger King on the way. But I will take a couple bottles upstairs." He grinned. "Have to remind myself not to flush the head. A flushing toilet has ruined more than one surveillance."

The kitchen wall clock showed a few minutes to seven when the phone rang. Alison's voice: "Honey, the studio is sending a car for me, but I thought I'd touch base with you."

"Well, I'm here, in charge, and enjoying the sunset."

"If you had a TV you could watch my performance—beginning at eight-thirty."

"For that very reason I brought one and I'm anticipating your cool, intellectual approach to today's intractable political problems."

"Oh, pooh, how you do go on." She broke into laughter. "You're a dear man to bring a set. Now we'll have entertainment in our spare time."

"If any."

"Hmm. Don't count on me for breakfast, okay? But lunch definitely."

After the call I watered my scotch and took Pat three Tuborgs. "Better get out of sight," I told him. "Abel could arrive any minute."

With him he took the receiver for the remote mike and I noticed the unit was attached to small earphones. Pat went up the stairs and I turned on all the living room lights to give the videocam a better view. Then I turned on my TV set and watched a boring game show until I heard a car turn in from the highway.

I activated our electronic array and went out to see Abel Green getting out of his car. Alone.

On the porch he said, "I'd forgotten how nice this place is." He didn't extend his hand—no false cordiality tonight—and followed me into the living room. I offered him a drink and he said he'd take a bourbon on ice, no water. I poured it in the kitchen, and when I came back he had the mantel decoy recorder in his hands. "I don't think we need this," he said, and switched it off.

"Bad idea," I said apologetically. "Sorry."

"Bad beginning," he said severely, "except for this excellent bourbon."

"Early Times," I said. "It aims to please the palate."

"All right, you asked for the meeting, what's on your mind?" He sat on the sofa facing the concealed videocam, and I sat on the other end.

"The senator and I have been wondering what's behind your endorsement of the exploratory committee chaired by your daughter. Particularly because the senator didn't authorize it."

"Very simple. I'd like Alison to get the nomination. She's popular in our state, and with proper handling and national exposure I think she could make a decent, even successful run."

"For the presidency."

He nodded. "That may be too big a bite at present, but I understand her not wanting to settle for the second spot."

"She's concerned about party competitors. As a party loyalist, she doesn't want to provoke or promote intraparty discord."

Green smiled indulgently. "That can be handled. When other would-be candidates compare their campaign war chests to hers they'll get discouraged."

"And campaign funding is—important."

"It's everything."

"And you assume substantial up-front funding by the senator herself."

He sipped his drink, smacked his lips and looked at me. "Two or three million, why not? She's got lots more."

"True. But I believe she's assuming very substantial party help."

"When she has the nomination she'll get it. Abundantly. The National Committee will hold nothing back. I'm vice-chairman and I can promise that."

I drank from my glass. "So what it comes down to is how much the senator wants to become president."

"Doesn't everyone?"

I smiled. "I didn't, don't."

"You're not a politician. But she trusts you, Bentley, confides in you. You could be a big help to her when the big money comes rolling in." He paused. "As it will."

I said, "She'll be glad to hear your projection. Of course, she'll have to leave the Senate."

"Unfortunately."

"And you'd appoint yourself to the seat."

"Yes, I would, and I don't mind admitting it." He gazed at me from under bushy white eyebrows. "You find fault with that?"

"Just with state law that requires a candidate to resign a Senate seat."

He spread his hands. "That's the way it is."

"I understand. And why shouldn't you occupy a vacant seat? You're the most prominent political figure in the state."

"Only until the senator's campaign gets going. Now, that brings us to your meeting with Sybil. She came to you on the senator's advice, to see if you would handle or advise on the regulatory aspects of exploratory funding. Instead, she said you attacked her verbally with crude, fantastic charges, none of which were true."

"Campaign funding is very complicated, Governor. I have no expertise in it and no wish to study the subject. There are, however, numerous Washington lawyers who know every dot and comma of the regs. The exploratory committee should retain one of them."

"You told Sybil that?"

"I intended to, but took up another subject."

"Which was?"

"The life and death of Andrew Bostick, thief and lover."

He winced. "What possible interest is that to you?"

"Because Bostick was hired to compromise Senator Bowman during a holiday vacation cruise. He made a videotape of their intimate encounters and used it to blackmail the senator."

His expression was shocked, "I knew the little scumbag was a thief—but a blackmailer?"

"Yes. His extortionate phone calls were recorded by the senator up to and including the day of his death. It was all there for the U.S. attorney, but his murder made them nugatory."

He drained his glass, sat forward. "I don't see what any of that has to do with my daughter."

"I think you do," I replied, and took his empty glass. "While I'm getting a refill, you ought to listen to what was recorded yesterday in my office." I pressed the Play button, got up and went to the kitchen. I took my time getting his bourbon and ice, more time to make myself a light scotch. When I returned to the living room the governor was sitting there, face lowered in his hands. I didn't enjoy his discomfort as he listened, or his groans at some of Sybil's words. And there were still long minutes to go.

To give him undistracted privacy I want out on the porch and lit a cigar. When it was half gone, I heard the end of the recording. As I went back to the living room Green was taking the tape from the recorder. "I'll take this," he said, "and you're a filthy human being to do that to her." The cassette disappeared in a pocket. He got out a handkerchief and wiped tears from his cheeks. "She hates me," he said brokenly. "And to find out like *this*—" He shook his white mane.

"That's your only concern?"

"The rest is only the fantasies of a sick young woman. No evidence she shot Bostick—*if* she did."

"She had motive and opportunity. I don't think the police need look further for Bostick's killer."

"They'll keep looking, Bentley, because without the tape they have nothing."

I smiled. "Ever occur to you copies exist, Governor? Take the tape with you, play it until it's worn out. Let Sybil hear it to refresh her memory."

Grimacing, he clenched his teeth. "What are you going to do about it?"

"That depends. Because we have to look back and consider the circumstances that brought Bostick to his death. I've mentioned Andy's cruise, his attempt to blackmail the senator. We both know he lacked money for a luxury sea excursion, so someone paid him and his expenses. Someone who had leverage over him because of an unreported jewelry theft. Sybil's jewelry."

"What are you getting at?"

"I thought you might be able to help identify Bostick's principal."

He eyed me. "What are you suggesting?"

"Had to be someone wanting to discredit the senator, blackmail her into resigning her Senate seat. Someone eager to take that seat and move on to the national scene." I paused. "Someone like you, Governor."

He grunted. "Speculation, unprovable."

"As I told your daughter, don't be too sure."

"What you have is Bostick's journal, and the videotape he made of—of—" He began choking. Tears welled in his eyes. "—of the two of them." He wiped tears from his cheeks again. "Unbelievable she could sully herself with a creature like that."

"Well, she thinks you didn't give her many—shall we say—social opportunities. That's part of her brief against you."

"I'll make it up to her," he said, "and now I want those things you took from Bostick's place. That should make her happy."

"You really think so? Anyway, I'm not surrendering anything to you. You're a blackmailing conspirator and your daughter is a murderer, but her crime doesn't bother you."

"It doesn't, you're right. If she killed that stinking little creep she had every reason to. And I applaud her courage."

"That from the state's sworn defender of the law? As long as murder's in the family you condone it?"

"Shut up. Give me the journal and Bostick's lewd tape."

"Take a walk, Governor."

His expression changed. "You're a cruel, heartless bastard. What do you want, money? Some kind of deal?"

"I want no more interference with the senator's career. I want Sybil off the committee, and you're to be responsive to the senator's desires. With what I've got on you and your daughter, forget taking over Alison's seat. I mean that. And to keep Sybil from shooting the senator again, I want her put away. She's dangerous, Abel, a murderous psychotic. Send her back to Sheppard-Pratt where the window bars are strong."

I'd raised my voice because I'd noticed a flash of motion outside the nearest window. Suddenly the pane smashed, a woman's voice screamed, "No. Not again. Not ever. I won't go, you can't make me!" Then two shots.

TWENTY-EIGHT

ONE BULLET WHISTLED past me, the second hit Abel
Green who yelped and clutched his neck. By then I was down,
Beretta in hand. I fired over her head and raced outside as Pat
Moran bolted down the stairs to join me outside, revolver in his
hand.

Sybil hadn't moved. She stood staring at her father, face working, foam bubbling from her lips, eyes vacant, unmoving. A revolver
hung at the end of her arm, pointing down.

"Drop it," I snapped, and she became aware of me. As I went
toward her, the muzzle lifted and the hammer clicked. Twice. I
jerked the gun from her hand. She looked at it curiously, as though
seeing it for the first time, and then she collapsed. She dropped to

the ground, drew her knees to her chest and began mewling. Re-gressing to infancy. Catatonic. To Pat I said, "Stay with her, don't let her bite or swallow her tongue."

I went back inside, pried Green's hand from his wound and saw the bullet had smashed his collarbone. Heart and lungs undam-aged. "You're losing blood," I snapped. "Without surgery you'll bleed to death."

"Help me," he groaned. "God, the pain!"

"I'll help you," I said, "if you'll agree to my conditions. Sybil in-stitutionalized, no Senate seat for you, and full cooperation with the senator."

"Yes," he breathed. "Yes. All that."

"Swear it, Abel."

"Swear it. God, *help me now.*"

"You're finished, you son of a bitch," I snapped. "Accept it, live with it, act accordingly."

As I went to the kitchen telephone I realized he'd never asked about Sybil. And while I was dialing 911, I glanced at my portable TV, and there was Alison seated in a semicircle with several famous talking heads. She looked composed and gorgeous. I'd muted the channel so I couldn't hear her words. But I knew she'd acquit her-self well, and become a sought-for guest as her political career gained broader dimensions.

The paramedics said they'd be there in ten minutes, try to stop the bleeding. So I folded a towel and told Green to press it against his wound. Hard. Then I went outside and found Pat kneeling be-side Sybil. He'd forced a rolled handkerchief between her jaws. Her eyes were open, fixed on some object I couldn't see. Or maybe noth-ing at all. Her body convulsed as from it rose the stench of expelled bodily wastes. Pat moved back to where I was standing, "Jesus, I never expected anything like this. Did you?"

"God, no—who could?" I glanced at the bullet-shattered win-dowpane. "But of course she wanted to know what we were talking about. And her self-preservation drive brought her here. I should have considered the possibility."

"Did she consciously shoot her father?"

"Who knows? Missed me and kept shooting. Maybe she only

wanted to kill me, not her father." I put her revolver in my pocket. "One bullet killed Bostick, another hit the Jaguar, and just now she fired twice. Four cartridges expended."

"From a six-shot cylinder."

"Maybe she fired a couple of practice shots before shooting Bostick. She's forgetful—told me so in my office, and now I believe her. Stay with her until the ambulance comes."

I returned to the kitchen and called Arthur Jensen's home, summarized what had happened, and suggested he inform the senator when she left the studio. "But keep her from coming to the farm. I'll call her later. I want Sean Elkins at the senator's apartment, and I need you here.

"All right."

"Somehow we have to keep the senator's name out of this, configure things for the least possible damage."

"I know that," he said testily, "and I hope you've got some bright ideas."

"Right now all I can think of is 'unfortunate, regrettable accident'—or 'episode' but I'll work on it." I saw lights flashing down the highway before I heard the ambulance siren.

I couldn't do more for Abel Green, didn't want to. So I went outside where Pat was guarding Sybil and said, "You'd better collect your gear before the cops get here."

"Right. Uh—was I here?"

"If you were I didn't see you. Take my car. We'll talk tomorrow." He hurried into the house, scooped up recorders, videocam, and mikes, dropped them in their cases, and was stowing them in his car when the Leesburg Rescue Squad arrived.

Just before the paramedics reached the porch I slapped Green's face to focus his attention. "If you're smart you'll say nothing. Someone will contact you tomorrow." From his pocket I removed the cassette he'd confiscated, and slipped it in mine. "You'll have lasting memories of tonight—the night your daughter tried to kill you."

They wheeled in a gurney, helped Green lie down on it, and trundled him away. Other paramedics were loading Sybil on a gurney, covering her with heavy blankets, assuming she was in shock, which, I guess, she was. Or having an epileptic seizure. I asked the chief medic where they were heading, and he said, "Loudon Hospital Center in town. Want to ride along?"

"No thanks, I couldn't add anything to the trip."

"Then you're not a relative?"

"Far from it. And thanks for the prompt response."

"That's our job."

While we were talking Pat Moran drove away in my car. If his equipment worked properly the whole scene would be recorded as it occurred. Valuable future leverage over Abel Green.

After the ambulance left, siren screeching, light bar flashing, I went into the house, took my glass from the coffee table and made a sturdy drink. As I surveyed the room I noticed where shards of glass from the smashed window had fallen on the floor. Their inside location was inconsistent with the story I'd begun to concoct so I picked up the pieces and tossed them outside where Sybil had been standing. Grains of glass I swept up and disposed of in the kitchen waste. Then I placed a sofa cushion over blood that had seeped into the fabric from the governor's back. If the bullet wasn't in his body it was lodged in the sofa. That Sybil, I thought, some crazy femme.

The television set was still tuned to the NBC channel but Alison's program was over and a movie about street gangs had begun. I left it on as incidental support for the story I was preparing to tell.

A car turned into the drive, light bar twinkling, but no siren. I swallowed more scotch and went out on the porch. The officer who got out of the car and came toward me was Sergeant Bottscher of recent memory. "Evening, sir." He touched the brim of his hat and mounted the steps. Squinting at me in the poor light, he said, "Seen you before. Name's—" He shook his head.

"Bentley," I supplied. "The senator's tax attorney."

"Ah, yes, I remember now. That phony tip about a body in the barn there." He half-turned to glance at it. "Senator around?"

"In Washington, doing a TV talk show. C'mon in, Sergeant."

"Thank you." He took off his hat as we entered the living room. "Mind if I sit?"

"Not at all. I can make coffee or offer you an adult beverage."

"No thanks." He cleared his throat. "Monitoring the Res-cue Squad channel, we heard of a shooting here. Care to tell me about it?"

"Well, I'd rather wait until the senator's attorney gets here—Arthur Jensen—but there's not a lot to tell, so I might as well go ahead."

"Obliged if you would." His gaze traveled to the broken win-dow.

"Don't know how closely you follow area politics, but Gover-nor Green endorsed the senator as a candidate for the presidency—that was a couple of weeks ago. To explore possibilities and raise initial funds a committee was formed, chaired by the governor's daughter, Sybil Green."

"I'm with you."

"Well, the senator was taking part in a network talk show, and the governor and his daughter decided to watch it from here." I ges-tured at the television set. "After the senator got here the plan was to discuss committee matters. Oh, I should add that father and daughter came separately. Anyway, Sybil was here, the three of us, when the program began."

"What time was that?"

"Eight-thirty. I was watching the senator on TV so I'm not clear on what exactly happened with the gun."

"Whose gun?"

"The daughter's." I took it from my pocket, set it on the coffee table. "She said she carried it when driving at night."

He picked up the revolver by the trigger guard and opened the cylinder. "Thirty-two caliber," he said. "All six shells expended. How many shots were fired?"

"One."

"Can you give me any details?"

"As I said, I was focused on the program. But I was vaguely aware that Sybil had taken the piece from her purse and was show-ing it to her father, the governor. Then I heard the gun explode. Sybil screamed and the governor grabbed at his neck. She was hys-terical, out of it. I got a kitchen towel, made a compress and had the governor hold it against his wound to slow the bleeding. Then I called nine-one-one. Maybe ten minutes later the Rescue Squad arrived and took both Greens away."

He nodded. "They say she's in worse shape than her father, rigid, unresponsive."

"She has a history of mental instability. You can imagine her reaction when she saw her father bleeding."

"Yeah. But who pulled the trigger?"

"Can't say. Maybe her finger got caught in the trigger guard or perhaps the governor moved the trigger taking the gun from Sybil. I don't know."

He frowned. "Too bad. Neither one is in condition to answer questions."

Headlights fanned across porch windows as another car came up the drive. "Should be Jensen," I remarked. "I thought he ought to be here to protect the senator's interests, if any need protecting. You know how the media hype any kind of incident involving prominent people—in this case a governor and a U.S. senator."

"Yeah, they'll do that, irresponsible bastards," he said bitterly and looked at the doorway as Arthur Jensen came in. After introductions Jensen said, "I could use a bracer, Steve," and followed me into the kitchen. While I was pouring scotch in a glass he said, "Mighty brief reprieve from Alison's problems."

"We serve at the pleasure of our clients, who pay exorbitant fees to compensate for inconvenience." I gave him his drink. He tasted it and asked, "So what's the situation?"

"Accidental shooting. Governor Green wounded, daughter in shock. Both taken to Loudon Hospital. Details when we're alone." We joined Sergeant Bottscher, who asked if the senator knew what had happened.

Jensen took a nearby chair. "She knows the governor was wounded in an accidental shooting, which is about all I know." He took a long pull from his glass. Bottscher said, "Mr. Bentley here has been very helpful in clarifying the incident. From what he said I don't believe any charges are likely to be filed against anyone—except possibly neglectful conduct, and that would be for the governor to decide. I hardly think he'll take that sort of minimal action against his daughter."

Jensen managed a thin smile. "Too many handguns around and mostly in the hands of inexperienced owners."

"That's the truth," Bottscher agreed, and got up. "I'll try to talk to the governor tomorrow—if he's available."

Jensen said, "I gather the wound isn't critical."

I said, "Looked to me like a broken collarbone, bullet deflected into the window." Both men glanced at it, then back at me. I said, "I'll have a glazier replace it tomorrow," and drank from my glass. Jensen said, "So it isn't clear who actually pressed the trigger, firing the revolver."

"Not yet," Bottscher said, "but I tend to think that regardless of particulars the governor will take responsibility."

"Probably," I said, "he's that kind of stand-up guy."

Bottscher picked up Sybil's revolver. "I'll take this along—formality. Want a receipt?"

Jensen shook his head and I said, "No, I'm not her lawyer."

"Then I'll be on my way. I believe everyone is fortunate nothing more serious happened here tonight." He left the room and we heard his heavy tread descending the porch steps. His car started and backed around. Arthur Jensen said, "Now, if it's not asking too much, Steve, I'd like to know what the hell happened."

I put the cassette copy back on the recorder from which Green had taken it, rewound the tape, and said, "After you've heard what was recorded in my office yesterday I'll supplement it with tonight's events. And while you're listening I'll call Alison."

"Good idea." He sat on the sofa, pressed the Play button, and I went to the kitchen phone. Sean Elkins answered and said the senator was not taking any calls, but after I gave my name Alison came to the phone. "Steve—are you all right?"

"Perfect. You?"

"Consumed with curiosity and foreboding. What happened? Why were Abel and Sybil at the farm?"

"It's all a pretty long story—the details can wait until you're here tomorrow. But, basically, Abel and Sybil wanted to discuss committee and eventful campaign financing, wouldn't take no for an answer. I didn't want to be hung up in town with them so I suggested they meet me at the farm and we'd watch your TV appearance together. Okay, so far?"

"I understand what you're saying."

"Then put Sean on an extension so I won't have to repeat myself, I've already gone through it with Sergeant Bottscher—remember him?—and I'll have to do the same for Arthur. Sean, you there?"

"I am, Mr. Bentley, and with your permission I'll tape the conversation. I'll need it for reference in preparing a press release."

"Tape away," I said, and told the women what I'd told Bottscher, emphasizing that I couldn't say who was holding the gun when it went off. "The very efficient Leesburg Rescue Squad was here in ten minutes and probably saved the life of the governor by its prompt action. Both Greens are in Loudon Hospital, but neither is in condition to answer inquiries."

Alison asked, "Has the governor's staff been notified?"

"Don't know, though the hospital may have, or the cops or the paramedics."

"Then I ought to make a call to the capital," Sean said, "if you concur, Senator."

"By all means—as a courtesy."

"Yes, we want to stay in front on this one." Sean said, "so I'll get on the other phone, then fax out a press statement."

To me, Alison said, "The whole thing sounds bizarre. Are you—"

"Sometimes its best to accept things at face value and not dig deep, okay? Now maybe you'll be here for breakfast?"

"Wouldn't miss it for the world. Good night, honey."

"Night, sweet." I strengthened my drink, made a repeat for Arthur and took them to the coffee table. My voice and Sybil's were coming from the recorder, and Arthur was listening absorbedly. I went over to the broken window and looked out at where Sybil had stood eavesdropping. How much had she heard? I wondered. Moonlight reflected on the shards below, making them look like chips of ice. Eventually, she'd emerge from her swoon but I doubted she would say much to clarify the shooting. If she even remembered it. As her father asserted, her psyche was fragile.

Calmer now, much less adrenaline in my veins, I turned from the window and scanned the opposite wall. The bullet that missed me had to be somewhere. I theorized a trajectory, walked from window to wall, and there it was, a hip-high puncture in the wallpaper. So the bullet was there, buried in plaster and wood, but I wasn't going to dig it out. If the cops wanted a specimen they could fire her .32 into a bucket of sand, only why would they want to? Sybil was not going to be charged with Bostick's murder; no one even suspected her of it. Pat Moran knew what I did—or guessed—and presently Arthur Jensen would. Plus the governor made four, but Green would keep that secret to his grave.

From the recorder came the sound of my office door closing on Sybil Green. Arthur looked up at me. "That it?"

I nodded.

"Quite a conversation," he said, and drank deeply from his glass. "But nothing to prove she killed her lover."

"I didn't have much to work with, Arthur, mainly hunch and speculation."

"With which you did very damn well. Should have been a prosecutor."

"Appreciate the compliment." I sat on the sofa and removed the cushion that concealed the bloodstains.

"Oh," he said, "you didn't show that to the sergeant."

"Of course I didn't. Because a bullet through Green and into the sofa couldn't have ricocheted from his collarbone and smashed yonder window. My stories may not be entirely factual but they have to be consistent."

Grudgingly he said, "Of course. Now what happened here this evening?"

"Before I go into that I have a confession to make. By the time Green got here I'd installed surveillance devices to record everything that transpired." I got up and went to the dining room table. "A minicam was hidden in the centerpiece. Its wide-angle lens covered most of the room, centered on the sofa. Two concealed minicorders taped the conversation. If I ever show you the video you'll see Sybil was never in the room."

"She wasn't?" Shock on his face.

"She was outside the window listening. When things got unbearable she fired her revolver. Missed me, fired again and wounded her father. The first shot is buried in the wall over there, the second is in the sofa behind all the blood."

"If she fired from outside there should be glass on the floor," he objected.

"There was. After the ambulance left and before Bottscher arrived I cleaned it up, dropped the pieces outside. For consistency."

"I'll be damned!"

"Anyway, I had Green listen to my office tape, and that broke him. Couldn't believe his little girl had done such an awful thing as murder. Actually, he believed it, he just didn't *want* to believe it."

"Denial."

"I charged him with hiring Bostick to blackmail the senator after a holiday cruise—during which he covertly videotaped them in the primal act that perpetuates the species. Uh—too euphemistic or do I make myself clear?"

"Appreciate your delicacy," he said wryly, "no coarse language here."

"Both of us being gentlemen."

"Thank you. Why would Green do such a rotten thing?"

"Because he lusts for Alison's Senate seat. He thought that having Bostick threaten her with the explicit tape would force her to resign from the Senate. Green appoints himself to her seat and grafts happily ever after." I downed the rest of my drink to moisten my pipes. "That fell apart when Bostick—in a moment of quasi-decency—took the videotape copies intending to deliver them to Alison in exchange for getaway money, but was shot by Sybil before he could." I paused. "Alison went down to the parking lot for their arranged meeting and found him dead in his car. She called me. Perhaps in an excess of caution I decided to move car and corpse to a far location with no possible connection to the senator, Reagan Airport. I took Bostick's bag of tapes from his car and brought them home where I destroyed them."

He stared at me. "My God, you've been busy."

"And that's only part of my protective services. The rest isn't relevant."

"That's a relief. If I knew I'd probably regret it."

"Then in sequence Doris Conlon, Harlan's mistress, was murdered. By whom you don't need to know. Then Harlan—"

"I told you what DOJ told me—the mob informant named Willie Coto as Harlan's killer."

"Very convenient. But until Coto confesses I'll believe Green ordered Harlan hit. I believe they were subterranean partners in dirty business and Harlan was becoming so irresponsible Green feared he would talk and implicate him in crimes of corruption. I'm not saying Coto wasn't the actual killer, just that he did it for Green, not the New Jersey casino mob."

"Alternate theory."

"My linked theory is that when next seen Willie Coto will be fished from the Narrows, too dead to talk."

Pensively, Jensen said, "You've given me a lot to think about."

"You don't need to think about it, Arthur. Most is history and so far the senator's image is unstained. That's the brief you and I have been working on." I drew in a deep breath. I'd been talking a long time and was beginning to feel deflated. "Water?" I asked, "or a refill?"

"Since I have to drive home, water."

I left long enough to fill a glass with ice water and pour a small amount of scotch in my glass, diluting it with ice water. Going back to Jensen, I said, "The main gain from the night's events redounds to the senator's advantage."

"It does? How so?" He drank thirstily.

"Because my recordings of what transpired here represent absolute leverage over Abel Green. Before the ambulance arrived I told him to forget occupying Alison's Senate seat. And I told him that I require his absolute cooperation in furthering her political goals, whatever they turn out to be. In a couple of days when he's lucid I'll also tell him that if I suspect he's engineering fresh plots to discredit or murder her those recordings go instantly public. He'll be revealed for the corrupt conniver he is, and Sybil as the killer of her lover."

Jensen grunted. "A twofer. Can't hardly do better than that."

"If you think of a codicil I'll add it. Meanwhile, I intend to store the take in your firm's vault. Safer there than my office. And if anything happens to me you'll know what to do with it."

He nodded.

"I'll review the stuff to make sure it contains all it should—including the shooting of the governor—and deliver it to you. That agreeable?"

"You know it is." He looked around the room. "I assume the senator is to be unwitting."

"Not that her psyche is fragile, but she doesn't need a lot of confusing garbage."

He drank more ice water. "She'll be here tomorrow. What will you tell her?"

"What I told Sergeant Bottscher. The only ones who can refute it are the Greens, and they're not going to. Abel squeezes out of this with a degree of public sympathy. And as a cloistered patient at Sheppard-Pratt, Sybil is devoid of credibility."

"You're having her committed?"

"Her father is, on my instructions. She's been there before so there's precedent."

"He glanced at the shattered window, then the bullet hole in the far wall. "You went up against a very powerful man, Steve. I'm not sure I have your kind of balls."

"Motivation," I remarked. "You've done assault landings under enemy fire so don't talk to me about balls."

He half smiled, downed the rest of his water, stood up and stretched. "Don't see anything I can do here, Steve. You managed everything before I arrived. But I'm a wiser man now, and in better position to guard our client's interests."

"I appreciate your coming, however inconvenient. And I'll tell Alison we owe you."

"Thanks." He moved toward the door, stopped and turned to me. "An indiscreet personal question: are you and Alison to be married?"

"Simple answer: I don't know."

"When Hod returns, how much will you tell him?"

"Maybe nothing. He has a good opinion of me now, I wouldn't want to hazard it."

"Don't sell him short, Steve. Thanks for the drinks. Good night."

I went out with him to his car. It was parked near the governor's official Marquis. We shook hands, and as he drove away his headlights revealed another car parked on the verge, out near the highway. Sybil's. Tomorrow I'd call Bottscher's office, request both cars be taken away. I didn't want them around provoking negative memories. I hadn't enough remaining energy to call him tonight.

I went back into the house, set the alarm system, turned off first-floor lights and trudged up to bed. My sleep was dreamless.

In the morning, much earlier than I wanted, I heard kitchen sounds, smelled the pungent mouth-watering aromas of coffee and frying country ham. The bathroom mirror reflected an unshaven, haggard face, ten years older than the day before. I made what improvements I could, got into a bathrobe and went downstairs. Alison hurried over to hug and kiss me. "Now, darling. I want you to tell me all about it. What really happened. Everything."

TWENTY-NINE

DURING BREAKFAST I dealt pretty much in generalities, telling Alison what I thought she ought to know of last night's events, broadening the story enough to satisfy anticipated questions.

She dabbed orange marmalade on an English muffin and said, "What a nightmare—for you, I mean. And you're always on hand when I need protection." She shook her head. "It's so sad about Sybil—poor girl never really had a chance at a normal life."

"Still, to be charitable we have to assume Abel tried to do the right things for his daughter. Uh—you have the number of the security firm?"

"On the refrigerator." She peeled off the magnetic strip and gave it to me. After identifying myself I asked them to send someone to the senator's farm for window replacement. "Not an attempted entry," I explained. "Happened during last night's accidental weapon discharge."

"Yeah, heard about it—Governor Green, right?"

"Right."

"We'll have someone there within an hour."

Next I called Bottscher's office and requested they remove the Greens' cars from the premises.

"And do what with them?" the clerk inquired.

"Whatever you usually do in similar cases. Just move them, okay?"

"Okay, sir. Towing involved?"

"Probably."

Sergeant Bottscher came on line then, and said, "We'll take care of it."

"How's the governor doing?" I glanced at Alison.

"Okay. Got a transfusion before setting his collarbone. I understand he'll be with us a couple of days, on the mend."

"And his daughter?"

"Heavily sedated. Haven't talked with the governor yet and I doubt Miss Green will be responsive until possibly tomorrow."

"Appreciate the information, Sergeant." I hung up, and told Alison what Bottscher had said. "Steve, shouldn't I go there and pay my respects to Abel? Express condolences?"

"Good idea, I'll go with you."

While Alison did our breakfast dishes I shaved, showered and dressed. The glazier arrived and accepted a mug of coffee from Alison before we went outside. Barely ten o'clock, but the sun was already warming the fields. In the distance we could glimpse and hear the tractor harrowing moist earth. I said, "I imagine he'll be seeding over the weekend, taking advantage of good weather."

As we strolled along the grassy border Alison said, "I'm sort of torn between things—getting a boat or keeping horses again."

"Can't you do both?"

"If you'd help with the boat. Then I need new stables, four to six stalls I've been thinking, paddock and riding ring. I can hire someone to muck out the stables and distribute hay and feed." She squinted at the distant farmer. "I'm going to talk with old John about planting hay and harvesting and bailing it for me. Oats and corn would be a blessing—horses love grain and eat a lot of it."

"Sounds like you'll need a manager for the farm."

She nodded. "Been thinking of that, too, because if I really go for the nomination I'll have to concentrate on it, exclude almost everything else." She pressed my hand. "Except you, dear."

"I've been thinking about that, too. Last night Abel and I discussed the ramifications, before he was wounded. I can guarantee he'll be fully cooperative with you if you want to make the run."

"That would be terrific. But with Sybil out of the picture the exploratory committee will have to be reorganized or reconstituted—whatever."

"That's something Sean Elkins can handle."

"Yes. Last night I told her I wanted her working full time for me and she seemed delighted. Hmm, I'll need campaign headquarters and a phone bank . . . It'll be like my campaign for the Senate but on a much larger scale."

"Much larger," I agreed, "with travel to all fifty states after you're nominated. Speaking engagements, TV interviews . . ." I broke off as a covey of whitetail doves erupted from cover and whirred away in the sunlight.

"It's daunting," Alison said, "but the prize . . ."

"The presidency of the United States. Many politicians see it as irresistible."

"Well, it's not irresistible to me—yet. But I've only begun thinking seriously about it. And I'd more than welcome your opinion."

"While you're out on the road I can keep your boat trim and seaworthy, look in on the farm from time to time."

"That would be wonderful. Wouldn't you go on the road with me?"

"Honey, I have an active practice that took years to build up. I couldn't take a year away from it, or even a couple of months. The sea closes over what's left untended."

"I understand. It's impractical and too much to ask."

I looked at my wristwatch. "Let's go see the shooting victim while he's still around."

* * *

One of Green's entourage was posted outside the door of his private room. He recognized Alison and said, "Senator, the governor will be glad to see you. Very good of you to come."

I asked, "How's he doing?"

"Very well. Tonight or tomorrow we'll move him back to the mansion."

"And Sybil?" Alison asked.

"I—I'm not sure what the plans are for her."

"The whole thing is terribly unfortunate," Alison said and we went in.

Green's upper chest was encasted, left arm in immobilizing plaster. His face was pale. After wetting his lips, he said, "It's nice to see you, Alison, good of you to come."

"Of course I'd come, Abel. And I'm sorry you were hurt last night."

He nodded slowly. "My poor daughter—she blames herself for everything. And you, Bentley, I have to thank your prompt action. Otherwise I'd probably have bled to death."

"I only did what seemed necessary," I said.

"I'm fortunate you were familiar with combat first aid."

I said, "I've been telling the senator some of what we discussed last night—your unequivocal offer to back her candidacy with all your influence."

His gaze lingered on me for a moment, before saying, "Entirely right. My mind's been a bit foggy from painkiller, but I absolutely verify that commitment." He breathed deeply, winced and said, "As for the possibility of my occupying a vacant Senate seat, I have no such ambitions. It's been dramatically brought home to me that I need to devote a good deal of time to caring for my daughter—compensate for past failure in that regard."

"Very commendable, Governor."

He said, "Should the senator leave the Senate I'm sure that she and I can agree on a satisfactory appointive substitute."

"I'm sure we can, Abel," she said, and touched his right hand. "But of course I've made no decision as regards a national candidacy."

"Don't delay, dear lady. In these maneuvers it's important to get out in front of the crowd."

"I understand, and I appreciate your advice." She paused. "Can I do anything for Sybil?"

"Afraid not, but it's good of you to offer."

"Since I'm here I'd at least like to look in on her."

"By all means."

Alison moved toward the door and I said, "Might not be convenient for me to look in, so I'll chat a bit with the governor."

When the door closed behind her, Green stared at me. "Satisfied, you bastard?"

"You recited your lines like an Eagle Scout, Abel, and to remind you not to backtrack and return to your old ways I'll be sending you a reminder. You're familiar with videotapes clandestinely recorded—this one stars you from your arrival to the farmhouse to your wounding."

"God, there's no end to you."

"One conspiracy begets another," I said harshly, "and you shouldn't discount the way I'm saving your ass—and your daughter's. I don't expect to see you again or communicate with you, unless you violate your pledges. Do that and you'll be consumed in a firestorm." I took two steps toward the door and looked back. "I'm not forgetting you had Harlan killed."

"Wha—what do you mean? How—?"

"Willie Coto talked," I said and left the room. Let him juggle that one, I thought, as I walked down the corridor to where Alison was waiting.

She took my hand, and together we left the hospital. When we were driving back in her Jaguar she said, "Sybil looks like a wax figure. I wonder if she'll ever be—?"

"Sane?"

"I was going to say her normal self."

"Which was never all that normal. Okay, time we lightened up. I vote for early lunch at the Laurel Brigade."

"Let's make it unanimous."

"Motion carries."

*   *   *

Later, while Alison was in the field talking with farmer John I phoned Pat Moran, who said, "What a night! When do we exchange cars?"

"Can you make it to my place in an hour? Bring along last night's take."

"Hour and a half, okay?"

"See you then."

When Alison came in I told her I had to return to my office for a while and would be back in plenty of time for dinner. She said that was fine, she'd take a nap in my absence; seeing the Greens had been stressful.

So after she went upstairs I got Pat's car from the barn and drove back through town. While we were lunching the Greens' cars had been taken away, a considerable improvement to the premises.

Until Pat arrived I went through two days' mail, built a drink and packed fresh clothing. Pat delivered video and audio recordings, and said, "From what I read and hear you put quite a spin on the shooting."

"The *accidental* shooting, Pat, never forget that."

"Sorry, I'll remember. How's the guv doin'?"

"In pain, which pleases me, but otherwise on the mend. The recordings are good quality?"

"Absolutely. How do you want everything billed?"

"External consultations."

He grunted. "Too bad you can't publish an audio transcript. The tabloids would eat it up."

"Hope I don't have to. But if Green makes trouble . . ."

"Say no more. Uh—the kid come 'round?"

"Not yet."

"Think she will?"

"I'm not a shrink."

"Coulda fooled me. Well, so long until next time. Right?"

We shook hands and he returned my car keys.

After he left I looked up the phone number of Walter Embry,

the computer consultant we'd hired to evaluate VanAlstine's process, and found him in his Falls Church office. After I gave my name he asked, "Everything going well with the doctor?"

"Yes, and thanks for your good and timely work, but that's not what I'm calling about. Let's say a home videotape was made and the maker wanted a particular individual's features blurred beyond recognition. Is that something you can do?"

"Easily, almost child's play. Done for TV programs all the time."

"That's what I have in mind. On a confidential basis."

"My work is usually of a confidential nature, Mr. Bentley. Such as evaluating the VanAlstine process. You have the videotape?"

"Yes, but it was made by minicam. The image would have to be transferred to a conventional VHS cassette."

"Entirely feasible. I'm relatively free today and tomorrow. When could you get the tape to my lab?"

"You have a courier service that works Saturdays?"

"I do—my son."

When Walter Embry Jr. arrived I gave him the minicam tape and told him I wanted my features removed, and an unretouched dupe of the original made. "I think your father understands."

"I'm sure he does—he's pretty sharp."

"That he is. The finished products can be delivered to my office on Monday."

"I'll tell him."

When I got back to the farm Alison was in bed asleep. I made fresh coffee and took her a cup, gently wakened her. Over cocktails she told me farmer John was greatly upset by her suggestion of planting corn and oats for stable consumption. "He's depended on income from selling crops he raises on my land and without it doesn't know how he'll exist. I suggested I pay him for planting and harvesting but he said that was far from meeting his needs. Now I don't know what to do."

"How about continuing your arrangement the rest of this year with the understanding you won't renew his lease."

"Seems cold, almost selfish, doesn't it? When I don't even have horses to feed."

"Meanwhile you could have stables renovated for when you do."

She sighed. "I was almost sure you were going to remind me a political campaign would consume all my time."

"It's so obvious. But a boat doesn't have to be fed or exercised. I'll check the ads in *Sailing*, maybe find something worth looking at within a few hours' drive. If not, give specs to a yacht brokerage, see what they come up with. Hod'll be back soon and can help with that."

"I miss him, don't you? And Mattie. What a great couple."

"Let's get Sean out here tomorrow, find out what she projects for a national campaign. That's a way to start—could be the demands are more than you'll be comfortable with."

"I'll call her now."

"Abel indicated you ought to invest a couple million in start-up funding—loaning to yourself is the strategy."

"How much is *he* going to come up with?"

"When you're nominated he opens party coffers to you. Big, big money. Until then you operate on your own money plus whatever the fundraisers provide."

She thought it over before saying, "I could do that, but I'd want reasonable assurance of gaining the nomination. Otherwise, it would be money down the drain."

"Don't minimize Green's considerable influence. And it's to his political advantage to place your name before the convention."

"I suppose so. And I'll confess the prospect makes me feel, well, shaky."

"Your whole career is a success story, why should you begin doubting your abilities?"

She sighed heavily. "I don't know. Maybe because the scope of everything involved is so enormous it's daunting."

I kissed her cheek. "Call Sean. Tell her we'll give her a country brunch tomorrow. Say you're ready to talk campaign."

THIRTY

SUNDAY MORNING SEAN Elkins drove up in her metallic-gold Lexus whose vanity plate read SPIN, and parked beside Alison's Jag. She was wearing tailored, artificially aged blue jeans, white silk blouse, denim jacket, and polished jodphur boots. Alison and I went down the porch steps to meet her, and after I was introduced she gave me a firm handclasp. Her dark hair was layered, and her face was fresh and unlined. "Senator," she said, "what a handsome spread you have. If it were mine I don't think I'd ever leave it for Washington."

We walked into the house where I poured three bloody Marys. After sipping, Sean said, "Senator, you can't know how I welcomed your call. I've been praying you'd positively consider a national campaign because there's nothing that makes my blood pump faster than devoting my full energy to a candidate. And I'm flattered you're consulting me."

I said, "You have a reputation for energy and creativity, and a great track record in circles that count."

"Thank you." As she sat she glanced around. "This is where the governor was wounded?"

"The very place."

"Yesterday," Alison said, "I visited Abel in the hospital. Stayed long enough to hear him commit to my candidacy."

"Wonderful. His backing will be enormously useful."

"Green also said the senator should be prepared to front a couple of million as seed money." I remarked.

"Well," Sean said, "it's gotta come from somewhere. To get things moving we need centrally located office space, office ma-chines and people to run them, a campaign manager, and an admin-istrator. Plus a telephone bank, travel coordinator, and so on."

"Also," I said, "a treasurer who's a financial watchdog."

Sean nodded. "To give us an idea of where we stand and how far we have to go, I want to commission two polls: one among the senator's state constituency for approval rating, the other national to determine name recognition percentage. You approve, Senator?"

"If you'll call me Alison."

"With pleasure." She looked at me. "I'm not sure I know Mr. Bentley's role."

Before Alison could reply I said, "Aside from being the sena-tor's tax adviser and attorney I'm a close friend and supporter. No role in her political activity or campaign."

"Too bad," Sean responded, "because you're very presentable."

"Well, thanks, and you should see me after I'm shaved and rested. Did you bring organizational charts? TO's?"

"In my car. I thought we'd get over preliminaries before going through the heavy stuff." She held out her empty glass and I refilled it from the pitcher.

"Which," said Alison, "we can get into after breakfast."

"My cue," I said, and left for the kitchen. I fried country ham slices and potatoes, made a platter of waffles and dollar pancakes,

and warmed cinnamon rolls. The dining room table was already set
with condiments, maple syrup, and butter. With coffee poured, our
country brunch was ready.

Sean tucked into the meal with an enthusiasm that made me
wonder how she kept her trim figure. "This is dee-licious," she pro-
nounced. "Alison, I've always dreamed of a good-looking in-house
chef, and by golly it turned out to be Steve. Except he's spoken for."

"Certainly is," Alison smiled. "Have to look elsewhere."

"That's how I spend free time—looking and looking. So far,
without result. And I can't understand why being successful in my
chosen vocation should turn men off—the desirable ones. If they're
intelligent enough to attract me, they ought to be smart enough to
want me permanently. Wouldn't you think?"

"I'd think," I said, and flashed to Lauri Nathanson. Although
she played the money game, Lauri was a lot like Sean. I wondered
who she'd take to Europe for the summer.

Meal over, I cleared the table for Sean's charts, and stacked
dishes in the machine while the women began serious discussion.
Washing pots and pans, I could hear large figures being mentioned
and was glad I wasn't involved. Sean was a focused no-nonsense ca-
reerist, and with her expert guidance Alison was going to enter a
national lottery for a single grand prize. The entrance fee was itself
a big-ticket item, beyond reach of the average player. But it was Alison's game and she was well qualified to play.

I went outside and walked down toward the barn where I'd
found Harlan's stiffened corpse. The episode seemed long ago, so
much had happened since, but it was only a month since my discovery. The alleged killer's name had been given me, but it was not
something Alison needed to know. Nor did she need to hear how
Sybil Green had killed their common lover, or who commissioned
the murder of Doris Conlon in her sad little refuge away from Harlan Bowman.

I got out a Montecristo, bit off the tip, and lighted the end
with a match. As I drew in satisfying smoke I reflected how effort-
lessly Alison had given up cigarettes. She had great strength of will,
and over the months ahead it was going to be tested in unforesee-
able ways.

Turning in through the grove of birch, I walked quietly toward the edge of the pool. Halted when I saw a raccoon on the other side washing food in the water. I watched in silence, knowing I would not see deer, which bedded down through the heat of the day. Even squirrels in a black walnut tree had ceased bickering in favor of taking things easy. I liked the pool and the unspoiled natural setting made me feel part of it, and as I watched, the raccoon munched its food, polished its whiskers and silently withdrew.

This was another world, far from Charley and Red, even more distant from the midnight pirates I'd repelled and the homicidal eruptions of Sybil Green. I didn't want to think about any of those things and hoped in time they would submerge deep in the dark depths of memory.

I dropped ash on the greensward, drew on my cigar.

When the breeze shifted I heard the tractor chuffing in the distance as farmer John readied the soil for perhaps his last spring planting. The thought saddened me until I realized that within a few months the landowner would have little or no time for horses or boats or any distraction at all. She might still come here to rest and untangle her thoughts, but those opportunities would be rare if her schedulers had their way. I admired Alison in many ways, and had done and risked much for her of things that she would never know. Nor did I want her to.

How would it all play out?

When the cigar stub warmed my fingers I strolled back toward the farmhouse. Sean and Alison were sitting on the back patio under a sun umbrella, chatting and laughing together.

Seeing me, Sean left the table and walked toward me.

"We're getting along famously," she said. "Alison is probably going to be the perfect client. But there's a personal area I need to know about—your relationship."

"Did you ask Alison?"

Sean shrugged. "She was evasive, said I should talk to you."

"I've always felt the lady sets the paradigm."

"Can't disagree with chivalry. But for planning purposes—to be blunt—I need to know if the two of you are planning to be married."

"In view of what's ahead for her I don't think it's practical."

"Emotion aside."

"Emotion aside," I repeated. "She knows I care deeply for her, and if she hadn't gotten into the nomination millrace I suppose we'd have been married."

"So it's accurate to say no present plans."

"None."

"Well, that clarifies the issue, and I appreciate your candor." She squeezed my hand.

"Probably the best favor in my power is staying out of her life while she pursues her political star."

She nodded. "That would be generous of you."

I looked at my watch. "Time I was getting back to town. The governor's shooting has made for a very long weekend. I'll tell our hostess."

Alison walked out to my car, said, "I hate to see you leave now, I thought we'd go back tonight."

"Well, I'm sort of a fifth wheel right now, and you and Sean can make better progress with your plans without distraction."

"She's good, isn't she? Very bright and enthusiastic."

"Just what the campaign needs," I said, kissed her and got into my car.

As I drove toward the highway I passed the spot where I'd seen the midnight watcher eyeballing the farm. Considering what happened later I'd decided the man was most likely Willie Coto, though Charley Winkowski had been an earlier choice.

Then back through Leesburg, over the river and into George-town, somnolent on a warm Sunday afternoon.

There was a call from Walter Embry on my machine. When I called back, he said, "Work's finished. I can arrange delivery today if you'd like."

"I'd like," I replied. "Have Junior bring your bill."

I made a double scotch with minor ice and hardly any water, wandered around my house recalling Sean's questions, and Alison's new resolve. We'd made no enduring commitment to each other, though skating close to the edge, and I'd always felt that Alison's af-fection—was it love?—for me was based on gratitude and secrets shared. Her guilty knowledge was far less than mine; even so she was enjoying the comfort of denial, a luxury denied me.

Embry Junior arrived, I took the package and wrote a check to cover his father's bill. Before taking it he asked, "Don't you want to check results?"

"I wouldn't have engaged your father if I hadn't full confidence in his ability."

"Thank you. He said he was sure you'd be satisfied." He took the check and slid it into a jacket pocket, opened the door and left.

The package was on my desk. For a while I stared at it, reflecting that the contents, though never seen by Alison, formed a sharp sword over Abel Green's head that guaranteed his continuous cooperation in fulfilling her aspirations.

The minicassette original I set aside with the VHS duplicate Embry had made. The digitally altered VHS was the one I slid into my VCR before settling back to watch.

There it was: the governor on the couch facing an unseen lens, and a man with his back to the camera. The sound of their voices was loud and clear. Each time the man moved in a direction that showed his profile, his blurred features were unrecognizable. The governor listened to the audio recording of his daughter and an unidentified male, covered his face and wept. Then he and the unknown man talked, their voices rose, the window smashed and a woman screamed. Two shots, one striking the governor. The man left camera range, returned and gave first aid, left again. The Rescue Squad arrived, took the governor away. Nothing more of interest.

Embry had done exactly what I wanted done. Through the filmed encounter my face was never revealed. The tape was ready for Abel Green's critical review. I rewound it and slipped it in an envelope, addressed it to Governor Abel Green. Tomorrow I'd turn it over to UPS for delivery at the gubernatorial mansion.

The minicassette and the audio tapes I put in another envelope for safekeeping by Arthur Jensen. That, too, I would have delivered tomorrow by Burton Michaels.

A good lawyer, Michaels, and a good man. I'd be doing myself a favor if I hired him as a permanent associate. In the next few days we'd work out an employment contract on the generous side.

I tried to think of other things that needed to be done: was Mrs. Altman due a raise? Office furniture refurbished? Carpet cleaned or replaced? Impressionist prints in the reception room . . . ? Remembering the Corcoran loaners in Alison's place brought my mind back to what I'd been avoiding: thinking of her.

I thought of her grace and intelligence, her soul-deep tropism to honesty, and the steep, incredibly difficult road she had chosen for herself. Ever since she began thinking seriously of the presidency I'd realized there was no long-range role for me. Had it all figured out before things came to a head today at her farm.

I was going to miss her, miss everything about her, and the worst part was yet to come—when I'd see her face and hear her voice on every TV channel in the land as her campaign accelerated toward nomination. With Sean's expertise and Green's applied influence, Alison Revelstoke Bowman was a shoo-in. And I could only wish her well.

My glass was empty. I made another drink, just scotch and ice, and thought that in my way I had probably contributed to a chapter in the history of our country. The first woman president? Why not? What had that string of male incompetents, grafters, and whore-masters done for us lately?

The phone rang. I didn't answer it and heard the message machine cut in. Alison's voice. Was everything okay? Would we dine together tomorrow? Please call.

Everything was not okay, and dinner would only postpone reality. She must know it was over, there could be no reprise. Still, I thought, it was nice to be missed by a departing love. And if she ever needed me again, truly needed me . . .

My hand trembled as I raised my glass.

Q Street was quiet, no official limousine in front of my house, no Willie Coto planting his bloody knife in my kitchen to frame me for a murder he had done. The house was quiet, too, and I liked it that way.

I was bone-tired. Too much thinking, too many drinks. Unsteadily I gripped the banister and went up the stairs to bed.

*   *   *

Next day I phoned Lauri Nathanson from my office, and found her at hers. "I've been thinking," I said, "and summer touring Europe's pleasure palaces sounds irresistible—if the offer's still on the table."

"It is," she said warmly, "and it's none too soon to make travel plans. Like Concorde over, QE2 back. How does that sound?"

"Regal. With that in mind I suggest dinner tonight—Army and Navy Club."

"Too stuffy. Counteroffer—Dominique's, on me."

"Save your money for Paris, we'll go to Clyde's."

"Too packed, too noisy. But since you're determined we'll compromise on Dominique's."

"Sly fox," I said. "Only to make travel arrangements, right?"

"Taking unfinished matters for resolution at my place. A client gave me a huge bottle of Dom Pérignon, but klutz that I am you'll have to open it."

"Macho chauvinist Steve lends a hand to li'l ultrafeminist Lauri?"

"Brute. And I suggest you be prepared to lend me more than a hand *ce soir*."

"Keep it clean, kid. *A quelle heure?*"

"*Huit* okay?"

"Transcendent."

So began an extended interlude with Lauri Nathanson whose cheerful hedonism was a welcome antidote to my loss of Alison. Until we left for Europe I was aware of the media groundswell favoring Alison for her party's nomination and the presidency itself. Then in July, when Lauri and I were enjoying historic Grecian sights and culture, I read that Alison had won nomination on the second round of voting. As anticipated, Governor Green had proposed her candidacy. Her real campaign would open later, and polls showed her with a slight edge over the opposition party's likely candidates, one of whom would be chosen in August.

At a sidewalk cafe in front of the Grand Bretagne Hotel, our Athens base, Lauri and I were taking midmorning coffee with retsina. I set aside the paper and watched passersby in Syntagma

Square, the white-tutued Evzone guard parading around the palace balcony above.

Lauri said, "Hello? You look pensive. Problem?"

"The retsina's bitter."

"So you said last week."

"I remember." My throat was tight with remembering.

Her hand covered mine. "Don't want to go home, do you?"

"By no means."

"Mm, I know the mood . . . Anything I can help you with?"

I looked at my watch. "Nearly time for blanket drill."

"You're right." She stood and grasped my hand. "That eider-down bed is marvelous—like making love in warm Jell-o. I've got to have one for my pad. Come along, now. You could have had her but you let her go—don't make me suffer, too."

I got up, laid drachmas on the table and followed Lauri to our suite. There, making love on the soft featherbed, I hardly thought of Alison at all.